MARK COBBS LEWIS

MASCOTS
&
MONUMENTS

ISBN: 979-8-89216-033-9 (Paperback)

Library of Congress Control Number: 2024917365

BookmarcAlliance
California, USA
www.bookmarcalliance.com

Table of Contents

PROLOGUE

A Short History; A Fight Between Brothers, A Mysterious Statue

North and South Dugganville had been founded as two separate villages, approximately five miles from either side of the Gage River. Although separated in the present day by only a river, the hatreds held by present day Dugganville citizens for inhabitants on the other side of that river, were as strong as they had been for their forebearers, nearly two centuries before. The story goes that two young brothers, named Duggan, had headed westward to make their fortunes and stake a claim in a young and rapidly growing country. Their boat had been swamped during a particularly heavy storm, and they had survived by swimming to an island in the middle of the broad waterway. The brothers fought over whose fault the sinking had been, and when the weather cleared, separated and swam to opposite banks, where each started a settlement.

As towns do, the villages grew toward the waterway, and would eventually meet again where the brothers had first separated. The rivalry between the Duggans, however, remained bitter. When the Civil war broke out, they fought again, and killed each other in armed conflict. The story of the Duggan brothers ends there, and history doesn't mention them again. Their legacy of discord continued, however, and on the island where the brothers had first separated, rose a statue and the legend of the apocryphal, Major Raeford Thaddeus Beaumont.

* ** **

Ownership of Beaumont Island had been a source of contention since the end of the Civil War. The island was no longer an island in the strictly geographical use of the term. Earlier in the Gage River's history, it had forked and surrounded the minimally elevated acreage before rejoining and continuing on its westward trek. Over time the normally lazily flowing water had chosen to pick a channel, leaving a dry shallow cut on either the island's north or south bank. Every century or so, flooding in the area had been severe enough that the river had changed its course, leaving the island to adjoin the opposite bank. The most spectacular of these floods had occurred near the end of the American Civil War and had, for a short time, covered the entire island.

Although the few acres of land were considered a trivial curiosity to most historians, even the origin of the name for the river running past them had long been the source of heated arguments among the inhabitants of the two small burgs. Most citizens on the north side, said it had been named for a British General, while South Dugganville inhabitants insisted that Gates was an Anglicization of Gigage, the Cherokee word for red.

After the floodwaters receded the Gates River had taken a northerly path, and the Island sat in Confederate territory. It would later become named for the larger than life, well carved statue that had mysteriously appeared at its center. Major Raeford Thaddeus Beaumont and his horse, or more accurately stated, their statue, are the only known occupants to have ever resided on the worthless spit of land. No records exist showing who, if anyone, may have owned the land, or who could have built the monument. The silent, gradually eroding silent figure on the stone horse is as enigmatic as had been the flesh and blood R.T. Beaumont over one hundred and fifty years before.

According to legend, he had been hailed as a hero and reviled as a villain by both sides. It seemed oddly appropriate that the unknown architects of his memorial had selected this one spot in the middle of a fickle river for its placement. Perhaps the placement was appropriate, but it had also sown the seeds of conflict and rivalry between the two Dugganvilles for over one and a half centuries following the American Civil War.

Neither North nor South Dugganville had any real use for the land that was minimally suited for building or growing. One of the many stories attached to the island was that the confederate officer who had purchased the land had done so with the stated purpose of turning it into a tobacco plantation. After the war, some believed the man had continued to secretly use and abuse slave laborers in his fields. A competing rumor was that Beaumont had been a convert to the abolitionist movement and had used the plantation as a front to hide its real purpose as a waystation for the underground railroad. If either legend held any truth, Beaumont had been a terrible planner since the island flooded regularly and only sparse vegetation grew on it.

Both sides wanted the island, not for the real estate, but for the legends that grew in the myth fertile soil surrounding the statue. Depending on the political climate of the decade and the most current mythology surrounding the Major, one side wanted to venerate and restore the statue while the other wanted to destroy it. Although two millennial celebrations had passed since the Major had supposedly been buried somewhere near the monument, the rivalrous conflict over its fate still spilled into every aspect of Dugganville life.

CHAPTER 1

The Present – The Protégé

It was the last match of the night, and the referee's face hovered only millimeters above the mat. As was typical with any competition between the towns sharing a name but divided by a river and over a century of history, the winner of tonight's bout would be decided in the last few seconds. North led going into the final match, but only by a point. If the South wrestler could pull off an upset, his team could still win.

An upset wasn't coming on this night, however. The referee's lips pursed tightly around the whistle, and he held his hand with open palm downward. Sweat dripped from the wrestler struggling on bottom, forming small puddles on the mat's latex surface. The South Dugganville wrestler, with his chin facing the ceiling and his head trapped ingloriously in the bend of the other's leg, struggled desperately to prevent his chin from being pulled toward his chest. The North wrestler, sensing the exhaustion of his opponent arched his back with greater intensity. The South Dugganville athlete could hold out no longer. His chin came forward causing both shoulders to touch the mat simultaneously. The referee's whistle exploded as his hand slapped the mat. The last match of the night was over, and North Dugganville had avenged its loss to South Dugganville from earlier in the season.

Students from both sides of the gym started to move on to the floor, but as was the norm when a contest took place between the two Dugganvilles, an extra police presence had been requested and all faculty from both schools were required to attend. Aside from an occasional faceless taunt, the exit went smoothly.

"Hey, R2! What did you think of my match tonight?" The wrestler who had only moments before had his hand raised in victory, sprinted toward the powerfully built man wearing a red North Dugganville Demons ball cap.

Franklin Bear looked at the young man strutting in front of him like the winning rooster of a cock fight. R2 was the nickname by which the wrestler and many of Bear's closest friends called him. He had been all but raised by a man named Tyrell Ramsey. The pair had grown so close that they were often referred to as Ramsey and Ramsey number two, or R2, for short. It had been Ramsey, who had introduced Frank Bear to the sport of wrestling.

Franklin, Frank, Bear was a legend in both Dugganvilles. He had been a three-time state champion and was a heavy favorite for a fourth title until an act of dastardly evil had destroyed his season as well as his hopes for a collegiate career. He was also a mentor to Jason Merritt. The high school senior already had two state championships under his belt and was considered the top contender in a talented 145-pound weight class for the current year. His only loss had come in the state finals during his freshman year.

"Who were you trying to impress, Jason – your buddies or those girls standing behind me watching their hot stud? I will tell you who you didn't impress, and that's the college scouts in the stands watching you. You put your team at risk hotdogging out there like that tonight. If I were your coach, you would be apologizing to every member of your team."

The cocky wrestler visibly deflated and looked away. "I know, R2. It's just that we had those guys the first match of the season, and their jerk heavyweight really hotdogged on Tommy in the last match of the night. Tommy was just coming out of football, and he's never really wrestled before. South needed a little reminder of who's on top."

Frank Bear looked at his protégé without responding. Jason tried to look back at his hero, but quickly withered and found the tops of his shoes to be a less intimidating sight.

The former wrestler began in the same calm manner he always used when making a point. "Now, that was spoken with the wisdom and maturity of a very bright human who is trying to get into an ivy league school. I wonder if that human has considered, however, that although he has the academic qualifications, he doesn't have the resources to pay for it without an athletic scholarship."

Merritt felt like shrinking into his shoes. "I'm really sorry, Mr. Bear. I shouldn't have let the trash talk get to me. I know I let you down."

Bear put his hands on the young man's shoulder. "Wow, I give you a little helpful advice, and suddenly it's Mr. Bear. Jason, it's not my team, and it's not my college career. Just make sure you stay focused. State is coming up in a few weeks, and you need to keep your head on straight. Now, go get dressed, and go straight home tonight. Somebody in town is going to try and start something, and neither you nor your mom need that."

"Yes, sir. I will," Jason answered, but as soon as Bear turned and walked away, the cheerleaders who had been standing behind him moved in on the night's hero. In addition to being the school's best athlete, Merritt was also incredibly handsome. As a young child, his skin had been so fair and his features so fine that he had often been misidentified as a girl. Now, at seventeen, he was almost universally considered to be an Adonis by the female half of North Dugganville high's student body. They quickly surrounded their idol, and just as quickly, he returned their attentions.

"JASON!" Jason Merritt and the fawning group of pubescent females surrounding him all jumped and turned to see a stone-faced Frank Bear. Jason had never even heard his mentor raise his voice, but something between a bark and a roar had just left the quiet man's throat. He stepped toward Jason, and the girls parted. The two men were almost identical in height and stood eye-to-eye. Frank's voice was soft, but held a slightly menacing tone. No one but Jason heard him. "When I said keep your head on straight, I meant the one that's above your belt. Now, go home."

"Yes sir, Mr. Bear, I mean, R2, I mean, yes sir." Without another glance at his entourage of stud worshipping groupies, Jason Merritt jogged to the locker room. He would be going straight home that night.

As Frank watched Merritt open the locker room door, he overheard the indignant comments of the hormone amped girls standing behind him. The intent of the frustrated females was easy to be discerned.

"Some legend."

"Who does he think he is?"

The last parting shot as they walked toward the exit was, "I'll tell you who he is. He's just a broken down ugly old man."

Rather than being offended, Bear laughed to himself. "*They got broken down and ugly right. I'm only thirty-eight, but I am starting to feel like they are probably right on that old part, too.*"

He was still chuckling as he walked across the gym floor toward the exit. He readjusted his hat on a head of jet black closely cropped hair. The big red pitchfork on his Demons tee shirt stretched tightly across his muscular chest. The only visible signs that Frank Bear wasn't still a top-notch athlete were the awkward limp with which he walked across the gym floor and an ugly scar that emerged from the hairline on the back of his head and ran down his neck until it disappeared beneath the crew neck of his t-shirt. The girls sneered at the team sponsor's logo, "Ramsey and Son Plumbing," stretched across Bear's back as he walked out the door. He felt their glares, and he considered turning back to smile and wave goodbye, but the vertebrae fused in his neck made the gesture not worth the effort.

CHAPTER 2

The Present – Old Rival, Old Friend

The next day was Saturday. Jason stopped by Frank's house to apologize again for being stupid and also to say thank you. His mentor had been right about trouble happening in town the night before. A big fight had occurred at one of the local teen hangouts, and several students had been taken to jail including one of the girls who had been waiting for him at the gym. It wasn't unusual for Merritt to stop by unannounced. He had spent much of his childhood with the Bear family. They had lived in the rambling farmhouse for as long as he had known them, but it had changed greatly since he was a child. Many of Jason's earliest memories had been created in the large comfortable home in need of some paint and a little TLC. The house, while still homey and comfortable, had grown even larger and had taken on the feel of an estate. Frank Bear had proven to be as successful of a businessman as he had been a wrestler, after inheriting a small plumbing business from Tyrell Ramsey. The business, once a one-man operation, had grown to become one of the largest plumbing and air-conditioning contractors in the two-state area. While Ramsey and Bear hadn't actually been related, their affection for each other was well known. Few who knew them had been surprised when Ramsey changed the name of his company to Ramsey and Son.

Shortly after he rang the doorbell, Tia, Bear's youngest daughter opened the door with the same effervescent enthusiasm she always displayed when her knight in shining armor came calling. "JASON," she squealed with delight and jumped into his arms.

"YAY, It's my Indian princess, TIA!" Merritt never failed to return the enthusiasm.

"Did you come to see me," she asked as the stars sparkled in her eyes.

"Well, of course I did, silly, but I need to talk to your dad, too. Is he here?" The boisterous laughter of two men erupted from the family room as he was asking the question.

"Yea, he's in the fambly room with his friend. He told me that if it was you, I'm supposed to take you to him. Everybody else went with Mommy and some lady shopping, but I didn't wanna go, so I stayed here. I don't know when they're coming back. I like Rachel."

Frank heard his daughter starting to ramble and called out. "Tia, sweetheart, are you going to stop talking and bring Jason back here so he can meet my friend?"

"OH! I forgot!" She grabbed the teenager's hand and pulled him into the house.

The family room was a large open space designed for joy and activity. It wouldn't have been described as total chaos, but a place for everything, everything in its place was definitely not the rule. Doll houses, play houses, and stuffed animals were situated throughout the room, as were tumbling mats, an indoor basketball hoop, and a ping pong table. The large French doors opened out to a spacious patio, also filled with randomly placed items, and a large activity pool. Visitors were always welcome, as long as they didn't mind sharing their chair with at least one of the two out-sized mongrel dogs, named Takedown and Reverse, who made it their duty to ensure that no visitor ever felt unwelcome.

Frank and the stranger were sitting at a game table in the middle of the room and still laughing, when Tia and Jason walked hand-in-hand into the room. The man was joyfully scratching two sets of floppy ears at once when he first saw Jason. He and Frank rose to greet the young man and his escort. Frank's friend was tall, a little over six feet. He wore a khaki safari shirt and blue denim pants that were clean, but had seen better days. The sparse ring of hair circling his bald pate, grew over his ears and stopped just short of his shoulders. His physique showed signs of neglect and wear. Shoulders that looked to be strong once were now slightly bent, and popping out in front of the thin frame covered by the shirt was a pot belly.

"Jason, I would like to introduce you to a very dear friend of mine, Hefner Briton." Briton smiled broadly and stuck out both hands to take Jason's, revealing bold tattoos on the inside of either arm written in block letters. On the left arm was the word REDEEMED, on the right, REBORN.

"I watched you wrestle last night, young man. It is uncanny how much you move like Frank out there on the mat. About the only difference is that you are a whole lot better looking."

"Says the man with a bald head and a pot belly," Frank broke in with an eye roll.

The comparison to the man he idolized made Jason smile. "Thank you, Mr. Briton."

"Just call me, Hef."

"Thank you, Hef. R2, I just came to," Jason started, but Bear interrupted.

"Jason," he paused and looked at the young man before continuing. "If you came here just to hear me, say I told you so, forget it. I already read about the trouble in town in the paper. I am just glad you made the right choice. Was your mom excited about your win?"

"No R2, she had the same opinion you did. She told me so when I got home. Her assignment was to watch the students exiting the side doors. She saw those girls waiting for me, and I think she was ready to leave her post, until she saw you. You probably saved me from a lot of embarrassment. I may be a state champion but, I'm still a teacher's little boy. I already catch a lot of grief from my teammates without being scolded in front of the whole school."

Briton was laughing so hard he could hardly contain himself. "Sheesh, Frank, I wish you had kept me out of trouble, but who the heck is R2. Is that like the robot in the movie?"

"No, that's just what most of the people around here who know me, call me."

"So Hef, if you didn't know everybody calls Mr. Bear, R2, how do you guys know each other?"

Hef reached out a long arm and put it on his friend's shoulder. "Frank, I do recall that you weren't real crazy about your surname, and as far as names go, Jason, I didn't care for mine either. As to how I know the newly christened R2, let's just say that if this fallen angel ever tries to tell you that he never lost a match during his high school career, it is time for him to get right with the Lord."

Frank rolled his eyes again, and both men laughed. Jason, looked on in confusion until the dawn of understanding rose on his face. "Wait, you're Carson Blake?"

"No, son. I was Carson Blake. That was another life before this." Briton held his arms out wide with palms turned outward, once again revealing the prominent tattoos on the insides of his forearms.

CHAPTER 3

The Past – The Spoiler

The undercurrent of animosity between North and South Dugganville had sucked many otherwise rational people under the mind drowning influence of bigotry and mistrust since before the Civil War and had continued to pull relationships down in the present day. Even the mascot names chosen sometime in the early twentieth century, had been designed to goad the other side into anger. Although no one openly admitted it, the Demons mascot had been selected on the north side in reference to a group of impoverished union sympathizers that had brutally terrorized rich southern landholders even before the war began. Likewise, the Red Raiders of the southside were named after a band of Indian Marauders who had fought for the confederacy and were known for their savagery. Many of the descendants of the mostly Cherokee band still lived in a poverty-stricken settlement officially known as Beaumont, but more commonly known as Indiantown, just a few miles away from the two Dugganvilles. Many of the indigenous residents in that reservation had the last name of Bear. It was where Frank Bear had spent his earliest years.

Now, a highly touted college prospect for North Dugganville high school, he had remained undefeated throughout his high school wrestling career, and by the time he was a senior there were no serious challengers to his wrestling supremacy. The river dividing

North and South Dugganville, being the state line, meant that the two teams competed in different athletic associations. This division did nothing to dampen the rivalry between the towns. In many ways, the winner of a North vs. South contest was more important to the communities than any state championship. The fact that North had a wrestler with whom no South athlete could compete did not sit well with Red Raider fans. Deepening the wound, no Red Raider had lasted past the first period with Frank Bear since his freshman year.

News traveled quickly throughout the athletics followers of both populations when a new wrestler moved into South Dugganville from the state of Oklahoma, just before wrestling season. Fingers on both sides of the river flew into Google search mode as soon as word got out that a three-time Oklahoma State Champion named Carson Blake had moved into South Dugganville and was in the same weight class as Frank Bear.

"Hey Mike, It's Barry. I just called to give you a heads-up. I don't know what is going on."

"Oh, really?" Mike Teige laughed. "I thought maybe my frenemy had suddenly gotten into the recruiting market with that huge athletic budget you guys on the south side have."

Barry Thomas returned the laugh. "Nah! That's you northern carpetbaggers who are into that sort of thing." Neither Mike Teige nor Barry Thomas had grown up in the area. They were the respective coaches for the North and South Dugganville wrestling teams and had been friends since their days in college. They were also among the few sane voices that could be heard when it came to discussing the rivalry.

He continued. "Mike, I probably don't know much more about the kid than you do. I am a little concerned though, because I think he is a bit of a hot head. I called his coach in Oklahoma today. He wasn't too excited about losing the talent, but also wasn't sad to see the dad go. The man is a single father and can apparently be pretty violent at times."

"So, what makes him move his kid out of a solid program his senior year? I read the write-ups on him. Both of the Oklahoma Schools are drooling!"

"Apparently, our local tire factory needs a new line supervisor. I heard through the grapevine that they offered a position with some pretty impressive blue-collar benefits to the dad, if he could move here before school started."

"Hmmm, let me think, Coach Thomas. Haven't I been hearing concerns from the union that Dugganville Rubber is laying people off, and now they need a new supervisor?"

Barry Thomas laughed again. "I don't know Coach Teige. You will have to take that up with the vice president of Dugganville Rubber, who also happens to be our booster club president."

"I will be sure and put that on my to do list," Teige said with a smirk. "I do have one favor Barry. I'm not worried about your kid being a hot head. You know Frank is unflappable."

"I do know. His nick-name should be Ice."

"Right. Unfortunately, none of our fans fit that description. We need to get together with our administrations before the match and map out some security plans. I don't want this to get out of hand."

"I agree. We can talk again before the season starts. In the meantime, get that grill cleaned up. I am ready for our clandestine loser-cooks bar-b-que, and you are going to have to cook this year."

"Oh, get over yourself, southern boy. My grill is going to completely rust out before I have to cook again."

NDHS and SDHS wrestled against each other twice each year with each school hosting once. The first match was traditionally the first match of the season for both teams and the last match was the last dual for each team before heading to their respective state tournaments. Since the rules were slightly different across state lines, it had been agreed from their earliest competitions that the state association rules of the host school would be followed.

The order in which weight classes competed, rotated throughout the year. This being the first match of the year, Bear and Blake, sitting in the 148lb weight class, would compete near the middle of the dual meet. Lighter weights would go first and the night would end with the heavy weights. The official colors for South were red and gray, while North's were red and blue. A few administrations over the history of the interstate rivalry had attempted to stop the competitions, if for no other reason, the symbolism of the colors.

Those administrations had experienced unfailingly short tenures. Interestingly, it was neither the blue nor the gray that caused problems, but the red. Ownership of the color in the stands was as intense as any competition in the gym or on the field. Security was often a problem because it was nearly impossible to identify which fans belonged on which side.

The night of the first dual meet of Frank's senior year saw a sea of red on both sides of the North Dugganville High School gym. As always, the teams were evenly matched and for the first time in four years, it wasn't assumed that Frank Bear would score a fall for his team. Faculties from both schools kept close watch on their student bodies while a noticeable police presence walked the aisles of the bleachers. It was not unusual for parents to get overly emotional during these competitions.

As expected, the score was close going into the middle weights. When Bear and Blake stepped onto the mat, only a couple of points separated the teams. The match that followed resulted in the first dual between the Dugganvilles in history to be halted and almost led to the end of the rivalry, and also to a long friendship between the coaches. If it were not for pressure from sportswriters in both states and scouts from several division I universities, the melee that ensued from the middle-weight match may well have ended the cross-state competition. Both groups had multiple representatives in the stands that night who all hailed it as a contest worthy of any NCAA championship. After watching the match, the coach for Iowa State University stated emphatically. "Both of these young men are contenders for collegiate championships, right now."

The differing sets of rules of the two state wrestling associations was one of two factors that led to the near catastrophe. If the match that night had been on the south side of the river, the contest would have continued having sudden death overtimes until a winner was crowned. North Dugganville's state association rules, however, limited a match to two overtimes. The first was a condensed version of a match with three shortened periods. The second was a two-minute sudden-death in which the first wrestler to score a takedown was awarded the victory. If no takedown was scored, the match would be declared a tie.

This rule difference might not have been an issue if not for an incident that had occurred earlier in the overtime periods. Bear had just evened the score, and thinking he had found a weakness in his exhausted opponent, attempted a similar move. The taller wrestler was able to catch Bear under the arms this time, and using his height picked the shorter man up over his head and slammed him to the mat out of bounds. The move was dangerous and could easily have drawn a disqualification. Instead, the referee stopped the match and issued a caution. Before the official could stand Blake up and show the symbol for a warning to the mat officials, the coaches from both sides were sprinting toward Frank Bear. He was obviously in distress. Coach Tiege's face was more panicked than that of his wrestler as he stood over him and worked to help him get his breath back. Coach Thomas stood over the pair and asked, "Is he OK?"

"Hell no, he's not OK. Control your wrestler, Thomas. That was bullshit."

"Come on coach. Both these guys are going full tilt."

"You heard me. Bullshit!"

What had started as an act of sportsmanship and concern by the south coach, quickly threatened to become a confrontation between the two long-time friends. The referee stepped in before Barry Thomas could respond. "Go to your chair coach," he said to Thomas.

"Coach Tiege, your wrestler has three minutes to decide if he can continue."

"What, after an illegal move?"

"Coach, he can forfeit the match now, if that's your decision," the referee responded, flatly.

"Coach, it's OK. I just got the wind knocked out of me. I will be fine." Frank Bear was as stoic as ever, but the fall had obviously taken something out of him. He held on till the end of the period hoping to gain his strength for the second and final overtime. By this time, both sides of the gymnasium were chanting. By the time the whistle blew to begin the final overtime, police and school staff had prepared to move quickly on to the gym floor.

Neither wrestler would be content with a tie, but time for the two-minute sudden death was quickly running out. Frank tried to get under Carson Blake's longer reach, but Blake was able to turn him, grab his waist and drive him to the mat. Bear's knee touched the mat just as the buzzer sounded and the south bleachers roared in jubilation thinking their wrestler had just scored the winning takedown over the mighty Frank Bear. It took several blasts of the loud speaker to get the gym quiet enough for anyone to realize that the referee had declared the buzzer had sounded before Frank's knee touched the mat. Therefore, the match had ended in a tie.

Barry Thomas threw his towel and sprinted toward the referee, crying foul as he did. Mike Teige also ran toward the referee to counter Thomas's protests. Pandemonium erupted in the gym. The assistant coaches from each school hustled their teams to their respective locker rooms as quickly as possible. Several fights broke out in the gym among both students and parents. Six weight classes remained to be wrestled, but police moved onto the gym floor and began moving people toward the exits. The administrations from both schools got on the loudspeaker and instructed everyone to go home. The match was over. It was the first time in the long contentious history of contests between North and South Dugganville that an event had been cancelled before completion.

It was three weeks before Mike Teige and Barry Thomas spoke with each other. Thomas started not to answer his phone when he saw the initials M.T. pop up, but took a deep breath and answered just before the call went to voice mail. "Barry, it's Mike. I just bought a new grill and some unbelievably expensive steaks. I was wondering if you and Caroline would come have dinner with us."

At first, Teige heard only silence on the phone. Then, "I would like to, but I don't think my wife is speaking to me right now. Wendy probably isn't talking to you, either."

"Nope."

"How is the couch?"

"Couch? The dog gets the couch. I get a blanket on the floor."

"Ouch. I thought my wife was mean. Mike, I don't know if I've ever felt this stupid in my entire life. We'll be happy to come if I can bring the beer."

"Bring a lot. It's a big football weekend, and I don't want to think about wrestling."

* * * * *

The coaches repaired their relationship and were among the voices calling for the second North/South competition of the year to be cancelled. They, along with their administrations, were drowned out by the noise of tradition and the desires of the public. Sports writers from both states called for a rematch and coaches from several Division I schools said the contest between Blake and Bear would be the best high school match in the nation. The police department even weighed in saying that they could handle the security. Sensing a financial boon, businesses on both sides of the river suggested that the last dual of the year should be held in the Dugganville arena. The arena was supported by tax revenue from both municipalities and usually hosted concerts, rodeos and semi-pro events such as basketball and ice hockey. The first match between Bear and Blake had generated so much buzz however, that businesses knew that people would be coming in from all over the area. Reluctantly, the coaches agreed to the site with three stipulations. The first stipulation was that Bear and Blake were to be the last match of the night. They didn't want their other wrestlers to have to contend with a mass exodus after their match or the chaos that might ensue if people didn't like the outcome. The second was that no one could enter the arena after the meet started, and the third was that concession areas and restrooms were to be constantly monitored by police. High school sports are notorious for trouble being caused by students seeking mischief in areas away from the immediate site of the contest.

Sporting events between North and South Dugganville had always been packed, but the night of the final dual of the year brought with it the air of a college championship. Not only had Bear and Blake maintained their perfect high school careers except for their one draw, both Dugganvilles had gone through the regular season undefeated. Local businesses were ecstatic as wrestling fans from across both states came to watch the showdown. The fiasco from earlier in the season had only served to intensify the hype and boost attendance. In spite of their misgivings, the coaches were also excited, because they knew that the heavy presence of college scouts in the arena would give their other wrestlers exposure that they would not otherwise have had.

As the coaches had agreed weeks earlier, they left the rest of their teams with assistant coaches immediately before the match began and took their two star-athletes to a small conference room away from everyone else. The four of them sat at a four-foot square table with Blake and Bear sitting directly across from one another. Both athletes had been warned that there would be no threats or posturing at the meeting. Carson Blake glared at his opponent. Frank sat impassive and stone-faced as always.

Mike Teige started. "Bear, Blake. Barry Thomas and I have been friends for a long time. We will be friends long after the two of you have moved on. Carson, I want you to know that I have already apologized to Coach Thomas for my behavior earlier this season."

"As I have, to Coach Teige," Thomas interjected.

"The final match tonight will be between quite probably the best two high school wrestlers in the nation. Any unsportsmanlike behavior on either of your parts, and we will end the match on the spot. It may cost us our jobs, but it will not cost our friendship. Coach Thomas?" Barry Thomas nodded in agreement.

"That's right. You both know that we are keeping you off the floor until time for your match. Carson, you will be in your room with coach Brown. Frank, Tyrell Ramsey will be sitting with you." "How come he doesn't have to sit with a coach," Blake protested.

Barry Thomas sighed slightly. "Carson, I gave you the option of sitting with your dad. You gave me an emphatic no. Mr. Ramsey has been in Frank's life for a long time, and he is a respected member of both communities. We aren't leaving either of you alone because of all the nonsense that has already gone on leading up to this rematch. You, OK with that?"

"It's cool." Blake said, tersely.

"Now, do either of you have any problem with anything I've said."

Carson looked directly at Frank while answering his coach. "I know that I'm better than him. All I am here for is to prove it to him and everyone else."

Coach Teige looked at his wrestler. "Frank?"

"I am only here to wrestle."

"Good," said coach Thomas. Before we leave this room, the two of you are going to shake hands.

Both wrestlers stood and stepped toward each other with straight faces. Even though they weighed the same, Blake stood a full head taller than Bear. Their handshake was firm.

"Good luck," Frank said.

Carson didn't reply.

*　*　*　*　*

Everything about the night had more the feel of a major entertainment event than that of two high school cross-town rivals trying to settle old scores. The arena was filled with red jerseys trimmed with blue and red jerseys trimmed in gray worn by fans who cared about the final point tally of the dual matches. Equally as many attendees came wearing clothes that reflected only a primal desire to watch what they hoped might be something akin to a championship wrestling spectacle. It had been agreed upon by the schools that only a few advance tickets would be allotted to each student as well as some VIP tickets to college scouts and the press. All other tickets had to be purchased at the gate before the first match started. This had been advertised for weeks in advance, but still more than a few people desiring to see only the final match went away angry, after being turned away when they showed up past the posted event time. Others, hoping to see or participate in a violent contest more interesting than the one on the mat, were put off by the rigorous monitoring of the concessions and bathroom areas. The reputations of the leaders of both communities were at stake, and every measure had been taken to hype the excitement while insuring an orderly event.

While Carson and Frank rested in their separate rooms with their chaperones, the coaches were in the locker rooms with their teams. Each coach gave essentially the same speech. Mike Teige looked at his wrestlers as they sat and relaxed as much as possible. "Don't let the locker rooms or that arena outside these doors put stars in your eyes and make you forget why you are here." The arena had been built to attract major sporting events and the dressing area was far more lavishly outfitted than to which any of them were accustomed. "A lot of people are out there tonight that normally wouldn't be coming to one of our matches or even to a North/South Dugganville contest. Some of them don't know or care anything about high school wrestling. That's not your concern. You can let it become a distraction, or you can let it get you pumped for state. Next week North and South will head to different state contests and this match has no bearing on our standings. It's about nothing but pride, and I want you guys to go out and show the Raiders and that crowd out there some DEMON PRIDE!"

If either coach was worried about the performances of their wrestlers that night, they need not have been. Everything about the dual had a collegiate feel, raising each competitor's desires to push himself harder than ever before. The two referees had been specially enlisted from a division I referee pool. Both stated, following the match, that they had been incredibly impressed at the level in which every wrestler that night had performed. The end result was that the Red Raiders and the Demons were in a tie heading into the final match of the night, only adding to the excitement of the main event.

A ten-minute intermission had been scheduled before the final match. During that time the teams hustled to the locker rooms, took a quick shower and returned wearing their team jackets and slacks. North wore red jackets with blue slacks. South wore the same outfits only with gray slacks. Concession sales were finalized and the stands closed. When the buzzer sounded and the last two contestants trotted out, each accompanied by a coach and chaperone, everyone in attendance at the event was sitting in the stands.

Blake and Bear walked to the center of the mat and the referee issued the standard pre-match instructions. After shaking hands, the wrestlers went to their starting positions. It became clear immediately after the starting whistle to anyone knowledgeable of amateur wrestling, that this match was going to deliver all that had been promised. The wrestlers had known each other only by reputation upon the start of their first encounter. They had been cautious at first. This time, each had first-hand experience of the other's style. They both knew that there would be no tie in this match. If neither had won by fall or points after the regulation and first overtime periods, sudden death overtime periods would occur until one wrestler scored a takedown and was awarded the victory.

Much of the first period in the first match had been spent with each opponent trying to adjust to the other's style which were as opposite as their dominant hands. Carson Blake was right-handed, but it was hard to tell because nearly everything about his approach was balanced, a textbook approach to stability. Frank had thought that he moved like a giant spider, he found it so difficult to find an opening. He had also thought that Blake, being so tall and skinny couldn't be very strong. He quickly discovered that he was wrong the first time the other wrestler grabbed his ankle. It had felt like a vice grip attached to a pneumatic hose.

Carson had also misjudged his northside rival during their first match. The left-handed Frank held his right foot so far back that he looked completely off-balance. Blake discovered two things about Frank's style when he tried to take advantage of the awkward looking stance and had suddenly found himself on bottom. He discovered that the short powerful wrestler's style was intended to throw his opponent off balance and that Frank Bear was the quickest wrestler he had ever encountered. Carson Blake was a hot head, but not a dirty wrestler. He had known that the move that had temporarily disabled Bear was a cheap shot, but he had lost his cool and had done it out of frustration. That didn't keep him from being angry over being denied a victory he felt he had clearly earned, and that anger had grown over the weeks following their first match.

He intended that there would be no doubt who the better wrestler was after that night and determined to put Bear on his back before the end of regulation. Carson Blake did not have a happy home-life, and school was a struggle for him. Wrestling had been the one endeavor where he hadn't been just good; he had been recognized as the best. He had felt that recognition threatened when his dad had told him about the move and used some crappy line about it being for a better life for them both. Then, on his very first match in a new state, this short ugly Indian jerk supposedly wrestled him to a tie. It wasn't fair. He had gone on to win every other match that season by fall, the majority of them in the first period, but the pile of crap in front of him had ruined a perfect four-year record. He was about to set the record straight.

Frank Bear had never had his confidence shaken, but he hadn't seen the move coming that nearly caused him to pass out. Unsportsmanlike or not, he should have seen it coming. For the rest of that first match, he had lost his fearlessness. Frank wasn't sure if his opponent really had taken him down in that last second, but he knew he had held back. It had been a long time since he hadn't been positive of the outcome before going into a match. Tonight, he was going to score a decisive victory for his team, but more importantly, for himself.

After the first whistle, few people in the stands would have ever believed that this match would ever last to the third period, much less go into overtime. The combatants weren't trying to just win; each was trying to assert dominance. Take downs, escapes, reverses, and near falls came at a furious pace. The collegiate referees that had been recruited for the night had alternated matches for the first eleven weight classes of the night. For this match, they alternated periods. At the end of the first period, Carson Blake led by two points, and the referees exchanged comments as they swapped places.

"I hope you wore your running shoes tonight. These guys are at least as good as anything you will see in the college ranks, and they aren't holding anything back."

"You don't need to tell me. I've been watching."

The score continued to see-saw throughout the second period but at the end Blake led again, this time by three points. Frank had started to become aware of something in his opponent's moves that he had also noticed in the first match before he had been addled by being slammed to the floor. Blake's stance was becoming less balanced as if his left side was growing tired more quickly than his right. Carson Blake had always taken his fitness regimen seriously, but he hadn't had to wrestle a full match all season. He also didn't run for the sheer joy of movement the way Frank had done for his entire life. Frank started to bait his slowly fading opponent by feinting for his right side before attacking his left. It worked on multiple occasions and with only seconds remaining in the final period, Bear was on top of Blake and led by four points.

Someone other than Frank Bear may have simply let his opponent escape. He could then play defense on his feet for the last few seconds. An escape is only worth one point and Frank would have still won by three. It would have been nearly impossible for his opponent to score anymore points in the remaining seconds. Frank Bear wasn't any wrestler, and this wasn't any match. Blake tried to tripod up to his hands and feet, and Frank sensed the opportunity to bring the contest to a decisive end by scoring a fall or at least a near fall. He moved his weight forward to go for the pin, but Blake ducked his shoulders under Frank and moved behind his opponent, momentarily turning his shoulders slightly toward the mat at the same time. Blake hadn't been as exhausted as he seemed, and Bear knew that it was he who had been baited this time. The sudden reversal occurred exactly as the buzzer sounded. The referee awarded Blake not only two points for a reversal, but also two points for a near fall, tying the match.

North Dugganville fans started to boo, but Frank held up an open palm toward the crowd signaling them to stop, before lowering his hand and offering it to his opponent. Blake took the hand.

"Good move." Frank said, evenly.

Blake nodded his head slightly in acknowledgement of the act of sportsmanship, before walking to his side of the mat to get ready for the first overtime period.

No one had moved from their seats when the buzzer sounded for the first overtime period to start. Some in the crowd, more familiar with the pseudo-sport of championship wrestling or the violence of MMA than amateur wrestling, were hoping the overtime period would result in a match ending injury; preferably graphic. The administrations of the schools wanted their side to win, but they were primarily hoping that it wouldn't go on too long so they could send their students home without incident.

The thing that became obvious to everyone in the arena was that neither wrestler was slowing down even though both had just run the equivalent of a six-minute sprint while pulling one hundred and fifty pounds of weight sprinting in the opposite direction. Perhaps, only one person in the arena noticed that one slight thing had changed. Frank had never wrestled anyone as mat-savvy as Carson Blake, and his last move to save the match had been genius. He had intended for Frank to make the move to his head. Blake was still tiring, however, and his moves weren't crisp.

The whistle blew, and the combatants immediately began circling looking for an advantage. Blake feinted toward the head and then dropped toward the legs. Bear grabbed him under the arm as if he were going to use his opponent's momentum to drag him off balance and then move behind him, just has he had done in the first match. Blake's countermove was also the same. He stopped his move short and attempted to reach under Bear's Thigh and pick him up off the mat. When he did so, he dropped one tired shoulder slightly. Frank had also changed his momentum and hooked the raised shoulder with his arm. Before Blake realized that he was no longer on his feet, the referee had slapped the mat and blown his whistle. Frank had won by fall.

It had happened so quickly, that it took the crowd a few seconds to realize that the match was over. Then, NDHS fans erupted in jubilation and SDHS fans breathed a collective deflated sigh before starting to the exits. A few new wrestling fans had been created that night and others left wondering what all the hype had been about. The ending, after all of the hoopla and stress leading up to the event, was slightly anti-climactic. Many in the stands didn't wait to watch the wrestlers shake hands or the referee raise Frank's arm in victory.

On the mat, Blake took Bear's hand and looked him in the eye. It was the first loss he had suffered in his wrestling career, and tears wanted to escape from his own eyes, but they didn't. "Bear, you won this one. I hope I get a chance to change that, someday."

"Me too." The strength of their handshake and the looks in their eyes indicated mutual respect.

The only exception to the orderly exit was one fan in the stands who had stayed and watched the final handshake with an angry glare. "Loser!" The fan screamed before throwing his program and storming toward the exit while muttering profanities to himself. Several fans gave him the side eye while moving away to create distance between themselves and the angry man. It was Blake's father, Anderson Blake.

The coaches had joined their wrestlers on the mat and were shaking their hands when the outburst occurred. Coach Thomas cursed slightly under his breath and put his arm around Blake's shoulder, but his wrestler stood stone-faced, acting as if he hadn't heard. Another round of handshakes was exchanged, and the athletes headed to their respective dressing rooms with their coaches.

"Frank, I've already told the rest of the team that it's probably a good idea if you wait until tomorrow night to celebrate. The boosters will be hosting a big party for you guys."

"You don't have to tell me coach. I am beyond exhausted. Tyrell is taking me home. I am taking a shower and going to bed."

Tyrell Ramsey had moved beside the pair and spoke. "You can go, coach. The rest of your team has already headed out. I will just wait outside the locker room for him to get dressed. I think my wife and his mom are planning on pampering their poor little boy when he gets home."

Frank reddened in spite of his exhaustion, and the coach laughed. "Must be rough, Bear to have so many good-looking women fawning over you all of the time. OK guys, I will see you tomorrow night."

The coach walked away, and Tyrell Ramsey sat down on a bench outside the locker room as Frank walked in. The automatic door closed behind him, and he walked toward where his street clothes were hanging. Suddenly, it was as if a sunburst had exploded inside of his head. The blast of light lasted only seconds before everything went dark. The elated but exhausted wrestler never saw who or what hit him across the back of his neck. Ramsey waited ten minutes before he started to get concerned. *It shouldn't take him this long just to get dressed,*" he thought. He waited only another minute before he stood and walked in to check on his surrogate son. What he saw horrified him and nearly sent his stomach through his throat. Frank lay unconscious on the floor with his mouth bleeding and his eyes blackened. His head was twisted in an awkward position, and his lower left leg looked like it had been torn off and put on backward. At first, Ramsey thought he might be dead until Frank groaned slightly. Ramsey shook himself from his shock and called 911. Looking for the perpetrator of such evil wasn't an option at the moment. Tyrell Ramsey had to stay with the young man whom he loved so dearly, until help arrived.

* * * * *

Frank Bear spent the next month in the hospital, part of that time in a medically induced coma. He was never left alone during the nightmarish time. His mother, Tyrell Ramsey, and Tabitha Ramsey took turns to ensure that he was always with someone. Rumors ran rampant as to who the perpetrators might be. It was no secret that betting on the match was heavy, and many thought the local mob was behind it. The person or persons responsible for the sadistic attack that night was never found, however. When Frank was finally wheeled out to be taken home, he still wore a neck halo, and his left leg was held straight by a contraption that looked like a medieval torture device. He hadn't spoken for weeks and it had been feared that he might suffer from permanent brain damage. Fortunately, brain scans had shown no permanent damage and it was hoped that he would, over time, return to normal functioning. His ability to walk normally however, would not return. The leg had been too badly damaged in the attack. The direction of Frank Bear's life had changed forever.

Hospital staff had treated their celebrity patient like royalty as they prepared him to go home. It was the first time that Emily, Lisa, Tunner and Rachel had seen their brother since that awful night. While struggling to keep in their tears, they led the way down the hospital corridors. The neurosurgeon pushed his wheelchair. Sophia and the Ramseys followed. Hospital staff lined the hallways and cheered as he rolled toward the exit. Many of them were wearing Dugganville High School Jerseys, both from the north and south sides of the river. When the doors opened, he thought for a moment that he truly had suffered lasting brain damage. *"Who were all of these people, and where had they come from?"* Both schools' student bodies lined the path to the chauffeured limousine that would take him home. Beyond them, stood a swarm of well-wishing humanity, it looked as if the entire Dugganville population had come to see him.

Standing in the middle of the path and directly in front of him was the teacher who, with the exception of the Ramseys and his mother, had been the most powerful influence on his young life. Because of Mrs. Amber Merritt, he had come to see himself as more than just a poor Indian kid who could wrestle. What the introverted young man hadn't realized was that he had also become a superstar among his peers. Having recognized a powerful but unchallenged intelligence in her student as a freshman, she had continuously pushed him toward a highly rigorous course of study. The end result was that, before this heinous tragedy, Frank was being courted by NCAA powerhouses and Ivy League schools alike. The Native American student, once shunned because he was considered dirty and ugly, had been elevated to unapproachable status because he was simply too athletic and too smart for normal students. That had all changed in just a few short minutes of evil, but for that instant, the smiling face in front of him and the love surrounding him was all that Frank Bear needed.

* * * * *

Frank wouldn't be able to return to school for the remainder of his senior year. Any talk of college was tabled. All of the young man's energy and his family's energy had to be devoted to his healing. He had been surprised when the limousine hadn't gone to his mother's subsidized apartment or to the Ramseys' modest two-bedroom home after they had left the hospital. Instead, the ride had headed a few miles south of South Dugganville toward the small village of Beaumont, known as Indian Town by the locals. It was the town where Frank's life had begun. Before quite reaching the town's outer edge, the limousine pulled up to a large old farmhouse sitting on forty acres. Frank recognized it. He had been there several times with Tyrell on plumbing jobs.

His mother, Sophia, was the first to speak. "What do you think, Frank? They wanted to give us a brand-new house in Dugganville, but I knew you would like it better here. Tyrell and Tabitha agreed."

Frank's injury fogged brain couldn't comprehend what was happening. "How? We can't afford; charity, don't like; confused."

Tyrell knelt in front of Frank. "Frank, look at me, take a deep breath, and don't try to understand everything right now. Here is all you need to know for the moment. You, your mother, your brother and sisters, Tabitha and I are all going to live together in that house."

"But, you can't afford –," Frank stammered.

"There is a lot to explain. Don't worry about it right now. I will tell you that a lot of business people in town are grateful that all that incident cost them was paying your medical bills and buying a place for you and your family to stay. That dressing room was supposed to be secured. Ambulance chasing lawyers moved in on Sophia almost before you got to the hospital. She was frightened and confused. She asked me to deal with it for her. You may remember coming here to do some work for the old couple who owned this place before they died. Every time we came here, your face lit up. It has been on the market for a while, and I knew the family just wanted out from under it, so I told the lawyer to work a deal with both town councils. The place needs some work, but it's a solid house on a great piece of land. There are way too many details to explain right now, but let's just say our fine leading citizens were more than happy to generously donate it to you and your family as long as you promise not to sue. I thought the deal might fall through when your mother refused to accept it at first. She agreed only after I agreed to have Tabitha's and my names put on the deed as well. That's enough information for now. You can rest for another week and let your siblings drive you crazy instead of me for a change. After that, your teachers have volunteered to come in and tutor you so you can graduate with your class. Of course, Mrs. Merritt has taken the lead on that effort."

* * * * *

Frank was quiet during the following week, saying nothing about the evil that had been done to him or about the drastic change in his surroundings. It was difficult to tell how much damage had Mascots and Monuments been done to his psyche, because he had been quiet by nature before the attack. He talked to his brother and sisters, but they quickly learned not to ask him personal questions, because he would act as if he hadn't heard them. The soon-to-be high school graduate talked mostly to his long-time mentor, Tyrell Ramsey, and that was primarily about plumbing. Frank had always been keenly interested in the technical aspects of plumbing, but now he started to ask questions about the business. Ramsey was delighted to spend so much time with Frank, and never attempted to delve into what was going on in the mind of the fragile young man he considered as his son.

It began to seem as if Frank might not acknowledge that the direction of his plans had been drastically altered if not completely derailed, until Sophia sat with him in his bedroom one night before bed. Getting in and out of bed was still a painful process and he needed assistance using his special lift.

"I love you very much, son. You will overcome this." She had said something similar every night and every morning since Frank had first woken up in the hospital. She expected that he would smile without response, as he had done each time she had spoken the words before.

"I know I will, Mom. I have been so ungrateful for everything that you've done for me. Did you know that you are the person I admire most in the world?"

The comment took Sophia by surprise, and left her stuttering. "Frank, what? No. I brought you into a horrible home. I couldn't take care of you. If it hadn't been for Tyrell and Tabitha we would still be in poverty and maybe still with that awful –"

Her son interrupted before she could finish the sentence. "Mom, stop! You raised me and my brother and sisters with so much courage. I learned that while working in Indian town for my senior project. I saw Bear there. He didn't recognize me, but I would know that ugly face anywhere. I see it in the mirror every morning. I wanted to hurt him for the way he had treated you and our family, but then I thought, no; My mother has already defeated that man. Tyrell told me how you set Bear up the first time he and Tabitha met you. That took so much courage, Mom. You taught my siblings and I how to be brave when we are attacked by cowards and bullies. Because of you, I am not going to let the cowards win this battle."

Sophia Bear tried to affect a laugh, but when she spoke it was through barely contained sobs. "Are you forgetting that Tyrell and Tabitha rescued us out of a pretty bad situation?"

"No, I will never forget that. Tyrell has shown me how to be a man. You like it here with them, don't you?"

"I do, Frank. It's not about the house. I didn't want it. I don't want it. They have done so much for us, and I realized that I could give them something back. I was a lonely lost teenager when I met Bear and wanted to belong somewhere. Now, we belong." She paused for a second, then asked, "Do you think you will be ready to start back with your studies soon?"

Frank broke into a broad grin, the first one she had seen since before he went into the hospital. "I am ready, now."

Sophia knew that her son was looking forward to seeing his favorite teacher again.

* * * * *

Frank Bear had one more set of visitors before his tutoring sessions started the following week. He was sitting in his wheelchair on the spacious deck during a warm afternoon when Tyrell came out to talk to him. "Hey, tough guy, Coach Tiege and Coach Thomas stopped by and wondered if you would be up to seeing people."

A small sigh escaped the wheelchair bound senior. He knew that he needed to start seeing people outside of his family, but he wasn't sure if he was ready for the awkward sympathy. Before he could answer, Tyrell added, "And Carson Blake is with them. It's up to you Frank. Nobody is going to fault you if you say you aren't ready for it."

Ramsey had expected that the news that Blake was with the coaches would be more than Frank was ready to deal with, and he was surprised when the revelation had the opposite effect. Bear perked up, "Yes, I would like to see them."

When the trio walked onto the deck, Blake stood a couple of steps behind the coaches. He bore the remnants of what had once been a significant black eye and was noticeably uncomfortable with the meeting. The initial exchanges between Bear and the coaches were mostly lighthearted small talk, to which Carson would nod and smile awkwardly without participating in the conversation. Seeing his discomfort, Frank made an effort to engage him.

"Hey, I saw your name in the paper, state champion. The competition must have been rugged. State was over a month ago, and that mouse on your eye still shows up pretty good."

"Not too bad. Nothing like what's on the north side of the river," Blake answered quietly with an uncomfortable smile.

Barry Thomas took Blake's response as a cue. "Frank, we are actually here because Carson wanted to see you. We just came along because we heard how good Tabitha's bar-b-que is. Of course, it has to be better than anything your coach can cook up. We are going to move out to the grill while you guys talk."

"Great, Coach Thomas. Thanks. Save us some. Tabitha's cooking is definitely better than Tyrell's." Carson and Frank listened for a few seconds to the good-natured bantering among the three men and watched them as they walked toward the barbeque pit to join their wives. When Frank turned to look at his former competitor, tears were rolling down Carson's face and he was shaking almost uncontrollably.

"Frank, I didn't have anything to do with what happened to you. I hate the stupid shit that goes on in this town. I wanted to beat you worse than anything, but you're a class act man."

Frank felt a bizarre urge to get up and hug the distraught athlete. He thought that it was probably a good thing that he couldn't yet walk. "Carson, I know that you didn't have anything to do with it. Don't forget, I grew up here, and I know that a lot of stupid shit goes on in this town. I heard about the fight, and I know that at least part of it was about you not letting a bunch of slimeballs badmouth me."

"You heard about that? What is the deal with that bullshit? I thought I left all of the bigots back home. I was just sitting in the cafeteria by myself when these four soft white guys surrounded my table and started saying a bunch of stupid shit. I guess with four on one odds they thought they could take me, but it didn't go well for them. The school officials told me that they cut me some slack because I had been under a lot of pressure, which is crap. They cut me some slack because I was minding my own business, not to mention, that I had just won state and they didn't want to expel their only first place winner; plus, it would look pretty bad after what had happened to you."

"It's pretty obvious that you aren't from around here, Carson. Your championship might have kept you from getting kicked out of school, but if you hadn't put a whipping on the son of the pastor of the biggest church in town, you would have been back in class the next day. Instead, they have you in that crappy alternative school which is nothing but a holding tank."

"I guess that explains a little, but I thought churches were supposed to preach against hatred and bigotry. That Talbot Appleton guy and his son Kirby are real pieces of work. They both tried to make it sound like I attacked that little shit with no provocation. He and three of his little gang buddies had me backed into a corner."

"I don't know about all churches. Mom and Tyrell's wife, Tabitha, both attend a small church in Beaumont. I think Talbot's church got really big because he preaches what a lot of people want to hear and not necessarily what they need to hear. I could tell you a whole lot of things, but it's not worth going into. I don't go to church, so I don't really know what gets taught. Hey, I have a question for you Mr. State Champion."

"What's that?"

"I know you didn't get that eye at state, and I don't see how a marshmallow like Kirby Appleton got one in on you. He's a Viking wannabe that couldn't lift a pen knife, much less a sword."

"He didn't. The eye is a gift from my loving father. He blames me for getting demoted because I lost to you. Then, when I nearly got kicked out of school, he said I was going to cost him his job. Great dad, huh? I am the only reason he has a job. I can't wait to get away from him."

Frank thought about his own biological father. "Carson, we might have more in common than you think. I know the feeling. So, you are going to Oklahoma State?"

"Yea, but I don't know how long I will last. I heard how smart you are, Frank. I'm not. I can barely keep up in school, and like you said, I ain't learning nothin' in alternative school. Wrestling doesn't bring in big money like football or basketball, so I don't think my performance is going to pay for my grades. Listen to me feel sorry for myself. You did everything right, and you still got screwed."

"No, Carson, I don't think we've been screwed. I just think that both of us have been body slammed pretty hard. We are both going to get our wind back, and we are going to make it. Hey, you are as close as I will ever come to wrestling an Olympic champion. I would like to stay in touch."

Blake winced slightly at the reference to their first match when he had illegally slammed Bear to the mat, but he answered with a sincere smile. "I feel the same way. I would have loved to have had a rematch with you at a collegiate national championship. I will call you after I go back to Oklahoma."

CHAPTER 4

The Present – A New Man

Jason Merritt looked at the man wearing the broad grin and religious tattoos standing in front of him. Frank Bear never spoke of his wrestling career, but everyone else in town did. Everything he had believed about Carson Blake, now known as Hefner Briton, had just been shattered.

"So, you see Jason, since I can't get Mr. Bear to admit to the error of his ways, I have been blackmailing him for years and forcing him to contribute to the mission where my family and I minister in Canada."

"Oh, I've heard R2 and Rose talk about your work. They are really impressed by the good you do. I just never knew you were-"Carson Blake," Briton said, finishing Merritt's sentence. He turned briefly to Frank. "Thank you, uhhh, R2. I see that I am not the only one with a name change." Bear nodded in acknowledgement, and the man reborn as Hefner Briton turned back to Jason. "Being Carson Blake nearly destroyed me. I dropped out of OSU before I ever wrestled my first match. A smaller school in Oklahoma City offered to tutor me so that I could wrestle for them, but no way was I going small potatoes after looking at fame and glory. Instead, I ended up frying potatoes at a fast-food joint. That, and a lot of other things that I went into after dropping out of school, never lasted long. I thank my Lord that my vanity never allowed me to get involved in drugs or alcohol. I was just too proud and too handsome to let that happen."

He sat up a little straighter, adjusted his paunch and slicked back his non-existent hair with an open palm, bringing an audible snicker from Frank. Briton winked at his old friend before continuing.

"Obviously, God's intervention, along with the beautiful woman you will meet soon, helped release me from my vanity and pride. So, I was stuck in Oklahoma City, lost, arrogant, vain, and probably close to suicidal. The last straw came when my father contacted me and needed money, telling me that I owed it to him since I had cost him everything. I decided to leave everything behind that had been me, including my name. There was an exit sign on the way out of town for Hefner and Briton Roads. I thought Hefner Briton had a bit of a ring to it, so I had my name legally changed. Unfortunately, that didn't change the direction of my downward spiral. It wasn't long before I found myself homeless and in trouble with the law for auto theft. I would go on, but I fear that my old friend might kick me out of the house if I make him sit through this very long story that he has heard too many times, and I think I see the angel that led me from jail to salvation coming down R2's extremely long driveway. Let me just end by saying that Hefner Briton's life has meaning now, and he is very happy. Oh, and Frank, you actually do look a little like that robot guy."

Briton hadn't been able to resist getting in one more jab on his old friend before the men heard car doors shutting and Tia squealing excitedly from the front porch, "Jason is here. Everybody, hurry and come see Jason."

Jason, Hefner, and Frank joined Tia on the front porch. The gang from the morning outing exited the mission van that Briton had driven from Canada. It didn't take but a moment for Jason to realize why the youngest member of the family had been left at home with the men. Standing in front of him were nine females, each wearing a smile, carrying bounty from their shopping trip and talking almost nonstop. Except when being enchanted by her handsome prince, Tia was far more interested in bugs and climbing the many trees on the property than she was in shopping.

Tia's grandmother, Sophia Bear was the first to give Jason a big hug and a kiss on the cheek. At fifty-five years old, she was still trim and attractive. Rose was next. Rose Bear was mildly overweight, but carried it with grace and an infectious smile, as well as a laugh that always bubbled near the surface. Each of Frank's girls followed in succession, adhering to a long-established ritual for greeting their favorite boy in the world. All of the girls had grown up with Jason, and each of them had gone through the same crush of which their youngest sister was now experiencing. Emily, at twelve had just been fitted for braces, which frustrated her greatly because she seemed to be the only member of the family without perfectly straight teeth. Casey, at ten, was an older version of her youngest sister which was probably why she and Tia often fought. They also adored each other. Nine-year-old Jasmine was the quiet intellectual member of the sisters. Frank had resisted allowing her to be tested for the school's gifted program until it became obvious that she needed more challenge in school. All of the girls favored Frank's mother or his wife in appearance, a fact for which he had always been grateful.

Developing an immediate crush on the high school heart throb standing in front of her was Hefner Briton's oldest daughter, Rachel; thirteen. She had been so enthralled by the handsome young man that she barely heard her mother, Sarah Briton, say, "Rachel, are you going to say hello to Jason?"

"Oh, hi! My name is Rachel."

"He already knows that, dippo. Mrs. Bear introduced you while you were standing their slobbering on yourself." Hefner's eleven-year-old daughter, Mary, had definitely inherited her father's traits. She was tall, slender, athletic, had an attitude, and didn't do well in school. Surprisingly, she and Jasmine, the quiet intellectual, had hit it off immediately.

Before her sister could respond, Hefner Briton's wife, Sarah, intervened. She wore little makeup and was plain in appearance, but possessed a gentle confidence that made her attractive. "Thank you, Rachel, for modeling the proper way to introduce yourself to someone for your sister. Frank and Rose, thank you so much for having us in your home. Your generosity has meant very much to our mission over the years, and Hef always speaks in glowing terms of you, Frank. Now, to finally meet your family after all these years is a wonderful blessing."

Rose and Sophia looked at each other, each of them wearing a grin. Frank stood and held out his arms, "Well everyone, with that introduction, I think it is time we fire up the grill. Jason, these girls are going to be really disappointed if you don't join us."

Tia held his hand in both of hers and looked up at him with big pleading eyes. He didn't notice, but the oldest Briton daughter had the same look. "It seems that I've been captured and don't have much choice. Thanks for the invitation. I would love to stay."

On the way into the house, Rose and Sophia Bear held back, giggling and whispering to each other.

Rose nodded toward Sarah Briton and said, "Wow, she's good. Never raised her voice, put her younger daughter in her place, saved Rachel from being embarrassed and changed the subject before anyone caught on. I am sending all of my girls to live with her."

Sophia giggled in response. "I know, where was she when I was raising my children?"

* * * * *

The invitation to dinner had been typical of the Bear clan. The Britons had planned on stopping only to say thank you and for his wife to meet the family that had contributed so much to their mission work. They didn't leave until two days later after Rose insisted that the Briton family needed more rest before their return to Canada, and a bond was forged between the two families. Frank Bear, or R2 as he was called by many in the community, had turned a small mom and pop venture into an incredibly successful widespread business. Each of Frank's younger siblings played active roles in Ramsey and Son Plumbing, Inc. His magnanimity was well known in the area and among his employees. The large but simple home and acreage that had once been deeded to Sophia Bear in an attempt to avoid a possible law suit was now a beautiful estate, but it had somehow managed to retain its warm and welcoming atmosphere. *Ramsey and Son* bar-b-ques on the large lawn covered with picnic tables were regular events for employees and their families. Anyone not knowing Frank's history might have believed that he had grown up as one of the old-elite of Dugganville.

A few days after the Britons had returned to Canada, Jason stopped at the house. He was surprised when Frank answered the door and he hadn't been swarmed by at least one of his daughters.

"Hi. I really came to talk to you R2, but where is my welcoming committee?"

Bear laughed. "I don't know how to break this to you, but not even the little one waits by the door every minute just hoping her knight in shining armor will come by. They are all on a girls' outing for the day or until Rose's patience wears out. I was doing some reading in the library. Come join me. I will get us some tea."

Unlike the family room, the library was neat and orderly. It was lined with texts of every ilk, from classic novels to science fiction to political documents including the constitution of the United States and Marx's communist manifesto. The primary text of every major religion also sat on the shelves, and Frank Bear had read them all at least once. Although Bear had never attended college, he was an insatiable student of humanity. Being invited into the library was a little like stepping on to holy ground. Even Tia seemed to grow up just a bit when she sat on her Daddy's lap in the library.

The pair sat with their drinks and the conversation meandered through the general topics they usually discussed, such as Merritt's preparation for the upcoming state tournament or how he and his mother, Amber Merritt, were doing. Ten minutes into the conversation, Frank looked at his young mentee and asked a question. "Jason, you know I could talk to you all day about anything, but I know you didn't come here to talk about wrestling. Why don't you ask me what you came here to ask, instead of walking around the edges?"

Merritt sighed, hesitated a bit while looking for the right words, and then began. "Ok, it has to do with what you just said to me. R2, you always know everything I'm thinking before I say it, and that's what has been chewing on me since this weekend. Before you say it, I do know you well enough to know what you are going to say after I ask my question. You don't talk about the past because you can't do anything about it. Everyone else in this town talks about your past though, and all I know about you is what they say. I thought Carson Blake was some monster whose dad had put a hit out on you because he couldn't beat you in wrestling. I had no idea that he was this really nice guy that you have kept in contact with for years; and a preacher at that. You don't even believe in God, and you certainly don't like preachers. You don't talk about it, but I've watched you walk away every time anyone even mentions the Reverend Talbot Appleton, his son Kirby, or their church. I knew you had been donating a lot of money for years to a group helping indigenous peoples in Canada, but I found out two days ago that it's a mission led by a Jesus Freak. I don't get it, R2. I know my dad can be kind of a creep, and I know he doesn't like you, but he won't tell me anything. Mom won't tell me anything, and you won't tell me anything. Whenever I ask you anything, you only tell me about R2, the man who was raised by Tyrell Ramsey. I know more about a man who I barely met before he died, than I do about the man who practically raised me, the one I look up to more than anyone on the planet. Whether you know it or not, You are my hero, but I don't know who you are. Who is Frank Bear?

CHAPTER 5

The Past – Young Frank Bear

Frank Bear's story was not a rags-to-riches fairy tale. It was an example of how dogged determination and not letting hard times get you down can lead to a successful life. It didn't hurt that he had been born with natural athletic talent and a keen intellect. As his last name might imply, Franklin Bear was a full blood Native American. More specifically, he was a member of the Cherokee nation. Throughout his lifetime he had dealt with both negative and positive stereotypes associated with his heritage. As a result, he would become an outspoken critic of automatically attaching traits to names or backgrounds.

Bear's early childhood had been devastatingly poor, the byproduct of generational and cultural poverty. His mother, Sophia Bear, tried her best to keep her home clean and her children fed, but without adequate financial resources or educational training, she was barely able to maintain the household from month to month with the small amount of government aide she received. Frank, her oldest child, couldn't remember ever having had any attachment to the man living in their dirty little house. The little boy didn't really care if the man he knew only as Bear was his father, since he had experienced no opportunity to develop a concept for the word. He couldn't remember having any interaction with the man until he was four years old. He had only remembered seeing him that day, because it had been his birthday and his mother had made him a beautiful birthday cake with real candles. The man had burst through the door screaming at his mother about the money she had wasted on the cake. She grabbed the cake handed it to her son and told him to run quickly out back. It was the first time he had escaped to his forest wilderness. He sat on a rock until he saw the man leave. When he went back in to tell her thank you, she smiled and told him she loved him and that she was proud of him. Both of her eyes were swollen.

A few months later, the man showed up and told his pregnant mother, two younger sisters and little brother that they were leaving their little town and moving to something called a government housing project in a place called North Dugganville. Soon, the little boy's big forest wilderness would be replaced by concrete and broken glass. Frank realized later that the man must come around sometime, or he wouldn't have so many little brothers and sisters. The newest baby turned out to be a girl. That same man was responsible for Frank starting kindergarten a year late. He had told Frank's mother that the whelp needed to stay home and pull his weight. If not for a visit from social services, school for the dirty little Indian boy might have been delayed indefinitely.

Frank Bear's life began to change immediately however, upon entering kindergarten. His teacher, Mrs. Tabitha Ramsey, also of Native American heritage, noticed how quickly that, although starting out behind the other students in the class, the bright eyes of little Frank picked up on every lesson. He soon outpaced the other students. His agility and strength were also impossible to keep from noticing. Unkempt and often smelling badly, little Frank spent most of his time on the playground alone. Mrs. Ramsey's heart went out to him, and she called her husband. "Tyrell, I think you should come meet this little boy. He is really pretty special."

Tyrell Ramsey owned a small plumbing shop in town and was a wrestling enthusiast. He volunteered as the coach for the afterschool wrestling program at his wife's school. He had a dazzling smile made all the more brilliant against the smooth blackness of his skin. In his early forties, he was still remarkably fit. Any visitation by Mrs. Ramsey's dark and handsome husband was a time of joy for her students. The little girls giggled when he winked at them, and the boys wanted to compare biceps with him.

"Ok, so where is the future star of North Dugganville Wrestling," he asked, as he sat down beside her on the playground and handed her a sack from the local drive-thru.

"He is out there on the playground, by himself."

"Why?"

"Because, kids can be cruel, and they say he smells bad."

"Well, does he?"

"Not too much. I have been helping him clean up after he gets here, but his clothes are a challenge."

"Sweetheart, I'm all in for trying to help this kid, but why did you pick him out for after school wrestling. I mean, the hygiene thing is a problem."

"Just watch him for a few minutes."

Frank sat by himself until the other children migrated away from the playground equipment to play a game. As soon as the last student drifted off, he sprinted toward the teeter-totter and ran up its wooden plank. Rather than run its full length, he went into a head roll as soon as his weight forced the board down, coming up on his feet at a full sprint. Mr. Ramsey was impressed by the move as well as surprised that his protective wife hadn't tried to stop her student. Frank ran straight for the merry-go-round and started pushing it as fast as he could. He jumped on and started to ride it like a surfboard. This time, Tabitha Ramsey did feel a sense of panic, but Frank jumped off before she could call out to him.

He ran straight for the gym bars that were configured in the shape of a giant Rubik's cube. Instead of simply climbing the structure, he frog-hopped up each level. Once on top, he started to hop from one side to the next. Tabitha Ramsey could stand no more. She stood and started to run to the gym bars. Just as she did, Frank lost his footing and fell from the top, landing flat on his back with an audible thud on the soft playground bedding below. Tyrell Ramsey passed her and reached the fallen daredevil first.

He looked down into the boy's face, and it was obvious the child was having difficulty breathing. "Try to relax, Frank. I want you to take a deep breath and hold it."

Frank followed the instruction keeping the breath for a second or two before a spasm forced it out.

"Good. Deep breath and hold it." This breath lasted a little longer. "Better. Deep breath and hold it."

The exercise lasted a few more repetitions until Frank's breathing began to return to normal. He looked up at the two concerned faces staring down at him. "Boy, Mrs. Ramsey, your husband is the blackest Indian I ever saw."

Both Ramseys' laughed, in spite of their concern. Tabitha had told Frank that her husband was coming to meet him, but she hadn't mentioned that he was African American. "And Frank Bear," Tyrell responded, "you may be the toughest little Indian, I ever saw. You weren't scared, were you?"

"Naw, I fall a lot. I've knocked my breath out before. It always comes back. Besides, this playground is a lot softer than the parking lot at our apartment."

"What does your mother say," Tabitha asked, while trying to fight back the tears forming in her eyes.

"Nothing, usually until I go back inside. She's too busy watching my brother and sisters. I think she always knows when I fall though, because she looks at me all over. I play by myself most of the time." "I think we may have to do something about that," Tyrell said, flashing his toothy grin.

The encounter on the playground was the beginning of a powerful bond between Frank Bear and the dark handsome Indian looking down at him. The Ramseys, both in their forties had wanted children, but had been unable to conceive. Fertility treatments were too costly for their modest incomes and navigating through adoption was tough enough when you weren't a biracial couple. Both of them had taken an immediate liking to the bright little boy in his crusty shell. They determined to try and play a role in Frank's life.

Tabitha had met Mrs. Bear once, and knew her to be a loving mother. She simply didn't have the resources to raise five children, all under the age of seven. All she knew about Mr. Bear was that he didn't have a job and was rarely in the picture. The Ramsey's devised what they thought would be a plan to help the little boy during his kindergarten year. It lasted much longer.

The first time Tyrell and Tabitha met Frank's mother together, they had taken Frank home from after-school wrestling instead of having him ride the activity bus. As with everything Frank did, he had proven to be a naturally talented wrestler, and the couple wanted to offer to sponsor him, i.e., buy his supplies. To their surprise, Mrs. Bear's husband was there. Neither of them would ever learn his full name. He surlily introduced himself only as, "Bear."

As soon as the Ramsey's began laying out their proposal to mentor the child, Bear interrupted. "Ain't gonna be no more after-school rasslin. Boy already misses enough of his chores goin to school. You people can go on home." He paused and sneered at Tabitha, "And what's wrong with you lady? Your people ain't good enough for you."

Tyrell, took a deep breath, ignored the insult, and was about to try and explain how the plan could work when he was again interrupted, this time by the usually silent, Mrs. Bear. As always, she spoke in a soft barely audible voice. "Bear, the county sheriff dropped by yesterday while you were out drinking. He wouldn't tell me much, but he said something about a warrant. I told him you would be here this evening. He should be here anytime."

Bear startled and jumped from his seat at the announcement. "BITCH!" He shouted. He started to reach for Frank's mother, but saw Tyrell's eyes widen and start to stand. He sat back down. He knew he had already touched a nerve with the powerfully built black man, and he quickly decided not to push his luck.

"Bear, your clothes are in a bag on the bed. You should go now," Sophia continued, sounding matter of fact.

"You can't throw me out," he replied, more whining now than demanding. He kept one eye on Tyrell.

"I don't think you have time to argue," she answered.

Without further words, the now terrified Bear stepped into the only bedroom in the apartment and grabbed a half-full dirty canvass bag. Without looking up, he ran back through the front room and exited the front door, slamming it behind him. Frank and his four younger siblings had witnessed the entire exchange.

Tabitha was stunned that none of them had shown an ounce of emotion. Even the youngest, slept peacefully in her crib.

"I apologize Mr. and Mrs. Ramsey, and thank you for being here. I am not afraid of Bear, but I was afraid he might hurt one of the little ones, if I was here by myself when I told him."

"Please, Mrs. Bear, call us Tyrell and Tabitha," Tabitha said, "but tell me, did the sheriff really stop by yesterday?"

"Oh no," she started with a hint of a smile. "I called them a few minutes before you got here and told them where he would be running. I will call you Tyrell and Tabitha, but you must call me Sophia. I know Frank likes you very much, because he normally doesn't talk much, but he tells me about both of you every day."

Then, for just a second, a small sob escaped her breast and a tear appeared in the corner of her eye. She wiped it quickly. "I am so sorry that my house and my children are dirty. I try hard, but Bear has always taken most of what little assistance we get. I am glad to be rid of that little worm. It would mean so much to Frank if he could stay in your program."

Tyrell knew immediately how Frank had come by his fearlessness and his toughness. After leaving Frank's family that evening, he and Tabitha made a commitment that their mentorship would extend beyond Frank, to his mother and siblings. They didn't have a lot of money, but they had connections and the benefit of an education. They researched and found better housing for the family, continuing education for Sophia, and early childhood programs for the children.

Frank grew quickly in school. His intellect was keen and athleticism obvious, but he was also quiet and somewhat apart from the other students. Although he soon had access to adequate hygiene and decent clothing, he would continue to be known as the stinky Indian kid throughout most of his early years in school. His long straight black hair, wide forehead and skin that looked like it was molded from clay only enhanced the image.

Frank would never become part of the "in-crowd" in the predominately white upper-socioeconomic community of North Dugganville, but by the time he was in middle school, his athletic skills brought him acceptance, although it never seemed to really matter to the introspective adolescent. His joy came in being with the Ramseys. The childless couple returned the love and embraced all of the Bears as part of their new-found family. Frank spent many of his afternoons helping Tyrell clean up his shop, and Sophia became Tabitha's unofficial aide by helping the teacher cut, paste and create for her classroom.

Frank's attachment to Tyrell diminished only slightly when he entered his freshman year in high school. Mike Tiege, the high school wrestling coach, had spent a lot of time talking to Frank about the possibilities that he might have as a wrestler of his caliber, but that wasn't what caused him to lose focus on the man he looked up to as a father figure. Although he hadn't shown it, Frank had been as bewildered and overcome by high school as every other freshman student on his first day of class. While some of the boys were trying to get noticed by the girls, the introverted teen was trying to make himself as invisible as possible. In addition to being surrounded by more students than he had ever seen before, he had also recently been beset by a strong case of adolescent acne. The bumps across his nose felt like golf balls trying to rupture through the skin, and he was positive that everyone who passed by was looking at them. Although exhausted and terrified by this new world, he continued to wear his ever-present mask of calmness when he walked into ninth-grade civics for his last class of the day. There, he was greeted by Mrs. Amber Merritt and found himself in dumbstruck awe. Never before had the teenager experienced having his breath knocked so completely from him.

"Good afternoon, class. I am so happy that you have almost made it through your first day of high school." Mrs. Merritt went on to explain that she was twenty-six and had been teaching for four years. She said something that made the class laugh, but Frank didn't hear it. Everything but the vision in front of him was lost in a fog. He was able to pay attention long enough to hear her explain that her husband had recently been elected to the state senate and that he would be visiting the class as a resource from time to time. He knew that she must have said something about class rules and the curriculum for the course, but Frank couldn't recall any of it. All he could remember about that last class of the day was the beautiful fair-skinned lady at the front of it. Frank Bear was deep in the throes of a crush.

It took him days to recover. Sophia Bear asked her son several times over the weekend if he was ok, as did Tyrell Ramsey. His normally sharp helper was clumsy and had a hard time following direction. Frank's siblings teased him that he had fallen on his head too many times. It was not until the Ramseys attended freshman open house with his mother that the cause of Frank's malaise became crystal clear. Frank had always breezed through any situation, but his discomfort became more and more apparent as they followed his student schedule through the evening. When time came to visit his last period class, the freshman student looked as if he might become physically ill.

"Tabitha, it's so good to see you. I thought you would be home getting ready for the little ones." Amber greeted her fellow teacher with a smile and a hug.

"What? They know each other," thought Frank in a panic. He shrunk even further.

Sophia looked at her son's discomfort and she realized immediately the cause of his sudden and strange affliction. He had been abused by his father and belittled by other students in school, but this was the first time she had ever witnessed her son not in control of his emotions. She couldn't suppress a slight giggle.

"It's good to see you, too, Amber. Ordinarily, I would be, but Tyrell and I are here with our unofficial but still as closely held family." With that beginning, Tabitha introduced Sophia to Frank's new teacher. If Mrs. Merritt had any intention of telling his mother about what a total air-head he had been in her class for the first week of school, she never let on. In fact, the freshman student seemed to be nearly forgotten in the adult conversation. Once again, Frank was finding it difficult to breath.

"Take a deep breath. Hold it. Take a deep breath. Hold it. You've had your breath knocked out before. It always comes back," he kept telling himself.

The next day in class Frank found himself finally able to focus on Mrs. Merritt's lesson instead of on her. Still more than a little taken by her attractiveness, he was able to concentrate, and after the fog had cleared, discovered that she was the best teacher he had ever had, except for Tyrell and Tabitha Ramsey. She did more than teach students a rote set of facts, which had always caused a struggle with boredom for the inquisitive student. The energetic teacher with the sparkling eyes challenged students to question why things were the way they were. The only area in which he continued to struggle was class discussions. The shy teenager listened intently, but even when other students made comments that he considered unintelligent, he remained reticent to contribute vocally. Expressing himself to others brought on a sense of near panic.

The inquisitive young student did thoroughly enjoy the guest speakers who Mrs. Merritt regularly brought into her class. He could not have known how one of those speakers would drastically change the course of his life. Only a week had passed since open house, when Mrs. Merritt introduced her husband, Robert Thomas Merritt, to her students. Merritt was eleven years older than his wife and a freshman state senator, considered to be a rising star among the progressive movement in an otherwise conservative state.

"The first thing you should know about me is that I am not Mr. Merritt or Senator Merritt, but simply R.T. I am not sure of the exact lineage, but I am an ancestor of R.T. Beaumont, who's statue protects us from the other side of the river. If my father had his way, I would have been named Raeford Thaddeus Merritt. I am so grateful to my mother." The class laughed at the oft delivered line from the senator.

"My father's revenge is that he still refuses to call me anything but R.T." Another chuckle arose from the students. The senator went on to explain that he would keep his discussions with them as politically neutral as possible. Mrs. Merritt had already explained that she would be inviting conservatives and progressives to her class to keep perspectives as balanced as possible. While speaking, he noticed the Indian kid with the broad face, thin lips and an acne problem sitting in the front row and taking notes. When R.T. Merritt opened the front door to his home later that evening, it was obvious that the businessman and state senator had been drinking, a practice that had become increasingly more frequent. He went to the well-stocked liquor cabinet in the home, poured a drink and after unsteadily sitting down, called to his wife. "Hey Sweet Cheeks, who was the greasy looking Indian kid in your class today."

He had also begun to call her disgusting pet names, and she hated it. "That was Frank Bear. He isn't greasy. He is a really hard-working kid with a lot of promise." Reluctantly, she continued and gave her husband a brief account of how Tyrell and Tabitha Ramsey had met her student and had taken the whole family under their wings.

"Interesting," he responded after digesting the story. "I wonder if," Amber interrupted, "R.T., please don't get any ideas. Frank is a great kid, and the Ramseys love him dearly. You promised when I invited you to speak to the class that you wouldn't use it to promote any of your agendas. He wants to wrestle and to work for Tyrell. He is also one of the few freshman students I have ever encountered that takes school seriously. I've heard Tyrell talking to the coach, and both of them think he could be good enough for a scholarship one day. And, please don't forget that the Ramseys aren't your biggest fans."

"Don't get so touchy," he said before swirling the ice in his glass and taking another drink. "If the kid weren't so homely, I might think you two had something going. How old did you say he was?" "He is fifteen. He started to school late. Please leave him and his mother alone, R.T."

"Fifteen. Eleven years difference between you and him. That's exactly the age difference between you and me. Maybe, I should be concerned."

It wasn't the first time her husband had made hurtful insinuations and Amber was growing tired of them. "For such a big shot senator, you can really be an insecure little prick sometimes. Leave them alone."

"This prick is who is keeping you in this big house. I noticed the little shit sat on the front row. How often do you bend over his desk to help him?"

Amber attempted to slap her husband as he sat in his chair, but he reached up, caught her wrist, and squeezed hard enough to make her wince. "You really need to calm down. I am just interested in our less served citizens, that's all."

Amber looked at R.T. in anger and confusion. *"What had happened,"* she thought. They had only been married for two years, but they had dated for two years before that, and he had never been like this until his election, and the sudden growth of the real estate business he owned with his father.

"Since you just made it clear that it's your big house. I will sleep in the guest room." She wanted to make another comment about the size of his manhood, but knew that would only make matters worse. His ego had also seemed to erase his memory, and she knew that reminding R.T. Merritt of how he had been able to start his business and purchase the house would only give him another chance to tout his greatness. When they first got married, the couple lived in a rented apartment and her new husband owned nothing but big ideas. His family touted its long history among the Dugganville elite, but that heritage hadn't translated into wealth. Amber's parents, who were modestly wealthy, had provided him with the start-up money for both the house and the business.

Merritt and his father had been equally charming and convincing in presenting how their business model would work. The parents, wanting nothing but happiness for their daughter, agreed to grant her inheritance money early with the idea that it would yield much more to her in the long run in an active business account. At the time, it had all seemed logical to the young school teacher since she and the dashing R.T. Merritt would be together forever.

* * * * *

Whereas before open house, Frank would say nothing to Tyrell or his mother about school or his civics teacher, he now couldn't stop talking about either. He rarely mentioned other students, but he talked about the new moves he was learning in wrestling and he talked about his classes; particularly civics. When he told Tyrell that R.T. had spoken to the class, Tyrell stopped him.

"R.T.? Who is R.T.," he asked, although he already knew the answer.

"Oh, he is Mrs. Merritt's husband. He's really smart and pretty cool for an old guy."

"Old guy? I am quite a bit older than him. What does that make me?"

Frank looked up sheepishly. Now in his fifties, Tyrell's waistline had started to expand slightly, and his once jet-black hair was peppered with gray. He still had the same impish twinkle in his eyes, and those eyes were looking down on Frank waiting for an answer.

"Uhhh, way cool?"

Tyrell laughed, but quickly asked Frank in a concerned voice, "Did this R.T. talk to you alone?"

"No, I had to hurry and get to wrestling practice, but he said he would like to talk with me sometime, and he gave me his card." The boy held the card up to his long-time mentor.

Tyrell frowned. "Frank, first of all, I have never heard you call your teacher anything but Mrs. Merritt. I don't think you should address her husband as anything but Mr. Merritt. Also, you have wrestling and school. You have to help your mother. And don't forget that you have to work for me if you want any spending money. Mrs. Merritt is a wonderful teacher, but don't get wrapped up in any side activities that the senator might have for you."

Frank looked confused, but answered, "Oh, OK Tyrell."

Ramsey didn't like or trust R.T. Merritt. The senator had once tried to use him and Tabitha as the faces for one of his progressive causes because of what they looked like. The couple considered Amber Merritt to be a close friend, but they had resented being used. Amber had apologized profusely to them as soon as she learned of her husband's actions.

Tyrell spoke to his wife that evening. "I don't like it, Tabitha. I've known R.T. his whole life and he's never given a damn about anybody but himself, just like his dad. Now, he's suddenly a crusader for the downtrodden minorities. How your friend Amber ever got fooled by that piece of human slime I don't know, but I am not going to let him suck Frank into any of his schemes. I've already had a taste of that, myself."

"I know you're worried Tyrell, but you have to calm down. I'm worried, too. Amber hasn't been the same lately. She is distant. Something is bothering her. We also have to remember, however, that we aren't Frank's legal guardians and Sophia thinks that, with the exception of you, Amber is the most wonderful thing that ever happened to Frank. She really thinks that her influence is what is going to inspire her son to want to go to college, and she may be right."

"I know," he answered through slightly gritted teeth. "I have to admit that I am a little jealous of that good-looking blonde friend of yours. I was sort of counting on adding, AND SON to the Ramsey's Plumbing sign."

Tabitha put her hands on her hips and stood in front of her husband in mock indignation. "Wait a minute, Mr. Ramsey. I am supposed to be the one jealous of good-looking women turning her men's heads, not you."

Tyrell put his head down and laughed, embarrassed by his own admission. His wife had always been able to make him look at himself and laugh. "You're right, Sweetheart. Sophia is his mom and a great mom at that, but she can also be pretty gullible, and I guess I am as protective of her as I am of Frank. If you get a chance to talk to Amber, will you please see if you can get her to tell you what is going on with her husband?"

"I will. I hope you remember that I am the one who first fell in love with that little boy and his family."

The Ramseys needn't have worried. Guest dignitaries still spoke in Mrs. Merritt's class, but Senator R.T. Merritt never returned.

Chapter 6

The Past – What I Am

Frank always looked forward to the last period of the day. In addition to getting see Mrs. Merritt, he was finally challenged to think after having spent the day breezing through a schedule that was ridiculously easy for him. One aspect of Civics class that continued to leave him stymied was his teacher's insistence that students participate in class discussions. Mrs. Merritt was skillful at bringing the most reluctant students into the conversation, but Bear invariably froze whenever he was asked to express an opinion.

She had established the practice of allowing the students to choose one discussion for each nine-week session as long as the topic was relevant to the class. The topic the students had chosen as the first session topic for each of her first three years of teaching had been team mascots. She had no reason to believe that the selection would be any different for the current year. It wasn't. She remembered from her time as a student at NDHS that the issue had come up every football season since the Reverend Talbot Appleton had become the pastor of a church in South Dugganville. It was then that Appleton chose to rant about the evils of choosing demons as a mascot. The choice of that topic had always made her a little nervous, but it was natural, considering that most of the members of the class were boys and athletes. For the most part, the discussions had been what she had considered to be surprisingly mature for her group of students. Only one near disaster had occurred during her second year of teaching when a student, who was also a member of the pastor's church, had been overly zealous in supporting the Reverend Allen.

Otherwise, she had been able to hook into the students' interest in athletics to explore current cultural issues behind the selection of mascots. Frank Bear was the first indigenous student who had been in her class, and she was again nervous about possible negative outcomes. Her fear came into being a few minutes into the class. Frank, as was his custom, had sat silently during the discussion.

"Well, since us Demons are playing the Red Raiders next week, I think we should hear from the Indian on that one. Or Frank, is a Native American what you are?" The question from the handsome student in the back of the room was obviously delivered with the intent of mocking the student sitting on the front row.

Like Frank, Braden Paxton was a year older than most of his classmates. He had been held back a year in elementary school, and continued to struggle academically. Also, like Frank, he was one of the outstanding athletes in the freshman class at NDHS. At the age of fifteen, he already stood 6'2" and weighed close to two hundred pounds. He consistently hid his lack of academic confidence in himself by demeaning others. He had, on more than one occasion, tried to bait Frank into a fight when they had been in middle school. Paxton was one of the few students with whom Amber Merritt found it difficult to make a connection. *Make a connection? Who am I kidding? I don't like that arrogant jerk,*" she had often thought. She was on the verge of breaking her self-imposed policy against berating students when Frank Bear quietly raised his hand.

"Yes, Frank?"

"I would like to answer that question, if it's OK, Ma'am."

"Oh, Dear God, I hope I don't have to break up a fight," was Amber Merritt's immediate thought, but her star student had never volunteered to participate in a discussion.

"OK, Frank. Go ahead."

Bear hesitated, before asking, "May I stand and look at Braden? It feels awkward to answer someone sitting behind me."

"*This could end so badly,*" she thought. "Ahh, umm, OK. Why don't you stand up here, at the lectern."

Most of the students knew Frank from elementary and middle school, but he had always been a silent fixture that no one really paid any attention to. They were as baffled by his behavior as had been the teacher.

Frank stood at the lectern and began. He sounded almost kind, as if he were explaining to a child who was struggling to grasp the obvious.

"It really doesn't matter whether you describe me as Native American or American Indian. Neither term accurately describes what I am. Braden and I were in the same American History class last year," Frank said, while looking over the class and then down at his teacher. She had taken his unoccupied seat.

"In that class, we learned that Christopher Columbus got lost and thought he hand landed on the coast of India, so he called my ancestors Indians. Later an Italian mapmaker, named Amerigo Vespucci, concluded that Columbus had discovered a new land, and this new land was named after him.

This land was not discovered by Christopher Columbus, and many groups of people had lived in it before it was named for a mapmaker. As with fair skinned Europeans, the inhabitants of this land were not one people, but many. They had systems of government, inter-tribal trade, religion, and they had families. Like the countries of Europe, the tribes here fought wars and committed atrocities against each other, and sometimes they took slaves. There was kindness and cruelty among them, as well as truth and lies. The only real new things that Europeans brought to this land were their vast numbers, powerful new weapons, total disregard for the land, and disease."

Bear concluded his short soliloquy with, "Like the Europeans and people everywhere, my ancestors and the ancestors of other people indigenous to this land, liked to think of themselves as special. I hear students in the hallway talk about what they are sometimes. They say they are Irish, German, English or French.

We all know that Braden is a proud Scot, because he often wears a shirt that says so." A ripple of laughter ran through the classroom. Even Paxton smiled and thumped his thumb on his chest.

"I have never heard anyone say only that they are European. My people, The Cherokee, refer to themselves as Aniyvwiya; which means, the real people. So, if you are asking me what I am, I will tell you what I am not, first. I am not European or from the subcontinent of India, and I am not a mascot. I am a person, I am an American, and I am Cherokee."

Frank quietly sat back down. The class remained silent for a few seconds until a loud whisper could be heard from near the back of the room. "Scalp!"

Mrs. Merritt almost corrected the student whom she knew had made the remark, but she didn't want to take the moment away from her terribly shy student, and she could tell from the body language and eye contact among the other students that Paxton, not Frank, had been its target. Beyond that, she had also found it humorous and oddly appropriate. The stud football player had been effectively put in his place. Still, she felt relieved when the bell sounded and students filed out of her classroom. It was impossible for her to miss that several students, including the whisperer and surprisingly, Braden Paxton, gave Frank a quick high five as they walked by.

"Frank, could you wait a few moments, before going to wrestling practice?"

Bear felt a sense of panic that he had said something to upset his teacher. "Yes Ma'am, I'm sorry if I shouldn't have said those things."

"Sorry? Frank, don't apologize. That was eloquent. I wish that several adults I know had heard it. Did you learn that from your mom or Tabitha?"

"A little from both, Ma'am, but mostly from Tyrell. I help him in his shop after practice, and we talk a lot. He says that it is very important that I never let anyone else define my heritage for me and, that in order to keep that from happening, I must learn my heritage. He also says to never let anyone else's ignorance hold me back. He and Tabitha teach all of us a lot more than we learn in school."

"Wow! You are very fortunate. I don't know many parents who make that type of commitment to their own children."

"I know. He and Tabitha help all of us, including Mom."

Amber Merritt smiled. "Tabitha thinks your mom is an amazing woman, and I think all of you are a pretty amazing group of people."

Before continuing, a concerned look came over her face. "Frank, has my husband tried to contact you or your mom?"

Frank returned the look. "No. Tyrell asked me that same question. Why?"

"Remember what you told me that Tyrell had said about not letting anyone define your heritage for you. Well, R.T. sometimes does that to other people. I don't want it happening to you."

* * * * *

Most of the rest of Frank's high school career went smoothly, and after achieving the extremely rare feat of winning the state championship as a freshman, he became somewhat of a celebrity on campus. When he walked on campus at the beginning of his sophomore year, he heard a group of incoming freshman girls whispering as he walked by, "That's him, that's him. Is he dating anyone? Of course! Who? I don't know, but he has to be?"

Frank had never had a date. He wasn't sure what you're supposed to do on a date. Girls had always been very blunt about how ugly they thought he was. He told Tyrell about the girls when he went to his shop that afternoon after practice. Tyrell laughed until he nearly cried. "Ah, my man. Welcome to the world of fame and athletic prowess. Both have a way of making a man better looking to the opposite sex."

He had seen girls hanging on their boyfriends, and the prospect frightened him. Frank quickly developed an aura of being aloof and someone you didn't want to mess with. He talked little, looked slightly menacing and had muscles that appeared to be spring-loaded. He had to cut his hair short for high school wrestling and now, except for the persistent acne problem, the sixteen-year-old student could have passed for a navy seal. What none of the students and very few adults realized, was that the hardened features and quietness of North Dugganville's star athlete masked a terribly shy young man who felt awkward trying to talk to other students. As a consequence, rumors about who the stud wrestler was dating or what he did outside of school surfaced often, but Frank's life outside of classwork consisted entirely of helping his mother with his siblings and working alongside Tyrell.

After winning state for a second year, Frank started receiving letters of interests from universities, some of them wrestling powerhouses. After showing them to his mother, Sophia told him that he should talk to Tyrell. Ramsey tried to act surprised when Frank showed him the letters before, shaking his head. "Frank, you are a two-time state champion before you go into your junior year of high school. Student athletes start making commitments their junior year. You don't think that schools are lining up to talk to you. I thought you were supposed to be smart. Believe me, this is just the beginning."

"What should I do, Tyrell?"

"What do you mean? What should you do?"

"I mean, no one in my family has ever gone to college. I never thought about it."

"Hmmm," said Tyrell while making an exaggerated expression as if he were trying to think. "I saw on your schedule request for next year that you listed an honors humanities course that is usually reserved for college bound students. You weren't thinking of college when you signed up for that course?"

"Yes; No; Well, maybe."

"Or, since you have never thought about going to college, could you possibly have noticed the name of the teacher assigned to the course."

Frank looked down and grinned before looking back up at Tyrell. "I know you and Mom aren't ever going to let me forget that, but she is still the best teacher I ever had and the only one that ever made me want to learn more than what the test covered."

"Well, there is your answer."

"Huh?"

"Don't just ask me. Talk to Mrs. Merritt and see what she thinks. She may give you some input that will help you think past high school."

"I hadn't thought of that. Thanks Tyrell. I will. Oh, and I told Tabitha she had nothing to worry about."

It was Tyrell's turn to say, "Huh?"

"She told me that you get all dreamy faced when you talk to Mrs. Merritt, too." Frank had already turned to go and was looking over his shoulder when he delivered his exit line.

"Go home. Get out of here!" Ramsey picked up a wrench and chased Frank out of his shop in mock anger. On the way back to his workbench, he mumbled to himself, "My wife put him up to that. I know she did."

A few days later, Bear got the chance to talk to his teacher after school. She glanced through the letters and, as Ramsey had done, asked him why he was taking an honors class if he wasn't planning on going to college. Tabitha had called her beforehand to let her know that Frank would be stopping by. She already had his high school transcripts on the top of her desk. They reflected a perfect GPA, but the humanities class was the first true college prep course, he had signed up for. Frank had never met with a high school counselor. Without regard for his future, he had automatically been placed in classes that guaranteed his greatest amount of success, so that he could wrestle. Amber had been furious the first time she learned of how grossly he was being underchallenged academically.

"Frank, since the first time Tabitha introduced me to you, I've heard stories of you taking risks and pushing yourself; to be better in wrestling, with helping your mom with your siblings, and while working with Tyrell. Why aren't you doing that in school, instead of taking all these easy courses that you can do in your sleep? The biggest question you have to ask yourself is, do you want your life to end after wrestling?"

It was a question he had never considered. In fact, he had never considered anything beyond the next day. It was still early in the year and not too late to change his schedule. Amber set up a meeting with the registrar and together, they crafted a true college prep course list. Frank was now even less involved in high school social life than before, but he had added another adjective to his description; college bound.

CHAPTER 7

The Present – Who I Am

rank looked at Jason long enough before responding, that the young man started to feel uncomfortable. Finally, he said, "Hero, huh? Jason, I am going to let you in on a little-known secret. Heroes are a bit like monuments and mascots. They aren't real. They are stories, myths, caricatures that society makes up because the truth is too complex to deal with. The same can be said of evil villains. They are like that eroding piece of rock that sits out in the middle of the river. Who knows whether the man supposedly sitting on that granite horse was a noble rescuer or the devil, himself. It depends largely on who's telling the story."

"You want to know who I am. Let me tell you who Hefner Briton is first. The man whom you knew by the evil name of Carson Blake, is just a man who was once a hot-headed high school wrestler; a damn good one, but still just a screwed-up kid trying to be good at something. He had a right to be an angry hothead when he got here. He had everything going for him where he came from, and people looked up to him because he was the best at something that was important to him. Just before his senior year in high school, the man who was supposed to care for him more than anyone on Earth, uprooted him and marooned him a thousand miles away in a nothing place called Dugganville. Do you know why?" Frank paused for a moment, knowing that Jason would have no answer.

"Carson Blake was brought here because Mr. Blake was offered a raise and moving expenses to come here, as long as he chose a home in the South Dugganville School District. Mr. Blake, who was perpetually on the verge of losing his job in Oklahoma, was suddenly promoted with the expectation that his son Carson, was going to beat the half-breed kid from North Dugganville. You did know that I am supposedly half-black, or should I use the term that I have heard more than once behind my back. What those bigoted idiots don't understand is that when they think they are hurling insults at me, they are paying me the highest compliment they could possibly offer. Tyrell Ramsey was the only real father I ever had, and I am proud to think that people believe his blood runs through my veins."

Jason couldn't miss that Frank never referred to the elder Blake as Carson's father. It stung because he had also never heard the man he adored, refer to his own dad as his father; only Mr. Merritt, or R.T. He stammered through a horrified response. "No R2, I, I know – that's not. I won't let anyone. I won't ask again. It doesn't matter, anyway."

Frank held up an open hand in a stop motion. "That's Ok. You wanted to know about your hero, and we will get to him in a little bit. We are still talking about the Jesus Freak, right now. Some of the stalwarts of our community on both sides of the river brought Carson here because they wanted to see a cockfight. You know the bastards that put roosters in a ring may put thousands of dollars into breeding and raising those birds, but they could care less about their welfare. As soon as that animal loses, it's thrown on a trash heap. Carson never had a chance once he left Oklahoma. He was never going to make it in college, scholarship or no scholarship. Do you think the outstanding leaders of our community or the loving Mr. Carson cared about a kid who could barely read when they moved him half-way across the country just to beat one stinking Indian kid? They may have had to spend some money putting a deadbeat on their payroll, but you've gotta ante up if you want to get the big bucks rolling."

"I really don't need to know." Jason wanted to melt into the floor.

The heat in Frank's voice, intensified. "No, Stud. You wanted to know about the match of the century; the one between two naïve high school kids held in the middle of nowhere, America. I am going to tell you about it."

The comment was obviously intended to hurt, and it made him feel like the man who had been so abusive to him and his mother when he was growing up. *"Why am I doing this to him? My son has a right know who his real father is, and all I can do is beat him up for wanting to know about some stupid prehistoric wrestling match."*

Frank wanted badly to wrap his arms around his son and tell him how much he loved him, but the bitter memories from the past pushed their way through. He continued, "The dignified elite of our little town have long been too sophisticated for cockfights. That's much too barbaric. Instead, they play golf. I have no doubt the spectacle that nearly ruined both of those two young men's lives was dreamt up after the first nine holes of a golf game by respectable gentlemen playing a friendly round of golf during a drunken Sunday afternoon had ended in a tie. Let's make this more interesting, they would have said. Why play for a few hundred when they could all walk away with thousands? I may never know the name of the person who ended my wrestling career and nearly my life, but I know who is responsible."

Jason knew he had opened a wound that had long been buried under the surface. He had always believed the man in front of him to be incapable of anger, but he was quickly coming to realize that his hero had long hidden incredibly deep and complex feelings. He took a deep breath and waited without responding, sensing that the lesson was not yet over.

"Why do I respect and care for a Jesus Freak? Look around the room, Jason. You see a lot of books, don't you? If you read them closely enough, you might discover that many of them are saying exactly the same thing, as long as you don't care who gets credit for saying it. Many of the works in this library are espousing the same faith, whether their followers realize it or not. Yet, those followers don't treat the lessons in those beautifully written texts as a way to live life. Instead, many of the so-called faithful use them as a magical talisman or a membership card, that somehow allows them to mistreat others and get out of jail free; or hell if you are playing a different kind of monopoly, as long as they chant the magical words– I believe. If you had a couple of years free time, I could show you just a few instances, but you have a state wrestling championship coming up next week, and you don't have that kind of time. Instead, I will share with you one short verse from that book the Jesus Freak likes to hit me with every time we talk."

Bear stood up and pulled a King James Bible down from one of the shelves. The shelf included The Torah, Koran, and Buddhism's Noble Eight-Fold Path among other religious texts. He opened the worn book and read. "Hebrews, chapter eleven, verse one. 'Now faith is the substance of things hoped for, the evidence of things not seen.'

You want to know what I believe? I believe that if a man's faith makes him hope for a better life for others and the substance of his life produces evidence of that hope, it's a good faith. Hef and I may not have the same god, and we definitely don't have the same religion, but we have the same faith. He lived through a crappy childhood, but instead of staying angry, he went on to make life better for a lot of people. Many of those people look like me, by the way! We share a faith that is more powerful than any religion. Both of us hope that kids have a safe place to grow up, and families a healthy place to live."

He put the book back on the shelf and sat down before continuing, taking a deep breath in an obvious attempt to maintain control before saying what he was about to say. "Now, if you are talking about the folks who run that church south of the river, who sell lies and practice bigotry in the name of religion, no, I don't believe in their god! Nor, do I share their faith!"

Jason winced and fought back tears. Never, had he seen R2 overtly show any emotion but joy. Jason knew that a father and son team of pastors had led the megachurch since before he was born, but he had no idea that the son, Pastor Kirby Appleton, had been pummeled by Carson Blake in high school for calling Frank Bear a derogatory name, or that Blake had been kicked out of school because of it.

He only knew that the man he believed to be his father had joined the church while his parents were going through their divorce. Jason vaguely remembered going to the church a couple of times with his father. There were a lot of kids his age there, and he had enjoyed that, but it didn't last very long. Nothing with his father ever had. It had all happened before Jason started elementary school. He knew a lot had happened that he didn't understand, but his mother had always refused to say anything bad about his father to him. In fact, she said little of anything about him. Jason rarely interacted with the man that he thought was his father, but his mother insured that he saw his paternal grandparents at least once a year. Their conversations were always cordial, and Jason wanted to feel closer to them, but the Merritts had never really added anything to his life.

Still, to hear the man he adored, speak so vehemently about his father and the church he attended, cut deeply. Jason had to resist the temptation to get up and run from the room, but the rueful teen felt like he had asked for it. Relief came when the front door opened and he heard Tia gleefully squeal his name.

Bear had also been caught by surprise by his burst of emotion. Anybody who knew the successful businessman and local philanthropist might have believed that he had suffered no emotional damage from the events in his early adulthood. Not even the three women who had suffered through so much pain with him were aware that Franklin Bear had to wake up each morning and recommit to the promise he had made to himself many years ago to not let his life end. He still dealt with intense pain, both physical and emotional. Bitterness, anger and the desire for revenge continued to creep up on him at unexpected times. On this evening, he had once again come face to face with the guilt he had felt daily for nearly twenty years over not being able to tell his own son who he was.

CHAPTER 8

The Past – Recovery

The shattered athlete had a lot to sort out as he lay in the emergency room unable to move or even communicate. Doctors, nurses, and even his family thought that he was unaware of their presence, but although barely able to feel his own body, he sensed the blur of motion and sound happening all around him. Only a few hours before, he had won a match that would likely have provided him with a full scholarship to any university he chose. Now he lay flat on his back again, helpless, just as he had been as a small boy when he fell from jungle gym. The blur cleared momentarily, and he found himself looking up into the faces of the same people who cared for him on that day. He would not, however, be jumping up after a few moments and brushing himself off as if nothing had happened.

Tyrell and Tabitha Ramsey didn't know it, but Frank saw them looking down on him and he felt Tabitha's tear fall on his cheek. He heard his mother's barely audible sobs just as he had many times as a child. *"What's different? Why is this different?"* Frank's thoughts in his confused state of mind caused time to run together. The past and the present seemed to be the same. Then it hit him. *"That was the beginning. This is the end."*

It was with that thought running through his head that he did lose awareness of his surroundings. He felt himself losing feeling of the few sensations that were left in his body, and he wasn't sure if he was becoming completely paralyzed or dying. The anesthesia being administered to his body through a drip line in his arm had taken effect quickly, and he was wheeled into surgery. When he woke in an ICU ward, he didn't know if he had been out for hours, days, or was even really alive. He was vaguely aware of movement around him and the sounds of beeps and people talking, but they seemed to be coming from somewhere far away, not next to his bed.

He saw a face look down into his; a woman's face. Then, someone moved his arm, and he could feel something cold and metal being pulled up beside him. A deep voice spoke in warped unintelligible tones, and he felt the bed starting to move. His next awareness came when he felt a familiar warmth against his cheek. He couldn't see her but he knew it was his mother. "I love you, Frank. We all do." She whispered softly to him, and he felt her tears on his face.

Bear spent the next several days in and out of awareness, but never spoke. The routine was the same each time. A soft beeping sound would slowly filter through the muck in his brain, not unlike the sound made by a barely audible reef buoy in a foggy ocean inlet. His eyes would open and he would find himself staring into a blurry image that he barely recognized. The faces were different, but the look was always the same; love, concern, and compassion. Over the days, he began to recognize the people they belonged to. His mother, Tyrell, Tabitha, and Mrs. Merritt all came and sat with him. The ICU was supposed to be for family only, but Sophia had insisted that the other three people were her family.

Slowly, Frank's thoughts started to return as well but, they weren't good thoughts. A mixture of bitterness and self-pity invaded his mind, as he thought back over his life again and again, in the hours and days that he lay trapped in his bed.

"What did I do to deserve to this? I've never hurt anyone. Why do people hate me?" Frank's angry questions to himself were generated by more than one evil act on a night when he should have been basking in glory. As a small child, he had stayed out of his house as much as possible because, when the man he would grow up to look like came home, it usually meant that he was going to be yelled at or worse. At his first school, children had constantly taunted him

and made fun of his smell and his clothes. Even after he had gained notoriety for his athletic prowess and later for his intelligence, Frank had experienced little genuine acceptance from his peers. He had heard more than a few rumors about his activities that had no basis in truth, such as supposedly beating up a kid from South for not showing respect to his sister. He had overheard a mother telling her daughter to stay away from him, because he had children by two different girls. After people realized how smart he was, a rumor had even been spread that he was part of some secret anti-government organization. The ones that had always hurt him the most were about the relationship between his mother, Tyrell, and Tabitha.

Still, he had always walked away, acting as if he hadn't heard. When he was a small child, and the man he knew as Bear came home, he had gone outside to play. In school, he had waited by himself on the playground until all the other children had moved away from it. Once, near the breaking point, he had almost exploded on a group of social thugs after one too many snide comments about Tyrell and his mother. Mrs. Merritt had seen the disaster coming and walked him away from it. Later, after speaking with Tyrell, he had decided to let it go and focused even more. As he had grown, he had developed an aura that said, *I'm not bothering you. Don't bother me.* Yet, here he lay.

For days, the same cancerous thoughts continued to eat away at his psyche. Each of those days, he slowly came into consciousness to the soft sound of beep, beep, beep. Then, a new sound stirred him from his empty darkness. No, it was a feeling. A weight on his chest. A sound was coming from the weight; sobbing and words. They didn't make sense. "I am so sorry, son. I should have been there. I wasn't there. You are here because of me. I failed you."

Frank opened his eyes and looked down to see a dark mass, a head. It was Tyrell's head. Tyrell raised his head and looked into Frank's face. "I know you can't see or hear me, but please wake up, son. I can call you son, can't I?"

"I want you to call me, son. It's all that I have wanted since I met you. What do you mean, I can't see or hear you? I am looking at you. Can't you hear me?" Frank screamed the thoughts from his mind and couldn't understand why Tyrell couldn't hear them.

At that moment, the door opened and Frank's mother walked in with Tabitha. Tyrell stood and the three of them embraced. Sophia, a strong believer in God spoke to Tyrell in her always quiet voice. "I know you don't believe, Tyrell, but God will deliver him to us. He sent you and Tabitha to me when I needed a strong man for my family, and he gave me much more. He made us all a family."

Tabitha looked into her husband's eyes and wiped the tears from his cheeks. Tyrell clasped her hand as he responded to Sophia. "Thank you, Sophia. If God will listen to anyone, he will listen to you. I will take any help I can get to bring that boy of yours back to us."

"Boy of ours, Tyrell. Boy of ours," Sophia said, nodding toward both Tyrell and Tabitha. "Remember, we are your family."

"Yes, I am your family." Frank screamed at them as he lay confused in addled panic. Why could they not see him looking at them? Why could they not hear him when he was yelling with all of his might?

"Uh, uh, uh," came a sound rising from his chest, barely escaping from his mouth. His eyes fluttered, and bright painful light forced its way into his brain. Frank hadn't physically opened his eyes or spoken to anyone in the preceding days. The images had been blurry because they had been only mental representations created by the touch and sounds of people he had been loved by for so long.

Tabitha was the first to react with a shriek that was a mixture of joy and surprise, before running out of the room to get a doctor. Tyrell collapsed in the chair beside him, and Sophia moved to his head and began whispering a prayer in his ear. In seconds, a team of doctors and nurses entered the room and gently ushered the family outside. As they sat in the waiting room waiting for what might come next, Sophia looked at Tyrell and said only, "I told you."

Tyrell later told his wife that Frank's mother had reminded him of a Cherokee version of the Mona Lisa. "Why does she always have that little smile, and what does she know that the rest of us don't?"

Frank's health improved rapidly over the next few days, and so did the clarity of his thoughts. He still spoke little as he tried to sort through the explosion of events that had occurred on the night he was brutally beaten. He barely remembered the match and still had no recollection of walking into the dressing room. At least, he no longer melted the past in with the present. The unjustness of the evil that nearly destroyed his life still threatened to pull him into a cesspool of bitterness, but each time he heard his mother's gentle voice pulling him back to safety. *"I love you, Frank. We all do."*

The seed of a new question formed and slowly sprouted. *"What did I do to deserve the love and compassion Mom, Tyrell, Tabitha and Mrs. Merritt have always shown me? I've never really done anything for them, but they have always been there for me."*

* * * * *

Frank's condition continued to improve steadily, and he was soon scheduled to be released from the hospital. Tyrell had neglected his business while watching Frank. Sophia eventually convinced both him and Tabitha to stay home and let her care for Frank until it was time for his release. Ramsey had always leaned toward obsessiveness when it came to organization in his shop and, sensing that Sophia's prophecy had been correct, returned to his home and went to putting his books and tools back in order. He was just getting started one morning when he heard a knock on his door and went to answer it.

"Amber, this is a nice surprise. I'm finally cleaning up this shop before people think I went out of business. I was about to put on coffee. Would you like –," he stopped mid-sentence after noticing she was pale and trembling slightly.

"Are you, OK?"

"No, Tyrell. I'm not. I'm not getting much sleep. Can we talk?"

"Certainly. Here, sit at the table. Let me get the coffee started, and I will be right back." His stomach twisted into a knot as he walked toward the pot. He thought he already knew what she had come to talk about.

"Let's see. It's a little bit of cream, no sugar. Right?"

"Thanks, Tyrell. You have a great memory." She tried to sound casual, but her voice quivered when she spoke.

Ordinarily, Ramsey would have sat down while coffee made, but he knew what was coming and needed the time to compose himself before he faced Amber. "I made a little bit of a mess over here. By the time I get it cleaned up, coffee will be ready. Fortunately, this new brewer that Tabitha bought is really fast."

"Thank you, Tyrell, and thank you for letting me barge in on you like this. I know you are busy."

Ramsey pretended to move a few things around on the counter before pouring the coffee and sitting across from Tabitha. They each took a sip. Ramsey waited, electing to let the trembling woman start the conversation.

She let out an uneven sigh. "Tyrell, I think R.T. may have had something to do with the attack on Frank. I am so sorry." She bit her lip, and tears flowed down her face.

"Amber, I knew what you were going to say. You aren't telling me anything that I didn't already suspect myself. Before we go any farther on this, I want you to know that you have been a dear friend to my family, and you mean the world to Frank. I am not sure what steps I am going to take next, but please believe me when I say that I don't want to lose your friendship; for our sakes, but especially for Frank's."

"Thank you, Tyrell. It has been really rough, the last couple of years. I don't know what I would do without you guys. I don't know what happened to Robert. He isn't the man I used to know."

"The man you thought you knew," Ramsey interjected before thinking. He started to apologize, but her look said that she knew that he was right. She nodded slightly, giving him tacit permission to continue.

"Amber, I have known your husband and his father far longer than you have. They are a product of the social inbreeding that has been endemic in Dugganville since long before the Civil War. I promised Tab that I wouldn't say anything about R.T. to you, but you need to know who you are dealing with. The old elite in this town play by a different set of rules than the rest of us. Sure, there has been explosive growth and a lot of big money to go with it, since the tech companies moved in, but it's the same old folks pulling the strings. All you have to do is look at the school boards on either side of the river to know who those folks are. Your husband has promoted himself as a beacon of progressiveness and brags about the new talented school administrations he brings in. Have you noticed that none of those administrations stay very long? Mark my words, both Dugganville high schools will be looking to replace some very fine administrators and wrestling coaches next school year. Your family came here when you were a little girl, and they have been very successful, but you will never be from Dugganville."

Ramsey watched Heather slump, and he kicked himself for going too far. "I am so sorry. You came here to talk, and I'm probably blowing everything out of proportion. R.T. probably had nothing to–"

"No, Tyrell. You are right. I am a grown, supposedly intelligent, woman. I didn't see who my husband is because I didn't want to. Neither did my parents. I am scared, and they are still clueless. In front of them, he puts on this big affectionate show, and I let him. I don't know why. Maybe, I am afraid to disappoint my parents, and Dad doesn't seem as sharp as he used to be. R.T. drops the charade before we can even get in the car and turns back into his old jerk of a self."

Ramsey gritted his teeth and clinched his fists. "Has he hurt you, Amber?"

"No, not physically, no. He just says really sick, nasty things about me, about Frank, and about you, Tabitha, and Sophia. Perverted things. Tyrell, the first time I saw him, he gave a speech to the new teachers at NDHS. I was one of them. He gave a beautiful speech about the need to embrace the diversity that was the new Dugganville. As I was growing up, my parents and I had often talked about that need. Yes, I will never be from Dugganville. Mom and Dad have expressed many times that, no matter how hard they try, they will never be fully accepted here. Fortunately, so many people have moved in that it is almost like there are three Dugganvilles now. Nearly all of their circle is in that third community, and they have almost nothing to do with Dugganville politics. It's harder for me, because most of the teachers have generational ties here. The only differences are coaches and administrators, because they are harder to find. And, as you have already pointed out, they don't last long. When the elegant R.T. Merritt stood up and told that same stupid joke that he opens every speech with, I thought he was the most magnificent man I had ever seen."

Tyrell scoffed. "That damned statue story. You know, there is no proof that Raeford Thaddeus Beaumont ever existed, except for that ugly piece of rock in the river. Daddy Merritt has been telling people about his supposed ancestor long before his baby boy was ever born. One part of that farce is true, however. Mama Merritt threatened to snip the possibility of any future heirs being created from its root if her son was named Raeford Thaddeus."

Though stressed, Amber couldn't refrain from laughing. The release felt good. "Thank you, I needed that. I have been worried that you might think," she paused before rephrasing. "I have been scared that you might hate me. Tyrell, I grew up here, but your family is the only part of this place that I truly love. If it weren't for you and my parents, I would have already left. I think that may be partly why R.T. hates you so much, and I feel dirty because of it."

Tears formed in Ramsey's eyes, and he reached across the table to take Amber's hand. "We love you, too! This town doesn't know what a great teacher they have in you, but we do. I want you make me some promises."

"What?"

"First of all, don't ever let that man abuse you. If you need some place to stay, you come here. You know that I am going to tell Tabitha about our conversation. It's a small house, but we have room."

"Oh, thank you. I will if -"

"Wait, I am not through. I want you to promise to ignore the slanders he makes about Frank's mom, Tabitha and me. Do you remember when you had to walk Frank away from a bunch of kids making stupidly bigoted comments? Frank told me about it. Those students didn't learn that type of hatred in a vacuum. It's endemic in Dugganville. I already know the type of hateful lies R.T. and his father spread while preaching the gospel of equality for all. It's all just a show to get something from the newcomers in town; like you and your parents. All you are going to accomplish by hitting him in the face with the truth is for him to hit you back with denial and lies."

"But Tyrell, what if –"

"And most importantly, you keep your suspicions about R.T.'s involvement in Frank's assault to yourself. Tell Tabitha or me if you must, but no one else. Amber, you've lived here most of your life, but you are still an outsider. You may think you are talking to only one person, but not in this town. Every pair of ears is connected to the send button. And, please don't say a word to Frank."

"Tyrell," her voice had a twinge of anger in it, the first in their conversation. "Surely, you know that I wouldn't. He has enough to deal with."

Ramsey knew the edge in his voice had sounded like he was talking down to Amber. "I know, Amber, and I apologize. I need to learn Sophia's secret for calmness. You will promise me the other things, though? If you hear anything, just come to me with it."

"Yes, you are right, and I promise."

Chapter 9

The Present – Rose's Love

Frank had stayed seated at his desk after Tia rescued him and Jason from the uncomfortable encounter. He was still sorting through the cause of his sudden outburst of emotion when he heard Jason say that he had to be going. He stood from his chair and walked out of the library to meet his protégé. An awkward silence came between them at first; an unseen barrier. Jason started to speak, but Frank took another step, wrapped his arms around him and whispered in his ear. "I never got around to telling you about me. We will talk again, soon. I promise."

"Thank you, I would really like that," Jason responded, quietly. The strength of Frank's embrace and the gentleness of his words had melted the barrier. Jason would have stood there longer, but he was afraid he would be overcome by emotion. Releasing himself from Frank, he turned to each of the female members of the family and began his traditional exit ceremony hugging each one, beginning with Frank's mother, Sophia, and worked his way down, saving his most enthusiastic hug for Tia.

After Jason left, Rose followed her husband back into his library and closed the door behind her. "That was intense. Care to tell me what it was all about?"

Frank sighed deeply and sat on the edge of his desk facing his wife. He motioned for her to come to him, and he wrapped his arms around her. "Oh Rose, I don't know how you let your Aunt Tabitha talk you into getting involved with this beat up pile of junk."

"She knew that I am a sucker for lost causes. I don't think I have ever seen you as shaky as you were when you came out of this room a few minutes ago. What came up between you two?"

"Rose, you know as much about my past as I do, the good parts and the not so good parts. Jason asked me about that past tonight. I didn't know what to tell him, partly because I don't know everything about my own life. I never realized it growing up, because reality stopped at the edge of my own little world, but I had always had an incredible set of adults looking out for my best interests for my entire life. I just hadn't seen it.

I was a dumb kid, full of himself, and thinking he could get up from anything. Then, my world got crushed and for the first time, I discovered that I am part of something bigger than me. Tyrell was helping me to understand where I fit in the world when," he hesitated, unable to finish the sentence.

Rose put her arms around him and kissed the tear running down his cheek. "It's OK, Frank. You don't have to go back to that time."

He continued without describing the event that took two of the most loved people in his life from him. "No, I do. Tonight, brought it all back to me. Tyrell was helping me sort things out, but he and Tabitha died before I ever knew fully what was going on. I don't know what to tell Jason."

"Frank, I love you with all of my heart, and I am with you always. You know that, so listen to me. You do know about the part of your past that is most important to Jason. He will eventually find out on his own, and probably in the not-too-distant future. It will be best for everyone if he learns it from you and his mother. Call Amber and tell her about your conversation with Jason," Rose paused and looked her husband directly in the eyes, "with your son, tonight. You and she see talk almost every week about Jason, and yet neither of you ever discuss how to let him know who he is. That isn't fair to Jason, and quite frankly, it isn't fair to his sisters. And by the way, Jason is my stepson! I want to call him that."

Frank felt like he had been hit in the stomach with a battering ram. "You know, I still can't even call her Amber. She has always been Ms. Merritt to me, even though I can't stand that name. She is one of the best people I've ever known. She was the first person to get me to look at where I came from, and not be ashamed of it. Now, I am afraid one day soon, my own son will look at me in shame."

Chapter 10

The Past – Old Home

Beaumont, historically known as Indiantown, was located a few miles to the east of South Dugganville. It was from this settlement that the infamous Red Raider forays across the river into North Dugganville had supposedly originated. In truth, the informal settlement was made up of individuals coming from a conflation of cultures and ethnicities; the common dominators bringing them there, being poverty and hard times. Although its fluctuating population did include indigenous members from several tribes, runaway slaves and deserters from both armies were also among its numbers. No one from the Union or the Confederacy really cared about the village of outcasts until after the war ended. It was shortly afterward that the settlement had endured several brutal raids at the hands of a group of vengeance minded thugs from North Dugganville. The group still calling themselves the Demons, included some of the same individuals who had rampaged through South Dugganville during the war.

As time progressed, other people displaced by the war moved to the settlement. The common denominator among all of the settlement's inhabitants continued to be poverty. Shortly before the turn of the twentieth century the settlement incorporated into a township and was named after the apocryphal Raeford Thaddeus Beaumont. Although not surrounded by a fickle river like Beaumont

Island, lore concerning R.T. Beaumont was as everchanging in the town bearing his name as it was about his statue.

It was there that Frank Bear had begun his life. When Mrs. Merritt had first suggested that a public service project in the depressed little village might be an impressive line on his curriculum vitae for college, he wasn't sure why. All he had remembered about his life there, was playing in a wilderness filled with a stream, trees, and grass just outside of town. To him, it had seemed like paradise compared to the glass covered asphalt he would make his playground after Bear later moved them to the projects in North Dugganville. Although less than twenty miles away from his new home, he had never returned. He had no need, especially since his family had been informally adopted by the Ramseys. His new paradise had become Tyrell's shop.

His first visit back to the community with his beloved teacher was an eye-opening experience for which he had not been prepared. Most of the small single-family homes were drab and in sore need of repair. Junky, undriveable vehicles sat in many of the yards. Streets were in poor condition and littered with cigarette butts and ragged plastic bags. The majority of the yards were overgrown with weeds. Those that weren't had been scalped to the ground. The local school had become the palate of choice for the graffiti artists of the local gangs. Frank's childhood paradise was, in fact, a community rotting from neglect.

Frank sat stone faced in his teacher's car after touring Beaumont. Only a tear at the corner of his eye betrayed the emotions that were boiling inside of him. He looked straight ahead when speaking to Mrs. Merritt. He couldn't bring himself to look at her. "I never knew. All I remember is the grass, and the trees, and the sound of the elk calling to me from the valley. How do people live like this?"

Amber Merritt was barely able to contain her own tears while witnessing the struggle going on within her student. She sat for what seemed like an eternity before attempting to answer his question. "Frank, you told me once that you were very angry with your mother for a long time because she had allowed your father – excuse me – because she had allowed the man you know as Bear to take you from your home. What made this place so special to you when you were a small child?"

Frank also sat for a long time before answering. "I just realized that I don't remember this town. I don't even remember my house or where it was, except that the back door opened out onto a field and trees. It must have been at the edge of town. I could run out the back door and escape all the shit – I'm sorry Mrs. Merritt. I didn't mean to say that."

"It's Ok, Frank. I have heard a lot worse. Keep talking."

"I could open that back door and get away from Bear and the grief he was always giving Mom. I could almost smell the alcohol before he walked in the front door, so I would just go out the back door as soon as he opened the front. We didn't have a back door at the projects, only a front. It opened to the parking lot. Whenever Bear would come home after we moved there, I couldn't get away. I was trapped – until Mom called Tyrell and Tabitha. He got scared and ran off. That was the best day of my life."

The teacher looked at her prized pupil. "So, tell me, Frank. What do you think that you might be able to do that would improve the lives of the little kids who live in Beaumont, like you once did?"

This time, his answer came immediately. "It doesn't take a rocket scientist to figure that one out Ma'am. I've lived it. When Frank and Tabitha first took us under their wing, they found us a better place to live and got Mom back in school. Most of all, they treated our whole family like we mattered to someone. This place looks like no one cares."

"Wow, Mr. Bear. You said it doesn't take a rocket scientist, but that sounds like the start of a genius plan to me. It occurs to me that a lot of schools will be very impressed with such an ambitious undertaking. Oh, and before we go, your mom told me exactly where your old house was. Would you like to see it?"

Frank hesitated. "I'm not sure."

"I think it would be a good idea if you did. You told me that as soon as Bear walked in the front door, you went out the back and nobody cared where you were, not even your mother – even though you were only four or five years old."

"Oh, Ok."

"Good, because we are parked in front of it."

Frank looked stunned and turned to see a tiny two-bedroom bungalow with a sagging roof. "The house is vacant now, and the landlord gave us permission to go in. Let's go see the big field you escaped to," Mrs. Merritt said with a gentle smile.

They exited the car and walked to the house. The door was unlocked, and they went in. Frank was shocked to see that less than fifteen feet separated the front and back doors. The giant field where he had escaped all humanity was, in reality, a large vacant lot with a tree and a small stream at one corner. He remembered his mother standing at the small kitchen window that looked out on the lot. His mother had always watched to make sure he was safe as she was being subjected to her drunken husband's outbursts. He had never been alone.

CHAPTER 11

The Present – The Mine

rank knew Rose was right. He had long known that Jason was his son, conceived during one confused emotionally charged night only days after Amber Merritt had been brutally raped by her husband. It had happened between a young man overcome with rage by the attack on a teacher he had idolized, and a woman whose entire sense of self-worth had been in danger of being destroyed by the physical helplessness of being unable to prevent the attack. Neither had ever talked about it after that night, and when Amber discovered she was pregnant, even her husband believed the child to be his. Both Frank and Amber had hoped that to be true while each secretly desired the opposite. Only they and those closest to Frank, knew the truth.

"I know you are right, Rose. I've known this day would come; have wanted it to come; for a long time. I can only hope that he can forgive his mother and me as you have."

"Frank, what are you talking about? I barely even knew you when that all happened. Both of you were adults, and you were no longer her student. You needed each other that night. What Robert Merritt did to Amber was a terrible criminal act, but he still would have made her life hell, if he knew what had happened between you and her. It was just as likely that Jason could have been R.T.'s son.

It's a good thing that looks are only skin deep, because once you get past the fair skin, blond hair, and blue eyes, that young man is you."

Frank did his best to laugh. "You are a kind human, Rose Bear. I noticed you didn't say Beauty is only skin deep."

The plump woman with the infectious smile wrapped her arms around her husband. "Oh honey, you don't think I married you for all those brains, do you? You are the hunkiest hunk, this Indian girl ever laid eyes on."

The gesture brought a smile to Frank, but also a moment of sadness. It had reminded him of the way Tabitha could get Tyrell to laugh, no matter how upset he was. He kissed her gently on the lips and held her tightly. "I love you, very, very, much!"

"You, know that I love you, even more. Why don't you go somewhere and clear your head? The answers will come to you."

"Good idea! It has been a while since I have been to Beaumont. I think I will visit the youth center and then do a little hiking."

"Don't forget to take your cane. Your idea of a little hiking usually means you are going to be barely walking by the time you are finished."

"Thank you, Tabitha Ramsey," he thought, "for introducing me to the most wonderful woman on the planet."

The town of Beaumont had changed little in the twenty years since he had sat in the car with Amber Merritt, with a few notable exceptions. Junk cars still served as landscaping for many of the yards, although not as many. Weeds still dominated the lawns, but most of them were now mowed, and not quite as many plastic bags could be seen blowing down Beaumont's streets. The most eye-catching changes to the community included a greatly improved school site and an ultra-modern youth and community center. The youth center sat on land that had once been the site of Frank's first home. The idea for the center was born when Amber Merritt had taken her student there, and Frank had first realized how much his mother loved him. The plans he had only begun to formulate had come to a screeching halt after the attack on his life during the first semester of his senior year. The idea for the center had never died, but had fallen into dormancy until the broken athlete had lain recovering in a hospital bed. His dream of a wrestling career and a college education had been crushed along with his leg and spine, but the dream had been replaced by having a purpose in life beyond sports and education.

Frank walked through the main door and, as always, was greeted by smiles from the adult workers and hugs from the kids. Not only had he been the primary driver of the center's creation, he still volunteered as a coach for the boys and girls wrestling teams. His daughter Casey had already announced that she was going to be the first girl's state wrestling champ from North Dugganville, and Frank was certain Tia would follow in her footsteps. He was thinking about his girls when Albert Floyd greeted him.

"Hey R2, what choo doin here? The little kids rasslin season is over. You ain't already scopin out the talent for next year are ya?" Albert was a small wiry descendant of non-landholding white southerners. He was around Frank's age. Albert was smart, but had been born into a situation even more impoverished than had been Frank's. His desperately poor parents had been killed in an accident when he was only two years old. After that, he had been raised by loving but equally as poor grandparents. After they both passed away shortly before the boy's seventh birthday, Albert was sent to live in a group home, where he would stay for the rest of his formative years. He had eventually earned his GED and had been hired originally at the center as its only janitor.

A near genius for organization and an ability to get along with anyone had quickly caught the attention of the center's board members. When the center grew and the need for a site manager became apparent, Albert's name had immediately moved to the forefront. He had been overwhelmingly grateful and threw himself into the position as if he were taking over a fortune 500 company. Although his writing skills were lacking, his new volunteer secretary, Rose Bear, always insured that written communication coming from the center was clear and efficient. It had been Rose who had suggested that Albert was the ideal candidate for the position.

"No, Albert, I just came to make sure that you are taking care of those new hiking trails. I can't have the rich folks from Dugganville complaining that you're letting unauthorized weeds get in with the wildflowers, now, can I?"

Albert scoffed. "Go on, R2. You are the rich folks from Dugganville. Sides, I tagged all those weeds last week to make sure they are properly licensed. Which trail you takin?"

"I haven't been on the new south loop for a while. I thought I might walk up those hills over there."

"Ok, but you better go back to your truck and get your cane first. I don't want Rose in a snit, because you fell down and hurt yourself."

Frank answered in a mock growl. "You and my wife."

"You just go ahead and growl. I ain't afraid of you, but I'm scared of that pretty lady."

Frank did as he was ordered and retrieved a trekking pole, what Albert and Rose had called a cane, from his truck before starting out on the trail. The idea for the trails had come about when Mrs. Merritt had shown him the wilderness, he thought he had been escaping to when he was a small child, only to find out he had never left his back yard. *"I guess all of us need to feel like it's just us and nature; God; whatever, sometimes," he had thought. "Even if Mama really is right there watching us the whole time."*

He had never let the idea go, and as soon as the business began to prosper, he purchased considerable acreage to the south of Beaumont. The rapidly growing list of employees at Ramsey and Son Plumbing were openly complimentary of the benefits of working for the magnanimous Native American plumber. Frank, however, had never grown out of being a quiet intellectual, and schmoozing to solicit donations and support for the center were out of his realm. Fortunately, Rose Bear and Albert Floyd were natural sales people. It hadn't taken them long to convince local hunting clubs and farmers that having their names associated with the center and the trails would be a great public relations move.

By the time he was thirty, the grand plan of a youth center and a hiking trail for the kids of Beaumont that he had formulated as a high school senior had blossomed into a community center used by the citizens not only of Beaumont, but also Dugganville and other surrounding communities. Nearly all of the staff were citizens of Beaumont, so the center had also had a positive economic impact on Indiantown, although not for Frank. The only revenue for the center came from minor usage fees, and that went entirely to pay the few staff who weren't volunteers. The majority of all other funding was provided by Ramsey and Son Plumbing. The board for the center consisted primarily of local farmers and sportsmen, and it was at one of the earliest meetings of the board when people had seen a rare flash of anger from Frank Bear. A board member, apparently not aware of the former wrestling star's history, had raised the issue of turning the center into an entertainment venue in order to create more revenue. Bear's words had been brief. "'Ramsey and Son' is a very profitable company, and this center needs no additional funding. I personally own the center and much of the land. If one for-profit event of any kind is held anywhere on these grounds, I will close the center the next day and sue this board for any revenue you may have collected. Are there any questions?"

No questions had been asked and the meeting had come to a rapid adjournment. Instead of losing support as may have been suspected, more donations of money and land had come in shortly afterward. It was to one of those later donated tracts that Frank was headed for. On it, was a two-mile looped trail still in its early stage of development. The inclines and descents of the trail were only moderately strenuous, but the hills were rocky and populated by tree roots in competition with the rocks for available ground. Temporary blazes had been placed along the route, but several had already fallen. He knew Rose wouldn't be happy with him for taking the trail by himself, but it was one of those times when he needed to feel like he was alone in the world, and the trail was as of yet, only sparsely trekked upon. Ironically, the land for the trail had been donated by a business interest of R.T. Merritt and his father after they had been approached by farmers on the board. The narrow path was bisected by a stream running through a valley between two hills. Any hiker taking the narrow rocky path had to ascend and descend the northern hill before crossing the stream and taking the opposing arc of the trail on the southern hill. A local scout troupe had only recently completed a picnic bench and a gazebo at the trial head. A map of the trail had been placed under a plexiglass covered sign board inside of the gazebo.

Bear sat at the bench, checked his water, and extended his "cane" as both Rose and Albert referred to it. The extendable trekking rod was actually standard hiking equipment, but his wife's use of terminology was her way of reminding him that he wasn't as invincible as he once had been. She had a point. Even now, a ten-foot drop or a six-foot crevice created temptation for the once agile man, but the reality of a neck that would barely turn and sometimes tenuous balance had somewhat cured him of daredevil risk taking. He would be careful and take his time.

"I suppose that I should have told her which trail I was taking. Nah, nothing is going to happen," he thought, before stepping out of the gazebo.

The dampness from the morning dew had made the trail slicker than he had anticipated, but he didn't mind. It had forced him to concentrate on taking each step while looking only far enough ahead to anticipate where his foot might next find steady ground. It was almost as it had been when he was a child planning his path around the playground equipment. For the next hour, the responsibilities of adulthood went away as he watched each step along the path. He barely looked up until he reached the point where the trail crossed the streamed and turned back for the return to the trail head. It was there that, for a few moments, Frank Bear once again fully became a small child alone in the universe and filled with wonder. He stood and let the tears flow down his cheeks as he became absorbed by what lay in front of him.

The trail made its turn at the edge of community center property and was marked by a boulder on which Frank now stood. Approximately a hundred yards beyond the boulder lay the source of the stream, a blue-gray marsh fringed lake shrouded in mist and nestled between the two sister hills. Just beyond the lake rose the mother of the hills, an ancient mountain that had long since lost the sharpness of youth and now wore the rounded edges of wisdom on her face. The arms of her base wrapped gently around the twins she had given birth to so long ago.

Bear breathed deeply and closed his eyes, waiting to be absorbed by the sounds that he knew would soon reach his ears. Frogs croaking from the across the lake sounded as if they were at his feet. A hawk, soaring high in the sky seemed to be just over his head, and then the sound he had been waiting for reached his ears like the call of a long-lost friend asking him to come out and play. The bugle of an elk came rolling down the mountain with such clarity that Frank imagined he could reach out and touch the animal.

The unique topography of the mountain family formed a sound stage that surpassed anything man had to offer. Frank had been enthralled by their music long before he had known from whence it came. It was one of the reasons he felt like he had escaped to another world from an abusive father as child. The valley between the hills formed a sound tunnel that had sometimes brought the call of the elk right up to his back door. His drunken father could belittle him all he wanted, but as long as little Frank Bear had been able to hear the elk, he had been alone in the wilderness.

He sighed again, opened his eyes, and allowed his thoughts to search for the reason he had made this hike. The lives of Amber and Jason Merritt were coming into focus when a new image, one that didn't belong, caught his attention. He hadn't noticed it when he first climbed on the rock, but the mist had lifted and he now saw what looked to be a newly cleared space almost halfway up the side of the mountain. *"What's that for,"* he thought. He continued to study the slope in the distance, and as he did, another new feature came into view; a rudimentary road or perhaps, just the beginnings of a road. The original purpose of his hike to the lake was lost as he viewed the disturbing sight.

The peak sat on land owned by the business interest that had donated the acreage for the new hiking trail. Frank had been suspicious of the donation from the beginning, but he felt like he had backed himself into a corner and had to accept it. The board had shown their support when he had said no to the idea of turning the center into an entertainment venue to generate funds. It was a coalition of farmers and hunters who had approached the Merritts about donating the land. *"If R. T. Merritt has anything to do with what is going on over there, it can't be good."* The universe had suddenly become crowded again. Frank's first instinct was to hike around the lake to investigate, but rational thinking prevailed. *"That would be pretty stupid, Frank. It would take you most of the day if you could still actually walk like a normal human. Go back to the center. Talk to Arnold."*

Bear turned his back on the scene and began his return on the other side of the stream. Ordinarily, the portion of the loop returning to the center would have been easier to walk. The changes in slope were more gradual and the path was less rocky. Frank found himself trying to hurry however, and had difficulty keeping his focus on the path at his feet. A sound startled him and he turned quickly, at first thinking that someone was chasing him with a chainsaw. The sudden twist caused him to misplace his trekking pole, and its tip hit a moss slickened rock instead of the gravel for which he was aiming. The tip skittered off the rock, causing him to fall, face first, towards its crystalline surface. An irrational memory of a dressing room from long ago flashed through his mind before he was able to react by dipping his shoulder and rolling through the fall as if performing an old wrestling move. His forehead had brushed the rock, but barely. It is sometimes said that humor was first born as a result of near tragedy. Frank sat up from his roll and looked down the slope where his hiking staff lay. Then, he looked at the rock, before laughing at himself. *"Whew! Go Demons! I've still got it."* Feeling the bump rising on his forehead, he laughed again. *"I am going to be in so much trouble when Rose sees this."*

While he sat and allowed his senses to completely return, he listened for the saw, but heard only silence. Then, the unmistakable sounds of human voices reached his ears. The voices weren't shouting, but the sound conduit created by the valley was so powerful that even at this distance he could tell they were angry voices. If he had still been standing near the lake, he probably could have understood what they were saying. He was too far away for that, but he was certain that one of the voices belonged to R.T. Merritt.

Frank carefully crab walked down the slope to recover his staff. A stiff neck and a twisted leg made getting back up the rocky slope treacherous, but Frank Bear had never let a fall keep him down. He had been able to attribute a great deal of his success to remaining calm and focusing on the path in front of him when others may have panicked. This was both a natural trait and one that had been further instilled in him by the man he would always consider his true father. By the time he reached the community center, his countenance was one of nonchalance. Arnold saw him as he was walking up the path and met him at the front door. "Ooooh, R2! I hope you've got a good story when you get home, because I don't think that bear you met on the trail is nearly as mean as the one, you're gonna deal with when you get home."

Frank belly laughed. "Ya think? Just wait until I tell her that you're the one that did this to me.

It was Arnold's turn to laugh. "Seriously, what happened?"

"No big deal. I just hit a slippery spot and went down. You are right about one thing. The real pain is going to start when I get home, if I don't get this cleaned up first."

"No problem. I have a well-stocked first aid kit. For a raise, I will make up a really good story about aliens for you."

Frank laughed again. He really liked the sharp-witted country boy that refused to be anything but happy. "Thanks, but I will have to man up and take the rest of my lumps when Rose sees me. But, speaking of aliens, do you know anything about what is going on across the lake?"

"Not really, R2. I just focus on my little world, but I heard something about the Merritts starting some kind of mining business over there."

"Oh, come on, Arnold. We both have blood lines that go back generations in this area. You and I both know how many people have lost their shirts digging for minerals around here, because these hills don't have anything worth digging for."

Arnold shrugged and offered a slight smirk. "And R2, neither of our bloodlines had shirts to begin with, so like them, I don't really pay attention to that nonsense. All I remember is hearing something about R.T. and his dad starting a; wait a minute – a bit coin mine. Yea, that was it. A bit coin mine."

Frank frowned.

"What's wrong, R2. You look like you just hit your head on that rock again."

"Nothing really, Arnold. I've just never been able to figure out how that pair always seem to be bankrupt and starting new businesses at the same time. No worries. I will figure it out later.

Hey, I almost forgot. I understand congratulations are in order, but I thought you and Mae weren't having any kids together."

"Damn it, Frank. It wasn't my fault. She snuck up on me when I had my pants down and wasn't looking." Arnold Floyd's protests did little to hide the looks of joy and pride beaming from his face. He had only met Mae two years before when she had started bringing her two little boys to the rec center. They had immediately adored the wiry little man with the big smile, and he had returned the feeling. Upon meeting their mother, he had been immediately smitten. She was five years older than Floyd and nearly a full head taller. Mae had escaped an abusive marriage in a nearby state and had moved to Beaumont to stay with relatives. Although tall, she was frail and timid, the product of years of abuse. Arnold's positive impact was clearly evident on both her and her sons.

"Frank, I'm not sure how a skinny little weasel like me could ever be so lucky," he continued. "I didn't figure I would ever get married or be able to support a family. Now I have a fantastic wife, two awesome sons, and a third baby on the way." Tears came to his eyes, and he looked away from Bear. Frank made a mental note to approach the board about raising Arnold's pay.

"Mae and your kids are very fortunate to have you, Arnold. If I know my wife, she is already planning on fattening up the lot of you. If you hear any more about the doings up on the mountain, let me know, will you?"

"Absolutely! I will take the boys on some hikes over that way."

CHAPTER 12

The Past – Meeting Mr. Wonderful

After recovering from his first experience with infatuation, Frank had fallen quickly into the high school routine to the point that it soon became unchallenging, teetering on boredom. Unlike the majority of his peers, he was not constantly distracted by trying to attract the attention of the opposite sex. His personal history had taught him that girls thought he was ugly. The recent onslaught of teenage acne had only served to intensify Frank's perception of himself. As a low-income racial minority attending a school in which the population was predominantly upper-middle class and Anglo-European, he had little opportunity to fall into a comfortable niche. The Native American student had always done well in school, but he had also always been placed in classes of low academic rigor. By the time he began his freshman year, Frank already had a reputation as a stellar athlete, and counselors placed him by default into basic classes so that he would have the greatest opportunity to participate in athletics.

Only two things in Frank's freshman year at NDHS held his attention; wrestling and Mrs. Merritt's Civics class. The class was a requirement for graduation from high school, meaning that all students had to take it regardless of their academic level. Frank had however been placed in a class with multiple students who were having to repeat the class, and many were at least one year overage, as was Frank because of his late start to school. He noticed that he had many of these same students in most of his classes. It was no secret that a block of low achieving students moved together through their daily schedule. Most of the new teachers at the school had at least one of these "baby-sitting" classes that were designed with the sole purpose of getting students who would otherwise drop out, through high school. Also peppered throughout the classes were a few star athletes with less than stellar academic records. Frank's biographical data almost guaranteed that he would be placed in the low achieving classes. He was an athlete, over-age, minority, and from a single-parent home.

The classes had all lived up to their reputations, until he walked into Mrs. Merritt's class that first day of school. Aside from being beautiful, she had incredibly high expectations for her students. After a day of completing worksheets, Frank had been immediately enthralled by this teacher who brought in guest speakers and engaged students in high-level thinking. After initially complaining that her class was too hard, even the students who had long been conditioned to a low level of challenge eventually became engaged. Other teachers entering her room were often surprised to see students labeled as troublemakers, actively involved in the class. He would learn later that, although she was popular among her students, she was not completely accepted by her peers. Amber Bronson had grown up in North Dugganville, but she had never completely fit. Most people had assumed that she wouldn't return after leaving for college, but her parents were there. She was also infected with the idealism of youth, causing her to believe that she could make a difference in the system.

The first months of her first year as a teacher had been daunting. The school district was growing quickly, and many new teachers had been hired along with her. Both NDHS and its sister school to the south followed the time-honored practice of assigning new teachers to the lowest functioning and least desirable classes. Unprepared, inexperienced, and receiving little support, many of the new teachers were destined to leave teaching by the end of the first year. The successes she enjoyed hadn't come without exhausting preparation. She was often faced by student frustration that was hidden behind a mask of apathy.

The thoughts of a challenging and unfruitful day had been on her mind when she first heard and saw the dynamic Robert Thomas Merritt. It was the night of the first school board meeting of the year, and she was determined to attend, in spite of her exhaustion. She had immediately perked up when the chairman of the school board, R.T. Merritt Sr., had introduced his son as the guest speaker. In his speech, Merritt Jr. had laid out the same principles for creating a strong inclusive community that she held dearly. The Merritt name was well known in the Dugganvilles, but Amber had never met the speaker or his father. Arthur Bronson, Amber's father, had met his daughter at the meeting. As a businessman, he felt that it was important to stay in touch with the workings of the school district. The explosive growth had brought a lot of newcomers like himself into the cities now separated only by the river, but the school districts on either side were still controlled by the families that had been there for over a century. The same could be said about community politics.

Mr. Bronson leaned over and whispered in Amber's ear as Merritt was finishing up his presentation. "Wow, progressive thinking. That's something you don't hear often in these parts. I wonder if he is serious, or if Merritt senior wants to impress a few outside business people like me. There is an election coming up, after all. He may need a few outsider votes."

"I hope not, Dad," she whispered back. "After today, I need to hear someone talk about looking forward instead of back. This is the most positive I've felt in weeks."

The comment caught her father by surprise. His daughter had always displayed a glowing upbeat countenance regardless of what might be going on underneath her perpetual smile. He took Amber's hand and squeezed it slightly. "Let's talk when we get home. I've barely seen you since you started your job."

He looked at her and winked. "You know, he is sort of a handsome guy, isn't he? I thought he was trying to get my attention, but I think he was probably looking at the new teacher sitting beside me."

Amber pinched her father's arm and gave a mock grimace before laughing slightly. "Would you stop? He was probably distracted by the glare coming off that bald head of yours."

Father and daughter laughed a little louder than they intended, drawing the attention of the people sitting near them. They had also been noticed by the speaker as he was making his concluding statements. The meeting drew to a close, and Amber told her father that she was going back to school to finish some paperwork and that she would meet him at home.

As she walked toward the door, she was met by R.T. Merritt. "I am happy that you found my speech about the challenges facing our community so amusing." His smile and stance gave away that he wasn't in the least angry, but looking to start a conversation.

"Oh, Mr. Merritt. Please forgive me. In truth, I found your talk inspiring, as did my father. He just has this way of making me laugh."

"R.T., please. Mr. Merritt is my father. So, you are Arthur Bronson's daughter. May I ask your name?"

Chapter 13

The Present – Crypto Crooks

Frank walked slowly up his driveway after returning from the Beaumont Community Center. The discovery that Merritt and his father might be planning something that could potentially cause more grief for Jason and his mother only deepened the emotional quagmire Frank had found himself in, about telling Jason the truth about his parenthood. For nearly two decades, he had worked to convince himself that his feelings for Amber Merritt were only those of an admiring student who had been inspired by an incredible teacher. He had reminded himself many times that the night Jason had been conceived had been an extraordinary circumstance bringing two emotionally distraught people together for a brief moment in time. He loved his wife and daughters dearly, and yet, still felt a connection to Amber Merritt that he couldn't deny. Painful thoughts from the past were still wrapping themselves around the present when he opened his front door. He had barely closed it when his thoughts were immediately interrupted by the sight of Rose standing in the middle of the room, her arms folded across her chest and one eye squinted.

"Hmmm, and do you have something you want to tell me?" she asked. The squinted eyed widened to match the other as she asked the question.

Bear shook himself back into the present. "Rose, it was just a little slip – no big deal."

"And, would this 'little slip' have occurred it you hadn't been on the new trail that's not even finished, yet?"

"Did Arnold call you? That rat," Frank growled as if his friend had betrayed a major trust.

"No, my spy didn't call me, but I knew where you would be going when you left here, even if you didn't bother to tell me."

Frank looked like a little boy who had been scolded for stealing a cookie. Rose inspected the bump on her husband's head before continuing. "Besides, I know Arnold's work. We need to add EMT to his job title and give him a raise."

"I know you two are in cahoots, now. He also mentioned a raise, which, by the way, I am going to bring up to the board. He is stoked about Mae being pregnant, but they are going to need some help, financially. We can talk later. Right now, I am going to my library and Face Time, Tunner."

Rose smirked. "Good luck getting him to answer. I love your little brother, but I've called him a dozen times about a computer issue we are having, and responsibility just doesn't seem to fit into his schedule."

Frank offered a knowing sigh. "I know, but I really need to talk to him. That is why I am Face Timing him. Sometimes, he gets the hint that it's urgent if I use that."

"Is this about Jason and Amber," Rose asked, concerned.

"Not directly, but it is about something that R.T. Merritt may be involved in. There has been a clearing cut out on his land across the lake, and I think it has something to do with crypto currency. My geek brother is the only person I know who might be able to explain it to me.

Tunner Bear was the second youngest of the Bear children and the only boy besides Frank. His biological father had shown up at the hospital just long enough to sign the birth certificate. He decided that his son should have a proud Indian name, and over Sophia Bear's quiet protests, wrote Thunder Bear on the certificate. Three-year-old Frank couldn't pronounce Thunder, and it came out Tunner. By the time Frank's younger brother started to school, the Bear family had been rescued by Tyrell and Tabitha Ramsey, and Sophia's husband was long gone. The name stuck, however, and Tunner was the only name by which he had ever been known. Except for possessing a keen intellect, he was the exact opposite of Frank and his sisters. Besides Frank, he was the only one of the Bear children who hadn't completed a college degree. After following his brother and two of his sisters through school, it was anticipated that he would be a serious student and an athlete. He was neither. He was, however, brilliant in the field of technology and after dropping out of college, went to work in the family business. He was the only one of his siblings who didn't manage a 'Ramsey and Son' branch, but was solely responsible for managing all things related to technology and marketing. He had a strong pension for being the life of the party and a tendency not to take anything seriously, a trait that caused him to often lose favor with his sister-in-law. He did jump a little faster if he knew that it was his brother contacting him. He answered the phone on its first ring.

"Hey Bro, don't let Rose get mad at me. I promise I am going to get that server problem worked out. What happened to your head? She isn't mad at you, is she?"

Frank had talked to his brother often, but hadn't seen him physically in months. He was shocked to see that his hair had grown long, almost to his shoulders. Behind his chair on the wall, hung what looked like a replica of a buffalo skin Indian shield and a bow.

"No, but she is pretty upset with you, Tunner. Mind telling me what's going on with the native look?"

"Wait a minute, Frank. My name is Thunder, Thunder Bear."

Frank growled slightly. "Ok, little brother. What's her name?"

"Sylvia Batten. She is an anthropology professor at the local college. When she found out that I am from the Bear Clan of Beaumont, she was really impressed."

Frank sighed and shook his head. "I'm not sure how, little brother, but I think you have managed to be guilty of the cultural appropriation of your own people. Has it ever come up that you are a vegetarian, hate camping, and can't stand the sight of blood? Wait, don't answer. Your love life is none of my business. I really need to talk to you about something that is going on south of the Beaumont Community center."

"Cultural what? Bro, you've got to stop using those big words on me." Tunner stopped his joking after seeing that his brother was serious. "Sure Frank. What can I help you with?"

"Do you know anything about Bit Coin?"

"Do you mean cryptocurrency? I know enough to hope that you aren't planning on getting involved with it. Big brother, you might as well go to Vegas. It's less risky."

"Don't worry. I'm not. I was more interested in finding out how it's made."

Tunner spent the next hour giving his older brother a primer on cryptocurrency. Frank had always liked to think of himself as being well read, and up on current events. He had never held an interest, however, in the gaming industry or making money from shady investments. According to Tunner, the two were linked, which had led to a boom of twenty-something year old millionaires. After taking notes for the hour, he had a greater appreciation for Arnold's attitude of not paying attention to a bunch of nonsense. Still, there was something strange happening on that mountain side. As he was finishing his short tutorial, Tunner gave him some websites for further research.

"So, bro, Sylvia is coming over in a few minutes and I gotta go, but tell Rose I will get it all taken care of."

"You had better, because if you don't, I am going to sic your baby sister on you."

"Oh, now that's just not fair. She will leave my nephews with me, and those two little hellions are savage."

Frank was still laughing when he hung up the phone, but his mood turned serious as he typed in the websites that Tunner had given him. He had already learned from Tunner that a Bit Coin Mine wasn't really a mine, but a collection of super powerful computers housed in what were essentially shipping containers. Depending on the number of shipping containers, the entire operation might not take up any more space than a large residential lot, which would explain the small size of the clearing being cut out at the base of the mountain. The computers did nothing but solve incredibly complex mathematical equations, with no purpose for the solutions that Frank could discern. The worthlessness of the output in conjunction with the mindboggling amounts of energy the process consumed was unfathomable to Frank. *"What does this do for anyone,"* he asked himself.

It was so different from the philosophy of the man who had raised him.

Chapter 14

The Past – Get Over Yourself

Frank had already earned enough credits to graduate, before the night of the attack. Technically, all he needed to do was complete two requirements that he had already nearly finished, and he could have graduated with his class. He didn't even need to take the advance courses for which he was already enrolled in the spring, especially in light of the fact that attending college was likely to be postponed indefinitely. It was a challenge though, and he was determined to prove to himself that he could still do it. He wasn't sure why, since everything about his life had changed.

After a few weeks of recovery, he was walking with the aid of a walker and awkwardly made his way down the path to the outbuilding that Tyrell had already converted to his plumbing shop, a vast improvement from the tiny one he had worked out of before. Ramsey was busy getting everything in order for the next day, and didn't hear Frank enter. Even though he dealt daily with sometimes filthy environments, the organization and cleanliness of his shop resembled a hospital operating room. Frank stumbled slightly as he tried to get his walker past the door, causing Tyrell to look up.

"Whoa, Buddy. I'm sorry. I didn't hear you open the door. Let me get that for you."

"It's ok, Tyrell. I have to start doing things for myself, eventually," he said aloud. To himself, he thought, *It has been that way my whole life. Everyone stops what they are doing, just so I can be me. I am going to finish those two courses and be done with it."*

"Eventually being the key word. I don't know of anyone who hasn't been amazed by your determination to get better. It's a long walk down here from the main house. Did you need something?"

Frank had walked to the shop to ask Tyrell what he thought about him continuing with his college plans, but he had already known the answer to that. The selfless man would have encouraged him to continue even though it would put more of a burden on him. "Nothing really. I just need the exercise, and Tunner is driving me crazy with his computer games."

He had hesitated too long before answering. Tyrell laughed with a slight air of sarcasm. "You know, I might find that easier to believe if I didn't know that your little brother was hiding from his sisters right now, because they are driving him crazy. Now, tell me what you want to talk about."

"I don't think I want to go to college, anymore," Frank blurted out.

"Now, hold on. You know that Tab, your mom, and I support you going to college, and you know that Mrs. Merritt will help you in any way that she can."

"I know, and that's just the point. I realized, while lying in the hospital that you and Tabitha have made everything about me since the day you first saw me. Mrs. Merritt has given up a lot of her time just for me, and I didn't know it until she took me to Beaumont and showed me our old house, but Mom has protected me since the day I was born. I turn twenty soon, Tyrell. It's time I did something for all of you."

Ramsey had been standing at a bench until that point. He wiped the wrench he had been holding with a cloth and set it in its rightful place. "Have I ever told you how I got to college?"

"No, and I've always been so busy worrying about me that I don't know much of anything about the most important people in my life."

Ramsey smiled and put his hand on Frank's shoulder. "That sounds almost exactly like something I said over thirty years ago, only I was a lot angrier and caused more trouble than you will ever be capable of. Unlike you, I was blessed by one of the wisest fathers that ever walked this planet. I was just too into myself to know it at the time. Do you remember the first thing you ever said to me?"

Frank laughed. "I couldn't help it. I had never seen anyone as dark as you, and there you were, smiling down at me."

"Don't feel bad. You've probably noticed since then that I am darker than even most African Americans. When I grew up and where I grew up, the darker you were meant the less intelligent you were, so that meant I was pretty much an idiot."

With that introduction, Tyrell Ramsey shared the story of his life with his young protégé. Ramsey's father had been light skinned, but his mother had been a beautiful woman with a complexion the color of fine ebony. It was from her that he had received his chiseled good looks and dark skin. His father had been devastated when she died only days after giving birth to Tyrell. He had also been incredibly angry. Largely self-educated, he had built a solid plumbing business and had been a reasonably successful black man with a mostly white clientele in the segregated south. He had been able to do so for two reasons; he was the best plumber in the area, and he knew how to subject himself to demeaning language without getting angry. Neither of those traits had benefitted him when seeking adequate post-natal health care for his wife after Tyrell had been born. His aging grandmother had helped him care for her great-grandson in those terrible days following the death of his wife.

The anger and grief nearly consumed him, but each time he had held his son he felt as if he was looking in the eyes of his beloved wife, and he made a conscious decision to survive for him and for the memory of the one he had loved so much. He also resigned himself to the belief that things were never going to change for black people, and that he had to teach his son how to play the game in order to live in a white man's world.

Tyrell had been born with a temper as hot as his skin was black, and an intellect that surpassed most of his regional peers of any race or culture. Schools in the Dugganville area were still segregated when he began his education. Yet, even in the all-black school he attended, he was channeled into lower achieving classes, because he was darker than his lighter skinned classmates. His father, other than taking repair orders, spoken in demeaning language from his clients, had little social interactions with anyone outside of his home. He spent the majority of his limited free time taking care of his son, and as time went by, his grandmother. The elder Ramsey spent time every day educating his son. Few people in his life would ever know how intelligent and well-read, Tyrell's father was. His experience had been that intelligence in a black man just made him a target, even among his peers. He had passed the knowledge of that experience on to his young son while insisting that he push himself to learn as much as possible. Most of the time, the younger Ramsey attempted to listen and grudgingly follow his father's instruction. Once, nearing the end of his junior year in high school, Tyrell decided to challenge the wisdom of his dad's lessons for life.

"You always want to be the smartest person in the room. You just don't want anyone else to know it."

He had heard his father make that statement many times, and the advice didn't sit well with the proud young black man. "So, I gotta listen to a bunch of ignorant black rednecks who don't know jack shit, while I act like a retarded N –,"

"DON'T SAY IT!" Tyrell's father raised the back of his hand and moved toward his son as if he were going to strike him down, but he paused and lowered his hand. The younger Ramsey had never witnessed such a flash of anger from his normally gentle dad. The man then spoke in a low carefully modulated tone. "You will hear that vulgar insult behind your back and to your face enough times in life, but the minute you say it out loud, that means you accept it as being OK! Is that what you want? That word spoken aloud, is one human's reminder to another that he believes himself superior and therefore has license to demean, enslave, rape, or even murder the one he believes to be inferior. I've seen terrible things that I hope you never have to see, Son. Things may have gotten better, but around here, a black man still has to be careful. I love you, and I am teaching you to survive the best way I know how. If you can think of a better way when you are on your own, you do it, but I made a promise to your mother before she died that you would grow up safe and become an educated man. Until you walk out that door and go on down the road, you will live under the promise I made to your mother. Do you hear me – boy!"

The elder Ramsey's emphasis on the word boy at the end of his reprimand caused his son to feel as if a knife had been jabbed between his ribs and twisted. His father was one of the most sought-after plumbers in the area. If he had been white, he could have demanded far more money and would have had to tolerate much less verbal abuse than what his son had witnessed. Tyrell had always assumed that his father had been afraid or accepted that he somehow deserved the demeaning behavior. Only then did he realize that his heartbroken father had spent every minute since the death of his mother keeping his promise to her. From reteaching the curriculum after receiving substandard instruction to maintaining a calm dignified composure regardless of the way he had been treated, Tyrell's father had been doing his best to ensure that his son remained safe and received a solid education.

"So, you see, Frank, that's why I ended up going to college; because a hard-headed light-skinned black man ate a lot of dirt so that his son could have a better life for himself. It turns out that being quiet and acting like I didn't know anything, even paid off. When I took the SATs, I outscored everyone in my class. State U was looking for promising underserved minority students to give academic scholarships. When they showed my scores to the administration, my teachers and counselors thought there must have been some kind of mistake. The university thought my, quote, poor academic performance must have been due to the hardships of being raised by an uneducated single father. It turns out that my daddy was more of a genius than I ever gave him credit for. I was given a full ride, as long as I kept my grades up."

Frank sat wide-eyed. "Wow, Tyrell! I never knew any of that about you – but, you went back to plumbing?"

Ramsey laughed and shook his head. "There is a lot you don't know about me young man. The story gets even more interesting after that. I had never been more than a few miles from Dugganville my entire life, and had only attended all-black schools. Suddenly I found myself a hundred miles from home in this big school with a whole bunch of white people. Talk about standing out! This shiny black skin caused more than a few people to turn their heads, and I started to wear it around like a super-hero costume. I found more acceptance on that mostly-white campus in my first two weeks of classes than I had found in my entire educational career at my all-black school. I don't doubt that some of my celebrity came because I was considered to be the token to liberalism, but it gave me a new attitude about myself and people in general. Now, do you want to know the big irony?"

Frank grinned and looked at Tyrell like he was about to be let in on a secret. "Sure, please, tell me!"

"So, I found myself walking around like the big man on campus." He grinned, slyly before continuing. "I mean, chicks, didn't matter what color, were really digging me. Professors were pointing my work out in classes as exemplary. You know how that Paxton kid struts around in school, because he thinks he is God's gift to women? That was me. I was just too cool to be angry anymore. I had decided within a week of arriving on campus that I was never returning to this bigoted backwater little town. Until, I got hit with a sledgehammer one day when I was sitting in the campus cafeteria, because that was the only place I could afford to eat.

Frank's eyes widened in shock. "A sledgehammer, really?"

"Well, a metaphorical one, but just as hard. I was eating lunch, and the most beautiful woman I had ever seen in my life sat across from me. I couldn't believe that I had never seen her before. There weren't many minority students on campus, and this girl would have stood out in any crowd. Do you know what she said to me?"

"What?"

"She gave me a sarcastic look through a pair of incredibly beautiful eyes, and said, 'You need to get over yourself, Tyrell Ramsey.' I was dumbfounded and confused. She acted like she knew me, but I didn't remember having seen her before."

"I tried every way I could think of, to figure out who she was without admitting that I didn't know who she was until I know she saw me squirming. Finally, she put me out of my misery, and asked 'You don't know who I am do, you?' All I could do was shrug and shake my head. 'Well, you would if you hadn't been such a bigoted little shit and had come in the house when you and your dad came to our house, three times, to fix my family's plumbing when we were little kids.'"

Frank grinned, "That sledgehammer sounds like Tabitha."

"You got it. I just looked at her and was finally able to stutter, are you a, Red Elk? 'Yes,' she said, 'Tabitha Red Elk. I came here last year on the same scholarship that you have.'"

Tyrell shook his head slightly before continuing. "She wasn't wrong, either. I was scared the first time we went to the Red Elks' home. They had, like, twelve children. The dad was crippled, and the mom spent most of her time trying to catch the kids. Dogs and chickens were everywhere. Their house was dirty and way undersized for such a big family. I had inherited my neat-freak tendencies from my father, and the chaos and dirt were more than I could handle. Most of their plumbing problems were outside the house, and I gladly stayed outside. I guess I was a little scary to them, too, because every time we came, all the kids ran into that tiny house. I can still remember a bunch of dirty little faces staring out at me. So, Tabitha had caught me in my own bigotry. I had felt just a little superior to this dirty Indian family with no money. I remember asking Dad why he kept going back when they barely paid him anything. His answer was short and to the point. He just looked down at me and said, 'White folk may pay me a little bit more, but the Red Elks treat me with respect.'"

Before continuing, Ramsey broke into a grin. "So, I am sitting across from this stunning woman, and I am trying to find the nearest hole to crawl into when she breaks out into this huge laugh that the whole cafeteria can hear, and she laughs until tears come to her eyes. She has been putting me in my place ever since. The irony is that I had to travel across the state to meet the woman who would make me want to come right back here."

A sentimental tear snuck from the corner of Frank's eye, which he wiped off quickly hoping Tyrell hadn't noticed. His brow furrowed slightly, as a question arose in his mind. "Wait, you didn't explain why you are plumbing still."

"Oh, that. Tabitha was studying to be a teacher, and after meeting her, I decided that was what I wanted to be, too. I was good in physics, so I got my degree in science education and planned to teach high school science. Several things happened at once that changed my career plans. We both wanted a family, and it wouldn't have been possible for her to stay home with me earning a teacher's salary. A bigger factor was my dad's health. I found myself helping him maintain his business more than I was preparing for classes. My relationship with Tabitha was missing out. Eventually, I stopped teaching and took over the business, full-time. This property was one of the accounts I took over from Dad."

Frank again realized that he knew very little about the man he idolized. "Didn't you tell me once that the owner used to be some kind of white-supremacist?"

"Hmmph. Probably still was the day he died. I can't say we ever liked each other, but we did eventually respect each other, thanks to his wife. He had a huge confederate flag in his front window. He called me out to his house, not long after Dad died. I stopped on the front driveway, got out, and leaned against my van. He looked out that flag-draped window for a long time, before he finally came to my car.

Tyrell affected the personality of the man before continuing.

"What's wrong with you, boy. I have a basement that's trying to flood. I don't have time for you to sit out here in the shade all day."

"One of my first actions after taking over Dad's business was to create a standard pricing list. After listening to him rant for a few seconds, I took the list out of my pocket and handed it to him. Mr. Taylor, I said. I have standardized all of my pricing, and this sheet is what I will develop my quote to you from. Also, my name is Mr. Ramsey; Tyrell, if you prefer, but not, boy. Finally, I will not come in your house as long as that flag is hanging in your window. Old man Taylor did not like being talked to like that by a black man. 'Why you insolent little – you will not talk to me like that. Leave this property. I will call someone else.' I left him with the price sheet in his hand. My final words to him were that I understood, but he knew my work and that I was still less expensive than anyone else he could find. A few days later his wife called, sounding really desperate and more than a little miffed with her husband."

Tyrell then played the role of Mrs. Taylor speaking on the phone. "Please, Mr. Ramsey, our house is going to be ruined if you don't take this job. I solemnly swear that Mr. Taylor will behave himself or it will be him who leaves, not you."

Frank laughed out loud at Tyrell's imitation of an angry housewife. Ramsey was obviously enjoying telling the story. "The first thing I noticed when I pulled in the driveway was that the flag was gone from the window. That old coot met me at the front door with his head down and his hand stuck out. Mrs. Taylor was standing a few feet behind him. 'Mr. Ramsey, I would be honored for you to call me Jackson, if I may call you Tyrell.' I shook his hand and told him that I would likewise be honored and tried to sound as much like a southern gentleman as possible. When I reached the basement, I was seriously tempted to jack the price up. It seems that after calling several plumbers and discovering that I was telling the truth, he had attempted to do the job himself. What a mess! I didn't though, and from then on, we had a cordial and respectful relationship."

Chapter 15

The Present – Decisions

Frank's mind was a maze of thought, and he wasn't sure what direction to take. He had two urgent situations to deal with. Before speaking with his little brother and doing research on the clearing on the mountain, Bear had already sensed that the activity across the lake represented an inherit threat to Beaumont. He was now convinced, and knowing that R.T. Merritt was behind it made his dis-calm even greater. He remembered vividly the first time Tyrell had expressed strong reservations about him having any kind of relationship with the then-state senator, but Ramsey had never fully explained why. Frank had also learned little from the teacher he adored. Even years after being brutally violated by her husband, she refused to divulge the full extent of his activities for fear of what might befall Jason, if he ever found out that her son had been fathered by Frank.

He could no longer speak with Tyrell or Tabitha. Asking his mother would be of no help, because the Ramsey's had protected her as much as they had Frank. He had to speak with the woman he still considered to be his teacher, even though they shared a son. He had to somehow fill in the blanks of his history after the one man who knew the answers had been killed in a tragic accident. He knew that Amber knew far more than she had ever shared. It was also time for the two of them to talk about Jason.

Frank Bear sat at his desk for a long time staring at the image of Amber Merritt on his phone before he could bring himself to touch the telephone number underneath. The picture was from his high school year book and depicted a much younger version of the person he was about to call. Finally, after a long sigh, he put his index finger on the blue number glowing from the screen.

Amber answered almost immediately. "Hi Frank, I thought you might call since state is coming up in a couple of days. Do you think Jason is ready?" Frank and Amber had communicated regularly over the years, mostly about Jason, but they had also developed an unspoken code in which neither referred to him as their son.

"Jason stopped by my house this week and asked me about my past. I think the time has come when we are going to have to deal with this."

The abruptness of his response startled Amber. Her thirty-seven-year-old former student had typically started conversations with, "Hi, Ms. Merritt," like he was walking into her class from the hallway, even after the drastic events that had occurred in their lives. At forty-eight, she was still beautiful, but the stress in her life had created a tiredness in her eyes that had largely the replaced the vibrancy that had been there before. She had known the time Frank spoke of was coming soon, because her son had started probing her with questions also.

"I know, Frank. He has a fine father, and should know who that man is. We have to wait until after the state tournament. He has enough on his mind, already."

"I agree. Do you think we could meet somewhere at the tournament?"

"Sure," Amber responded, but after a pause, added, "Are you sure, Rose is OK with this?"

"Without a doubt. She is the one who has been pushing me to do this. She loves Jason, and she is more than a little worried that one of our daughters might really fall in love with him without knowing that he is their brother. If I hadn't called you, she probably would have. We have to talk about your ex-husband, also. He is up to no-good, and I want to know what it is. Sometimes, I feel as clueless as Jason about what went on between you and him, and I know that neither Tyrell nor you ever told me everything that was going on with R.T. I know that both of you were protecting me, but now I need to know it in order to protect you and my family."

The Relationship between Amber and R.T. Merritt had been somewhat of a marital cold war following the night of his brutal sexual attack on her. Neither side was willing to launch an all-out assault, because neither knew the full capabilities or vulnerabilities of the other. If her ex-husband had excelled at anything, it was at hiding his finances. While, on paper, it appeared that he was near bankruptcy, she knew that he turned over huge amounts of money – or at least that is what he had constantly bragged to her. Her unwillingness to press the issue in divorce court would result in his paying a pittance in child support.

The reason behind her reluctance, lay in the true identity of her son's father. Merritt carried a lot of societal weight around Dugganville, and he could easily ruin her and her parents if he ever found out. Merritt believed however believed that Jason was his son. Amber was a smart woman, and he feared that she may have somehow videotaped the whole rape and kept it as ammunition for future use. Even before the attack, he had returned home on more than one occasion after a night of womanizing and too much alcohol. Upon waking the next day, he would find his wife in an all-too-calm mood and oozing with mock compassion. He was never sure what he had said or how he had behaved the night before, and his wife would purposefully pick up her phone from the table as he sat down to breakfast, implying that she had something to show. He had feared that she had recorded him bragging about his sexual infidelity. He didn't think he ever had, *"but, God, that woman should have been a professional gambler, the way she carries a bluff,"* Merritt had often thought.

What he had disclosed, was far worse in Amber's mind. It was what had brought the fearful woman to Tyrell's shop following the attack on Frank. He had spoken a name; Bubba Raines. In a drunken stupor, Merritt had told her that Raines wanted to play rough with her toad of a boyfriend. Amber hadn't understood what it had meant, but there had been seething maliciousness in his voice. Amber was now mortified thinking what Merritt might do to Jason, if he found out that he was Frank's son.

Fortunately for Amber, except for her son being shorter than either she or her husband, he bore little physical resemblance to his biological father when he was child. By the time Jason began to display personality characteristics of Frank Bear, R.T. Merritt bitterly assumed it was because his ex-wife had alienated him from his son, and Bear had become his role model. The cat and mouse game went on for years with each assuming that the other might find out something that would expose the other. For Amber, the paralyzing fear was that her ex-husband might do something to harm not only her child, but also the Bear family, whom she loved dearly, if he ever found out that Jason was not his son.

"You are right about that too, Frank. Tyrell and Tabitha loved you so much. He made me promise not to burden you with too much information while you were still trying to heal."

"I wasn't a child, Ms. Merritt," his voice broke in.

"No, you weren't and aren't, so there is one thing I am going to insist on when we are talking about our son and anything involving him. I need you to drop the polite student crap and call me Amber. I know that you still call most of your teachers by their titles, and believe me, I get that you still feel guilty about what happened between us so many years ago. Don't forget that I was the one in a position to be labeled as a predator, not you. If we are going to make decisions about our child, we are going to do it as equals."

Frank heard the anger in her voice and felt deeply wounded. His eyes burned, and his lip quivered. Her phone was silent, and she thought that he might have hung up. Finally, she heard a deep sigh. "I agree, Amber. We have lived with this lie for over seventeen years and have learned to adapt. Everything our son has believed about his life of the past seventeen years is going to change in one devastating conversation. That change may prove to be dangerous for him and you."

"And for you and your family, Frank."

"I suppose. As I said earlier, there are things that neither you nor Tyrell ever told me. As long as we are talking about our son, we will be Frank and Amber. You are mistaken about one thing, and I need to tell you. My insistence on calling you Ms. Merritt, even though I despise the name, for all of these years has nothing to do with guilt or politeness. I love my wife and my daughters, and I am forever grateful for my family. I never want to do anything that will cause harm to my relationship with them. I call you Ms. Merritt to make sure that I never forget that blessing."

Amber could hear the shakiness in his voice as he spoke. Suddenly, she did feel like a predator. She had loved and still loved Frank Bear for what he had always been; a beautiful human being. Had she selfishly used him in a moment of weakness?

He waited for a response, but none came. When Frank next spoke, his voice was calm and steady. "I can tell by the long pause that it's taking you a while to digest the bombshell I just dropped on you. To answer the question, I know you are asking yourself, no, you never did anything to lead me on. I know you know that you were my first and only infatuation with anyone. The Ramsey's and Mom gave me a lot of grief over it. After that, I turned you into some kind of superhuman in my mind. The night that bastard did what he did to you was the first time I have ever wanted to hurt someone. For the first time, I realized that you weren't a goddess or a superhero. You needed me. It was the first time that I ever felt like anyone needed me. So, Amber, I have experienced a lot of firsts because of you. Rose already knows what I am about to say, because she is the one who made me see it first. I love you deeply, and you will always have a part of me. You don't need to feel any guilt. I don't. I cherish the family Rose and I have together, and I cherish the son you and I share."

Frank could hear Amber sniffling when she answered. "Frank, do you remember the day we drove to Beaumont? Neither before, nor since, have I allowed myself to be in a car alone with a student, male or female. You are special. When I found out I was pregnant, part of me was terrified that the child might be yours, but the bigger part prayed that it would be. I don't know how Jason will react when he finds out, but I do know that he has a father he can be proud of. When you hang up, please tell Rose, thank you and please talk with her more. This is going to be a drastic change, not only for Jason's life, but also for your daughters."

"I know. Rose and I have already been talking."

CHAPTER 16

The Present – Historical Connections

Robert Thomas Merritt sat nervously tapping the fingers of his left hand on an oversized desk while holding a glass of scotch in his right hand and staring at the miniature replica of the R.T. Beaumont monument displayed on the corner of his desk. He could see the full-sized Raeford Thaddeus in all of his eroded glory from the office window overlooking the river. As he had been for decades, the major was currently on the southern side of the river, but it had been predicted that this would be a particularly rainy year, so who knew if Beaumont might once again change sides and be a Yankee by the end of the season. Next to the statuette and standing proudly between a set of mahogany bookends was an eleven by seventeen-inch tome entitled, "The Legend of Raeford Thaddeus Beaumont," by Robert Thomas Merritt, Sr. The worn-out story that both father and son had so often told about their own names, held about as much factual basis as the oversize volume sitting on his desk. The book held mostly black-and-white copies of pictures from the American Civil War. A few had been collected from local sources, but the majority could be found in public domain and were largely unattributable to any specific source. Interspersed between the faded images were testimonials, narratives, and other anecdotal records; none of them verified; from people on both sides of the conflict who had supposedly served with the major.

Most of the stories came from Merritt's paternal grandmother, whose maiden name had been Gloria Margaret Beaumont before she had married his grandfather. Gloria Margaret had claimed to be descended from Dugganville royalty and, since she was a rather imposing woman, few had ever dared challenge her claim. R.T. Jr. remembered being fascinated by her stories as a child and then becoming slightly incredulous as he began to notice that important details tended to change, each time she told them. He had long supposed that his father had simply settled on the version he liked best before adding them to the book.

Junior had inherited his grandmother's talent for story-telling and his father's tendency to label hearsay as gospel truth, if the labeling advanced his cause. That inherited tendency was the engine powering Merritt's nervous tapping on the desk's surface. The lack of truth behind his recent financial claims was beginning to overshadow his talent for making them sound valid. He had promised local investors that placing the bit coin mine at the base of the mountain towering over the valley leading to Beaumont would have little environmental impact while earning them huge profits from cryptocurrency.

Some of those investors were the same hunters and farmers on either side of the mountain who had convinced him to cede part of the valley to the Beaumont Civic Center. Father and son had agreed with the understanding that they would be placing a small data plant at the base of the mountain that over looked the valley between the Twin Sisters; the name given to the hills at the foot of the mountain. They had confidently promised that the entire operation would only take up an area about the size of a football field and require but one small road to transport equipment and run powerlines. R.T. had painted a beautiful image of his company, the farmers, and the hunt clubs being in full partnership to help the small low-income community of Beaumont, while they raked in huge profits.

Of course, he had known enough about the noise created by the huge supercomputers required for bitcoin mining to understand that it could potentially create a nuisance for Beaumont, but he had convinced himself that they would find it worth the small sacrifice. He had also convinced himself that it was Frank Bear's fault that he barely knew his own son and that his wife had divorced him. *"Maybe the noise will keep that Indian shit up at night while he is trying to sleep in that big house that he doesn't deserve,"* he had thought. Now, it was he who was losing sleep, as he reconsidered the people to whom he had made promises.

"I don't know if it's worse to be a fictional Beaumont or a real live, Merritt."

Civil war era Dugganville had not been unlike any other community in history that had found themselves on the border of a major social conflict. Families and friendships that had been previously believed to be strong were suddenly and cruelly split apart by the sharp heavy wedge of ideological differences. The two Dugganvilles had been founded by brothers. As is often the case with siblings, their similarities separated them as much as their differences. Until the time that war had been openly declared between the union and the confederate states, there had been little distinction between North and South Dugganville. Separated only by a few miles and a river, the citizens of each of the villages often traded and socialized with the other. Almost overnight, the north side of the river became blue and the south turned to gray, with the only common color being the blood-red water in the middle.

The American Civil war, like any other armed conflict, also provided a great deal of opportunity for those less encumbered by the chains of ideology and more attuned to the possibility of profit, a lot of profit. Among them were politicians, businessmen and clergy who by day condemned the warmongers from the other side, but by night in the shadows of candlelight, shook hands over stacks of money with those same warmongers. There were also laborers, poor farmers and even some slaves who, fully understanding their impotence in the conflict, cast their loyalties with those who afforded some material security.

Over a century later, the loyalties hadn't changed a great deal in Dugganville, even after the influx of "trannies" as a result of the growth in the tech industry. Tranny was a derogatory term that had nothing to do with a person's sexual orientation. Depending on who was explaining the term, it stood for transplant or sometimes, transient, because of the newcomers often short-lived tenures in the booming city. Either way, the established culture of Dugganville tended to view the newcomers as invasive noxious weeds. The north side, with its greater emphasis on industry, had generally fared better financially than the agriculturally oriented south, but the power structure had barely changed since the confederacy had been brought back into the union.

The true origins of R.T. Merritt's Grandmother Beaumont may have remained a mystery, but the branches of the Merritt family tree were well documented and their roles in Dugganville had changed little. While in the daylight, the Merritt's had been small business people on the northern side of the river in the second tier of the Dugganville elite, not quite laborers, but not invited to the social gatherings of the aristocracy either. In the shadows, they had been rumored to supply arms to both blue and gray armies.

He knew of at least one direct ancestor that had disappeared under mysterious circumstances, and, as he sat pondering the developments on the mountain, he hoped that his family's tendency to play both sides wouldn't leave the young man he believed to be his son inheriting a pocketful of nothing, long before he was finished trying to turn his financial fantasies into real money.

The alcohol Merrit had been consuming was taking him quickly down the road of self-pity. *"Who am I kidding,"* he thought. *"Jason will probably be glad to see me go. I know his mother will. Ms. Noble-High and Mighty, thinks I have been holding out on her all of these years. She doesn't know how hard it is to run a business in this town. Damn, I get drunk and forget to wear a condom one time, and I will be paying for it the rest of my life. And the kid's a wrestler. Just stick the knife in me and twist it, Amber."*

Merritt had never wanted children, and had never really wanted to be married. Amber Bronson's beautiful smile and witty intelligence had left him vulnerable for the first time in his life, and for a brief time he had felt a little like the noble person she had seen in him. As soon as it had become obvious that she wasn't going to be one of his season-long flings, his mother had become excited about the possibility of grandchildren. By the time the handsome couple had married, Merritt was already becoming inured to the charms of his beautiful, but naively cause driven young wife. For him, the marriage soon became a means to an end. In the beginning, he had wanted to be the believer in worthy causes that he had portrayed to Amber and her parents, but the chilling effect of responsibility for another human being had left him feeling shackled by the relationship. Still, he had to play the role. The Bronson's were influential in the tranny community and they had access to big purse strings.

The longer he sat at the desk, the more pitiful and angry his musings became. Before long, he forewent taking time to pour his drink into the glass and began drinking straight from one of the multiple bottles in his liquor cabinet. By the time he finally passed out, Major Beaumont's shadow had stretched eastward up the river into a long thin line, before vanishing with the sunset.

The fog hung heavily when Merritt awoke the next morning, both over the river and in his head. Addled and feeling the beginnings of a horrific hangover, he tried to make sense of his surroundings. His office, an overturned bottle of vodka on the expensively carpeted floor, the smell of vomit, and his body, fully clothed in a rumpled and stinking suit, came painfully into focus as he tried to shake himself from his stupor.

He glanced at his watch. 10:30 AM. "Damn, what's her name is probably already in the office. I have to send her on an errand, to give myself time to get cleaned up," He mumbled to the statuette on the desk.

He punched the call button on his desk. "Uhmm, Uhmmm,"

"It's JoAnne," Mr. Merritt.

"JoAnne, right. Listen, I was up here working all night. I need you to run and get me a breakfast sandwich and some coffee. Also, stop by the drugstore and pick up some headache medicine. I have a bad one." Merritt never ate breakfast, and he had a Keurig. His medicine cabinet was fully stocked. For this one time, he felt like he needed to clean up his mess before she came in.

"Yes sir, Mr. Merritt. I will be back in an hour," she said in a voice tinged with disrespect.

Merritt stood and looked around the office, trying to decide if he should clean up the mess first or take a shower. He decided to clean himself up first, not wanting to be seen or smelled in his current state, and was about to get undressed when a light tap came on the door.

"Shit! I will open the door just wide enough to see what she needs," he thought, and went to the door.

After barely turning the knob, a huge hand slapped the door with a force hard enough to send Merritt stumbling backward. He caught himself without falling and saw a huge hulk-like figure filling the door frame. "I want my money!"

"Damn it, Bubba! You aren't supposed to be here. Did my secretary see you come in the building?"

Raines answered with a gravelly sneer. "Yea, she saw me. Nearly shit herself tryin' to get out of my way. Now, where is my money?"

Bubba was the man with whom Frank Bear had heard Merritt arguing after he had been startled by the sound of the chain saw a few days before. The logger had just started his chain saw to clear some brush when the man who had contracted his services, Merritt, pulled up in his Land Rover to check on progress. The conversation had grown heated almost immediately when Bubba had asked when he was going to receive compensation. Snorting like an angry bull, the big man had stormed off and made it profanely clear that neither his grader nor his saw would be started until he received payment for what had already been done. That was why Frank hadn't heard the saw again after it had startled him and caused him to hit his head on the rock.

William "Bubba" Raines, a.k.a. Back Door Bill, Bubba Dump, and a host of other unflattering nick names was also an integral part of the multi-generational shadow culture that had long thrived in the Dugganville area, although in a much lower caste than the Merritt family. He was a big man in height and girth. Powerful muscles laid under several inches of flab. Although Raines generally listed Caucasian on any forms requiring race, arguing that it was as close as any other, blue eyes, tightly curled black hair and mocha-tinted skin betrayed his multi-racial heritage. Among his ancestors were escaped slaves who had later acted as spies for the confederate army; for pay of course. During prohibition, another branch of the Raines family had run bootleg liquor while also acting as informants for the feds; again, for pay. He and Albert Floyd were second or third cousins depending on which branch of the family tree you followed, and the two families had held animosities against each other dating back to the Civil War.

Bubba had continued his family's legacy of not letting ideology get in the way of a fast buck, and he had honed it to the blunt edge of an iron pipe held in a huge ham-handed fist. Anyone doing business with Raines understood that if his name was ever mentioned, the pipe would be payment for any difficulties he had with the law. Population growth, much of it from the coasts, had brought with it increasing government oversight and subsequently, tighter legislative regulations concerning land usage.

Most of the trannies accepted the increased regulations as a consequence of the growing economy, but a few had been introduced to BFG and its owner, Bubba Raines. BFG stood for Bubba's Fencing and Grading. It was important to Raines that he be treated with respect by the wealthy, and in his mind, the only way to do that was to have a "Bona Fide" company. He even made out handwritten invoices that he made customers sign. None of BFG's business dealings were ever bona fide. Many unpermitted private roads and illegal fences had been laid by BFG, and thanks to most of the local rural residents being part of the century old system, nobody really cared. Even if a less informed newcomer complained about an encroachment on their newly purchased acreage or an illegal dump on their property, they were generally met with a shrug and a yawn by the local authorities.

For a few select customers he went beyond the confines of breaking petty permitting laws. The Merritts, father and son, had profited from a long business relationship with Bubba and were well aware that he was a violent man. He had spent time in prison for beating a man to death in a fit of rage. R.T. Merritt had been thankful that Raines had chosen to storm off on the day of their encounter, rather than taking his aggression out on him.

"Now listen, Bubba. I told you that you would get your money, but I don't keep that kind of cash here. Give me a day, and I will put it in your box."

"You're lyin' Merritt. I know you always keep cash close to you. Pay me, or you're going to be chokin' on your guts."

"Alright. Take it easy. I'll get it." Merritt turned and removed a picture from a wall that had been concealing a small wall safe. He opened the safe and started counted counting cash.

"Ah, hell, forget it," he said and removed the entire contents of the safe. "That's about $300 extra, and it's all I've got for now. That enough advance payment to get you started again?" He had lied. The small safe was where he kept the slush money for offering quick bribes. A larger safe with considerably more money was hidden under the floor. Bubba believed that he stood on an even ground with the power players of the area, but he was actually only considered to be a dangerous nuisance who sometimes proved to be useful.

"Maybe," was all he said before turning and walking out the door, leaving it standing open wide. Merritt shakily went to the door and closed it. His head pounded and his stomach ached, but alcohol wasn't the cause.

Raines was only part of the reason for Merritt's alcohol fueled pity party from the night before. The few who were knowledgeable of the process, understood that bitcoin mining was nothing more than one big digital pyramid scheme. With little or no government regulation, the world of crypto investments held the potential for enormous profits, but also for equally enormous losses. With his golden tongue, however, Merritt had convinced many of the local elite to lay down big sums of money. Most of his investors were from Dugganville and beyond, and weren't overly concerned about any negative environmental impacts the bit coin mine might have on a small rural community. After all, he had assured the investors, they weren't putting any pollutants in the air or water. A few, however, had been among the same hunters and farmers who had approached him about donating the land for the Beaumont Community Center, and they were starting to ask uncomfortable questions.

On top of all his other troubles, his mother had all but broken ties with him because of, as she had put it, "his immoral ways." In reality, R.T. Merritt Sr. was easily as crooked and licentious as his name-sake son, but he and his wife were teetotalers and had long been put off by their son's drinking and open carousing. The family matriarch hadn't been enthusiastic about her son's infatuation with the beautiful young woman from out of town or her high-minded ways, but that changed when Amber had given her a grandson. After the divorce, it seemed to R.T. Junior, that his parents had turned on him overnight. It had been Amber, not he, who had insured that they be given time to see Jason. Merritt was still lamenting the growing pile of undeserved ills to which he had been subjected when his phone rang. He looked at the caller ID.

"Damn, can this day get any worse," he thought, before tapping the accept call button on his phone.

"Hey, what's up?" Although he wanted to scream at his father to leave him alone, Merritt answered the phone, impassively.

"God damn it, Junior, you have really stuck your pecker in a deep bucket of horse shit this time."

Merritt didn't know what he hated worse; his father's meaningless vulgar folkisms, or being called Junior by the man with whom he shared a name. The moniker and the banal profanity usually came in the same sentence or at least in the same paragraph. For as long as he could remember, Merritt Sr. had never once called his son Junior in a show of pride, as one might expect a father with a namesake son to do. No, on the extremely rare occasions when his father had expressed overt pride, he had stretched out his full name, Robert Thomas Merritt, my son, almost as if he just enjoyed hearing the sound of his own name.

Junior was reserved for those times when his son needed reminding that all of the privileges he had enjoyed in life, came only through the sacrifices of his parents. To Junior's knowledge, Senior had never imbibed, but he was certainly often drunk on his own self-worth. It was during these self-importance binges that R.T. Merritt Sr. often felt the need to express himself through folksy and meaningless metaphors.

Merritt had seldom acknowledged his father's parental title, even as a child, when responding to one of Seniors rants. "R.T., If you could wait two seconds and let me talk before you go off, I would appreciate it. You are probably calling about some kind of noise you've heard going on with Bubba. I've already talked to him, and he won't be a problem." He tried to sound as sharp as possible, even though every word created a painful reverberation in his skull.

"Damn it, Junior."

"My name is, Robert." The younger Merritt cut him off.

Merritt could hear his father take in a deep breath, hold it and blow it out in a long slow exhale before continuing. "Ok, Robert," he said, with obvious spite in his voice. "It's good to know that you think you have that sadistic Cajun under control, which I doubt, but he is the least of your problems; or should I say, the least of our problems, since you hooked me into your latest hair-brained dumb ass scheme."

Another one of his father's finer qualities had just surfaced, that of being all-in for an idea and then finding a way to divert blame as soon as difficulties arose. Still, Merritt couldn't help but detect the note of real fear in the older man's voice.

"Ok, so what's going on," he asked, probing. The combination of too much alcohol from the night before and the second explosive confrontation in less than an hour caused Merritt's head to pound and his speech to slur.

"You've been drunk again," haven't you?

"Yes, Mr. Merritt, I've been drunk. I had an unpleasant encounter with Bubba yesterday and another this morning about his pay for clearing the mine area. He may not be very intelligent, but we both know that when he talks about pulling your asshole through your throat, he isn't speaking metaphorically. I guess that I let it get to me."

"You're playing a dangerous game, Robert," his dad said in a slightly softened tone. "I know that you think you can control that gorilla because he admitted to you that he is responsible for the Ramseys' death, but I see no good outcome coming from it. Don't forget that it was you who made sure the back door was open to the arena dressing room when Raines crippled Frank Bear for life and nearly killed him."

"Damn it," Dad," Merritt said through gritted teeth, "you know that wasn't supposed to happen. He told me that he was only going to rough him up enough to knock him off his high horse. Regardless, I can't change any of it now. What is the bigger problem, you are talking about?" Merritt Jr. asked the question although he already knew the answer.

"Have you checked to see what your sure bet investment is doing," his father answered. "Anything cryptocurrency is tanking, because the government is stepping in. Some of the people I talk to, doubt that it's coming back. You convinced me to talk a lot of heavy hitters into this fantasy money."

"There it is. If something doesn't work, it was all my idea," the younger Merritt thought, and shot his father a look through the phone that bordered on hatred.

Merritt senior thought he could actually feel his phone get hotter from the look he knew that his son must be giving him. "Ok, I will admit, it looked good on paper, and more than a few people came to me interested. The problem is, Robert, that every aspect of cryptocurrency seems to be turning to poison at the same time. The government is starting to get their fingers into it and talking about imposing regulations. You and I both know that everything the feds touch, turns to shit for hard working people like us. The arrangement we've had ever since you came up with your grand scheme to present yourself as the defender of the underrepresented classes in the area, was that you work the new money while I make sure that the established elites of Dugganville are still content."

"So, how has any of that changed," the younger Merritt shot back.

"You're not listening, Junior." The father made no attempt to hide the point he was trying to make by referring to his son with the demeaning moniker.

He continued. "Crypto isn't the wild west anymore. People are paying attention. Now, I don't give a damn about some dirt-poor town full of coloreds, mixed breeds and white trash, but those overgrown computers you call mines aren't even running yet, and I have already had hunters coming to me saying that the game animals are being affected. Farmers have told me that they are seeing a change in the behavior of their livestock. You know the Indians say that valley is ruled by some kind of spirit, because the way sound is amplified between those hills. If Bubba's road-grading equipment causes enough noise to upset the wildlife, what do you think the monster computers you call data mines are going to do? Yes, SON, I have done my homework. Those things make enough ruckus to shake shit out of rock. We both know that the new elite moving into town is not one bit different than the bastards the Merritts have been sucking up to for generations. They want Beaumont to look like it's doing a little better, but only if it means that their own bank accounts are getting a lot fatter. This thing you've got going now could well put those worthless ignorant people you pretend to care so much for, flat on their back and take a lot of money out of some very rich people's pockets at the same time. Damn, if my son ain't brilliant! Oh, and did I forget to mention, that you may manage to keep your mother from ever seeing her grandson again!"

"ENOUGH," Merritt screamed into his phone. If he had been in the physical presence of his father, he had no doubt that he would have slugged him or worse. The head ache was gone, as was the slurred speech. All that remained was angry focused clarity. "You leave my son out of this, and no way in hell am I going to let you hide behind Mother's skirts, you, spineless prick. If it hadn't been for me sucking up to Amber's parents, we wouldn't have near the real estate holdings we do. And as for poor Mom, she hated Amber, until she found out that she was going to be a grandmother. Now, this is what you are going to do. Start talking to the local landowners. Tell them that, after the initial start-up phase, the computers will tone down, and we will continue to mitigate any negative effects on the environment."

"What? How am I going to do that? I don't know anything about this stuff."

"That has never stopped you before. Lie, you dumb shit. It's what you do best."

"Ok, genius, what are you going to do," his father shot back. "What our family has always done. Play both sides against each other."

Chapter 17

The Past – Promoting Minority Business

Bubba Raines fell somewhere between Merritt Junior and Frank Bear in age. Raines had not always been the graying and scarred flabby behemoth that would one day argue with Merritt at the site of the bit coin mine. As a younger man, he had been handsome to the point of being beautiful, a darker more muscular version of DaVinci's, David. Narrow hips and a flat stomach had angled sharply upward to a powerfully built chest and muscular arms. In spite of his impressive height and heavily muscled body, he had moved with the grace of a dancer. Jet black deeply curled hair covered his head in ringlets. Flawless mocha skin framed a pair of deep-set blue eyes and perfect teeth. Women of many ages and backgrounds had tried to coyly catch the attention of the young William Raines only to be met with the same murderous glare he had turned on practically everyone he had ever met. Hopes of a romantic tryst had quickly turned to discomfort, if not out-and-out fear as each had hurried away to escape the glare.

Raines hated everyone, including himself. He hated his father for being too black, his mixed-race mother for not being white enough, and his teachers at school for being too white. His family was poor, and he hated the system for making him poor. He hated school because he couldn't learn a curriculum that seemed pointless to him, and he hated being placed in special classes. He hated coaches for constantly trying to recruit him for athletic activities in which he held no interest. He did, however, have one talent in which he excelled. He could intimidate anyone, and he worked to develop that talent daily. Mandatory attendance laws required that students attend school until they were sixteen, but no one looked for the handsome oversized student when he walked out of the school at age twelve and never went back.

Neither of his parents had ever asked why he wasn't in school, because he was also rarely home. Bubba's earliest memories of his father were of him constantly sniveling about not having enough money to feed the rapidly growing child with his meager government check. One thing Raines had never been was lazy, and he had earned money even as a small child undertaking every mindless dirty job in the area for landowners who might have helped him more, had he not been so angry all of the time. In the beginning, his father required that he surrender some of his earnings for room and board, but by the time Bubba turned eleven, the older, but barely larger man dared not ask.

Bubba would never be accused of being bright, but necessity required that he quickly learn how to handle money, and he soon discovered that he had another talent; how to pick the right customers. If a farmer wanted him to shovel shit out of his barn and spread it on his field, he could make more working at the fast-food place in town. If that same farmer wanted the shit dumped in the river without anyone knowing, he got paid much more for making an illegal dump and for keeping his mouth shut. It would be impossible to tell from the dirty hovel in which he lived, but by the time William Raines turned eighteen, he had already amassed enough money to buy the rocky acre upon which sat his broken-down shack.

William Bubba Raines and Tyrell Ramsey entered R.T. Merritt's life at approximately the same time. Ramsey Plumbing had grown slowly but steadily since the death of his father, primarily through word-of-mouth advertising. Unlike his father, Tyrell refused to accept substandard pay for quality work, and he had been able to provide a comfortable, although modest, standard of living for Tabitha and himself. In the beginning, he had lost a few of his father's customers for his "uppity" attitude, but the more elite of Dugganville society appreciated the quality of his work enough to overlook the new standard pricing sheet he had implemented without apologies. R.T. Merritt Sr. had even become a regular customer. Tyrell saw his business begin to grow at a more rapid pace with the influx of new residents from the north and east. The telegenic black man with a degree in science and relaxed openness toward the newcomers, had been a refreshing change for many of the new highly educated residents. Accustomed to the polished vehicles and the professional manner of the service technicians from whence they had come, the aging trucks, dirty overalls, and we'll-see pricing of their new culture had often made them less than comfortable in letting service techs into their pristine homes. Tyrell's time attending the university had served him well among the increasing population of highly educated people moving into the area from other parts of the country. He had quickly found himself in the position of having to turn away business. His father had devoted himself to ensuring that his son could compete with anyone academically, but the concept of growing a business beyond what was necessary to meet his family's daily needs had been foreign to him. Tyrell had no background to see himself beyond his one-man operation. This lack of worldly business knowledge combined with R.T. Merritt Jr.'s desire to inculcate himself into the new money moving into Dugganville, had been the catalyst for Ramsey's initial confrontation with Merritt.

* * * * *

"Hello, Tyrell. I suppose it won't be long before my parents have to add an extra room with as much time as you've been spending here at their house," Merritt Jr. said to Ramsey as he was packing his tools up after a long day digging a trench in the Merritt mansion's back yard. The huge antebellum style house had been purchased by Merritt Sr. when his son was still a boy. As with everything that Merritt's father undertook, he had spent a great deal of money creating the illusion of a beautiful estate while allowing critical maintenance on the house to deteriorate until he often found himself in crisis mode.

Tyrell sighed slightly and managed a less-than-genuine smile before answering. "If your father doesn't break down and do a complete overhaul of the plumbing on this place, it may be cheaper for him to build me a cottage rather than having me come out every time something breaks."

Merritt smiled broadly and laughed out loud, acting as if he was truly entertained by the comment. "I've been telling that old codger that you can only repair clay pipes for a hundred years or so, before they finally just go back to lake bottom."

Neither man liked the other. Tyrell was approximately midway between the father and son in age. Ramsey had watched the elder Merritt display his condescending arrogance toward his father while acting as if he were doing the single hard-working black man a favor by giving him work, even though his dad was, by far, the more intelligent person. As the younger Merritt matured, Tyrell had often thought he was watching a slightly smarter clone of the father emerge.

Conversely, Merritt Jr., had felt loathing mixed with an uncomfortable feeling of ineptitude when around Ramsey since he had been a child. Merritt had never seen Ramsey display anything but amiable respect toward his family, but behind the man's glistening eyes, R.T. had often sensed a feeling, not of gratitude, but of smug superiority. Ramsey was a successful and educated black man, however, and well respected among the growing tranny population. His wife was also a minority, and had quickly established a reputation as one of the most effective primary teachers in Dugganville. Merritt knew he had to establish a working relationship with Ramsey, in order to appear separate from the old elite of Dugganville.

Merritt acted as if a sudden thought had occurred to him, and then continued talking to Ramsey. "You know, Tyrell, that option might save my poor short-sighted father a little money, but would probably cost you a lot of money in the long run."

Ramsey looked confused, but didn't respond.

"I see that I have your attention. Tyrell, what you've done with your dad's business is nothing short of amazing. Hell, you've even got old man Taylor saying that you're not only the best plumber, but one of the finest gentlemen in Dugganville," and you and I both know that old bigot doesn't say anything nice about black folk."

It was all Ramsey could do to keep his expression neutral. *"Now, isn't that the proverbial pot calling the kettle black,"* he thought. He nodded slightly, indicating for Merritt to continue.

"You are good, Tyrell, very good, and in a prime position to establish yourself as the go to plumber in a rapidly growing market, but in order to do that, you have to grow with the market. Otherwise, you are going to get swallowed up by a bigger company with a broader name recognition."

Tyrell didn't like what he was hearing, but it made sense. He had seen solid Mom-and-Pop shops go under before, because they just couldn't compete with the big guys. "Ok, I am listening. Just how do you propose I grow my business? I only have so many hours in a day, and a lot of them are spent trying to maintain pipes for people who are too cheap to update their plumbing," he said, taking an obvious dig at Merritt's father, only superficially disguising it as humor.

Merritt took the comment without breaking stride. "That is exactly my point, Mr. Ramsey." Merritt went into full salesman mode, elevating Tyrell's status to Mr. Ramsey. "Why are you digging ditches instead of hiring manual labor and training a future workforce at the same time?"

Tyrell held up a hand. "Wait a minute. I learned everything I know about plumbing from my dad. I might be able to take on an apprentice like he did me, but all that is going to do is keep me from getting quite as dirty."

Merritt displayed a slightly incredulous frown. "I thought your degree was in science education. Are you telling me that you can teach a bunch of bored kids, chemistry, but you can't teach a motivated work force how to make more money?"

Tyrell hated to admit it to himself, but Merritt was making sense. He rubbed the back of his head and started to say something, but Merritt interrupted, "I tell you what, Tyrell. You know that I am a businessman, but I also have a stake in this community. Give some thought as to what a bigger Ramsey Plumbing company might look like and come by to see me at my office in a week. I might have some ideas for you."

The ideas Merritt would work on, however, before next meeting with Ramsey wouldn't be about helping the black owner of a small plumbing shop to expand his business. Much of the influx coming into the Dugganville were of a more liberal mindset than the established community, and a significant portion of the newcomers were minority. Merritt saw promoting Ramsey's business among the transient population as a safe way to build his connection with them without alienating the established elite. Expanding Ramsey plumbing might even increase business for some of the local companies. Although, on a less nefarious level, it wasn't unlike the activity some of his family had participated in during the American Civil War, namely, act as agents for the underground railroad while simultaneously providing information to slave owners about runaways.

Like his ancestors, Merritt was not going to let ideology get in the way of profit. As with his forefathers, he understood that the coming change was inevitable, even if he didn't like it. He also knew that being on the bleeding edge of that change wasn't profitable. He had been as incensed as old man Taylor, that Ramsey had forgotten his station in life since receiving his education and had demanded pay commensurate that of a white man. He also recognized that, with the influx of highly educated and more liberal newcomers, things were only going to get worse – unless he could profit from the change.

* * * * *

Merritt watched as the angular physique of William Raines climbed down from his ancient road grader, shirtless and wearing a pair of loose-fitting overalls. Another talent Raines prided himself in, was the ability to make virtually anything run. He had put the grader together from salvaged and stolen parts not long after leaving school. Bubba was now eighteen, and the machine still ran flawlessly. Merritt thought he looked like the mulatto version of L'il Abner, except a lot scarier.

"Whadda ya want, R.T. Unless, yer payin more than you did last time, I'm busy."

Merritt held up his hands in mock submission. "Whoa, Bubba, give me a chance. That was a misunderstanding. Tell you what. Hear me out, and I will give you double what I already paid you, just for listening."

"Double of damn near nuthin, still ain't very much, but go ahead. I'm listenin."

"I agree, Bubba. I made it clear to that transient that we were clearing that land without a permit, but he still backed out on me and left me holding the bag. But, that's my problem. Here is another hundred, on top of what I already said I would pay you for listening," he said, while holding out five twenties to Raines.

The deal Merritt was referring to, hadn't actually cost him anything. He hadn't made as much as he had hoped, but he was still well within his cost/benefit margin when he held the bills out to Raines. He thought he could almost detect the slightest glimmer of a smile on the young giant's face. Bubba inspected and counted the bills before stuffing them into his pocket. Wordlessly, he looked up and waited for Merritt to begin.

"Dealing with the Trannies moving into the area is a pain in the ass, Bubba, but there is still a lot of money to be made off of them, if we play it right. Hell, you might even be able to buy a grader that wasn't held together with bubble gum and bailing wire."

Bubba scowled, and Merritt feared that insulting the big man's pride and joy may have gone too far. "All I've heard so far, R.T. sounds like more of the smoke that you're constantly blowin out of your ass. What's this plan yer proposin?"

Merritt prided himself in making cow manure smell like roses waiting to be planted, but he knew Raines would be a tough sell. He would have to convince the multiracial bigot to train under, not only an African-American, but one wearing very dark skin. Beyond that, he was going to have to sell the idea to Bubba that he should work under Ramsey for a short period of time until he could establish himself with the Tranny community. One thing that generations of Merritts understood was that greed knew nothing of borders, politics, culture, or religion. It was always possible in any group to find someone who wanted to make an easy buck. All he had to do was convince Bubba that big money could be made from working with people the big man despised. That part would be easy, because Raines hated everyone. Every dollar he had ever made came from people whom he hated. The challenge would come in getting Raines to see the wisdom of working with a man who was nearly idolized for his honesty and trustworthiness.

He finished his spiel with, "So, you see, Bubba, setting this up to look good to all those rich transients moving is going to pay off big bucks in the long run. They may talk all high and mighty, but they're just like us folks who grew up here. They are going to hire you and Ramsey, because that looks good, but when they want something done that doesn't look good, they're going to step out back and talk to you. You and I both know that's where your big money is."

Merritt stopped and studied the emotionless face looking back at him. The man was so incredibly handsome that he almost didn't look real. Not a single blemish marred his skin to betray the rough life he lived. Perfectly balanced, clear blue eyes could not, however, hide the bitter hatred that burned behind them. The businessman found himself growing increasingly uncomfortable and was about to break the silence when Bubba spoke.

"Did you say Ramsey? I ain't workin for that black son of a bitch! I don't know what you and your daddy tryin to work up with that darkie and his Indian bitch wife, but you keep 'em away from me. Now, if you're through wasting my time, I'm busy. I'll take the rest of my money and be on my way."

Raines held out an open hand in a manner that said he expected it to be filled quickly. The abruptness of Bubba's refusal caught R.T. by surprise, but he had worked with him enough to know that the conversation was over and quickly paid him the agreed upon amount. Merritt thought that he knew every simmering feud that existed on either side of the state line, but the flash of anger he had witnessed from Raines was coming from more than his normal anti-social self. Beyond resenting Tyrell Ramsey for being a member of the human species, Bubba hated Ramsey and his wife on a personal level.

Merritt had always felt that Raines wasn't the angry simpleton everyone believed him to be. The barely literate giant had created a profitable shadow market before he was old enough to drive. He had hoped that Bubba would see the benefits of putting on the front of having a legitimate business arrangement with someone as solidly liked in the newcomer community as Tyrell Ramsey. Merritt had seen the appearance of a budding minority business supported by him as a powerful springboard into his newest scheme for generating profit; politics. He had decided to run for the state senate. The newcomers tended to be far more liberal in thought than the population that had been in Dugganville for generations. If he could position himself to be seen as a champion of opportunities for underserved populations, he would win the transient vote, hands down.

Bubba's vitriol toward the Ramseys was a snag he hadn't anticipated. Still, it may be something he could make use of, if he could find out why Raines's hatred of Tyrell Ramsey was so strong. Merritt remembered that Bubba had some distant cousins in the Beaumont area with the last name of Floyd and that the families had never been on good terms. He figured that if they knew anything about the bad blood between Bubba and the Ramseys, they would be willing to share. A trip to the poverty-stricken little community seemed like an oddly profitable idea.

The next day, Merritt pulled his new Escalade up to a house that seemed barely bigger than his car. A single wire ran from a power pole to the house, and a small hut stood behind the house that he was sure served as an outhouse."*At least there are no empty milk jugs or junk cars laying around,*" he thought, as he knocked on the badly splintered and poorly hung front door. A tiny boy answered, and Merritt was surprised that he had even been able to open the door. Then he noticed that the boy had pulled a small step stool to the door in order to do so.

The boy sported a broad grin and what appeared to be perpetually happy eyes. He looked almost small enough to be crawling, but the child's obvious confidence gave the impression of a teenager. His ragged, but clean clothes, were those of a toddler.

"Hi Mithtuh, ma name ith Albut. Whad yo uhs?"

Merritt hoped he had understood the child. "Hi Albert. People call me R.T. Can I ask you how old you are?"

"I free, but almost fo uh."

Merritt had been looking into the house for adults as the child spoke, but seeing none, asked, "Wow, you're a big guy Albert. Where might your mama be?"

"She in the gahden with my papa. Wan go talk to 'em?" Albert raised his tiny hand to Merritt's.

R.T. was impressed with the child, in spite of his discomfort in the surroundings. The little boy took his hand confidently, and together they walked over a small hill overlooking a garden struggling to survive in poor soil. *Just like everything else around here,* Merritt thought. He was startled out of his thoughts by an aging couple walking from the shade of a tree. There was no question of why Albert was so tiny. The woman was rail thin and under five feet tall. Her husband was only slightly larger.

"Albert, who you got there," asked the man.

"Thith here, ith R.T. He wan talk to you," answered Albert with his gap toothed lisp.

"Hello Mr. Floyd. My name is R.T. Merritt. I am very impressed with your son. He has all the attributes of a born leader."

"Thank you, Mr. Merrit." Mr. Floyd started to say something, but Merritt cut him off.

"R.T., please call me R.T., Mr. Floyd."

"Alright, R.T. My name is Sam, and my wife is Bertha." Bertha nodded and moved beside her husband. "As I was about to say. We are proud of Albert, but he is really our grandson. He calls us Mama and Papa because his parents were killed before he was old enough to remember them. I've heard of you, but what are you coming all the way out here to talk to a couple of nobodies like us?"

Merritt offered them the customary condolences for their loss, and the next few minutes were spent in preparatory small talk designed to make the question he had come there to ask seem like a natural part of the conversation. After praising the closely knit nature of Beaumont, he continued with, "You know, Sam, a lot of the families around Beaumont have been here for a long time. Well, I'll just come out with it. I am trying to encourage more business opportunities in Dugganville and the surrounding area for people like you and that sharp young grandson of yours.

He looked at Sam and could tell the older man was listening. "In order to do that, I need cooperation from local folks. The Floyds, Red Elks, and Ramseys have all been here for generations. So has the Raines clan. I know your family and Bubba's have never had a great relationship, even though you are kin. What I don't know is why Bubba hates Tabitha Red Elk and her husband, Tyrell, so much."

The old man eyed Merritt with a look that bordered between suspicion and interest. Both men had generations of history in the area and each understood the unwritten laws of the caste system ingrained in that history. Still, times change, even in the culturally entrenched area surrounding Dugganville. Sam Floyd, uneducated and barely literate, was trying to decide if the man standing in front of him was sincere or simply continuing a practice that had long been used in the valley south of the river; making false promises to the poor as a means to take advantage.

"I don't understand what old family feuds have to do with your plan. Go on," he said.

Uneducated, maybe, but Merritt could see that Sam Floyd wasn't stupid or gullible. If he were going to get information from the old farmer, he knew he had to make his story sound good. "Sam, listen, I know that I've had a lot of privileges in life given to me that I don't deserve, just because of the family I was born into."

He paused, hoping that the humility of his statement would sink in. "But I'm not among the super-rich, either. I do have to work to keep what I have. I figure that if I can create some opportunities for folks not as fortunate as I have been, I can make life better for myself in the process."

Merritt could see that he still had Floyd's attention. "I am still listening," the old man said. "How do Bubba, Tabitha and Tyrell figure in this?"

"Well, Tyrell, as you may know, has started to build a pretty good business."

Sam interrupted him. "I am aware of that. He will still do work for me though – even gives me a big break on that price sheet he carries around."

Merritt steamed internally at the comment. *"Impudent darkie never budged a penny for Dad. He needs to learn who butters his bread,"* he thought, before continuing with an enthusiastic smile. "That is exactly my point, Sam. Tyrell has solidly established himself in the area by treating people right, but his business will never grow without help. I tried to team him up with Bubba, but that was a total no-go. What is it between those two?"

Floyd shook his head. "You know Bubba, R.T. He hates everybody. That boy was just born mean. The only thing the Ramseys did wrong was try to help his family get him back in school. Tabitha has a soft heart for every creature she thinks has been given a raw deal. When Bubba blew up, quit school and ran away from home, she tried to work her magic on him. I don't know if you've ever been around that woman, but everything about her makes you feel like the world is a better place than it really is."

"I've noticed that she even puts a little pep in your step," his wife interjected while pretending to look away.

Floyd uttered a fake growl and continued, "Anyway, Tabitha tried to get involved. She went to the family, the school, and finally the sheriff, trying to get Bubba back in school. The next thing you know, Tyrell has his truck vandalized. After that, Tabitha told her husband that she thought someone was following her. Tyrell Ramsey is one of the nicest men I know of any color, but he ain't someone you want to make mad, and I think Bubba decided it was better to back off. Anyway, he stays completely away from the Red Elks and the Ramseys."

"I see," said Merritt.

"By the way, there's other local folks in this valley tryin' to run businesses who could use some help. Why don't you contact them," Floyd asked.

"I need minorities," Merritt mumbled, mostly to himself. He had already realized his blunder before Floyd responded.

"Why, you sorry sum bitch! I shoulda' knowd it. You don't give a shit about the poor folk in this valley. Yer just tryin' to make yourself look good. Git off my property, now!"

Merritt turned and walked quickly to his car. He wasn't overly concerned that he had offended the old man. He was of no importance to his plans, and he had obtained the information he came after. Apparently, Floyd wasn't concerned with the more affluent man's opinion of him, either. Merritt could hear his grandson howling with laughter while the farmer chased him through the garden.

An epiphany came to Merritt on his drive back to Dugganville. He had been working too hard. The old man's words rang in his ears. *"Yer just tryin' to make yourself look good."* That old dirt farmer was absolutely right. Merritt had learned enough of the newcomers to know that, looking good to their peers was all most of them really cared about as well. Sure, there may be a few who had moved into the area that were actually concerned about the welfare of the generational poor, but the majority had moved into the region for the same reason that people like him had stayed; to make money. All he had to do was say the right words, and he could use the transients the same way his caste had always used the poor folks of the region. He could make it look like he was on their side. It was time for R.T. Merritt to throw his hat into the political ring.

Chapter 18

The Present – Problem Solved

Few people can appreciate how much talent it takes to lie constantly, and yet remain honestly sincere in your words. Merritt hadn't been ousted from his seat in the state senate. Finding the public nature of being consistently "on the record," too restrictive, he had simply decided not to run again. He preferred being able to state conflicting lies without some obviously biased media personality trying to misconstrue his words.

Merritt had begun the practice of keeping a spare change of clothes in his office while cheating on Amber. He stripped from the ones he wore the night before and, rendering them hopeless, tossed them into the trash. His office had a private shower, another perk he had found advantageous during his adulterous trysts. After cleaning up and changing into fresh clothes, he sat at his desk to manage the task at hand. His stomach burned like he had swallowed battery acid, but his mind was clear and focused. He was not going to allow Bubba Raines, his father, or some eastern syndicate to deny him the wealth he deserved.

Merritt was well aware of his position in life. He was never going to be a true power player in the community. His short time as a state senator had convinced him of that. He preferred presenting a highly visible image of compassion for the public well-being, while working quietly in the shadows to fill his own personal coffers.

His marriage to Amber would have worked well for that purpose if she hadn't been such a high-minded bitch who actually believed in something called the greater good. He cursed himself for the nth time for having temporarily allowed her beauty to choke his ambition with her altruistic noose.

Merritt thought briefly of his son, Jason. *"It's a shame that little shit couldn't have been taller. He probably would have been a great quarterback instead of a dipshit wrestler following Frank Bear around. Damn! He must have taken after someone on his mother's side of the family."*

Merritt cursed again, shuddered, and brought himself back to the task at hand. He knew that he was swimming in treacherous waters, but he also saw the potential for great profit. He hadn't realized it, but while he had been thinking, his hand had been subconsciously drawing circles and taking notes on a piece of paper. When he looked down, he realized that he had solved his problem. Looking back at him was a set of four circles. Written in one circle was the name, Bubba. In another were the words "Newcomers and syndicate." In a third were the words, "Farmers, Hunters." Finally, in the fourth circle was a single word written in capital letters and heavily outlined, "**ME.**"

What had intrigued Merritt was not the occupants of each of the four circles. After all, his father had vividly reminded him that any of the other three circles would happily shorten his time on Earth if this deal went south. To his own surprise, he had not placed the "**ME**" circle in the center of the paper. Instead, the biggest circle was reserved for the name, "Bubba," and each of the other circles had arrows drawn to and from it.

"I'm not the key player, in this drama," he thought. "That big dumb mongrel is causing problems for all of us."

Merritt knew that Raines wasn't the violent half-wit that most people in the area believed him to be. He was intelligent and savvy in the ways of business, even though his definition of business was almost always illicit. Few people other than Merritt could come close to assessing how much money Bubba actually had. Raines was probably more adept at hiding money than anyone in the area, except for himself. Bubba's problem had always been that he was so filled with hatred, he didn't know how to enjoy his wealth. In his mind, living in apparent squalor while flipping the finger at the area elite who believed they were using him, was his means of getting revenge on the arrogant bastards. He had no concept that the easiest way to stick a knife in someone's back was to crawl in bed with them. Bubba's blatant hostility toward anyone that breathed would ultimately be his downfall.

Merritt looked down at the circles once more. *"And, my salvation,"* he thought. *"That idiot knows enough about all of us to be a pain in the ass. I am the only one that knows enough about him to send him back to prison for a very long time, and he can't prove anything on me."*

Merritt's headache had subsided and he felt suddenly hungry. He was disgusted with himself for letting a minor hiccup get the better of him. Before leaving his office to get something to eat, he checked his calendar. "State Wrestling Tournament," was scribbled in for the next weekend. *"Damn, that's a nuisance, but I guess I should go watch Jason's final hurrah. And, since I've never been to one before, I might have the chance to piss off Amber and that ugly troll, she adores so much. This is going to be a good day, after all."*

He suddenly felt a spring in his step and nearly knocked the coffee and bagged breakfast from his secretary's hands when he opened the door. She stepped back and raised the Styrofoam cup to keep it from spilling. Merritt looked confused. "Ms. Ahhh, can I help you?"

The secretary bit her upper lip slightly before responding. "It's JoAnne. You sent me after breakfast and something for your headache."

He had forgotten the errand as soon as Bubba had shown up. "I did, didn't I. I am feeling much better now, so keep the breakfast and the coffee."

"I paid for them with my money."

"Oh. Well, in that case, here's ten dollars, and take the rest of the day off."

"Thank you," she said, while thinking, *"It will give me a chance to look for a new job."*

CHAPTER 19

The Present – Strategic Planning

North Dugganville High School had advanced seven wrestlers to the state tournament, and were considered to be one of the strongest contenders to take the state title in Jason Merritt's final season as a high school competitor. Wrestling is an individual sport, however, and Merritt knew that the only way he could advance the cause of his team was to earn his own state championship. If he did, it would be his third in four years. He was favored in the 145lb weight class by virtue of his previous successes, but he found himself more nervous than he had been in any other tournament. The past season had been a hard one for him emotionally. His driving force had always been to live up to the man whose skill in the sport and compassion for others he admired so much, but in the past few weeks he had learned that the man he idolized was much more complex than he had ever realized.

He struggled with understanding why pleasing Frank Bear meant so much to him while making his own father proud, meant so little. Part of it he understood. The local wrestling legend had always made himself a part of Merritt's life while his dad, had made obligatory appearances. Still, a son should yearn for his father's attention, but Jason didn't. The weight of his dilemma had come crashing in on him the night of his confrontation with Bear over how little he knew of his past. Bear's displeasure had left him distraught, but that wasn't what had left him shaken to the core. It had been the hug and that last statement R2 had made as he was leaving that night. *"I never got around to telling you about me."*

The University had provided dorm rooms for the contestants during the week of the state tournament. Merritt was laying on his bed in the room when his roommate entered. "Bro, you look sick. You gonna be able to wrestle, tomorrow?"

Jason sat up, and responded without revealing the true reason for his malaise. "Yea, I'm fine. Just nerves."

His roommate was Brad Smith, a promising sophomore who had been tutored by the senior wrestler all year. "Nerves? I am the one who should be nervous. This stuff is probably old hat to you by now."

Jason chuckled, "No way, Soph. If you ever get so cocky you aren't nervous, count on losing."

* * * * *

At approximately the same time Jason was talking to Brad Smith, Frank saw Amber Merritt sitting alone at a small square table in the corner of the restaurant. After taking a deep breath and letting it out slowly, he walked toward her. She looked up after hearing him talking to parents sitting at another table. He had come a long way from the introverted young athlete she had first met in her class so many years before. Back then, it would have taken him less than a minute to cross the large seating area, once he had spotted an empty table. He would keep his eyes forward, and, once sitting, would have arranged himself so as to say that he wasn't interested in company.

Now, it seemed to take him an eternity to reach her table as he stopped several times to chat briefly with parents from Dugganville and around the state to say something positive about their athletes and to wish them luck. Bear had learned the art of making people feel important. He was only a few feet away from Amber, when they made eye contact. His demeanor changed instantly. The broad toothy smile smoothed to thoughtfulness as he nodded, took another deep breath, and sat across from her.

"Hi Amber." Bear had a wife and four daughters, a highly successful business, and was an influential member of the community, but in the eighteen years since Jason had been conceived, this was the first time he had ever called her by her first name in public.

"Hi Frank." She had always called him Frank, but somehow, her voice sounded different now, also. She realized that Frank hadn't been the only one playing a role stuck in the distant past. Although he had been an active father without claiming the title and had helped her and her parents over the years, she had always reverted to talking to Frank, the high school student, when talking to him directly.

Her hands were palm-down on the table, and he leaned forward as if to take them in his, then thought better of it. Amber realized that she had sent the signal for him to take her hands and withdrew them to her lap. "Amber, Jason draws a bye in the first round, because he is first seed and won't be wrestling tomorrow," Bear said, trying to act casual. "There is a lake just a few miles from here. I thought maybe we could pick up some lunch and take a walk."

"I think that is a very good idea. It's going to be hard to talk, here;" she agreed. "You are sure that Rose is OK with us talking, aren't you?"

"She is," he paused. "My wife and I are closer than ever. We will talk more about that tomorrow." Frank had used the term wife as a reminder to himself.

She smiled and was about to say something about the tournament when a voice startled them both. "Well, look who I just happened to run into. Wow, these state tournaments are really a big deal. Lot of high school parents, here. Mind if I join you two? What do you think my boy's chances are, Chief?"

Without waiting for them to answer, R.T. sat at one of the two remaining empty chairs. His appearance had caught them by surprise, both wondering if he somehow knew what they were discussing. Amber's face was red and she could feel her heart racing. Frank's face immediately molded into a blank emotionless stare, which he turned upon the unwelcome intruder. Merritt had hoped to make them both miserable, but instead found himself becoming uncomfortable.

"I mean, what time is his first match tomorrow? I thought we could all root for him together," he said with a slight laugh, trying to regain the advantage.

Frank kept his voice low and almost monotone. "Do you have a smart phone, Junior?"

His address to Merritt as, Junior, caught both Amber and her ex-husband by surprise. She had told Frank how much he hated the moniker. She looked quickly at Frank and involuntarily widened her eyes before looking around to see if anyone in the room was watching. R.T. started to raise his voice in a vulgar response, but realized that if he did, many people would hear his outburst. The former wrestler was still very good at keeping his opponent off balance.

"Yes, so what," he answered, keeping his voice low.

"Oh, I just assumed that, since you haven't attended a single match in four years that you've been following him on your phone. Or, that maybe your mama and daddy had been keeping you up on his success. They have been to many of his matches, but I guess you weren't invited to come with them." Bear never turned his gaze from Merritt as he spoke. The stiffness of the wrestler's neck made his stare feel even more piercing.

Merritt tried to maintain some bravado, but this encounter was not going as he had hoped. He answered with unconvincing nonchalance. "Well, it looks like I've wasted my time coming here. Maybe I should head on back to Dugganville and leave you two to whisper sweet nothings in the corner."

Frank ignored the implication. "I think that is an excellent idea. In fact, I will walk you to your car." For the first time since Merritt had sat down, Bear turned to Amber. "Ms. Merritt, keep your seat. I will be right back after I walk little Robert Thomas outside."

Amber's face showed no emotion, but it wasn't because she was calm. She was frozen in place; paralyzed with the fear of what might be about to happen. Frank's face also showed no emotion and his voice was calm, but his eyes were those of an alpha male preparing to attack a threat to his pack. Amber had seen it only once before, and Frank was much stronger now than he had been then.

Merritt felt it, too. "Now, no use in getting your panties in a wad. I will head on back and come back up for the championship match," he said, knowing that he wouldn't. He turned, and walked to the door, giving several Dugganvillites a cursory nod, as he headed for the exit as quickly as possible.

Frank and Amber sat at the table, looking at each but saying nothing. Finally, Amber managed to say, only, "Frank?"

Frank's hard expression softened slightly, as did his voice, when he spoke. "I will be glad when this tournament is over. It may be hard for him to accept, but it is time that Jason understands that he is our son. And Amber," Bear lowered his voice so much that she could barely hear him, even though she was only inches away from his face. "If R.T. ever hurts you or our son again, I will kill him."

Amber wanted badly to wrap her arms around him to comfort him, as he had once done for her. It was impossible in the open dining area, however. Instead, she looked at him through eyes on the verge of tears, and said, quietly, "I know."

* * * * *

Frank called Rose that night and told her everything that had happened.

"Are you, OK, Frank?" She asked.

"Yes. I am glad he showed up, today. It will make tomorrow easier. Rose, I don't deserve you. You've lived with this, all these years."

She cut him off. "Frank, Stop! Jason is a part of this family, and always has been. He needs to know, and his sisters need to know just how much a part of it he really is. I know you still love Amber, and I am not worried or jealous. She is a part of this family, too. Now, stop your whining. We need you to be strong. Jason needs you to be strong. Amber needs you to be strong." She paused before adding, "You're right. You don't deserve me. You big Wuss."

Her confidence in their relationship was what he had needed to hear.

* * * * *

The lake where Frank had chosen to meet was ordinarily a popular site for fishing and pic-nicking. Unusually high rains, strong winds and a cold day had caused it to be virtually deserted. It was the reason that Frank had chosen it to meet with Amber. Her car was already in the parking area when he pulled his truck in next to her. They exited their vehicles at the same time. Although wearing a heavy coat, she was shivering when he walked up to her. He then surprised her by putting his arm around her waist before pointing her to a covered pavilion.

"There is a propane grill behind that wall. We can light it and stay a little warmer. We will also be out of the wind." All of her former student was gone. He was in charge. He lit the grill, pulled off his stocking hat and sat across from her.

Before he could say anything, she started with the speech she had been practicing in the car on the way there. "Frank, before we start, I need to say thank you."

"Amber," he interrupted, "you've probably said thank you every time I've seen you for the past twenty years."

"No, Frank. I haven't. I've told my student, the boy, thank you, many, many times. I've never said thank you to the man. Even after you saved me from Robert's abuse and then practically raised Jason under completely unfair circumstances, I still saw you as a high school student that I cared for, but one who could cause me to lose my job and my reputation because people believed, because I believed, I had seduced him. I realized after you sent Robert running yesterday, that I have been such a hypocrite. You weren't the only one who had to maintain a distance in order to keep the lines clear. Frank, Jason and I have relied on you all these years, and yet, somehow, I convinced myself that you were just a student, because I was afraid of what the Merritts might do to me, Jason, and to you. Yes, I am ready to proudly tell Jason who his father is, and I am no longer afraid of R.T. Merritt or his family."

Frank smiled and took her hand. For the next five hours they sat and talked. The weather was cold, but they were too engaged to notice. They discussed multiple scenarios in which they could break the news to their son. At times, they role played how they might handle different reactions he might have. They talked about

Rose and the impact on his daughters. Nearly an hour was spent discussing how to protect themselves from the Merritts. Amber had already accepted that she would have to resign from the district and move. With Jason graduating and her parents planning to retire and move for health reasons, she had no difficulty in making that decision.

Frank also asked that Amber tell him things that Tyrell and Tabitha never had. She told him about her meeting with Tyrell and her fears that her ex-husband and a man named Bubba Raines may have had something to with Frank being assaulted after his second match with Carson Blake.

"Bubba? I only met him once, and Tyrell told me to stay far away from him. He didn't have to convince me. That guy was scary, but what made you think he had something to do with me getting mugged?"

"Robert came home drunk a lot, and when he was drunk, he bragged; usually about how he could have any woman he wanted, but also about how powerful he was. Sometimes, he would make disgusting accusations about us, even when you were just a freshman. It was during your senior year that Robert came home drunk and angry with me. He told me that if I didn't learn to show him some respect, he would send this, Bubba, to –," she stopped. "I can't repeat it. It was so vile and ugly. I dismissed it at the time, because that kind of drunken speech had become so common with him. After you were hurt so badly, I wanted to go to the local police, but Tyrell wouldn't let me."

Amber started to quiver, but not from the cold. Frank put his hands over hers. "If Tyrell told you not to go to the police, he had a reason. Dugganville has changed a lot since I was a kid, but the Merritts are still part of a culture that we will never understand. Tyrell told me once, that Bubba and Albert Floyd are related somehow. That seems really hard to believe, but I will talk to Albert and see if he knows anything."

Amber looked down at her watch. "Frank, I need to go. The coach is meeting with his wrestlers and their parents in an hour. Are you going to come."

"No, after four years of us coming to this tournament, you should know that I don't attend those meetings. It is important that the wrestlers and parents look at the coach and not to me."

"Yes, I knew that. Just thought I would ask." Amber leaned over and took Frank's hands, again. "Frank, the look on your face when you were talking to Robert, chilled me to the bone. If anyone ever deserved a terrible end, it's him, but don't do anything that will get you in trouble or worse. We all need you."

He shook his head. "Damn, I really do feel like I have two wives. You sound like, Rose."

She stood, leaned over, and gave him a quick kiss on the lips before leaving. "And, we both love you, very much."

CHAPTER 20

The Present – Reckoning

The Demons finished in a disappointing fourth place at the tournament. The heavyweight who had been trounced earlier in the season by South Dugganville finished third, and Brad Smith, Jason's sophomore roommate surprised everyone with a strong second place finish. As expected, Jason won his weight class in convincing manner. Almost immediately he began receiving congratulations from the coaches and athletic directors of schools who had been courting him for their programs. He knew he should have been more excited, but recent events had dampened his enthusiasm for wrestling at the college level. Smith had told him after the tournament that his mother had seen Jason's mother talking to R.T. Merritt and Frank Bear at a restaurant. She had told Brad that whatever Frank Bear had said to Jason's dad, had caused him to leave in a hurry. *"What was that all about,"* he had thought.

The pensive teenager was lying on his back in his room one early Saturday morning following the tournament, when his mother knocked on the door. His mother had told him the night before that she wanted to visit the Bear family.

"Jason, are you ready? May I come in?"

"Sure, Mom."

She entered the room and Jason sat up. He was shirtless, barefooted and wearing a pair of fashionably tattered Jeans.

Muscles rippled across a flat stomach and broad chest, only causing his mother to worry even more about the choices he might make after learning of his true heritage. He reminded her of another man whom she cared for deeply. "Jason, I would like to start early. Put on a shirt, and we can grab something to eat on the way."

"Sure, Mom. What's going on?" Frank, Rose, and Amber had chosen that day as the time to reveal everything to Jason. Rose had taken the girls to visit her family for a few days. The parental trio had agreed that Jason's sisters shouldn't know anything until Jason was ready.

Amber reached in Jason's closet, pulled out a shirt and held it up to her son, before answering as casually as she could. "Jason, I know that Brad's mother saw R.T. leave the restaurant pretty quickly at the tournament, and that he never came back to watch you wrestle."

Jason thought little of his mother calling his dad, R.T. She usually did; either that or Robert. He also hadn't thought anything of his father not staying to watch the tournament. He was more surprised that he had showed up at all. "Mom, if you are trying to tell me something, would you just come out and say it."

"I am son. That is why we are going to see, Frank. We need to talk."

"Is it about me wrestling?"

"No, Jason it's not." Her voice quivered, slightly. "I don't mean to make this sound so ominous. It's just a matter that the three of us need to talk about, together."

"Am I in some kind of trouble?"

"No, no, no, Jason. Not at all. Please, let's get in the car and go see Frank."

The drive to the Bear estate was quiet. Jason noticed immediately as he pulled into the long driveway to the house that Rose's car wasn't there. The only person remaining on the property, other than Frank, was Sophia. She had walked to a stream on the back half of the acreage to pray.

The door to the house opened before Jason and his mother reached the front porch. "Hi Jason. Hi Amber. I've been waiting for you. Come in and sit down."

The greeting seemed somehow ominous and Jason's knees started to shake, in spite of his efforts to control his emotions. He had never heard Frank Bear call his mother by her first name.

"Ok, guys. I'm getting scared. Are y'all having an affair?"

Both Frank and Amber were stunned. The question would have been laughable if there hadn't been such an odd sense of truth to it. Bear took control, once again. "Jason, the answer to your question is, no. Your mother and I are about to tell you some things, however, that will be very hard to grasp. I promised you, a while back, that I would one day tell you who I was, and am. Today is that day.

With that introduction, Frank and Amber told Jason how they came to be his parents.

CHAPTER 21

The Past – Marital Rape

Frank was nineteen years old when he crossed the graduation stage with his cohort class. If not for a biological father who had held him out of school at a young age and a brutal attack by an unknown assailant during his senior year, the academic standout would have graduated with enough credits to enter college as a sophomore. That hadn't happened, but it didn't matter to the cheering crowd of seniors and their parents as he stood from his wheelchair and haltingly walked across the stage to accept his diploma. After shaking hands with the school superintendent, the quiet superstar did something totally out of character. He requested the microphone, and after taking it, turned to the audience, who were still standing.

"Thank you. I know that our senior class is anxious to go out and celebrate, and that our parents are anxious to go home and worry, so I will be brief." A short respectful laugh arose from the audience. "Most of you really don't know me, and I admit that I really don't know you, either. Until a few weeks ago, that wasn't very important to me. Then, immediately after overcoming what I thought had been an unfair challenge to my plans for my future – my plans, my future," he had repeated the words more to himself than to the audience. He refocused his attention on the auditorium. "Anyway, I felt that a terrible injustice had been done to me, and my self-absorbed world came crashing in around me. It was only then that I realized that I have been surrounded and protected my entire life by the love of an amazing group of people. My mother, Tyrell and Tabitha Ramsey, and someone you all know, Mrs. Amber Merritt, have taught me that the most powerful accomplishment you can ever achieve is to give of yourself out of love. In the last few weeks, I have experienced that love coming from many of you. Thank you again, and best wishes."

Frank handed the microphone back to the superintendent, and limped quietly back to his wheelchair. The superintendent was obviously choked up and struggled to continue. After a few moments, he was helped by the crowd as a swell of applause began slowly and reached a crescendo as Frank reached the ramp, where he was helped by Tyrell. The superintendent pointed toward Frank, who waved one last time at the crowd, before the next graduating seniors name was called.

As is customary with graduation proceedings, the local school board was seated on stage. All of the board members, except for the president, had applauded heartily at Frank's short speech. Robert Thomas Merritt Sr. hadn't heard the speech. His mind had been preoccupied with his son's behavior. As soon as Frank had started to speak, Merritt Jr., had stood up at the back of the auditorium and stormed out in obvious anger, rather than listen to what the now-beloved senior had to say.

* * * * *

Frank's interest in going to college for any reason had seemed to vanish. Instead, he became intensely involved in family and in Tyrell's plumbing business. While still physically unable to be of much assistance to Tyrell on job sites, he displayed a natural talent for improving his surrogate father's business practices. Although Tyrell was a perfectionist in the field and in his shop, he was not a skillful businessman. The standard pricing sheet had been a great practice, but he only held people to it, if he felt like they were trying to take advantage of him. He often did more than customers requested without asking for more money, and he insisted on doing everything himself. This was one reason why he had become so popular, but it had also kept him from growing his business.

When Frank first approached him with the idea of taking on an apprentice, Tyrell had balked. The memory of R.T. Merritt's attempted manipulation had still been bitterly simmering in his brain. Frank continued to promote the idea and Tyrell eventually relented, hiring two of Frank's non-college bound classmates. Their first job was to have been at the home of R.T. and Amber Merritt. Tyrell wouldn't openly admit it, but the selection of the job site was a purposeful slap at R.T. Merritt. Both of the young men were white, and they would be working for a black man. He was nervous about the job. He had never worked with anyone other than Frank, and the role of supervisor wasn't something he fell naturally into. On the day before the job was scheduled, he went to the Merritt home to talk to Amber and to determine how he could best use the young men.

He became immediately alarmed upon approaching the front door. It had been broken open. The door wasn't massive, but it would have taken multiple forceful kicks to do the amount of damage he saw. After pausing for only a second, he rushed into the door and called Amber's name. "Amber, Amber! Are you, OK?"

He waited to hear a response, so as to decide what direction to take. At first, he heard nothing, but soon the sound of muffled sobbing came to his ears. It was coming from the breakfast patio. The patio was a small glassed-in enclosure with a southern exposure, designed to catch maximum sunlight on chili winter mornings. Amber had it built to off-set the darkness of the old mansion that her husband had insisted on buying. To get to it, it was necessary to walk through the house and out the back door of the kitchen.

Tyrell sprinted through the house and out the open back door. As soon as he crossed the doorway, Amber looked up. "Tyrell, I am so, sorry. I –."

"Sorry for what?" He said, as he quickly walked toward her. "What did he do to you?" He asked the question, but he already knew the answer.

"Claimed his rights as a husband, is what he told me. Oh, Tyrell, I never thought he would," She stopped without finishing the sentence. "I am so scared."

Tyrell's immediate instinct was to find Merritt and leave him so bloody and battered he would never be tempted to hurt his wife again, but he knew how that would likely end. Secondly, he thought of calling the local police, but again, that would not go well. "Wait a minute. Has this got something to do with my bringing those two kids over here to work on the job."

"No, not directly." She answered. "I told him about your apprentice idea yesterday morning. I foolishly thought he would like the plan, because it would make him look good, but when he found out that they were two of Frank's friends, he stormed off in a rage. He came home around two this morning, still furious, but on top of that, he was drunk. He pounded repeatedly on the door and screamed at me to let him in. Tyrell, he has a key. I decided that, if he was too drunk to know how to use it, I wasn't about to let him in. I told him, no, not in his drunken state. A few minutes later, I heard the door being kicked in, and then." She paused without finishing the sentence, but skipped to the aftermath.

"He was smart to leave. I would have called the police if he had stayed much longer, and he wouldn't have been able to deny anything at that point, but he is so good at sobering up. If he walked through that door right now, he would probably look as if he had a good night's sleep with nothing but warm milk to drink before going to bed. Tyrell, the only thing I know to do is divorce him and leave town. Dad isn't doing well, anyway. His company is trying to work with him, but his memory lapses are making him unable to do his job any longer."

Tyrell looked at the shattered beautiful woman sitting in front of him. Only a few months before, she had been sitting in his shop apologizing for an act over which she had no control. Now, it was Ramsey who felt the need to apologize. He had told her to let him deal with the attack on Frank so she wouldn't get hurt. She had trusted him, and he felt that he had failed her, as he had failed the young man he looked on as his son.

It took all of his emotional strength to respond calmly. "Amber, I am going to make some calls. I made a few friends at the university that know how to proceed with an investigation without going through the local police."

"Tyrell, don't. That is too dangerous for you and Tabitha. Too many people owe the Merritts favors in this town."

"No, Amber, it's not. My father was an incredible man, but he believed you could only survive by kowtowing to the privileged. It would be too dangerous for me to try and survive like he did. I will be careful. In the mean-time, do you want to come and stay at our place? We have lots of room, now."

"No, I am not going to allow him to make me live in fear. I've already decided that, like you, I am not going to kowtow to the privileged. I've already called someone to have the locks changed, and this time when he comes home drunk and abusive, I am calling the police, so they can see firsthand."

* * * * *

The incident had shaken Tyrell as much as it had Amber. He drove home trying to decide what to do, next.

"Oh, Shit! The interns," he thought. *"They are supposed to show up at Amber's place in the morning, with Frank."*

Tyrell felt a dizzy sensation come over him and pulled his van to the side of the road. He had wanted badly to protect Frank from the emotional trauma of knowing the danger that his beloved teacher was in, but he realized that would now be an impossibility. *"Frank is a man,"* he kept telling himself, as he tried to convince himself that the young man whom he loved so much was well enough to cope with harshness of the situation. He called Tabitha and asked her to meet him in his shop, alone. As it had been since the first time they met, only she would be able to bring his mind into focus, so that he could make the right decision.

She was already there when he opened the door. The look on her face betrayed that she knew that something serious had happened. Tyrell told her everything that had happened, starting with his finding Amber's front door broken open. He ended with his realization that he was going to have to tell Frank, also. She stood in front of him while he sat on a shop stool, looking up in her eyes. She pulled his head to her breast and kissed the top of his head.

"I love you," had just left her lips when the shop door opened and Frank walked in, now using only a cane for support.

"I called Jeff and Braden, and told them that the job is on hold for right now. Either of you want to tell me what is going on?" Frank looked in both of their faces waiting for an answer, but receiving none, continued. "Tyrell, if you remember, you were going to call me and have me meet you at Mrs. Merritt's house so I could show her my new truck. That was supposed to happen about three hours ago. Then, Tabitha hurries out here to your shop before you get home, without saying a word to anyone. Finally, I walk in just now, and Tyrell is paler than a white man. Now, look!" The last word came out louder than Frank had intended, and it was the closest thing to a show of anger as the young man had ever displayed to the people he loved so dearly.

"Look." His voice softened. "I know both of you are only trying to protect me, but if I am going to be a partner in this business, you have to let me know what is going on."

At that moment, Tyrell realized what his father must have felt the first time that he understood that he could no longer protect his son from the evils of the world. He knew that there were many things that he would have to tell Frank, including Merritt's attempt to manipulate him and Bubba Ramsey into falling for one of his schemes, the high-stakes betting going on before Frank's match with Carson Blake, and most importantly, Amber's suspicion that her husband had been behind the attack on Frank after the match. There wasn't time for that at the moment. The most immediate things that Frank needed to know, were that Amber Merritt had been brutally sexually attacked by her husband and that he was a dangerous man. He relayed the events of the day clearly and slowly to Frank, as he had done only moments before to Tabitha.

Frank sat quietly after Ramsey finished describing what had taken place earlier in the day. Images of what his mother must have had to endure when he was a young child popped involuntarily into his mind. Anger churned like angry worms in his brain and in his heart; anger toward Bear for abusing his mother, anger toward Merritt for abusing his teacher, and anger toward himself for being powerless to stop any of it. Tyrell's next words startled him. They sounded as if he had known what Frank was thinking.

"Frank, you are my son in my heart, and the pain you are feeling, I feel. I never met my mother, but I know that my father's heart broke every time he looked at me. He had wanted badly to save her, but he couldn't. Her abuser hadn't been a man, but a system. I never understood the crap he put up with, day in and day out, until one day, I realized that he did it so I wouldn't have to. Right now, you probably want to find R.T. Merritt and beat his brains in, as I did earlier today, and as my father wanted to with every doctor who refused to take my mother because she was the wrong color. You are a man now, and you have to decide what actions to take as a man, not as an angry child."

Frank looked at Tyrell. He knew that the man he had looked up to for so long was right. He usually was. That didn't help with Frank's frustration over his current weak physical state, nor did it ease his rage toward physically stronger men abusing better but less powerful women. "What are you going to do?" He asked, Tyrell.

"Tabitha and I are going to the capitol tomorrow to meet with a friend of mine from the university. He is a state senator and became acquainted with R.T. during his short time in office, and he knows the Merritt family, by reputation." Ramsey paused, "And he knows the history of Dugganville."

Frank looked pensive. "Does Mom know anything?"

Tabitha answered. "Frank, sweetheart. How could she? You got here almost as fast as I did."

Frank nodded his head, as if to say, of course. "Good. I know you and Tyrell were probably talking about how to break the news to me. Mom needs to know, also. She is going to want to console, Mrs. Merritt. It's just her nature. I need to see her first, though. We can tell Mom after you get back from the capitol."

Neither of the Ramsey's were able to hide their discomfort over the thought of Frank placing himself in a dangerous situation. Frank looked at one and then the other, waiting for a response.

When none came, he continued. "I make my own decisions. I will go over in the morning, after you leave. I can wait there with her until the locksmith comes to fix the door. From what you said, R.T. probably won't show up, but somebody needs to be there if he does."

"OK," Tyrell, answered. "Should I call Amber and let her know that you know what happened?"

"No need. I can tell her myself."

* * * * *

Sophia had established a morning breakfast routine from the first day that the Bear family and the Ramseys had moved into the big farm house. Each day, she would rise before the rest of the family and prepare breakfast with her dog, Wally, at her feet. Wally was a huge multi-colored Newfoundland/Labrador mix that had been rescued from the county animal shelter. The dog and making breakfast in her kitchen had met two of her three requests she had made to the Ramseys before accepting the deal for the large country estate. She wanted a dog, because she had never been able to have one, and she wanted to be able to make breakfast for her family in a nice kitchen. The third request was that Tyrell and Tabitha Ramsey be placed on the deed as co-owners.

The routine felt awkward for all of the Bears at first, because none of them had ever experienced so much stability and comfort. Neither had Wally. He had been malnourished when Sophia first saw and fell in love with him. The big dog adapted quickly, however, and had taken the lead in making sure that everyone felt comfortable in their new home. When Frank had first arrived from the hospital, it had been Wally who insured that the fragile athlete touch something warm and loving every day. The Bear Clan accepted the giant teddy bear as an extension of their mother, because he seemed to understand their feelings as well as she did.

Wally wasn't his normal joyful self, trying to give overly-wet kisses, on the morning that Tabitha and Tyrell were to drive to the state capitol and Frank planned to visit Mrs. Merritt. On practically every other morning, he blocked the kitchen door not allowing anyone to pass until he got a neck hug. Not even Tyrell or Tabitha was exempt. On this morning, he merely sat at the doorway as each of Frank's four teenage siblings walked by.

"What's up with the slobber machine," Tunner asked his mother.

Sophia offered an unconvincing giggle. "Oh, he is probably tired of so many people hanging all over him."

When the Ramseys walked into the kitchen, both dressed in business casual attire, Wally did stand, but just stood between the couple as they sat down.

"Thank for respecting the threads, big guy. Tabitha and I have important business today, and I would rather not be wearing a dog hair suit today." It was part of his routine to try and say something approaching funny at the breakfast table, at which Tunner usually laughed and the girls groaned. That morning he had sensed that his timing was off and that Wally had noticed.

Finally, Frank limped into the kitchen without his cane, wearing slacks and a new polo shirt that Sophia had never seen. Wally left the Ramseys and stood by Frank, waiting for him to sit down. As soon as he did, the dog laid his head, which was roughly the width of a dinner plate in his lap, and sighed deeply. Frank looked down at Wally, who was looking up at him through huge sad brown eyes. Frank looked up, and saw his mother looking at him through equally huge sad brown eyes. Frank looked away from her and realized that everyone was looking at him.

"What?" he asked to no one in particular, before looking down at Wally and asking, again, "What?" The question prompted Wally to show his affection by jumping into Frank's lap and stretching the full length of his long-wet tongue across the young man's face several times. The sudden move broke the tension and everyone laughed at the oldest Bear sibling as he tried to get Wally out of his lap while wiping the slobber from his face at the same time. Even Tyrell and Tabitha found themselves wiping happy tears from their eyes, in spite of the tension they were feeling.

"Well, son," Sophia started, still trying to suppress a giggle. "We don't often, see you come to breakfast looking so sharp. You have a brand-new truck, and I think that Wally was afraid you were about to run away."

Frank had already researched a speech and practiced it several times about where he was going and why he was dressed up. He had been nervous about giving it until the family pet had left everyone in stitches, including him.

"And I was going to explain all of that, before this big furball attacked me and gave me a bath without a towel." Wally had resumed his position on the floor beside Frank. His head lay in Frank's lap as the young man talked. Frank continued to stroke the huge pate as he talked, finding courage in its warmth.

"So, explain," Sophia prompted.

He turned to Tyrell. "Tyrell, one of things that all of your customers really admire about you is that you show up on the site, looking really sharp. You look like a business, even though you don't really have any employees. I am wearing a simple outfit, but Mom just said that I look sharp. I think it would be worth it if we bought Braden and Jeff outfits just like these, but with 'Ramsey and Son Plumbing' embroidered on the left breast."

Ramsey understood what he was doing, and picked up on it. "OK, good idea, but isn't a polo shirt a little dressy for field work. What if we get them a t-shirt, also with our logo across the back of the shirt."

Tunner asked, "You guys have a logo?"

Ramsey answered, "We don't yet, but we are working on it. Frank, here is your first official duty as co-partner. I was supposed to go to Mrs. Merritt's house today, but I can't. Go there, express my apologies, and get her opinion on the shirts."

Frank's oldest sister, Emily, was only a year younger than him and a beautiful near-clone of her mother. The pair had always been close, and he would eventually name his oldest daughter after her. She had graduated in the same class as he, but had never shown any resentment for his fame. Emily was attending college on an athletic and an academic scholarship for business and mathematics. She was home for fall break. Rolling her eyes dramatically, his little sister stated, "Like he needs an excuse to go to Mrs. Merritt's house."

Frank feigned a mock sigh and retorted, "you are so lame, little sis."

The rest of the breakfast fell into what had become standard Bear family banter, and Wally seemed satisfied that everything was going to be OK. Tyrell and Tabitha stood to leave and Frank walked them to their car.

"Thank you, Tyrell. I really appreciate what you did in there."

Tyrell tried to make light of it. "I just hope those shirts don't cost too much. Hey, be careful, and don't try to fix Amber's problems. She is a strong woman."

"I know, and I will be careful," Frank said before returning to the kitchen and finding that his mother and Wally were the only two of his family members remaining.

"Frank, can you come here a minute, before you leave. I would like help drying the dishes."

Frank noticed that there were only two plates left in the drainer and knew that wasn't why she had made the request. He walked around the table and toward where his mother was standing at the sink. She was a petit woman and had just stepped off a small step stool that she used for putting dishes away. He found himself nearly shaking when he looked down into her face and said, "Sure Mom, this is about the lightest KP duty I ever got away with."

Sophia giggled in her customary way before reaching up and caressing Frank's cheek with the palm of her hand. "I love you son. We all do."

"I know, Mom. How could I not know?"

"And I know that Mrs. Merritt's husband is not a good man, just as I came to know that Bear was not a good man. You are a good man, and I am very proud to call you, my son." She moved the hand stroking his cheek to the back of his neck and pulled his head down so she could kiss him on the forehead. "That is my little blessing. You look really sharp in that outfit, by the way."

Frank stood for a moment, before realizing that he had been released without having to explain anything or defend his decision. "Thanks, Mom. I should be home in time for dinner tonight."

Frank went to the driveway and climbed into his new Chevy Silverado. The vehicle wasn't actually new, but it was late model and in great condition. The truck hadn't been part of the settlement Tyrell had made with the two city councils. Rather, it had been a gift to Frank from the student bodies of the two Dugganville High Schools, paid for through a go fund me effort spearheaded by none other than Amber Merritt. The four-wheel drive vehicle had been specially equipped with extra-wide mirrors to accommodate the disabled athlete's inability to turn his head and extra hand-holds to help him climb into the truck more easily.

He still felt a sense of guilt for having it, but his mind wasn't on the truck today. It was on how he was going to explain to his teacher that he knew what had happened to her, without exposing Tyrell for having betrayed a confidence. He was still mulling over the best approach when he pulled up to the front door and immediately saw that it was standing open. R.T. Merritt's escalade was parked in the circular driveway. He pulled his truck to a quick stop behind the luxury SUV.

Without thinking, he opened his door and jumped to the ground. The sensation of pain running up his spine caused him to almost lose consciousness. He involuntarily sat on the truck's running board for a few seconds. Slowly, he reached into the front seat and grabbed his cane. The pain subsided with each step, and by the time he reached the front door, he was no longer using the cane as a support, but carrying it like a club.

He stopped momentarily just inside the front door, listening. The first voice he heard coming from the den belonged to R.T. "Listen, Amber. I am sorry about last night. I know I went too far. We can work this out."

Frank paused only long enough to take a deep breath before walking stealthily to the den. The next voice he heard belonged to Amber.

"Get out, Frank, or I will call the police!"

"And tell them what? That, I broke into my own house. Come on, sweetheart. Be reasonable. It had been a while since you even let me touch you."

"Don't ever call me that, again. You raped me. Get Out!" Amber was on the verge of screaming.

"Amber, you need to calm down." R.T. sounded like a parent lecturing an angry teenage daughter.

"I heard Mrs. Merritt tell you twice to leave. Now leave!"

Frank's voice startled both R.T. and Amber. They quickly turned to see him standing in the doorway of the den. His knees were slightly bent and he held the cane at shoulder level in his left hand with the tip pointed toward the astonished R.T. His face was expressionless, but the look in his eyes was deadly.

It took a moment for Merritt to recover his composure, but finally said, "What are you going to do, you ugly little toad. You're trespassing. I can either call the police or break your scrawny neck, myself."

Frank's voice remained flat, but he quickly flipped the cane around and held it with the crooked end in the air. "Either works for me," he said, and took a painful step toward Merritt.

"Aw, shit. You aren't worth my time," he said while walking toward the door, making sure he gave Frank and the cane a wide berth. "Just make sure you don't try anything, little boy, or I will make life hell for you and that black asshole you kiss up too. Amber, my lawyers will be calling you. You are going to lose this house and everything I ever gave you."

Frank followed him out of the door, still carrying the cane like a club. As soon as he felt sure that Merritt had driven off, he returned to the den and saw his former teacher sitting on the couch and looking up at him. The strength, humor, and wisdom he had always seen in her had vanished. She was crushed, helpless. "Frank, I'm so sorry," she said, barely above a whisper.

With the aid of his cane, Frank stiffly knelt down in front of her. "Sorry? I know what that sorry excuse of a man did to you, and now he has the nerve to come back. We need to call the police."

"No, he is too smart and has already protected himself. I called Wilson's Security Service to change the locks and add cameras. I told them it was an emergency. How could I have been so stupid?"

Frank looked confused. "What do you mean?"

"Oh, Frank," she said, while looking into a face made taut with concern. "This is Dugganville. The first thing the manager did was call R.T. to find out what had happened. He told him not to worry about it, and that it had just been some of my students playing a prank. I was barely dressed this morning when he came walking into the den, gloating."

The pair looked at each other, she on the couch, and he on his knees looking up into her face. He wanted badly to hold and console her, and she wanted nothing more than to be held, but even though he was now twenty and was no longer her student, each was held back by taboos of social barriers.

They stayed in that position, until Amber finally took his hand and pulled him to the couch beside her. "Frank, you're supposed to be smart. Staying in that position is going to set you back on your progress," she said through the beginnings of a sniffle. "How did you know," she asked.

"I overheard Tyrell and Tabitha talking last night. He didn't want to tell me, but I twisted it out of him. He and Tabitha are on their way to the capitol, now."

Emotionally exhausted and without thinking, she lay her head on his shoulder. The weight of her head and the smell of her hair on his shoulder were both terrifying and electrifying. He froze in place, afraid to move. In only moments, he realized that she was crying. His fear melted into tenderness, and he put his arm around her.

"Oh, Frank," she sobbed, relaxing into his embrace. "I am so tired. I have always tried to do everything right, and I thought I was so smart. How could I have been so wrong and so naive?"

Frank didn't answer, but pulled her closer to him and kissed her gently on the top of her head. The fragrance of her shampoo and the vulnerability of her sobs had aroused conflicting emotions within him. She was not the beautiful seemingly invincible vision he had first met nearly five years earlier. A feeling of trespass came over him after the kiss, but she looked up and pulled his face close to hers. He tasted the saltiness of her tears the first time she kissed him.

Not another word was spoken. Amber slid off the couch. It was now she who knelt in front of him. She pulled his face down to hers, and kissed him again. While his body was bent forward, she gently pulled the polo shirt over his shoulders. The motion took them both to the floor where they gently undressed each other.

Frank had been on top of her only moments when he was hit by a sense of true panic, as he felt himself start to climax. He tried to pull himself off, but Amber wrapped her arms and legs around him tightly. He felt her body tremble under his. The trembling resided before growing stronger again, until finally erupting into uncontrollable sobs. He tried to ask her if she was ok, but she couldn't speak and only held on more tightly. Eventually, the sobs subsided, and her embrace slowly relaxed, allowing Frank to roll off of her. She sat up, pulled a throw from the couch, and wrapped it around herself. Frank sat up too, and now being embarrassed by his nakedness, self-consciously pulled his shirt over his private parts.

"May I use your bathroom?" Frank thought his soft, almost timid, voice sounded like it belonged to someone else. The pair had just shared in sexual intimacy, but it now seemed totally inappropriate to Frank for him to dress in front of his teacher.

She nodded and pulled the throw more tightly around herself. Her mind and her emotions were screaming in rage and confusion at each other. *What have I done? It has been so long since I have felt tenderness. Does R. T. have someone watching me already?"*

She pointed to her right and said quietly, "It's down the hall. There are towels and washcloths in the closet."

"Thank you." While keeping his shirt in front of him and carrying his pants behind him, he stepped quickly into the bathroom. He wanted to shower for fear that someone, his mother, might be able to smell sex on his body, but the fear of being caught in the Merritt shower was even stronger. He found the washcloths and soap, cleaned himself up, and dressed as quickly as possible. Like any young man, he had wondered what his first time would be like, but this brought no joy or satisfaction, only guilt and questions. Guilt for doing something that he felt was wrong and questions about how to help the teacher who had always been there for him.

When he walked slowly back into the den, Amber Merritt was already dressed. She handed him a glass of water. "Frank, I –."

"No, it was my fault."

"Frank, I wasn't about to apologize." He could hear a slight shakiness in her voice, but she continued, steadily. "I was about to say thank you for being here and for standing up to my husband. You put yourself at great risk. I don't know many people who would have done that. When you leave, walk out like you haven't done anything wrong, because you haven't. You protected me. Thank you."

"I am coming back this afternoon."

A look of confusion, bordering on alarm appeared in Amber's eyes, and Frank knew he had to explain. "You aren't safe from your husband or anyone else as long as that door is busted. Even shut, you can tell it's broken. I don't think he is going to hurry and try to get it fixed properly. He wants to control you. Tabitha's brother is a handyman in Beaumont. Tyrell has done a lot of work for him at no charge. He won't be able to install a security system, but he can change your locks and secure your doors so that your drunk," Frank bit his lip and took a breath before continuing. "So that Merritt, won't be able to kick them in. We can have it done, today."

In spite of the trauma of the events of the day, Amber couldn't help but look at the quick-thinking young man in admiration. Both of them had been knocked flat that day, but he was already breathing, already looking forward. "Thank you, again. How much do I owe –,"

Frank held up his hands before she could finish as if to say, *"stop, this one's on me."*

Frank called Tabitha's brother as soon as he got in his truck, told him that he had an emergency door repair, and asked him how long it would take him to get the needed supplies and drive to North Dugganville. The Red Elks were a close family, and Tabitha's brother considered Frank to be a part of that family. Later that afternoon, they met back at the Merritts' house. Tabitha's brother was skilled, and working with Frank, was able to quickly repair the door and replace three other outside door locks.

The sun had set before they finished the last door and Frank, unaccustomed to so much exertion, was exhausted. He thanked Tabitha's brother, said goodbye to Amber as if he were talking to a customer at the end of a job, and drove home. So as not to alarm his family, because of his long absence during the day, he texted the Ramseys and his mother letting them know about the door repair. Tyrone texted him back with a thumbs up for thinking about the repair.

Later that evening, when he walked into the kitchen through the back door, Frank, Tabitha, and Sophia were waiting for him. He knew they would be and hoped they wouldn't ask too many questions about the morning. The straightforward young man was not good at hiding the truth. He looked at them and said, too nonchalantly, "Hey guys, were you worried?"

Bear felt instantly from the looks on his families faces that he had telegraphed his guilt. He tried to look away, as his mother approached him, but she placed both hands on his face and looked into his eyes. She asked simply, "Is Mrs. Merritt, OK?"

"yes'm," he mumbled, still wanting to look away.

"Are you, OK?" She asked her son.

"I'm fine."

Sophia asked Frank another question. "Frank, what about Mr. Merritt?"

The question caught him by surprise. Her son looked directly into her face and in clipped tones, said, "Mom. It's not what you might think. That son of a bitch was in her house when I got there. Nobody got hurt, this time. I will sort it out. I don't want to talk about it right now."

Neither Tyrell nor Tabitha had ever heard Frank talk to his mother so brusquely or use such strong language. They looked at each other, the alarm apparent on their faces. Frank had said nothing about Merritt being at the house or what had happened afterward, in the text he had sent before his arrival, and his loved ones had no way of knowing what he had just been through. Tyrell was about to intervene, but Tabitha touched his arm and shot him a 'stay-out-of-it' look. Ramsey held his tongue.

Sophia answered, calmly and with no hint of hurt or anger in her voice. "Frank, you are an adult, and you don't ever have to talk to me about it if you choose not to. I know you are strong, but you may be in a very dangerous situation. After Tabitha and I leave, I think it would be a very good idea if you trusted Tyrell and talked to him. You cannot do this on your own."

"He needs you," was all Tabitha said to her husband, before taking Sophia's arm and walking out of the kitchen.

Tyrell had still been clueless to what Sophia had known intuitively, until Frank quietly relayed the events of the day to him. Although already late, they sat up for several more hours, sometimes talking and sometimes just being together. Finally, noticing the exhaustion in the young man's face, Tyrell told him to go to bed. The ordeal had taken more out of him, physically and emotionally than he had realized, and Frank spent the next week at home, resting and talking to no one, except Tyrell.

Tyrell, however, visited Amber Merritt every day for the next two weeks. He wanted to make sure that R.T. knew that someone was checking on her. At the end of the second week, she called and told him that she wasn't feeling well and asked if Tabitha could take her to the doctor. The doctor was relatively new in the area, but his nurse's family had been in Dugganville for generations. The news of Amber's pregnancy spread quickly and reached Merritt's mother and father before it reached him.

Amber Merritt had come to detest her husband, and the feeling was mutual, but the awkward timing of the pregnancy prevented either from moving forward with the divorce. R.T.'s mother had been ecstatic when she called her son to tell him congratulations. He had learned from years of experience how not to tip his mother that he had no clue as to what she was talking about. He called the Dr.'s office, rather than Amber, and discovered that she was indeed, pregnant.

The couple tried for the next year to at least make a pretense of remaining in the marriage. They stayed in the house together, although sleeping in separate bedrooms. R.T. had planned on being present the evening the child he believed to be his son was born, but important business with a female client had kept him occupied. Both of his parents had been there.

The inevitable occurred before Jason reached his first birthday. The couple applied for a divorce on the grounds of incompatibility. Merritt's original plan had been to take everything that she owned, claiming that she had denied him any marital intimacy throughout their marriage. The birth of a child belied that claim. Moreover, he had no desire to be responsible for any part of Jason's life, and he knew his parents would lobby for him to challenge for custody, if he pushed too hard.

"Count your losses, and move on. You were stupid to think a woman was ever worth the trouble." Merritt would have rather slammed his soon-to-be ex-wife on social media and bragged about his sexual

exploits at the same time, but he was too much of a businessman to underestimate the power of appearances. Instead, he joined the mega-church in South Dugganville led by the father and son pastor team of Talbot and Kirby Appleton.

CHAPTER 22

The Past – 'Profit' of Redemption

The reverend Talbot Appleton beamed from his seat as he sat on the stage and looked out into the huge congregation. He hadn't always worn a high collared pastor's robe, but he had decided long ago that the more-saintly attire better represented the importance of his position to the community. The new glistening worship center stood on the same site as had the dying rural church populated by a few old women and even fewer old men, where he had preached his first sermon after arriving in South Dugganville almost twenty years before. The church now boasted an attendance approaching seven thousand on Sunday morning, and that didn't include the thousands more who viewed the sermon via television or the internet. The incredible growth of the church over the past twenty years had left him with a great sense of gratitude for God's greatness as well as a sense of glowing pride for his own accomplishments. He could barely contain his tears as he watched the greatest of those accomplishments walk down the long center aisle of the sanctuary toward the solid glass pulpit.

Kirby Appleton didn't look much like his father, except for a large nose that had obviously been genetically inherited. Dr. Talbot Appleton was tall, rail thin and of swarthy complexion. His twenty-year-old son was much shorter, stocky, leaning toward pudginess, and fair to the point of being anemic looking. Rather than a robe, he sported designer jeans topped by a black silk shirt opened several buttons past the collar and revealing a heavy gold cross shining from a hairless chest. He assured himself as he looked in the mirror each morning that his daily regimen of weight training was improving his physique, and yet his expensive body-shaping underwear was not completely successful in preventing a roll of flab from sneaking over the top of his belt. Still, he strode toward the dais with the confidence of a pious rock star, occasionally pausing to shake hands with a member of the congregation or run his fingers through his wavy shoulder-length blonde hair.

The elder Appleton had been forty years old when his son was born. At the time of his birth, Talbot Appleton had believed that he had been struck down by God and that his life might be over. He had long been stuck in the position of youth pastor in a church on west coast that was even larger than the church he had built. He had tried to convince himself that it was God's will that he fell in love with the fragile young high school student who had been abused by her family. He had even tried to do the right thing after he left the church, by marrying the girl, even though she was barely seventeen. The stress had been too great for the emotionally distraught teen, however, and shortly after his son was born, he found his child bride hanging from a tree branch in their back yard.

He had gathered up the remainder of his few belongings and, with his infant son, he traveled across the country until he came to the rural church outside of Dugganville. There he had found fertile ground upon which the seeds of his oratory fell and he realized that this had all been a part of God's plan. Almost instantly, people in the area recognized the power of his story. Here was a man who had fathered a child with his wife after years of being childless. He never revealed that his son had been conceived out of wedlock or that the mother was barely out of childhood, herself. Then, shortly after the miracle of birth, the child's mother had died suddenly and was called home by God, according to Talbot Appleton. The small rural congregation never learned that Kirby's mother had taken her own life.

The story resonated with many in the often tragedy-stricken area, who had also suffered from the ravages of poor health care.

Interested listeners began to trickle into the church at first, until the trickle became a flow, and finally a powerful river. Talbot Appleton had found his true calling. After establishing himself as a sympathetic character among the hard scrabble members of the community, he had shifted his message to the blessings that come with turning away from sin, receiving redemption, and giving to the faith. It became necessary to build a new sanctuary and then another. The models of the cars in the parking lot became more expensive, the congregants grew younger and wealthier, and Pastor Talbot Appleton morphed from being a sympathetic figure to saintly one.

Little Kirby Appleton continued to grow, and, although he had never known his mother, he was continually reminded of what a brave young man he was for facing such a harsh life every day without her blessed presence. Meanwhile, the comforts of that harsh life became more and more plush as the church and the tithes continued to grow. It wasn't long before Kirby Appleton realized how special he was.

After all, he had faced life without a mother. The endless stream of gray-haired women wishing to be called Nana and mothers of young children making sure he was always not only included, but first in line, simply couldn't fill the void of his tragic life. As for the possibility of another mother for Kirby, his father had steadfastly decided that he wasn't about to tempt the Lord's will. An occasional foray into pornography and a rare counseling session with an out-of-town prostitute would have to meet any less-than-Godly needs he may have. Outside of those minor needs for worldly maintenance, the Reverend Talbot had become wholly committed to growing God's church and to maintaining his own twenty-acre estate.

As a result, he grew apart from his miracle child for a period of time. Kirby had never known his mother, but when puberty struck somewhere during his middle school years, he began noticing the distinct difference in appearance between the man he called father and his own. Norse mythology was popular in the media, and Kirby decided that his mother must have been of Scandinavian Royalty.

The hair touching his shoulders or the Viking shield tattooed on Kirby's upper arm may have caused a bigger rift between the father and his teenage son if the tattoo had been larger or if Talbot Appleton hadn't been too busy to notice. After a DWI charge and a rumor told to him by a member of his congregation that his son might be involved in a gang, the reverend had finally confronted his son directly. Kirby had learned the lessons of his father's example well and fell down before him in extreme remorse, saying that he was sorry and that it would never happen again.

Talbot Appleton was once again overwhelmed by God's grace and convinced that his son had turned from the dark ways of Satan. Talbot's church continued to expand, his lawn continued to grow, and all was well until Kirby's senior year when the reverend received a phone call from the school saying that his son had sustained injuries in a fight.

After arriving at the school, he was taken immediately to the nurse's office where he looked at a face that was barely recognizable through the bruised eyes and bloody nose. The pastor never saw the faces of the three other young men sitting in an office down the hall, all of whom suffered from similar facial alterations. Nor, did he ever meet the young man waiting in the Dean's office with clinched fists and looking for more.

"What is this travesty," the pastor bellowed, loudly enough for several teachers to poke their heads into the hallway. "Where is the devil that did this to my son?"

The principal floundered for a response. The school nurse did the only thing she could think to do and quickly closed her door.

"What type of organization are you running here, where innocent children are beaten and maimed," Talbot Appleton, growled through gritted teeth, the veins on his neck, bulging a dangerous shade of purple.

The principal was a member of Appleton's congregation as a matter of social propriety, but he didn't particularly care for the man who made a lot more money than he did with far fewer headaches. Still, administrative positions in Dugganville were usually short of tenure, and he knew it was important to tread softly with someone who held such a powerful social influence.

"Pastor Talbot, I assure you that, if I thought my son had been attacked for no reason, I would be at least as angry as you are now," he said using the line he had used in many situations before. *"Oh great, listen to me trying to bullshit the master bullshitter,"* he thought.

Still, the line usually worked to calm an angry parent, and the reverend seemed to relax his jaw. Seizing the moment, the principal asked Appleton to walk across the hall with him to his office in order to talk about the situation.

"Shouldn't you be calling an ambulance," Appleton asked, his voice a mixture of simmering anger and growing concern.

"Nurse Jenkins has already talked to Kirby and the other boys. They are quite lucid and insist that they don't need treatment. In fact, your son didn't want us to call you. We will leave the decision whether or not to take him to the hospital up to you."

The principal had barely finished the last sentence when the Reverend snapped back at him. "Other boys? Do you mean to tell me that more than one of these heathens jumped my son?"

It was a struggle for the principal to keep from smiling. "No sir. It appears that your son and three other boys may have backed one of our athletes into a corner during the lunch period. The young man in question comes from a rather harsh background and didn't hesitate to defend himself."

The expression on Appleton's face went into neutral as he processed the information. "You are trying to tell me that my son acted as the aggressor with three other students, and he looks like he does now. I find that hard to believe."

"Reverend Appleton, I understand your concerns. We tried to get Kirby to call you and tell you about the fight, but he refused. It was witnessed by several teachers and most of the students in the cafeteria. Everything happened very fast. The other student was sitting by himself when Kirby and his friends surrounded his table. His name, you will find it out anyway, is Carson Blake. He stood up, and several students heard your son say a racial slur to him. Teachers were already walking toward the table, when Blake responded with a vulgar sexual term. Every witness agrees that all of the boys, including your son, went after Blake at the same time. Unfortunately, some of our other students impeded staff members from getting to the fight quickly enough to stop it immediately. Those students are being dealt with. By the time teachers reached the fight, your son and the others were on the ground. Fortunately, Blake's coach was near the cafeteria at the time. He yelled for Blake to stop, and he did so without further action. Blake and the coach walked together to the Dean's office where they sit, now.

Appleton pondered the principal's account before finally saying, "Blake? Isn't he the thug the local mafia brought in from Oklahoma to beat the Indian kid from North? Then, when he couldn't, his dad nearly killed the kid in the locker room."

Social influence or not, the remark was over the top, and the principal felt himself losing his temper when a light tap was made on his office door, and a battered Kirby Appleton walked in and sat in a chair beside his father. He looked up at his father through battered and tear-filled eyes before saying, "Dad, the fight was all my fault. I started it. I am so ashamed of myself, and I want to change."

The open admission shocked both the reverend and the principal. What neither had known was that Kirby had been sitting with his phone while in the nurse's office, and for the past hour that phone had been dinging constantly with taunts and threats. Nobody really cared for Carson Blake, but they didn't like Kirby Appleton or his gang of Viking Wannabes, either. Watching the four of them get pummeled by the stud athlete was an open invitation for the wolves to move in. The tears in Kirby Appleton's eyes as he sat in the principal office weren't tears of shame, but of terror.

The principal was still seething at the pastor, but the son's admission had allowed him to gain control of his mouth. The pastor was still angry at the school for allowing his precious son to get beaten, but also realized that it was better not to press the issue after his son's confession. Kirby Appleton just wanted to go home as quickly as possible.

Of the five combatants in the school cafeteria that day, three were sent to alternative school to finish their senior years, Carson Blake and two of the other boys. They stayed as far away from him as possible. One of the boys dropped out of school. Kirby Appleton finished his senior year at home, through an on-line Christian Education Program. The principal accepted a position in another state.

* * * * *

Kirby Appleton changed his life as soon as he walked out of South Dugganville High School that day. He became actively involved in his father's church, spending almost all of his time there, or in his room studying. His father had told him that he had made a deal with the principal whereby he could return to SDHS if he was worried about Carson Blake's presence at the alternative school. Either site sounded like a death sentence to the high school senior who had been branded as a social pariah by practically every student in the area. He told his father that he needed to spend the rest of his senior year atoning for his sins.

Talbot Appleton had been overwhelmed by his son's transformation and the depth of his repentance. Soon, father and son, were working together on every aspect of the church, and Talbot recognized something that he had never seen in his child before. Kirby Appleton possessed the same silver tongue as his dad. "Dad, I would like to start giving my testimony in church and to groups outside of the church." Talbot had been thrilled but thought he should have discussed dress with his son the first time he had entered the church's small chapel to share his story with a group of elderly congregation members. The looks on their faces mirrored that on his father's.

His blonde hair, still uncut, fell to his shoulders instead of being pulled back in its customary pony tail. He wore tight jeans, black military boots, and a black t-shirt. Covering his upper left arm was the tattoo of a Viking shield, now largely obscured by one of a Christian cross. Kirby emerged from the curtains and walked, not to the plain wooden dais, but stepped down from the stage and stood directly in front of his father. A space shorter than the length of his arm separated him from the one hundred plus members of the senior worship service, ages sixty and over. He had purposely directed an overbright stage light to the spot where he would be standing. The harsh glare created by the light bouncing off his fare skin and blond hair made it impossible for the audience to look at the soft-bodied young man without squinting. This had been his intention, as had been the slight background static in the microphone. He had created an oddly ominous effect for a church testimonial.

"The person you see standing before you," Kirby began, "is not the person that my father or my heavenly father intended me to be."

Talbot Appleton had instructed his son that he had only ten minutes to give his testimony to the audience of senior citizens. The one subject the younger Appleton had excelled in before leaving SDHS had been drama, and he intended to use his theatrical skills to create a permanent imprint in those minutes. His head drooped to his chest, and the microphone held just below his chin picked up the sound of sobbing. After a few seconds, he looked first back at his father, before turning again to the audience.

"I have brought shame to my church, to my dad, and to my god. I won't shock you by enumerating all of the shameful actions that I have hidden from Dad, and from you."

Talbot Appleton's emotions were fluctuating between fear that he may have been raising a career criminal in his home without having a clue what his son had been doing, and relief that his congregation wouldn't learn of his son's deeds as he was hearing of them for the first time. The majority of the audience, however, experienced a let-down after hearing that they would be denied hearing the juicy details. The spoiled preacher's kid was often the object of discussion at checker boards and quilting circles, but most folks gave him a pass for his entitled behavior. After all, the poor child had been raised, motherless. But now, standing in front of them, was this dangerous looking Viking figure. Kirby Appleton had grabbed their attention before informing them that they wouldn't be hearing of his monstrous sins.

"Just know that I have been in trouble with the law. I have been a gang member, and I have inflicted violence on another human being."

What they would never learn was that Appleton's most egregious sin was that he had earned the reputation of being the spoiled arrogant jerk who they already knew him to be. Before the incident in the cafeteria, he had been pulled over one time for drunk driving, but had been let go, after the sheriff had recognized who he was. His gang, the Valhalla Force, had inspired nothing more than eye-rolls except from the most timid of incoming freshmen, and he had been involved in one fight; which he lost, badly.

"All of this was before God broke me and sent me to my knees." The audience hadn't noticed but the volume of the speakers had lowered and the static had disappeared. Kirby raised his eyes to the ceiling. The spotlight dimmed, and the house lights came up. The audience, including Talbot Appleton blinked several times to allow their eyes to adjust to the change in light. Standing in front of them was his son, drenched from head to toe in his own perspiration. His once wild mane of hair, now hung limply on his scalp. The spotlight had done its job, creating the image of a morally penitent sinner.

He concluded by pointing to the tattoo on his arm and explaining, "Once my eyes were opened, and I realized that I had been fighting against my true god, I considered having the pagan symbol of a Viking shield removed, hoping that my father and you would never know that it existed. Then I realized that Jesus has covered all of my sins, and I had the symbol of the cross added to show that God can use even the most abased of his children. I kneel down now before you, and I am asking for your prayers."

With his last words, Appleton dropped the mic and went to his knees, sobbing. Audience members looked at each other, not quite sure what to do until the Reverend Talbot Appleton rose from his seat and stood by his son.

Tears flowed down his cheeks as he raised his hand and beckoned the audience, "Please, come and offer prayers for my child as he begins his new journey in Christ."

One by one, the audience, some of them using walkers or in wheelchairs, came to the front of the chapel to offer a prayer for the newly found child of God. Kirby, with his head bowed, smiled inwardly. *"A performance, well done,"* he thought.

* * * * *

That heartrending testimony from his son had been delivered barely a year before, and the blessings from heaven had flowed like the opening of a celestial floodgate, since. Talbot had long struggled with guilt for not telling his son more about his mother or how she had died, but he could now see that it had all been in God's plan. At sixty, he had felt his own health start to wane, but his young son had turned into a dynamo for the word of God. The church had been growing steadily for years, but Kirby's vitality and appearance, along with his talent for marketing and spectacle, had created an explosion in the growth of attendance by young adults in the church. Other recent graduates of SDHS suddenly remembered how scary it had been to pass him in the hallways before his conversion. Even students who had been in the cafeteria the day of fight with Carson Blake recalled it as being a mass riot instigated by Kirby and his Valhalla gang.

The Church of God's Redemption had become a local phenomenon drawing in young and old, rich and poor, generational families and newly relocated transients. It was in those dichotomies of the church membership that the son had recognized a fertile field to be plowed, which his father had missed. Talbot Appleton had brought a story with him, when he moved to the small church on the south side of the river with his infant son that the inhabitants of the depressed area had recognized, and one for which they held great empathy. Inspired by his courage under such great adversity, the small congregation had given deeply of their time and meager resources.

Talbot Appleton's message had been consistent throughout his service at the Church of God's Redemption. Humble yourself, and keep not for yourself. His target audience, however, had grown throughout the years, spreading out toward the wealthier suburban areas of the Dugganvilles. The acquisition of a new house, expensive wardrobe, and several new cars using church funds had all been for the purpose of increasing that outreach. He had always believed that he had been giving his utmost for God's mission, but now, watching his son walk down the church aisle as if led by angels, he realized that his ultimate purpose had been to raise a successor. *"Talbot has saved his thousands, Kirby will save his tens of thousands,"* he said to himself.

Although he had never been to seminary or any form of higher education, most people in the audience already referred to him as reverend or pastor Kirby, titles he never bothered to correct. He had felt himself called to represent the new age of evangelism. He stepped to the dais that had been designed to his specifications and crafted by a local glass artisan. This would be its first test. Taking a deep breath, he opened his palms and laid them simultaneously on the surface of the high-tech lectern. A single beam of light shot from the ceiling and illuminated Appleton. The dais had prisms strategically cut into its corners. Upon striking the dais, the beam burst into a shower of multicolored light droplets that fell on the audience and immediately disappeared as if melting like magical snowflakes. Joyful sighs of wonderment arose from young and old alike, and heads throughout the auditorium turned upward to watch the lights travel across the high domed ceiling.

It was exactly the effect that Kirby had hoped for. "This is the way that God wants you to be," he started, while slowly raising his hands from the lectern. The light show faded, and all eyes turned to the man standing at the pulpit.

*　*　*　*　*

Earlier in the week, Pastor Kirby had been sitting in his temporary office at the church struggling with the message he would deliver for his first sermon to the entire church. The space had been converted from a classroom until an office with a more befitting aura could be constructed. He had always loved to perform drama on stage and that was why he had convinced his dad to commission the outlandishly expensive glass pulpit. He had never acted in front of such a large audience before, and suddenly found himself with a growing sense of terror that he might not know his lines.

He stared at the blank screen in front of him. "Brothers and Sisters in Christ," he wrote.

"*No, that sounds like my dad,*" he thought.

"Friends," he started after deleting what he had written. "*No, most of these people barely know me.*"

"Dearly Beloved," he typed on his third try. "*Damn it. It's not a frigging wedding.*"

In frustration, he started typing meaningless profanity and thought about going to his car where he kept a bottle of scotch whiskey hidden. Suddenly, the door to his office opened. In a panic, he held his finger on the delete button and looked toward the door.

"Pastor Kirby," came a booming voice from the tall handsome man stepping in his office. "Or is it, Reverend Appleton? Hell, son. How should I address you?"

"Excuse me, sir. I wasn't expecting, anyone." Suddenly, Kirby felt like he was back in school and had just been caught smoking in the bathroom by the school dean.

Without being invited in, R.T. Merritt strode across carpeted floor, pulled up a folding chair that had been leaning against a wall next to the desk, and sat down. His demeanor quickly changed from swaggering to humble. "Pastor, your father sent me here. My name is R.T. Merritt. You may have heard of me. I have lived a successful life, but recently I have recognized a need to make some changes. After I shared a little of my story with the senior pastor, he told me that I might want to talk with you. You see, I too have realized that God almighty has more in store for me than the path I have been following."

After his initial panic, Kirby had recognized the state senator from the north side of the river. His face had been plastered on bill boards and commercial ads during the election. Now, as he sat listening, he was also recognizing a fellow thespian. What he didn't know was that Merritt had known everything about the reason for his sudden exit from SDHS, before coming to the church that day. It had been Merritt that had asked the senior Appleton to speak with his son, and not the reverse.

"Pastor Appleton, my marriage, I am afraid, is irretrievably broken, and I am seeking your wisdom," Merritt began, effectively stroking the younger man's ego.

"Senator Merritt, I appreciate your candor with me, but I don't know much about marriage counseling."

"Oh, don't misunderstand me, Reverend. As I said, the marriage is broken. I am looking to make a new start, and I would like to do so by helping to build your church," Merritt said, purposefully assigning ownership of the church to the naively egotistical young man sitting across the desk.

Kirby Appleton quickly took the bait, and listened intently to the senator as he described his plan for his own redemption for the next hour, carefully describing how that plan would usher what was now the largest church in the area into a new era.

"You see, Reverend Appleton, your father has done a marvelous thing for this river town, but look at our congregation," Merritt said, although he had yet to join the church.

He continued. "It's almost exclusively white, most of our members are from the south side, and almost none of them come are a part of the influx of very wealthy people moving into the area. I fear that a very fertile field is being left to lay fallow, while waiting to be plowed by someone else."

The light bulb that turned on in Kirby's head was visibly noticeable. Nodding thoughtfully, he added to Merritt's last statement. "If the church is to prosper as God has planned, we must reach out to the prosperous newcomers in our community. We cannot be held back by the past." the younger man had verbally completed the thought that Merritt was trying to implant in his brain.

Merritt smiled. "Thank you, Pastor Appleton. You humble me with your wisdom. It goes far beyond your youth. If there is anything that this servant can do, please, tell me."

Both men were smiling when Merritt left Kirby Appleton's makeshift office. Merritt had accomplished two goals. Both police departments were comprised mostly of generational Dugganvillites, and many of them were members of the church. His attendance would provide him with a barrier if Amber ever decided to press charges. More importantly, he hoped that he had created an avenue for bringing old and new money together under the shade of the church. He and his father would no longer need Amber or her parents.

The Pastor Kirby Appleton had been given a vision and the text of his first sermon before the full church.

Chapter 23

The Present – Divine Intervention

Kirby Appleton sat smilingly in front of his computer inspecting the revenues for the church from the preceding month. They had continued to skyrocket since the launch of The Church of God's Redemption social media platform. He leaned back in the office chair fashioned from imported mahogany and nubuck leather and patted the swell of his belly as it pushed against the buttons of his designer shirt. Long since departed from his thinking, was any sense of need to portray himself as a former Viking rebel. Designer shirts and lavishly expensive business haircuts were more in line with his current sense of mission. The only reminder of his former image as a fallen angel was the tattoo on his shoulder, and that never saw the light of day. He would have had it removed, but he hated pain.

The thirty-six-year-old pastor had not, however, lost his skills in the arts of drama and theater. Without them the masses hadn't the capacity to maintain their attention during a long sermon, no matter how impassioned.

"Hit hard with shock and awe, then dazzle with joy and wonderment." He slapped the desk for emphasis, although he was the only person in the office.

It was the formula he had used since his first testimonial in front of the senior citizens of the church. The result had been explosive growth, and the church had quickly morphed from its status as the largest regional church under his father, to having a growing national and international influence.

"And my teachers, said I didn't understand chemistry," Appleton chuckled to himself.

"Reverend, reverend," a petite attractive blond wearing a silk dress and too much makeup said softly, as she touched him softly on the hand covering his computer mouse.

Appleton startled, and looked up from the computer. "Oh? Lacey, I'm so sorry. I was, um, praying about my next message and didn't hear you come in."

The church secretary kept her hand on Appleton's another moment before sliding it off, seductively. The startled look on the reverend's face melted into another smile and a small sigh when she leaned forward farther than necessary to give him a message. "It's ok, Reverend. I didn't mean to interrupt your work. Mr. Merritt is in the front office and says it is very important that he talk to you."

A puzzled look came over Appleton's face. "Which one?"

"Merritt, Jr., the son."

The Reverend sighed again, this one neither lustful nor pleasant. *"What does he want,"* Appleton grumbled to himself.

Lacey noticed the change. "Are you OK, Kirby, I mean, Reverend," she asked while sliding her hand over his, once again.

"Yes, I am fine," he said, quickly returning to his serene state. "But, how are you, Lacey. Are you still alone?"

"OK, I guess. My husband will be overseas for over a month, and I am feeling terribly lonely." The twinkle in her eyed belied the sadness of her words.

"I am so sorry to hear that, Lacey," he said, while sandwiching her hand between the two his. "Please, ask Mr. Merritt to come in."

The secretary left the office without further words, but the code had been sent and decoded. It was one she and the saintly pastor had used since shortly after taking her new job. Little did she know, or perhaps she was fully aware, that the celibate pastor had similar communication systems with other women in the church.

Kirby Appleton had never learned the true identity of his mother, but he had long suspected that there was a great deal more to the story than what his father had shared with him or anyone else. Almost immediately upon his commitment to the full service of God, however, the elder pastor began schooling his son in the fine art of priestly celibacy. Time had left his father behind in many ways, and the Reverend Talbot Appleton had never been able to grasp the power of technology in building a church. When it came to the fine art of creating an image in the absence of reality, however, his father had been among the best.

Kirby Appleton had learned many valuable lessons from his father and mentor since his revelation as a senior in high school, but those lessons had come to a halt only a few months before. In addition to his worsening physical health, the senior pastor had begun to experience memory lapses from the pulpit and would sometimes digress into odd ramblings. The difficult decision to retire his father from the pulpit came when the senior pastor had broken down into a tearful delusional confession about his son being conceived out of wedlock with a minor. Thankfully, Kirby had been on the stage with his father and had quickly escorted the sobbing pastor away from the pulpit, while simultaneously swerving the service to a song filled hour of praise.

Appleton knew that the man who would be entering his office in the next few moments was another master of illusion. When they had first met nearly two decades before, Appleton had not been prepared for a duel of deception with a seasoned veteran. While the relationship of the past twenty years had been profitable for both men, the reverend had matured and had learned not to swallow the dangling bait too quickly. It would have been so much easier if he could just say, *"Look, you sorry son of a bitch. What do you want, and what am I going to get out of it?"* Such open candor would have broken the rules of the game, however, and both men were masters in the art of rhetorical fencing.

"Reverend Appleton," Merritt said, in an uncharacteristically soft voice while standing politely at the pastor's doorway waiting to be beckoned in; also uncharacteristic of the bombastic businessman. *En Garde.*

Appleton picked up on the change and felt an immediate need to be wary. "R.T., what a pleasant surprise. I wasn't expecting you.

Come in." He stood and walked over to a pair of comfortable straight back chairs that had been arranged for informal meetings. He motioned for Merritt to join him, as he did. *En Garde*

Merritt began his performance as he sat down. "Thank you, Reverend." *Advance.*

"Why so formal, R.T.? Please, call me Kirby." *Retreat*

"You are right, and I apologize for being so stiff. I must admit that one of my weaknesses has always been the inability to find the proper words to express my heartfelt concern for people going through trying times. I will just come out and ask, how is your dad?" *Feint.*

The question, on its face, was innocent. He had answered it countless times, already. Questions coming from R.T. Merritt, however, usually had dollar signs for punctuation rather than question marks. Kirby offered his standard rote response. "He is resting better lately, but I am afraid he won't be returning to the pulpit. This change in his journey has been very difficult for a man who has been doing the Lord's work for so long. For his own wellbeing I have had to hire someone to take care of him. He dearly loves his flock, but his health will not allow him to be in the public eye any longer." *Parry.*

Merritt sat for long ticking seconds without responding to the reverend. He thoughtfully placed his fingertips on his lips, and Appleton noticed the faint beginnings of a tear in his left eye.

"Damn, he's good!" Appleton thought.

Finally, "I try not to get angry with God, reverend; excuse me, I mean Kirby. What I am trying to say is, I don't understand the justice in God's thinking. Your father is a great man, and to be reduced to making such an embarrassing confession in front of so many people is simply not fair." *Parry and thrust.*

Talbot Appleton's words from the pulpit had been barely intelligible, and his son had hustled him from the stage so quickly, that he had thought that one really understood what he had been saying. He couldn't see how could Merritt have made any sense of his father's few rambling statements so quickly. More importantly, why was Merritt bringing it up now, in his office. He had heard no mutterings about the contents his father's errant sermon, and he would have. Lacey, in addition to being the church secretary and his secret mistress, had proven to be the most efficient rumor radar a man could have. Nothing got past her.

"R.T., I must admit, that I am concerned as well as confused. I fail to see how my father's dementia induced ramblings constitute some type of confession. I was on the stage with him, and I barely understood what he said. He has been the pastor of a very large church for a great many years, and that last rambling statement was likely the assimilation of the hundreds or thousands of confessions he has heard over those years." *Parry, retreat.*

"I certainly hope so, son, but that's not what it sounded like!" Merritt's voice had become deeper and slightly louder. He was now leaning toward the younger man. Appleton sensed that R.T. was moving in for the final thrust. He knew that, once again, the older game player had come into his office knowing the final outcome of this contest before it had begun. It was time to end it. He sighed and thought, *"Go ahead and get it over with, bastard."*

"Mr. Merritt, you and I both know that you aren't here to express concern for my father's well-being. Perhaps you could elaborate on your true purpose."

"Why, Kirby, I am shocked that you would think that I have any motives beyond protecting the legacies of you and your father. Did you and the reverend ever spend time together looking at pictures of your mother?" Merritt knew the match was over but enjoyed toying with his prey.

"Huh? No, the subject has always been too emotional." Kirby felt his intestines twisting into a knot.

"That's too bad. Every child should know its mother," Merritt said while reaching into his jacket pocket. He pulled out an old color photograph of a pale young woman. She had limp blond hair and was obviously several months pregnant. The sad look on her face accentuated the planeness of her appearance.

Kirby tried to act nonchalant, but, except for her nose, the face staring back at him could have been a female version of himself in high school. He felt the bile that had been trapped at the knot in his stomach start to rise up into his throat. "Look, I don't where you are going with this, but I don't see how an old photograph from who knows where, has anything to do with me or my father."

Merritt jumped on the last statement. "Ok, Kirby, I do apologize for the age of the photograph. You see, I have had it in my possession for nearly twenty years."

Kirby was worried that he might pass out.

Merritt went into full merciless attack mode. "Why, young man, you look a bit confused or ill; quite possibly, both. Let me ease your discomfort by explaining. You see, you may have grown up here, but you will never be from here and will never understand the way Dugganville works. Are you following me?"

Merritt waited with insincere politeness for a response. Kirby realized that he hadn't been breathing while the older man was talking. Tears had formed in the corners of his eyes. He took a deep breath in and let it out before saying, "go ahead."

Merritt nodded at Kirby and began. "Have you ever heard the story of my great ancestor, Raeford Thaddeus Beaumont, Reverend Appleton? I know you've seen his statue sitting on that beautiful horse in the middle of the river. Now, a lot of people coming here from places like California, don't believe that the stories about the Major are true. That doesn't matter to those of us with deep roots in Dugganville, because we really don't care what people from somewhere else think.

Now you may find this hard to accept, but some of us don't believe all of the stories that those transients from other parts of the world bring to our little corner of paradise. We usually don't check them out, because, like I said, we really don't care. But I learned a long time ago that, as a businessman, it never hurts to know a little bit of background about the people coming into our fine community. Are you still following me?" *Slash and Thrust.*

Kirby had never pressed his father to tell him the full story about his mother. As an incredibly egocentric human being, it hadn't really mattered to him. The stories he had created in his own mind about his mother being a beautiful Norse superwoman who had been struck down in the prime of life, had been far more gratifying than discovering that she may have been just another pitifully sad human being trying to find her way in life. Yet, the picture staring up at him from his desk, said that was exactly who she had been. He nodded at Merritt once again while trying to betray as little of the fear he was feeling as possible.

"As I have already said, multiple times, the locals don't really care what transient folks such as your father bring with them, but apparently a rather large church on the west coast was very upset about the relationship a certain youth pastor had with the child in that photo."

Merritt paused for dramatic effect. "Especially after that child took her own life shortly after she gave birth to the child, not yet born in that photograph" *Touche', and match!*

Appleton felt himself being overcome by nausea and looked quickly for the trash can under his desk. He lay his head on his desk and held one hand up, making a silent request for Merritt to stop.

"Oh, I am so sorry, young reverend. I know this news is terribly difficult. Please, take your time. I am in no hurry"

Kirby slowly felt his stomach starting to settle and his breathing returning to near normal. Finally, he raised his head from the desk and asked in a shaky voice, "So, if you knew this for all these years, why are you waiting until now to blackmail me?"

Merritt laughed out loud. "Blackmail? Son, who said anything about blackmail? A good businessman just knows not to spend his capital too early. If I had wanted to ruin your life, I would have done it back then. I merely want our fine church to grow, reach the masses, and prosper; now more than ever. Why this fine tabernacle of God could bring even greater wealth to this growing community than it has experienced over the past thirty years. You and your father have been a powerful force toward pulling the north and the south sides of the river together. I only share this information with you to let you know that evil forces also exist among us that would love to drive a wedge and destroy everything you've accomplished. Please believe me when I tell you that I meant no disrespect when I said that you will never be from here. It is just a fact of life that many of us have long been entrenched in this culture of between worlds, and sometimes you have to make deals with the other side in order to survive. Those deals may go back generations, a circumstance that prevents newcomers such as yourself, from participating. In most instances, nobody gets hurt, but occasionally, a player forgets the rules. When that happens, drastic measures must sometimes be taken for the good of all involved."

Kirby had found momentary relief upon hearing that he wasn't being targeted for blackmail, but Merritt's last statement had caused his discomfort to return. "But I don't see how that affects me. You already said that I am an outsider, and not involved."

"You are absolutely right, young man." Kirby noticed that Merritt's addresses to him had migrated from Reverend and Kirby to son and young man. *"He is working me, and I am powerless to stop it."*

"Yes, you are absolutely right, and that is exactly why I have never mentioned your unfortunate mother to you or anyone else until a few minutes ago. Do you remember when I told you that people from Dugganville don't care what people from somewhere else think?"

"Yes," Kirby answered warily.

"Well, that all worked out very well for us poor little backwoods folks for a long time, because nobody from anywhere else cared what happens in this little river town. Now, with this explosion of people coming from all over the map, we find ourselves not to be so little anymore, and there are more of you than there are of us. The old folks among us, still see North and South Dugganville as two distinctly separate entities, but you new folks don't even seem to recognize that there is a river between us.

Suddenly, we are on the map, and people are paying attention. Your father came here thirty years ago with a story. It was a good story, even if it lacked in factual basis. It inspired a lot of folks on the south side of the river, and the church grew. Then, a decade or so later, you approached the church with another powerful story, also with no basis in truth."

Kirby felt the knot in his stomach dissolve as everything in him turned to jelly. *"Does Merritt know everything about me?"*

"Don't look so pale, Reverend Appleton," Merritt said, raising Kirby's status once again. "I have been following your career for a long time, and I am an admirer. It matters not one whit that the old guard, such as my family, don't like it that the newcomers are going to eventually take over. It is going to happen. There are already more of you than there are of us. My goal is simply to survive. If helping you grow your church and bring more newcomers into the area helps me do that, I am your faithful servant."

For the first time since Merritt had walked into his office, Kirby Appleton started to feel hopeful. He had known since his first meeting with the smooth-talking businessman, that any offer from him came at a cost. Church coffers sometimes grew and depleted overnight unexpectedly. No one had seemed to mind, nor could they question the church's explosive growth. He had, on occasion wondered how Lacey had missed the anomalies. In addition to her other attributes, she had proven to be a top-notch book keeper. *"Don't worry about it, now. One crisis at a time," he thought.*

"Reverend Appleton, are you with me? You seem to be wandering off?"

"Uh, yes, um, sir, I mean R.T. I am just trying to process a lot of information and got lost in the weeds for a few moments. What is it exactly that you want me to do?"

"Not much, really. I would just like to you make a slight change in the focus of your message. You are the master of the feel-good sermon. Every time I leave this holy place, I am ready to tackle the world. It's one of the reasons your popularity has risen so quickly among the youth and the transient population, as well as the old guard."

"And when was the last time you were in this holy place, except to lean on me for one thing or another," Appleton mulled to himself.

Almost as if reading his thoughts, Merritt smiled before continuing. "There are populations on either side of the river, however, who will never hear your powerful messages of hope. I need you to bring the activities of those populations to the attention of your church." It was the first time that Merritt had changed the possessive pronoun. No longer, "our church," he had just given full ownership back to Kirby. Appleton knew what that meant.

R.T. Merritt spent the next thirty minutes outlining the situation for Appleton, before ending with, "Now don't worry. With your gift of oratory this will be little more than a high school speech contest.

We will get together soon, and I will give you the exact information you need to do God's will."

Merritt stood and shook the preacher's hand as if he really meant good will. He turned and walked out the door, closing it behind him. Appleton sat for what seemed like a long time trying to contemplate everything that had just happened. When he looked up at the clock, he realized that only a few minutes had passed. His next thought was a happy one. He would be seeing Lacey that night. With a new found lightness in his step, he walked to the door and opened it.

The lightness quickly grew heavy. His first sight was of Lacey, standing with her breasts fully pressed against Merritt's arm as he leaned over to whisper something in her ear. Both turned their attentions to the direction of the door. A guilty giggle escaped from the church secretary before she let go of the business man's arm and sat back at her desk.

"Yes sir, Mr. Merritt. The pastor is available next Friday afternoon. I will put you on his schedule."

CHAPTER 24

The Present – Bugle Call

Amber and Frank had chosen the kitchen as the place to break the news to their son. It had served as the setting for many family gatherings over the course of Jason's life. Amber had been at several of those gatherings as a family friend, and the sunlit breakfast area felt like the natural place to discuss family. There was a small breakfast bar underneath a large picture window, and on this day, Frank and Amber sat next to each other on one side of the bar. They had never done so, before. Jason sat facing them on the opposite side.

Amber had narrated most of the long brutally difficult story, while Frank sat impassively listening. They hadn't known what reactions to expect from their son, and had talked beforehand about how to deal with the possibility of angry outbursts or violent accusations. Instead, he had mirrored the face of his father sitting across the table from him, sitting quietly, showing no emotion, and asking no questions.

Amber stopped talking and waited for Jason to finally respond. "How do you know for sure," was the only question he asked.

"Not long after you were born, I took you on a trip to Connecticut, where I saw my childhood doctor. The DNA test confirmed that you are Frank's son."

"But?" Jason waived his hand over his face and raised a lock of hair, silently indicating that he didn't see how it was possible.

Frank responded to the question asked in sign language. "Yes, your fair skin, blue eyes, and blonde hair, hide your Cherokee heritage. I know what you have just been told is hard to accept. I can only explain by saying that Europeans and Indigenous peoples have been mixing since those first three boats landed, centuries ago. I guess genes sometimes lay hidden for a long time."

All three sat silently, until Jason spoke again, saying only, "I am going to take a walk."

Amber started to reach across the table to hold her son, but Frank placed his hand on her leg under the table. She pulled her arms back to her side.

Never had Frank's emotions been so tortuously shredded. When Amber had been attacked by her husband, Frank had been ready to kill to protect her, but now he felt like it was he who had brutally damaged his own son. He wanted to wrap his arms around him and tell him how much he had been loved through all of the years of deceit. Instead, "OK," was the only word that left his lips.

Jason stood and walked toward the kitchen door leading out to the patio. He tried to appear calm, but had to stop and lean against the door frame for a few seconds before stepping outside. He feared that his legs might not hold him up.

Without conscious thought; he was too numb to think; he walked toward a small stream that cut across the back corner of the Bear Family acreage. The spot was only a mile from Frank Bear's first home in Beaumont. He and Frank had come there often, listening for the sounds of the elk bugling through the valley between the twin sisters. It was perhaps his favorite place on earth, but he couldn't see it, now. The blood pounded in his head, and with each thump a painful pulse of light blurred his vision. Feeling himself dizzy, he sat on a large rock near the stream, the same rock on which he had sat many times before.

Confusion swirled around him, and he thought, *Am I angry, sad, bitter? Who with; Mom, Frank, my dad. No, wait R.T. isn't my dad, anymore – never was my dad. Why didn't they tell me before?"*

While he sat, the soft bugle of an elk flowed through the valley, mixing with his turbulent thoughts. The sound calmed him, but momentarily. Quickly, the sound he had always associated with Frank Bear, whom he had loved possibly even more than his mother, entwined itself with the other questions torturing his soul.

The torture continued until Jason could take it no more. He stood and screamed back at the elk. "HYAAAAAAH!"

Bugle call,

"HYAAAAAAAAAAAAAAAAAAAH!"

Bugle call,

"HYAAAAAAAAAAAAAAAAAAAAAAAAAAAAAAAAA!"

The call and response continued until Jason sat back on the rock, exhausted. No matter how loudly and angrily he had screamed, each time the elk had responded, seemingly saying the same thing, "You are home."

Everything he thought to be real had suddenly grown dark. He sat numbly on the rock for a long time, staring into nothingness, until he felt a presence. He twisted on his seat and looked over his shoulder. There, stood Sophia Bear. She wore a simple beige shift tied at the waist with a rope belt. Her long silver-streaked black hair was tied in a pony tail. She was looking at Jason through wisdom saddened eyes and her trademark enigmatic smile.

"How long have you been standing there," he asked weakly.

"All of your life, Grandson."

"Sheeesh, does everyone know but me."

"No, only your parents, me and Rose. Frank and Tabitha knew when they were alive."

A few seconds passed, before Sophia asked, "May I sit with you?"

Jason was exhausted, confused, and suddenly lonely. For as long as he could remember, Frank's mother had made the world a better placed simply by walking into the room. He needed her presence. He didn't resist or pull away when his newly discovered grandmother sat and put her arm around him. Instead, he crumpled and buried his face in her midsection before breaking into an uncontrollable sob. She held him for a long time, while swaying gently back and forth and softly singing a Cherokee lullaby, as if she was comforting a distraught infant. She was finally getting to hold her first grandchild.

He finally sat up and asked, "How did you know I would be here?"

"You see the top of the old mother mountain over there," she asked while pointing due south.

"Yes."

"Between here and that mountain is your father's first home. It was where the Beaumont recreation center sits now. We had a very hard life when Frank was young, and when things got bad, he would go into our back yard and listen to the elk. You are his son."

"Grandma Sophie?" Her heart sang upon hearing the title. It was what her granddaughters had always called her, and he had also, because that was her title in the Bear household. Hearing it then, wrapped her heart in the joy of fulfilled hope.

"Yes, Grandson?"

"I didn't know how to let them know when they told me." He paused and started to tremble, before taking a deep shaky breath. "I didn't, uh. I didn't, unnh. In my heart, I have always seen your son as my dad. Your family has always been my family. Now, that I know the truth, I am terrified I might lose that family. I don't think I believe in God, but I still used to pray to him that somehow this fair skin and blonde hair was a mistake and that I was really an Indian inside, the son of Frank Bear. Now, it has happened and I am afraid God is going to take it away because I don't believe. Are the Merritts going to hurt Mom when they find out?"

She took his chin in her hand and looked into his face as she might a small child. "No." She said flatly. "Tyrell and Tabitha died when you were very small, but they still loved you as their grandchild, just as I do. You would have known much sooner who your real family was if it hadn't been for the car accident. Tyrell was beginning to tell your father everything about the Merritt family when he and Tabitha died. Frank was still not very strong. A few weeks before she died, Tabitha had introduced Frank to her niece, Rose."

A puzzled impatient look came on his face. "How will that keep my mother from getting hurt?"

There it was; the all-knowing smile that Tyrell Ramsey had witnessed when Sophia Bear had told him that her son was going to be, okay. "There is much for you to learn, Jason. It will take time. Your father has always had strong feelings for your mother, and when he thought he had been responsible for her getting hurt, he was devastated. Tabitha knew that Rose and Frank would be a strong pair, and Tyrell knew that my son would one day be able to protect your mother. That terrible day they died, changed the timing but, not the final outcome. We are family!"

"R2," Jason started, but then paused. He waited a second before continuing, as if wanting to savor the next word that would come out of his mouth. "Dad, has told me very little about himself, but he talks all of the time about the Ramseys. I almost feel like I know them better than I do, him. All I know about the accident was that it happened during a terrible rainstorm on a mountain road that is hard to drive even in good weather. What were they doing out?"

"Tabitha had received a phone call from a family she had tried to help before. She told me before they left that the woman had said that it was an emergency. Tabitha was unable to turn down someone who needed help, even if it might mean danger to herself. Rose was the one who took the call when the highway patrol found them the next day."

Sophia's voice had trailed off, and Jason felt his eyes starting to burn. "I wish I could have known them. I am so sorry, Grandma Sophie, about the accident."

"If it was an accident," she said, barely audibly. Her voice had been so soft that Jason hadn't been sure that he had heard her correctly.

* * * * *

It was the first time since Jason had been conceived that Amber and Frank had sat together as a father and mother, worrying about the welfare of their son. More than once, Amber had checked to make sure that her car was still in the driveway, and Frank had repeatedly walked toward the kitchen door, before she would call him back.

Eventually, they sat across from each other at the breakfast bar and held hands, each praying and hoping inwardly.

"Would it be better if one or both of us went to look for him," Amber finally said aloud.

"We can't. He is an adult," Frank responded, not convincing himself.

Both snapped their attention quickly to the door when it opened softly and Sophia Bear walked in.

"Mom?" Frank asked, half fearing that something had happened to his son.

"Your son is waiting for both of you in the family room," she announced calmly through the ever-present smile.

They froze in place while gripping each other's hands more tightly.

"I really think you should go see him," she said, her smile broadening.

While trying to maintain some restraint, Amber and Frank walked excitedly to the family room. Upon opening the door, they immediately witnessed the mongrels, Takedown and Reverse, jumping happily on Jason as he sat on the floor with his legs crossed. Emotionally exhausted, but at peace, their son greeted them with, "I can't believe you kept my dogs locked up this entire afternoon."

The western sky glowed orange by the time that Frank and Amber entered the family room with Sophia Bear trailing a few steps behind. Frank had difficulty convincing himself that it had only been a day. He felt as if he had just relived the past eighteen years all over again. A quick glance at Amber let him know that she too was totally exhausted from the stress of releasing the secret she had carried since her son's conception. The confusion on Jason's face hadn't totally disappeared, but surprisingly he seemed to bear no bitterness. Only Sophia seemed to be completely at peace, as if she had just lived through another day.

It was she who had filled in many of the gaps for her grandson, and helped him to understand his parents' decision to withhold the truth for so long. As she had spoken and listened to him throughout the day, things that he had difficulty reconciling before, began to make sense. Merritt's parents had always doted on him, but he had still felt little connection to them. In truth, he never really liked R.T.'s mother or father. He had in the past reckoned that it was merely a generational difference. He hadn't felt close to his mother's parents either, but both of them had been in failing health for nearly as long as he could remember. He had never felt close to R.T. Merritt, but, *"Yea, the man I used to know as my father, is a rapist and general all-around jerk. What was there to love?"*

That was one of the thoughts that Sophia had helped Jason to begin to cope with during the afternoon. Although she had never been fully aware of Tyrell's concerns or of his conversations with Amber, she had known that he was working on a plan to have the truth come out so that Frank could claim Jason as his son without destroying Amber. In a tragically terrible irony, Tyrell and Tabitha had been traveling the mountain road on the night they died to see the mother of Bubba Raines. She had called Tabitha and said that her son had come to their home and told his father that he needed his help.

After Tabitha had calmed the distraught woman down enough for her to explain the situation, Mrs. Raines had ended with, "Mrs. Ramsey, Bubba's mean. My husband was afraid not to go, and they've been gone a long time."

Tyrell had long suspected that Bubba had something to do with the attack on Frank and hadn't hesitated to agree to check on the woman. "You can stay here, and I'll go," he had told his wife, but she had insisted that Mrs. Raines would need her comfort." Tyrell and Tabitha Ramsey had said nothing of this conversation to Sophia Bear, telling her only that they were going to help a friend. It was the last words she had exchanged with her adoptive family, and they had haunted her since that night.

She might never learn the answers to some of her questions about what had happened to the couple whom she loved so dearly, but she could help the loved ones standing in front her to heal. Frank and Amber had moved to either side of Jason, each of them petting and scratching an appreciative dog on the ears while looking down at their son. Takedown and Reverse felt none of the awkwardness experienced by their human loved ones. Nor did they hear the unspoken question that pervaded the room. *"What was R.T. Merritt going to do, once he found out the truth?"*

* * * * *

The revelation to Jason had gone better than either Amber or Frank had dared to hope for. Their son had actually seemed relieved as if he had been released from the lie as much as they. It would take time to grow this new relationship, but each was ready.

Frank called Rose and told her to come home the next day, two days earlier than had been planned. Her parents were disappointed, but Rose had promised to comeback soon. When the girls had asked why, Rose had explained by saying simply, "That big wus of a dad you have, misses us and wants us to come home."

Rose's four daughters noticed the car belonging to Amber Merritt as soon as they pulled into the driveway the next day. Casey and Tia raced to the house in order to get the first shot at their favorite athlete. Tia was intercepted by both dogs and Casey was already in a mock wrestling match with Jason by the time the remaining three females walked in the house. Rose raced to Amber and the two women nearly collided in an embrace. Both began crying happily and profusely. Emily and Jasmine stood back, giving each other a "that's weird," look.

The effervescent Rose then ran to Jason, nearly knocking Casey over, and began hugging and kissing him. Her stepson resisted only a few seconds before wrapping both arms around her and picking her up off the floor. Now, all four girls exchanged, "what's going on here," looks, before Tia, the youngest, took charge.

"Dad, would you mind telling your daughters why everyone is crying, and what have you done to our mother?"

Frank had never fully realized until that moment how much his loving wife had held her emotions back for his sake. *"Will there ever come a day when I give as much as I get?"*

He wiped the tears from his eyes, and looked around. Even his own normally calm mother was sobbing. Jason now stood between Amber and Rose, hugging them both.

"Well girls, I am glad you came home early, because I think that this might be another long day," was all he could manage to say without choking up.

CHAPTER 25

The Past – Road Rage

Ramsey sighed as he looked at the image staring back at him from the bathroom mirror. In just the last two years his hair had turned completely white and stood in stark contrast against his dark skin. His wife had told him that his colorless locks had made him look even more distinguished. *"No, Tab. Throw in the circles under my eyes, and they just make me look even older than I feel, which is pretty damn old."*

"So, how are we going to fix this, old man," he said to the image in the mirror. Jason was going to turn one in a few weeks, and Tyrell Ramsey was as proud as any grandfather could be of a grandson. Only, he was unable to tell anyone that the fair skinned infant was the child of the young man he had long considered to be his own son. Amber Merritt and her husband had finally filed for divorce on the grounds of irreconcilable differences.

"Amber has talked about moving with her parents to Florida. R.T. probably wouldn't fight it, but if she goes, that takes Jason away from Frank; and from me."

Tyrell's thoughts drifted back to Tabitha and the time she had first introduced him to the dirty but fearless little boy on the playground. *"My wife has always felt a need to salvage every sad case she comes across."* He laughed to himself. *"Starting with me."*

The brief moment of mirth quickly melted back into the stress that had been growing steadily since the day Frank had shared what had happened when he walked in on Amber and R.T. Two weeks later, Amber had learned that she was pregnant and only a short time after her baby was born, had it confirmed that Frank was the child's father. Before learning the news, Ramsey had been working on a plan to expose Merritt's brutal attack and bring him down. Learning that Amber was carrying Frank's child had not only complicated the issue, but placed people he dearly loved at risk. As long as Merritt believed that his criminal action had resulted in the conception of a child, he would be cautious.

Amber had been somewhat protected because Merritt's parents had wanted a grandchild so badly. As soon as any of them learned that Jason was Frank's child, Merritt would be able to deny the attack and accuse his wife of infidelity. Tyrell had kicked himself again and again for not being quicker thinking after he had discovered that Amber had been attacked. He had let the ridiculous rumors concerning him and Frank's mother cloud his judgement, and had been worried over what kind of trash Merritt might spread. He was a black man who had just walked in on a white woman who had been raped by her husband, but who would have believed him or her. She hadn't called in the attack immediately, and why would Merritt kick in the door to his own house? Merritt was the master at working the system.

In the face of all that was happening, the woman who he loved more than anything in life had taken on another hopeless cause; but this was a very dangerous one. Tabitha Ramsey had maintained contact with the parents of Bubba Raines, even after the ill-fated manipulation attempt by R.T. Merritt to have Tyrell take Bubba on as an apprentice. Tyrell was one of the few people who showed no fear of the violence prone hulk, and Bubba Raines hated him all the more for it. In spite of that, Tabitha still checked in on his parents, sometimes bringing them food or taking them to the doctor. Neither Mr. nor Mrs. Raines had been blessed with a great deal of intelligence or ambition, but, *they aren't bad people, and they don't ask for much,* "Tabitha had told Tyrell."

She had walked into his shop that morning and said, "I am going to see the Raines. Mrs. Raines called, worried about her husband."

"Is he ill," Tyrell had asked.

"No. His son picked him up last night. He said it was for a job, but Bubba never has anything to do with either of his parents. Her husband didn't come home last night."

"Tab, you can't go!"

"Tyrell, I am going. If you could have heard that poor woman crying on the phone –." Ramsey had held up his hands in surrender before she could finish the sentence.

He had known from the moment she had first opened her mouth that there was no point arguing, and he had also known that he was going with his wife to the decaying trailer the Raines called home. He could only hope that the old man would be there when they arrived or, at least that Bubba wouldn't show up while they were there. Before leaving the bathroom, he looked down and patted the rounding swell that had once been washboard abs. "Sophia sure *feeds me well*," he thought. The thought was subconscious acknowledgement that he might no longer have the physical ability to confront Bubba Raines.

Tabitha met him at the door and held his raincoat out to him. "We will need these. It's starting to come down pretty hard."

Tyrell made one last effort to dissuade his wife. "Tab, you stay here. Let me go by myself. I can help her."

Tabitha twisted her mouth into a smirk and shook her head. "You? My sweet, but clueless husband is going to comfort a distraught woman. Now, put your raincoat on, and let's go."

"*This isn't good*," he thought, before saying, "Well, you succeeded at last."

A quizzical look came over his wife's face. "Succeeded?"

"I think I am finally over myself," he said, referring to the comment she had made to him on their very first meeting.

She laughed with tears in her eyes and threw her arms around his neck. "And it was worth the effort. I love you!"

Huddling under an umbrella, they ran toward the car. What Tabitha hadn't heard on the phone, was the voice talking to Mrs. Raines after she had hung up. "I always knew you were a good mama," Raines mockingly cooed at his mother. "And, a smart one, too, ain't ya Mama?"

Sobbing uncontrollably in fear, Mrs. Raines had been unable to answer.

Bubba knelt in front of his mother, his face only inches from hers. The face staring up at her had once been an image of near perfection, but was now lined, scarred, and bloated. The cold soulless eyes were the same she had seen each time she had looked at him since he had been a child. "Mama, cat got ya tongue? You smart, ain't ya?"

The terrified woman had managed to nod her head and mutter something approaching, "yes" through her sobs. Without another word, Raines had stood and walked out of the trailer.

The winding road up the mountain to the home of Bubba's parents was difficult on a clear day. In the rain, it was treacherous. Blind switchbacks and occasional sharp downturns in the grade of the road, combined with poor maintenance and little signage had resulted in several fatal accidents over the years. All of the fatalities had been attributed to driving at unsafe speeds or driving under the influence. Tyrell wondered to himself if anyone had ever died from being stupid enough to drive the road during a rainstorm. *"No, just go slow. Pay attention. We'll be fine."*

Ramsey had taken the road many times over the years, and he knew it well. He really wasn't concerned with driving the road even in the rain except for one spot that was particularly tricky. After climbing for several hundred feet, a driver would find himself looking into nothing but sky before dropping drastically for another hundred feet. At the bottom of the drop, the road bent sharply the other direction. The inside of the bend was tree covered mountainside, the outside; a sheer cliff. *"The idiot who designed that must have been an out-of-work roller coaster engineer,"* he had often thought.

Tyrell felt it as soon as he topped the upgrade and started down the other side. The road was unusually slick. He took a deep breath and took his foot off the gas. Immediately, he looked for a spot to turn into the upward slope of the U, if he felt himself start to slide. Suddenly, a man stumbled from behind a tree as if he had been pushed. Tyrell had no choice. He turned away from the man, while tapping his breaks in hopes of staying on the road and missing the man. The car immediately started to spin. Ramsey tried to correct the spin, but there was no room on the narrow mountain road. The last thing he heard before going over the edge was the rear of his car thudding against Bubba Raines' father. Mr. Raines got hooked in the bumper and was taken off the cliff with Tyrell and Tabitha.

It was still raining heavily, but Raines couldn't resist climbing down to inspect his work. Decades earlier, Ramsey had kept him from finishing his work on Frank Bear. Now, he had finally been able to enact his revenge. The first thing he saw was his father's mangled body partially laying partially under the car. *"Nobody will miss him."* He could tell from standing by the driver side door that Ramsey's seatbelt had done him no good. The steering column had been driven through his chest, killing him instantly.

"Damn! I wish he could have suffered a little more." After taking a few seconds to admire the sight, he stooped to see how Tabitha had died. To his surprise, her eyes were open, and she motioned weakly for him to come closer.

"Sheeeut! This otta be good. The bitch wants to beg for mercy," he said out loud to the trees, before walking to the other side of the car. The impact had popped the door partially open. Raines jerked it the rest of the way back, leaned in toward Tabitha, and placed a hand heavily on her shoulder. "Yea, sweetheart, is there something you wanted to tell this pitiful little mix-breed boy?"

She motioned weakly for him to come closer, and he leaned in with his ear next to her lips. She spoke, and with what strength she had left, took his hand in hers. Raines jerked away from the dying woman and acted as if she had bitten him. Although too weak to speak, she mouthed the words again. Raines screamed and twisted Tabitha's head so forcefully that it lay on her chest, grotesquely looking up at the ceiling of the car.

The wreck was discovered the next day. No one knew why the Ramseys had attempted to travel the mountain road in the storm. All Tabitha had told Sophia was that they were going to check on a friend. The blood alcohol level in the deceased man's body pinned under the wreckage had told the story of what happened on that tragic night. Obviously, he had stumbled drunkenly in front of the Ramsey's car at a spot where it would have been impossible for them to miss him. Bubba's mother died alone in her derelict trailer a few weeks later. Coroners were unsure whether to list starvation, exposure to the weather, or lack of necessary medicine as the cause. The official cause of death was eventually listed simply as natural causes.

* * * * *

Many of the members of the Red Elk extended family came to the farmhouse north of Beaumont in the days following Tabitha's death. Some slept in the shop, and others brought small campers. They had grown up accustomed to tight conditions, but more importantly, to supporting each other. Frank's sister took a leave of absence from the university and came home immediately. Amber brought her baby to the house, and Sophia asked her to stay a few days, saying that they could share her room.

Tabitha's niece, Rose, was there. Sophia and her family weren't related to Tabitha or Tyrell, and the highway patrol had called her to inform her of the accident. Tabitha had introduced her to Frank a few weeks after the attack on Amber. The pair had quickly fallen into a comfortable friendship. She was the only girl his age outside of his sisters that Frank hadn't felt awkward being around. Unknown to him at the time, Tabitha had told Rose that Jason was his son, before she had introduced her niece to him. Both Rose and Frank were very special to her, and she felt she knew when two people were right for each other. Had she lived, Tabitha would have eventually told Frank that she had shared his secret with one very special person.

The memorial service was a private affair attended only by the Red Elk and Bear families, along with Amber Merritt and her infant son. Tyrell had no living relatives. It had been expressed by Tabitha to her family that she wanted a natural burial. Tyrell had never expressed any preferences to anyone, so the pair were wrapped in linens and buried under a tree very near the spot that Jason Merritt would scream in anguish nearly eighteen years later.

That evening, Frank and his siblings, Sophia Bear, and Rose sat around the kitchen table. A feeling of loss and emptiness pervaded the room. The stoic Bear family had shed few tears, but each was feeling the deep pain of losing two loved ones who had meant so much to their lives. No one spoke.

It was Frank's sister, Emily who finally broke the silence. They were barely ten months apart in age. Like Frank, she was extremely intelligent and an outstanding athlete. She was attending college on dual academic and athletic scholarships. She had always been the most focused of the Bear children and was very close to her older brother.

"What about, "Ramsey and Son Plumbing," she asked flatly.

"Are you kidding, sis? Now?" Tunner Bear was the only openly emotional member of the family, and his siblings had openly teased him while growing up for being an odd Bear.

"No, she's right," Frank said absently. He could feel the weight of what might happen to them all, squeezing on his chest. It felt like his lungs might collapse. "We have college expenses, upkeep on this place, a lot of things. We have figure out what to do, and I don't see any way to keep going without keeping the business running."

Silence again filled the room as each of the siblings looked at each other. Frank spoke again. "We may need to think about changing the name of the company."

"NO!" The explosive response came in unison from every person sitting at the table including Sophia and Rose. It was the first time either had spoken.

Rose jumped into the conversation. She didn't share the stoicism of the Bear family, and it was obvious that she was struggling to keep her emotions in check. Still, she had an aura about her that inspired confidence even in the worst of times. It was a trait she had shared with her aunt. "First of all, thank you for including me. I have known you for such a short time. Tabitha was in love with all of you."

Rose had to stop for a few moments to gain her composure. "She called me a lot when I was a kid, and she always talked about this wonderful family that God had brought into her and Tyrell's lives."

She stopped again and took a deep breath. "Anyway, I am just trying to tell you that I know my aunt, and I know Tyrell. Both of them worked very hard to earn respect for this family, and for my family, the Red Elks. We all owe them, and we need to build this business to respect what they have done for us. We cannot allow others to destroy what they have built."

"Finally!" Lisa said, with an emphasis that surprised even her. She was the planner of the family and hated indecision. "We have someone at this table who knows how to talk sense."

Sophia spoke almost as if to herself. All eyes turned her way. She had always been revered as their protector, and, aside from Frank, she had been the closest to Tyrell and Tabitha. Her voice was soft, as always. "I don't know how, but I think that Tabitha knew that she and Tyrell weren't coming home when they left that night. Tabitha always told me where she was going, but that night she just said that she and Tyrell were going to visit someone in trouble. She hugged me before she left and said that she was so proud of us all. We must honor their love for us by growing Ramsey and Son Plumbing."

Everyone at the table looked at Frank. It took him a few moments to realize that he had been thrust into the role of head of family. He felt slightly dizzy. *"OK, hypocrite. You wanted to take care of your family the way they have always taken care of you. Now is your chance. Step up."*

Suddenly the image of a young Tyrell Ramsey leaning against a truck and holding out a standardized pricing sheet to a bigoted old man sprang into his mind's eye. Any doubt or fear he may have had, left him at that moment. It was now time for him to take the lead. He spoke as the patriarch of his family.

"Just about everyone in Dugganville has already assumed that we will be going out of business. At least one of them and a few of his cronies are getting drunk in celebration of that event while I am talking to you." No one interrupted to ask who. They all knew.

"That is not going to happen. Three years ago, I was attacked from behind by a coward. Everyone thought I would die, but no one in this family would let me give up, and we aren't going to give up, now. A lot of people don't think we deserve this big ol' house or all of this land. They think it's charity for a bunch of lazy Indians. They think our mother had five kids to collect more welfare. I can guarantee you that once those people got over their grand sense of altruism for helping out the poor Indian kid, they started bitching about all of the free handouts we were getting.

No one remembers that, even with my injuries, only one person in my class had a higher GPA than me, and that was my little sister. No one cares that she is now among the top in her college class and majoring in business administration. She is an Indian, so she had to have it handed to her. No matter how much Lisa and Janie accomplish, a lot of folks in this town will always see it as being handed to them because they are poor lazy Indians."

"And Tunner," Frank lowered his head and shook it slightly before continuing. "I get it. You know more about technology than most of the people in this town, and school just isn't your thing. But, if you were going to do the homework for half the white girls in your class, you could have at least tried to do some of your own." Tunner looked away and his younger sister, Janie, gave him a slap on the arm with a little too much force to be considered playful.

"My point is this. People around here think that we are too young, too lazy, and too Indian to be successful. And because they think that, is exactly the reason that we are going to become the largest home services company in Dugganville and the surrounding area. It was only two years ago that we hired our first two trainees. Now, we have ten. People think Tyrell put that in place. I started that effort, and Emily and I have been managing it. I say Emily and I. Lisa has been handling the scheduling and new accounts. Tunner set us up in our business software, and Janie, you came up with the plan to include HVAC. We were going to – "He paused for effect and then continued more forcefully. "No, we are going to start that this year! Imagine that; a bunch of lazy Indian kids, running a successful company while they are still in school.

We may mourn, be we don't have the luxury to mourn idly. My guess is that we have already lost a few accounts just because people assume we will be closing shop. As soon as we get up in the morning, all of us have to get on the phone. Before that, Tunner, you and Janie have a job. Put together a message for every client and supplier we currently have and assure them that Ramsey and Son will continue to offer the best service in the area.

Frank continued. "I know the technical side, and I have a pretty good handle on the personnel we are going to need if we plan to expand out of this area. Emily, you are almost done with school, and I know that you are itching to exercise those business chops. Start working on our new business model."

He looked at his second sister. She shared his passion for American government and was close to finishing a degree in political science. She was also seriously dating a local farmer. "Lisa, are you still planning on going to law school?"

"Absolutely! Somebody is going to have keep *Ramsey and Son,* and my little brother out of trouble."

"Mom, I need some help, here." Sophia merely smiled at her younger son's mock distress. Inwardly, she was grateful that her children could keep their playful relationship, even in the face of tragedy.

"I was hoping you would say that, Lisa. I think we were all a little worried that we might lose you to the farm."

"No way. If I let Stuart stick around, he is going to have to learn how to use a pipe wrench."

Next, Frank turned to his little brother. "Tunner, we need you! You know social media and tech better than anyone of us. In current reality, you may be the difference between Ramsey and Son, succeeding or falling flat."

Tunner had never liked responsibility and found himself squirming under the heat of everyone else's glare. After a few uncomfortable seconds, "Got it! C'mon Bro. I may not be a stud athlete or an academic nerd like the rest of you guys, but I am still my mama's baby boy. Ramsey and Son Plumbing is going to have the rockinest tech on the planet!"

Everyone laughed, and the youngest sibling, Janie, stood behind Tunner and put him in a headlock. "Thank you, Janie," Frank continued. "You have just demonstrated one of the two primary functions you will add to our company. First of all, you are the only person in this family that our brother is afraid of. Keep him in line. Secondly, and almost as important, you are the one who is constantly looking for new ways to open a cereal box. We have to stay innovative if we are going to compete. You will be our director of innovation."

"Already on it, big brother. Emily, you need to include corporate accounts in our business model. There are a lot of new start-ups coming into this town, and we can clean up, if we get in early on that market."

Janie felt the smiles of her siblings as they looked on her in slight amazement at how quickly she had already come up with an idea. "What can I say? Innovation is what I do."

Finally, Frank turned to Rose. "If we are going to expand, our best chance is to go south first, because that is the area of greatest need."

Rose stopped him by holding up an open palm. "Okay Bear, you don't have to say anything else. If you need a workforce, the Red Elks are in, and as you were about to say, there are a lot of us."

The evening, although a time of great sadness, had been good for the entire family. It had helped them to move forward. One by one, each member of the family migrated to bed until Rose and Frank sat alone at the table.

"I am proud of you Bear," Rose began, but was quickly interrupted by Frank.

"Rose, I know that I have never told you this. I am very proud of my family, but I really don't like being called Bear. The man who wrote his name on my birth certificate is not a good man. He hurt my mother. I had hoped that she might change our names to her birth name, but she refuses. She says that a strong name can't be ruined by one man, but I still don't like it."

"Frank Bear! We have known each other for two years, and this is the first time I have to admit that I am a little disappointed. Your mom is right. A name doesn't bring a person honor or dishonor. That responsibility belongs to the holder of the name."

Frank tried to maintain a neutral expression as he looked at Rose, but he finally shut his eyes and the unmistakable glisten of a tear slid down his cheek. "I know," he said, keeping his eyes closed. "I also know that Tabitha put you and me together. I don't want you to be ashamed of me, but I can't blame my actions on the man whose name I share."

"BEAR!" The forcefulness of Rose's interruption caused Frank to sit board straight and stare at the woman across the table from him. "I know that Jason is your son. You are about to take charge of a family and they need you very much. It is time for you to quit living in your own little world. I was about to say before you interrupted me so rudely, that I am proud of you for the love and responsibility you showed for your family tonight. I would very much like to be a part of that family, and yes, I will marry you; IF, you understand that you cannot do this by yourself. You need me!"

"You know about, Jason?"

"Yes, I've known everything about you since you first met my aunt."

"She knows?" For two years, Frank had felt his feelings growing for Rose. He had wanted more from their relationship, but had always feared that she would reject him if she knew the truth. In his own mind, what had happened was unforgiveable. He felt himself getting lightheaded.

"Well?"

Frank startled, "Well, what?"

"I've said, yes. It might be a good idea if you asked me."

Realization finally sparked for the befuddled young man. He pushed away from the table and nearly fell as he turned to walk around it to Rose. A bowl of apples sat at the end of the breakfast bar. He grabbed the bowl as he made the turn and limped with his awkward gait toward the woman with whom he would spend the rest of his life. Holding the bowl awkwardly in one arm, he used his free arm to brace himself against the table and slowly lowered to one knee. He then took the bowl in both hands, held it up to her and asked sincerely, with no humor intended. "Rose Red Elk, will you marry me?"

Rose laughed out loud through her tears. "I already said yes, you wus. The one thing my aunt never told me about the man she set me up with, was that he is an incurable romantic – and so smooth."

C𝐻𝐴𝑃𝑇𝐸𝑅 26

The Present – A New Family,
A New Danger

The people sitting around Frank and Rose Bears' table looked much the same as the group that had met twenty years prior, following the deaths of Tyrell and Tabitha Ramsey. The family members had kept the table as their center of operations even after becoming the largest plumbing and air conditioning business across a two-state area. The size of the family business meeting had grown over the years and now included a gathering of children playing in the family room or on the grounds. Every person in the room, save two, were still under the age of 40.

Frank's oldest sister, Emily, had married a banker and they had two children, a boy and a girl. Her husband handled the business accounts for the company. Lisa married the farmer she had been dating at the time of the Ramseys' death. He didn't play an active role in the business, but had proven to be a positive contributor during the meetings. Tunner had never shown an interest in marriage, but his current relationship with Sylvia Batten, a college professor, was his longest and most serious. Janie had never married, but had twin sons from a relationship with a Chinese graduate student she had while in college. When he had asked her to return to China with him, she had refused to leave her family. He hadn't fought to take

216

the boys with him. Much to Tunner's dismay, his young nephews adored him.

As she had at every meeting, Sophia sat next to Frank. She said very little, but her presence was still felt as the cohesive force for the family. Attending the meeting for the first time was Amber Merritt. She had been in the house during the fateful meeting following the Ramsey's deaths, but had been in Sophia's room with Jason, while the Bear family had discussed their future. She sat next to Rose Bear. The two women held hands and leaned into each other in a nonverbal display of sisterhood.

Frank had invited Jason to attend, saying that he had a right to be there.

"No, Dad, Tia and I need talk to my cousins. I may be a lot older, but I want the chance to be a part of them." Jason was more surprised than Frank that the word, Dad, had flowed out so naturally. It seemed as if he was finally directing the term to the right person, and it felt good. Tia, after getting over her initial shock, had been the most enthusiastic about welcoming Jason into the family, because, "having Jason for a brother is way cooler than having him for a boyfriend!"

Of the adults, it was Emily who had been the most uncomfortable with the news that the blond headed boy she had known for his entire life was her nephew. She also had been in a class taught by Ms. Merritt and had adored the teacher almost as much as had her brother. Only a year apart, they had gone through school together, because he had started school a year late. Although attractive, intelligent, and athletic, she had never been popular in school. Any boys that may have wanted to ask the pretty girl out were discouraged by the unfounded rumors surrounding her dangerous looking brother.

She may have also been stuck in unchallenging classes if Amber Merritt hadn't taken an interest in the entire family. Although sometimes teasing her brother about his crush on the teacher, she had always seen Ms. Merritt through the same lens of perfection as had he. Now, looking across at the woman, trembling slightly and leaning into her sister-in-law, Emily was only now witnessing the frailness that Frank had first seen almost two decades before. This was the first time she had seen her high school teacher since Rose had broken the news to each of them by phone. She wrapped her arm around her husband's, grateful for the gentle man she had met in college.

Aside from the presence of Amber Merritt and the obvious reason for which the meeting had been called, the rest of the participants seemed to be in standard Bear Clan mode. Sophia hopped up whenever she sensed that someone might need a snack or something to drink. Each time she did the monster sized mutts, Takedown and Reverse, rose with her hoping she might get something for them also. Lisa and her husband, Stuart, talked with each other and other members of the family. Janie antagonized Tunner. It had been her role since they were small children. He loved it.

"Hey big brother, is that some muscle tone I'm seeing in those arms? I guess that pretty white lady professor has you working out. Your nephews thought she was really cool, the one time you brought her to my house. When are you going to make her a part of this group?"

"Bite me, Sis!" He answered, somewhere between irritation and laughter. "I told you; we aren't serious."

"Oh, yea. Not serious. I saw the book on indigenous cultures in your car, and my poor boys think that Uncle Tunner doesn't love them anymore, because he never comes around."

"That's because I'm afraid they will tie me to the stake," he growled.

"Hey big brother. The twins are in middle school now. Admit it. You're just afraid that you can't beat them in video games anymore."

As nervous as she was, Amber couldn't help but smile at the banter. It reminded her of the relationship she had with her father before his memory was slowly eaten away and before R.T. Merritt had robbed her of most of the joy in her life. She was brought quickly to the present by the sound of Frank's voice.

"Thanks everybody for coming on short notice, and thank you for clearing your calendars so you can stay a few days. Obviously, there is a lot you don't know about what happened twenty years ago. There are things I still don't understand. Tyrell died before he had a chance to explain it all to me. Amber and I are going to tell you about the events that led to us conceiving our son, Jason. Rose has always known. Tabitha told her about it, before she ever introduced us."

"Amber and I both have one request. Please don't refer to her as Ms. Merritt. She only kept that name after the divorce, because of the very complicated situation. It will be a while before we can make this all public, but as soon as we do, she is changing her name back to Bronson. In fact, she will be Dr. Amber Bronson, since she has just completed her PhD in spite of all the road blocks put in her way by R.T. Merritt. Jason has already told us that he wants to be known as Jason Bear. Since we can prove that he is my son, we can legally have his birth certificate changed."

Frank hesitated, not knowing what to say next, and a few awkward congratulations for Amber could be heard around the room. An even more awkward silence started to grow in the room until, "Amber, you and Jason are our family."

Sophia had been standing in the kitchen. Everyone looked at her as she walked to the table and sat down and started speaking in her calm quiet voice. "Tyrell and Tabitha were our family. They were my brother and sister, like you are all brothers and sisters. They tried to keep me from worrying about the bad things that were happening, but a mother knows when her children are in danger. As Frank has said, there are things we will never know, because my brother and sister were taken from us too soon. I know more than either your brother or your new sister, however, and I will tell you what I know."

With that introduction, Sophia began retelling the events of the past in remarkable detail. Frank and Amber found themselves looking at each other in awe. His mother knew about the years of emotional abuse Amber had suffered from her then husband, and she knew of Amber's visit to Tyrell after the attack on Frank. Frank looked at Amber in a mixture of questioning and confusion. He hadn't known of the visit. Amber nodded back slightly and dipped her head to one side as if to say, *"I have no idea how she knew."*

Sophia concluded with, "When Tyrell and Tabitha died, Tyrell was trying get help from a friend he had met in college. I don't know his name. The friend was in state government and knew Robert Merritt. The web of deceit in Dugganville is very old and very tightly woven, but Tyrell was trying to get information that would expose the Merritt family and others for their crimes. He had wanted to tell the world that he had a grandson and hoped the information would keep the Merritts from doing anything bad to Amber or any of us."

The word, grandson, hit Frank hard. There was no blood test, name change, or adoption paper that could make him feel any stronger about Tyrell Ramsey being his true father. Before that moment, he had never considered the pain the man he considered to be his dad must have been in, because he couldn't hold his grandson. Their oldest brother then did something none of his family had ever witnessed. The stoic Frank Bear bowed his head and cried, openly.

Rose started to stand and go to her husband, but Sophia raised her hand, indicating that she should sit back down. Rose sat and the family waited silently for Frank to regain his composure. After a few moments, they looked on as a huge sigh escaped his chest and he raised his head. Looking back at them was an older, sadder, wiser, and stronger, Franklin Bear.

"Amber, will you ask our son to come in. He should be a part of this."

Chapter 27

The Present – Unsettled Scores

No human culture or creed is exempt from the sin of greed. No one knew that better than Bubba Raines, and he used it. He had never given a shit about the money, but he knew that when people owed him, they feared him. Fear had always been his capital. He worked in the shadows, and just about everyone in the area with any money, whether it be the old elite or the new transient rich, owed him.

On this day, he stood outside of his dirty little hovel chopping firewood. The stack already stood higher than the house, but he continued to chop. Raines had never been lazy, and that was one of the many things that made him dangerous. A potential client or victim never knew when he might show up, but the where would always be in the shadows and on his terms.

A drop of sweat from his scarred brow fell into his eye and he cursed the sting. He considered the scar as a trophy, even if it had earned him extra time in prison for a courtyard brawl. *"That sum bitch ain't gonna cut nobody else with that hand,"* he liked to tell himself each time he ran his hand over the jagged line running down his face.

Not unlike many people, Bubba's mind frequently jumped back to events of the past, but Bubba's thoughts were never joyful or sad. They dealt only with scores settled and those to be repaid. For the most part, he could return those thoughts to the repaid file, as he did each time that he touched the white scar running down his brown face. When he couldn't, he cut wood. On this morning, the bloody image of Tabitha Ramsey had ruthlessly invaded his thoughts of the past.

WHACK, "I hate you, bitch!"

CHOP, "Die, whore!"

CRACK, "Look at your dead husband!"

He chopped, cursed, and chopped again, until exhaustion set in and he fell to his knees. In the end, his desire for revenge would be unmet, and all he had to show for his efforts was a larger pile of wood. Ironically, the woman he hated so badly had been indirectly responsible for warming his filthy hut over the course of many winters.

He had to get her out of his head, and the only way to do that was to intimidate someone else. You can't scare the dead. To calm himself, he walked to his road grader. After wiping the seats, he carefully checked all of the fluid levels. It was the only material thing he had ever cared about, and it had always responded to his every wish. As he worked, he thought.

"That damn R.T. is up to somethin. Their ain't nuthin up there worth makin a road for, an he's scared. I could go see that little weasel of a cousin of mine. He might know. Aw, shit!"

Raines looked back toward the axe buried in a stump as the second unsettled score of the morning popped into his head. *"Damn it! This is gonna be a bad day!"*

Bubba had been released from prison at the age of twenty-six after having served seven years for manslaughter. Sam and Bertha Floyd had been distant relatives of Raines. It had been Sam Floyd's testimony that had sent him there, and he had vowed to pay the old man back. Both of the Floyds died of old age before Raines could honor that vow. Making the bile particularly bitter was the image of Tyrell Ramsey sitting in court with Bertha Floyd and his then four-year-old cousin, Albert, while the old man testified that he had witnessed Bubba brutally beating a man to death while the victim was pleading for mercy. Ramsey had kept his gaze locked on Bubba throughout the trial to ensure that he made no attempt to intimidate either the old woman or her young grandson. It was the first time in his life that Raines had himself felt intimidated.

The public defender had been successful in getting the judge to sentence Raines for the lesser charge of manslaughter over murder. He had argued that the Floyd family had a long running feud with that of the Raines, and that had tainted the old man's testimony. No one could prove that Bubba had intentionally killed the man. As instructed by his lawyer, Raines had kept his mouth shut throughout the trial, even though thinking, *"Like hell, I didn't mean to kill him."*

Bubba walked toward the axe, but looked at the wood pile hiding the side of the house and decided, *"Forget it. It's time to settle some scores. I'm tired of choppin wood."*

* * * *

"Hey cousin, Albert," Bubba said in a low drawl while making a weak attempt at a friendly face as he walked toward the slightly built man standing at the entrance of the Beaumont Recreation Center. Raines was incapable of projecting goodwill, even falsely.

"Whadda ya want, Bubba?"

"What makes ya think I want sumthin?"

"Cause ya never called me cousin. Hell, ya never called me Albert. State what ya got in mind. I'm busy."

"Why you cantankerous little shit. I just thought you might know what's goin on up on the mountain."

"Don't know, Don't care. Ain't none of my business. Now mind, yores."

Bubba wanted to charge the little man and stomp him until his guts spilled on the ground, but he saw the host of little faces and those of their adult counselors looking from the plate glass windows at the front of the rec center. He couldn't even subtly hint at a threat to his cousin without possibly being arrested.

"Alright, cousin. I'll be seein ya."

Bubba turned and walked away. Inwardly, he cursed himself for being stupid enough to approach Floyd in such a public place. Allowing his temper to go explosive in a public place was what had landed him in prison the first time. It had been the testimony of his dipshit cousin's grandfather that had sent him there. He was still on parole, and it was public knowledge that he had threatened the Floyd family for being responsible for his imprisonment. *"You won't always be surrounded by snot faced kids, cousin. I'll get my chance."*

The only person more dangerous to his freedom than Albert Floyd, was R.T. Merritt. All he had to do to keep Floyd from sending him back to prison was not be seen around him in public and he had blown it. Merritt, however, knew things about him that no one else knew. Bubba knew that he had long played a dangerous game with the smooth-talking con man. No one doubted that when Raines made a threat, he had the will and the means to carry it out, and that was the problem. Bubba had never learned the art of a bluff or the rules of high stakes poker. R.T. Merritt was a master of the game.

After leaving the recreation center, he drove to the trailhead at the base of the Twin Sisters Hills and got out of his truck, an old ford. He stood at the sight where Frank Bear had stood only a few days before, but a small pavilion and a new map of the trail had been erected since then. *"What a waste of firewood,"* he thought before stepping into the pavilion and studying the map. After muttering a few profanities about the stupidity of townspeople, he started walking the lower half of the trail. Albert and his team of kids had taken great care to cut the trail through places of interest and beauty on the hills, but Bubba cared nothing for that. After the first few turns, *"screw this."* He left the trail and tromped through the brush to the point where the trail turned back to the pavilion. Scratching his head, he looked up the slope of the mountain where Merritt had paid him to bulldoze a road.

From the same point where Frank Bear had viewed the mountain earlier, he could see the clearing and the road that led to it. *"Don't make no sense. That clearing ain't big nuff to do jack shit."* There were times when Bubba hated himself as much as he hated everyone else. He hated it anytime someone made him feel stupid, and now he felt stupid. *"Powerlines. Merritt said he was going to run a lot of power to the flat where I cleared the trees. What could those be for?"*

Raines decided to make his second visit to foreign territory in a day. After nearly causing a scene at the recreation center, the big man cautioned himself to stay calm when he went to the Dugganville library. While incarcerated, he had learned how to use a computer as a part of the prison's vocational education program. He hadn't seen any use in learning the skill, because the rudimentary electricity coming from the single line he had illegally run to his shack would have been insufficient to power anything beyond a few lights and a small refrigerator. He took the program anyway to have something to do, and had gone to the library a few times after getting out. It hadn't taken many trips to Dugganville for him to decide, *"this bullshit gets me nuthin."*

Now he needed information, and the only way he could think to find it was by using the library's computers. His card had expired long ago, *"but hell, they ain't gonna forgit my face."*

Two hours later, the Dugganville librarian's heart sank when he looked up from his desk and saw Bubba lumbering through the front door. He did indeed remember the profane foul-smelling behemoth. "Hello Mr. Raines, it has been a while," he said while trying to remain as professionally courteous as possible.

Bubba immediately felt as if the man was talking down to him. An ever-present problem with living a life intimidating others is that one finds one's own self constantly in a state of paranoia. "So what?"

"Uh, nothing, sir. How can I help you?"

To himself, *"Stupid, stupid, stupid. Play their game, get what you need, and get out of here."*

To the librarian, "I need to use one of your computers."

"Certainly, Mr. Raines, but your card has expired. It's free, but you will need to fill out an application for a new one."

Bubba sighed, barely able to contain his anger driven impatience, but managed to say calmly, "I only need to use it one time. I won't be back."

The librarian started to cite the library's no exceptions policy, but made an immediate administrative decision that an exception could be made in this instance.

"Yes sir, I understand. We have an open carrel in the back corner of the library."

Bubba struggled to ask the next question. He had neither the vocabulary nor the mindset to ask for help. "ahhmm, it's been a while. Could someone help me look up some information?"

At this point, the librarian was willing to do about anything to get the odiferous man away from his desk. "Yes. Ms. Hightower," he said to a young college intern walking past. "Could you help Mr. Raines with a computer search?"

The attractive young woman paused only momentarily before saying, "why certainly, Mr. Raines. I would love too." The student's temporary loss of composure had been barely perceptible before she motioned for the revolting creature to follow her to the computer carrel. He sat at the computer. She stood as far as possible from Raines while still being able to see the computer.

"I need information on the slut and her bastards." Using offensive language to purposefully intimidate women was a habit that Raines had found impossible to break.

"Excuse me?" The intern wanted to turn and run.

"Ahhh damn," he mumbled under his breath. "Sorry, It's a local term. I mean that I need to look up any recent news about Twin Sisters Mountain."

In spite of her revulsion, she suddenly felt a sense of compassion for the man sitting befuddled in front of the computer. The intern could never have known that, had she seen Bubba before he went to prison, all he would have had to do is smile and scoot over, and she would have happily slid in beside him. She would have been met with the same angry glare as had been many hopeful young women, before they scurried away in fear. Raines was asexual, and beyond that, couldn't stand to be touched by another human being. Now, his mechanical attempt at apologetic pleasantries elicited only pity. Bubba felt the change of attitude from the intern, and it made him hate her and himself all the more. "I have heard my father talk about the Merritt family mining bit coin in that area," he heard her say.

"Mining what?" the scowl on his face portrayed a mixture of anger and confusion.

The intern took a couple of nervous steps backward. "I don't know much about cryptomining, except that it uses really powerful computers, needs a lot of energy to run, and is supposedly very noisy. I can help you pull up some information on the computer, if you would like."

"That worthless bastard is running a scam and cutting me out of it." He seethed inwardly.

Bubba stood quickly, nearly knocking the chair and the intern over at the same time. He glared at her before turning and walking toward the front entrance, mumbling the whole way. She hadn't understood what he'd said, but was certain that his comments were vulgar and directed toward her.

* * * * *

Merritt looked down at the caller ID on his vibrating phone. *"Damn, why can't that old man learn how to text?"* "Yea, what's up?"

"I just thought you might like to know that Bubba was seen at the library," Merritt senior answered.

"That Cretin? What's he doing at the library? I'm not even sure Bubba can read."

"Well, apparently he went there to look up information on your little mining operation."

"There he goes again," Merritt thought, *"I'm pretty sure that when this goes through, he is going to want his share of the profits from my mining operation."*

"How do you know that?"

"Bob Hightower called me. His daughter was an intern there until this afternoon. She told her dad that the smelliest ugliest man she had ever seen came in needing help on the computer. When she asked what he needed, he said he was looking for information on what was happening up on the twin sisters; using Bubba's highly colorful language of course."

"yea, it sounds a little like yours, Dad." Merrit thought to himself

"Hightower's daughter was getting nauseated just from Bubba's smell, but she still tried to help him. Instead of helping him use the computer, she just told him what she knew, which is pretty much what anyone could find out if they picked up a newspaper. Bubba took off like a rocket. I think they are still trying to fumigate the place. Hightower's daughter was so upset that she went home and told her parents that she was quitting her internship and changing her major. Bob's pretty protective of his little girl, and he's asking me what you are going to do."

A long silence came over the phone before Merritt senior finally asked, "You still there?"

"I'm still here, Daddy" he said sarcastically. Thank you for sharing that very interesting information. For now, just let Mr. Hightower know that I am also concerned about Bubba Raines. I will get back to you later."

Merritt hung up, leaving his father feeling confused and increasingly uneasy about the events unfolding around him. The rift between him and his son was growing ever wider, but that didn't mean that he should keep him in the dark. *Junior's going to get us both killed, if he isn't careful."*

* * * * *

Bubba drove straight back to his shack. The name Hightower had immediately registered with him when he heard the librarian call the intern's name, and she had said that her father had told her that Merritt had something going on, at the mountain. The pieces of his memory started to fall into place as he drove. It had been a long time, but he had done work for Hightower before, and he remembered that the farmer and Merritt had occasional business dealings.

He had also kept a detailed log of every illegal deal he had ever made since leaving his parents' home at the age of twelve. The only gap in the log came during the time he had been in prison. Every neatly handwritten entry included who, what, where, when, and how much. He had never cared about the why. The logbook was Bubba's version of a trophy, but also his insurance that, if he went to jail, someone else was going with him.

Raines walked past the shack and to an earthen cellar in the back. He pulled open the counterweighted door and walked down steps. The inside of the cellar was surprisingly dry and smelled better than his house. The ceiling was low and he had to stoop slightly to walk to a canvas, draped over something in the back. Bubba pulled off the canvas and revealed the second aberration to his filthy lifestyle. As with the road grader, the safe in front of him and the contents within it had been meticulously cared for. Bubba took great pride in anything he felt gave him power over those who looked down on him. Inside the large safe were four clean and well oiled, but illegally owned guns; an AR17, Vietnam era M16, Glock 19 and a double-barrel twelve-gauge shotgun. The barrels had been sawn off just a few inches beyond the stock. Neat stacks of cash arranged according to denomination took up most of the room on the shelves in the safe. He had rarely needed to spend any of his trophy money. On the top shelf, in the upper right-hand corner sat two large three-ring binders containing a collection of spiral notebooks. He had started the first notebook, shortly after being released from prison. After having quickly amassed enough business to fill it, he began the practice of placing the completed notebooks in binders. He took the newest from its binder and turned immediately to the page he remembered.

johnson	barel dump	Bomont lake	6/22	$1,000
merit	fince line	bomont rek	6/30	$1,500
hitower	lost cows	H ranch	7/1	$3,000
merit	trees	Bomont rek	7/10	$1,000

The records were a combination of orderliness, poor spelling, and Bubba's shorthand. The transactions between Johnson and Hightower so close together had given him one of his few moments of merriment. The two men hated each other.

Johnson had been one of the first transients to move into Dugganville who had been rude enough not to leave. He was a member of one of the prominent hunting clubs in the area and owned large tracts of land to the north of the Twin Sisters. He had pushed hard for the reintroduction of wolves into the area, arguing that they had been a part of the natural ecosystem. He also wanted their population to grow to the point where they could be legally hunted, although he had never argued that point publicly.

His stance on introducing the wolves as well those he had pushed on other ecological issues had set him immediately at odds with Hightower, a multigenerational rancher and farmer whose landholdings butted up against those of Johnson in many places. Johnson frequently complained that Hightower's farm chemicals were harming wildlife, while the farmer argued that the reintroduction of wolves would eventually destroy his livelihood.

Bubba looked at the ledger and laughed to himself. *"And those arrogant pricks think I'm stupid."* Bubba never asked why he did a job as long as he got paid, but he always knew. The fence line for Merritt had taken him close to a week working a few hours each night. Merritt wanted to reclaim some of the land he had supposedly donated to the Beaumont community center. Immediately after the land had been surveyed, Raines went out and quietly moved survey stakes. The other job had taken him only a couple of hours. Merritt didn't like some of the trees that sat on a portion of the donated land that he intended to eventually reclaim. "Dose them with a slow acting poison, something that will look like a fungus," Bubba remembered Merritt telling him.

"Stupid white people," Raines thought while looking at the jobs for Hightower and Johnson. The rancher had paid him to kill a couple of his own cows and make it looked like they had been killed by wolves. The hunter had paid him to poison one of the streams that ran onto his land from Hightower's ranch with agricultural waste.

Raines looked at the ledger for a few moments and then flipped to the last page. He growled at the X's indicating that the job hadn't been completed.

Merit   rode   mountin   XXX   XXX

"Those two stupid white boys would have to agree for a road to come across their land if a road up on that mountin is goin to be good for anything. The only way they would agree to that is if they both stood to make a lot of money. I think it it's time I paid a visit to Mr. high and mighty Merritt."

Chapter 28

The Present – Boundaries

Albert Floyed smiled broadly when he saw Frank, Lisa and Tunner walk into the Foyer of the community center. "Hi y'all! It's about time that Frank brought some of the good-lookin' members of his family with him."

Tunner shook his hand, and Lisa gave the little man a heartfelt hug. "My big brother tells me that you have done some pretty impressive work on the trails."

"Aw, the kids did the work. I just carried the water," Floyd said with his typical modesty.

"Albert, we're going to hike up to a couple of the turnouts so I can show Lisa and Tunner the boundaries of our property."

"Ok! Hey, wait a minute. Let me get one of the new spotting scopes. You can see a lot more with that. The kids love watching the wildlife with them."

Floyd left the trio standing in the foyer for a few moments before returning with a black case. He set the case on a nearby table and opened it. Inside the case was a high-quality spotting scope. "Let me show you how to use it. These things are awesome!"

Frank looked down at the instrument. "Scopes? Albert that thing looks expensive. How many of these do we own?"

"Five."

"Are you sure the center can afford five?"

"Oh, the center didn't pay for them Frank. You did. When I was tellin Rose about my idea, she said to get good ones and to get enough so more than one kid at a time could use them."

"You could run those ideas by me, too, you know." Floyd smiled innocently at Frank's remark while Tunner and Lisa made little attempt to hide their smirks.

* * * * *

It had taken close to an hour to reach Frank's primary destination. After leaving the trailhead they hiked, not on the trail, but up a difficult climb so that they could see where a road would have to cross from Hightower's land to Johnson's before reaching the Merritt holdings on the mountain. Lisa and Frank were both surprised that their younger brother had taken the lead throughout the climb, even while carrying the scope. Tunner had never before been overly fond of exerting himself. He already had it set up on the outcropping by the time they arrived.

"Check down there, Frank. You can see the markers they have set for the road."

He peered through the scope and scratched his head. "Why would Merritt be building the road on the mountain before grading the access road to it? That doesn't make sense.

"I don't know," Lisa said. "I can call Stuart. Since the roads are all on private land, you probably aren't going to find out much from public records. Farmers talk though, and if Hightower has something going on, he may have told my husband."

"Here, Sis," Tunner said, as she reached for her phone. "The signal is going to be spotty up here, and you probably aren't going to have much luck with the relic that you carry around."

Lisa gave Tunner an incredulous look, before taking the phone and responding, "Thank you, oh great wizard. Frank, who is this imposter that has kidnapped our little brother?" She then dialed her husband, and spoke only a few moments before handing the phone back to Tunner. "Stuart said that he and Hightower haven't talked in a while, but he had heard that his daughter got hassled by Bubba Raines in the Dugganville Library. She almost quit her internship over it."

Tunner looked at his brother and sister, not needing to voice the unspoken thought that each was having. The Bear family had long suspected that Raines had been involved in the attack on Frank. They knew he had hated the Ramseys, but Tyrell had not shared his own suspicions with them before he died.

While Tunner was breaking down the spotting scope, Frank answered his sister. "That's a shame. Phyllis Hightower is a nice kid, even if her dad can be a total jerk. Are you two ready to do some more hiking?"

Tunner already had the scope packed away and slung around his shoulder. "Let's do it!"

Lisa punched her little brother on the arm. "Seriously, Frank. Who is this guy?"

In less than an hour, they were standing at the spot where Frank had heard the argument between R.T. Merritt and the person who he now believed to be, Bubba Raines. They stood looking sadly at the scar on the mountain that had been created by Bubba's road grader. In only a few moments, as if in an attempt to salve their sorrow, the sound of an Elk bugle came rolling down the mountain. They couldn't see the animal, but it was as if they were standing next to it.

After the bugle ended, Tunner spoke in a serious tone that was uncommon for their little brother. "Frank, I know why they are building the road on the mountain, first."

His siblings looked at him, indicating that he should go on.

"You can't appreciate how incredibly loud the computers that run a crypto-mine are until you've actually heard them. Unetlanvhi created the Twin Sisters in a very special way."

Tunner had used the Cherokee word they had heard their mother use when speaking of The Great Spirit.

"When those computers are powered up, it will no longer be the elk and the geese that speak to the people of Beaumont. Everyone living there will be subjected to constant, gut rumbling roar. Merritt is trying to get everything in place for his mine before it is to late to stop it. He was able to make the deal with Hightower and Johnson, by telling them that, because of its location, they wouldn't be able to see it and that the road would be minimally used. I am sure that he also promised them a sizeable share of what he said would be significant profits. What they don't understand, is that their livestock and the wildlife are going to be seriously screwed."

Lisa looked at Tunner, once again, in amazement. "Oh, my God! Frank, he's right! There is a case in Tennessee right now involving bit coin mining. The plaintiffs in that case were only told that the operation would need a very small footprint, and that it would help the economics of the area. Now, the quality of life for the people who had chosen to live there because of its beauty and solitude is largely destroyed by noise pollution, while big money players elsewhere rake in the profits. The case could take years to settle. The problem would be exponentially worse here, and the people in Beaumont don't have the money to fight it."

"Damn! Those two idiots never let their hatred for each other get in the way of making a few bucks. The only other time I ever heard them agree on anything was when they cooked up some scheme with R.T. Merritt to try and turn the Beaumont Community Center into a high profit entertainment venue. When I kicked them off the board, they both claimed that it had been the other's idea. Now, that bastard has sucked him into another of his schemes."

Lisa spoke. "Johnson has some pretty scary connections back from where he came. If his hunting buddies start seeing a decline in game, R.T. could have a lot bigger problems than Bob Hightower or Bubba Raines being upset with him."

It was late before they returned to the Bear Estate, and everyone agreed to wait until the next morning to discuss what they had seen that day. Bear took Jason aside before going to bed and asked his son to join them as an adult in all further meetings. He felt that it was imperative that Jason hear everything, firsthand.

"Jason, you may hear some pretty damning information about R.T."

"It's not a problem, Dad." He found himself enjoying the sound of the word more each time he said it. "I know what kind of a man

R.T. is, and I have always been a little worried that I might turn out like him. It feels good, knowing that I don't have that in me.

* * * * *

The next morning at breakfast, there was one addition to the group sitting around the table. Jason sat between Amber and Rose at breakfast and was obviously nervous. Frank began the meeting by asking Lisa to recount the events of the day before. His second sister would eventually become an outstanding lawyer possessing exemplary skills in recall and an uncanny ability to create a clear narrative in courtroom situations. She left out no detail, but stopped at one point in her narration to lay heavy praise on Tunner for his performance the day before. For the first time in his life, he didn't have a quick retort and could only blush. Janie chucked her brother on shoulder.

He quickly deflected the attention away from himself. "Hey, I think we should welcome my nephew to the table. I gotta warn you kid; you have never seen the brutal side of this family." Everyone laughed and Rose gave Jason a big kiss on the cheek, causing her stepson to turn several shades of red.

After the laughter subsided, Frank stood and moved to the purpose of the meeting. "We need to talk about what's happening on The Mountain of the Twin Sisters."

Chapter 29

The Present – Flood of the Century

Friday

Morning sunrise lay hidden behind an ominous shroud of gray. The storm had been building for days. It had taken nearly a week for the bright blue of morning to darken to the hue of a starless night. An incoming front continued to creep forward slowly like a predator sneaking up on its prey before unleashing its furious attack.

Merritt looked up from his desk overlooking the river. *"Damn, it looks like the forecasters may finally get one right. That sky is going to dump a lot of water, once it finally lets go."*

He walked to his refrigerator and grabbed a bottle of Perrier. The businessman hadn't touched a drop of alcohol since the day of his last confrontation with Bubba Raines. He opened the water and walked back to the window overlooking the river. Although the sun was now well above the horizon, Merritt could barely see the statue on the island below him in the gloom.

He raised his bottle in a salute. "Better keep your powder dry, major. You may be a damn Yankee again after this one rolls through."

Merritt pressed the call button on his desk and said, "I am leaving in a few minutes to see a potential client and won't be back until Monday.

"OK," came the reply. JoAnne had already given her two weeks notice.

Merritt rarely kept a secretary long enough to bother learning her name. He didn't pay much, but he didn't expect much. He had three rules.

1. Never hire a male. Even the thought was repulsive.

2. Don't hire a woman who thinks or ask questions. That's not what they're here for. File and take messages. That's it.

3. Above all, never sleep with a woman that works for you. For some reason, she will think that she can get in your business just because you are in her pants.

"Too bad for the Reverend Kirby Appleton that he never learned rules 2 and 3," Merritt thought as he grabbed his raincoat and umbrella.

* * * * *

Merritt's raincoat was still dry when he walked into Kirby's office and handed it to the church secretary. As he did, he leaned over and gave her a kiss on the cheek that lasted too long to be a friendly peck. After standing, he held a finger to his lips indicating that she shouldn't let the pastor know he was there. Lacey blew him a kiss in response.

Appleton startled and closed his computer in a panic when Merritt walked in his office and closed the door with a loud click. His secretary had been cool to him lately, and the pastor had resorted to an occasional foray onto carnal websites.

"Now, now, Reverend Appleton, what would your flock say about that?" After asking the question, Merritt leaned over Appleton's desk to make sure that the speaker to his secretary's office was turned off.

"I have no idea what you are talking about. I am finishing up on this Sunday's sermon," Appleton replied, but the guilty look and bright red face had betrayed him. *Why do I always feel like such a child around that man?*

"Well, Rev, I hate to do this to you, but I am afraid you are going to have to scrap that sermon and write a new one. It seems that you have been suddenly inspired by God to alert your people to the evil that resides among us."

"I can't! It's too late," the preacher said, disgusted with himself for the obvious whine in his voice.

"No pastor, it is not. You see, back when I was a state senator, I became somewhat of a sermon writer myself." Merritt dropped the manuscript he had been holding in his hand on Appleton's desk.

"All you have to do is memorize it, add a few of those rhetorical flourishes at which you excel and deliver it to our congregation on Sunday. Now, I must admit that I have been rather backslidden as of late, but I assure you that I will be there in person to be inspired. Is there any problem with that?"

"No sir," Appleton said, once again sounding like a chastened school boy. Merritt, not his father, was the only person who had ever been able to make him feel repentant for his sinful life.

Merritt leaned, once again over Appleton's desk and turned the speaker back on. "Lacey, would you please ensure that the reverend isn't bothered for the rest of the afternoon. He will be working very diligently on his sermon for Sunday."

"Yes sir, Mr. Merritt."

Before leaving the pastor's office, Merrit made one more comment to further demoralize Allen in front of his secretary. "Oh, and don't worry if you hear something that sounds as if he may be in distress. Those are just the moanings of the spirit coming from our pastor as he seeks leadership from on high."

A barely stifled giggle came over the speaker. "Oh, yes sir, Mr. Merritt. I know all about the pastor's moanings."

Merritt stood and closed the door, this time softly, behind himself when he left. Lacey handed him his raincoat, and he gave her a suggestive wink as he walked out the front door of the church. The beast had pounced, and the rain was now coming down in torrential sheets. He cursed himself slightly for not taking his umbrella into the church, but a little rain wasn't going to dampen his very good mood.

Appleton stayed in his office without opening his door, until he was sure that his secretary had left for the day.

Saturday

The deluge had continued throughout the night. Life in Dugganville had come to a virtual halt. Before it would end later that evening, more rain would fall in Dugganville and the surrounding area than had been recorded for a single twenty-four-hour period at any other time in history. Multiple flooding deaths would be recorded, and municipal services would be strained for weeks afterward.

Merritt awoke from the couch in his office, and stretched. The couch had been folded flat into a bed. After standing, he neatly folded the sheets and placed them into a closet before returning the couch to its original position. Sleeping in his office had become standard practice as of late. He owned a well-furnished town house in North Dugganville but, unless he planned on entertaining someone for the evening, he had felt no need to travel the bridge to the other side of the river. The office had all the trappings of a modern efficiency, including a kitchenette and shower.

He smiled as he looked at the continuing barrage of heavy rain continuing to fall from the black atmospheric ceiling that hung only feet away from the top of his office building. *"God must love me,"* he thought, as he unconsciously began to whistle Dixie.

Only days before, he had been looking at the likelihood of his scheme blowing up in his face and the literal possibility of his body being ripped apart by Bubba Raines. Now, while most of the citizens of Dugganville saw gloom, R.T. Merritt saw only sunshine.

"Bubba, you stupid simian brute. You may be able to hide as long as the good folks of our fair city have a use for you, but you threatened the wrong farmer's daughter. It's a shame that you don't go to church. If you did, you might understand why that farmer is going to be coming after you."

He chuckled happily to himself and continued in his mental conversation. *"And Mr. Benjamin Johnson, I know that, as an atheist, you don't believe in the almighty, but it's a shame you can't hear that powerful message also. I fear that angry farmer may also be planning a salvation experience for any transient non-believer.*

An idea had suddenly come to Merritt, and he pulled his phone from its charging station. After pressing the name, he waited for a response.

"Hello."

"Hey Ben, I know you don't read the Bible, but you might want to start building an ark."

"Yea, I've seen the rain, and I know the story. What's up Merritt?" Ben Johnson had never played the local good ol' boy game with R.T. He knew that if Merritt called, the perpetual manipulator had a scheme worked up. On occasion, some of Merrit's schemes had proven to be profitable, but Johnson had no desire to exchange small talk with him."

Merritt was well aware of Johnson's get-down-to-business attitude, and that was precisely why he had chosen to open the conversation with an allusion to religion. "Alright, Ben. I will get straight to the point. I think Bob Hightower and the preacher at that monstrosity of a church he attends are cooking something up."

"You go to that church."

"And you know that I have to for social propriety. A lot of people with whom I deal, expect me to be a member. One of those people is Hightower. Now, that preacher has enriched himself greatly by convincing his followers that God's blessings will flow freely to them if only they contribute greatly to his church, and I deal with those people as well."

Johnson interrupted. "Yea, I know. I think they used call it selling snake oil."

"Ben, let's not pull punches. Kirby Appleton, you, Bob Hightower, I and many others in this town are selling the same damn oil and putting a different label on it. Like any other good salesman, we are just competing for market share. I am afraid that preacher and his disciples are moving into a new tactic; that being, if you destroy the competition, you no longer have to compete." Merritt waited for Johnson's response. He knew he had transient's attention.

"Ok, go ahead."

"The Reverend Kirby Appleton's sermons have always focused on a happily ever after fairy tale. He knows how to make people feel good about giving him their money. He has suddenly shifted his attention to the sin and moral decay that is present in and around Dugganville. His focus lately has been on the people living on the edges, like Bubba Raines and on the non-generational wealthy folks," Merritt paused for emphasis, "like you living in the county. He has lost several of his newer followers because of that shift, but the old money and the fine Christian Southerners who joined that church under the Senior Reverend Allen, are eating it up."

"Still not quite sure where you are going with this."

"I heard that Hightower has been spending a lot of time in the pastor's office. Call his secretary if you don't believe me. Bubba got ugly with our farmer friend's daughter a few days ago. After that, Hightower calls me and says he wants out of the deal. If you want further proof, tune into Appleton's sermon in the morning. He will be preaching from that glass spaceship he calls a pulpit, even if he has to move it to the ark."

Johnson puzzled over Merritt's last remark. He was totally disinterested in anything to do with religion or the church and, if he had heard about the famous speaking platform, he hadn't given it a thought. Still, if what Merritt said was true, he probably should look into what was going on. "Alright, when does it air? And, what's that secretary's number?"

Merritt gave Johnson the information, hung up and fist pumped the air. *"YES! Get them to fight each other and they will forget about me. None of the investors will come for me after those three are through with each other. This flood will wash away any work that has been done on the mountain, and before I'm finished, Bubba's even going to get blamed for the rain that did it."* He might not make any profit this time, but R.T. Merritt felt like he had potentially escaped with his life.

He stood and walked to the window. *"And look at that. I do believe that this rain may stop in time for the faithful among us to go to church!"*

* * * * *

A family of Bears had also not been bothered by the torrential onslaught. Their large comfortable farm-house had often served as a cozy den for the whole clan for long periods of time. The addition of two new members to the family had only seemed to make the gathering more complete. The only person feeling any strain at all in the family free-for-all was Jason, as he felt himself constantly being pulled between adults who wanted to dote on him and new siblings and cousins who felt that he had the responsibility to be with them. It was a feeling greater than any championship he had ever won.

Tia finally ended the tug-o-war. "Listen, big people! Y'all had my brother all day, yesterday. It's our turn! Jason, you have to play with us."

Tunner howled. "Welcome to the family, nephew. I have been bossed around like that my whole life. Good luck!"

Before being dragged away by his youngest sister, Frank hooked his son by the arm and said, "Tia may I borrow your brother for two minutes. I promise that I will give him right back."

She looked at her dad in what was a five-year-old's version of the stink eye, before nodding in agreement. Frank walked out to the covered patio with his son. Even with the awning and the screen, rain was still splashing on the ceramic floor.

"Everything else can wait. Grandma Sophie, would tell you that God put this rain here to give us time to be here as a family. I have told you many times that I am proud of you."

"Dad, stop. If I walk out there crying, Tia is going to think that you beat me, and Tunner is going to tell her that she is right. We will get together later this afternoon."

Frank laughed and hugged his son. "Go on before your little sister revolts. I will be in, in a few minutes."

After Jason walked in, Frank continued to look out into the rain. It had let up, but was still coming down steadily. One other person knew the truth, and he had kept that person a secret from everyone else. Over the years, Frank Bear had often felt the need to share a pain in his heart that he wasn't sure, even his beloved mother would understand. He looked down at his phone and touched the number.

"Hello."

"Hef, we are a whole family."

Frank Bear had first met Heffner Britton when he was known as Carson Blake. The pair had been pitted against each other by the powerful, with the intent of using them for sport and gambling. Instead, they found a common bond and even though separated by a continent, that bond had grown ever closer.

Briton's response was short. "God, bless you brother! We will talk soon. Now go enjoy your family."

* * * * *

At least one person did not find joy in the rain. Being completely closed up in his small dirty shack reminded Bubba Raines of his time in prison. Beyond that, he was already seething after his experience in the library. After unsuccessfully trying to seal a number of leaks in the dilapidated structure's sagging ceiling, he cursed loudly and decided, *"I'll stay in the cellar until this goes over."* Once again, cursing loudly, he threw some canned goods in a sack, put on an old poncho and walked into the rain.

He nearly fell down the steps trying to open and close the angled door to the cellar quickly enough to keep the rain from pouring in. Once at the bottom of the steps, he cursed upon noticing that the earthen walls in the cellar felt damp. Everything in the world he cared about except for the road grader was in the cellar. Twenty years earlier, he had dug the pit for his underground sanctuary from the limestone enclosing it using only a pick and shovel. After running his hands over the walls to examine them for leaks, he assured himself that they would hold. He opened the safe and took out each gun to wipe and re-oil it, although they were already clean. Next, he carefully counted and restacked the money, before placing each stack neatly back on its shelf. Finally, Raines pulled out the newest ledger, but the increasingly agitated hulk found himself unable to look at the figures for long without going into a rage. Those bastards had cheated him, and he hated them now even more than he had before.

He paced in the small cellar like the caged predator that he was. *"Get the grader. Knock down that stupid pavilion at the trailhead."* It was the only thing that Bubba could think of to do that might momentarily quench his thirst for revenge. The pavilion had nothing to do with Merritt or Hightower, but it was an easy target and his worm of a cousin had pissed him off earlier. He tried to raise the counter-weighted door, but water immediately poured in,

and he realized that he wasn't going anywhere for a while.

One more binder sat on the shelves. He took it down, opened the cover, and pulled out a neatly folded sheet of paper that had been tucked in the pocket of the binder. The paper was a handwritten receipt that had been created by Raines two decades earlier. It had recorded the transaction, that had earned the cash he had used to purchase the shack and the land upon which it sat.

Chapter 30

The Past – Blood Money

"You stupid block skulled Precambrian troglodyte. All you were supposed to do was rough him up a little, and you may have killed him."

Bubba Raines hated the feeling of being inferior, and nothing made him feel more inferior than people using words he didn't understand. His truck was parked facing R.T. Merritt's SUV. They were meeting on a remote road near a mountain lake where they sometimes did business. Without responding, he walked to the back of his truck and started to reach into the bed where Merritt knew that he kept a short length of pipe, specifically for the purpose of settling arguments. He likely had used the same pipe when he had attacked Frank Bear only the night before.

"Oh, don't even try that, pretty boy." Merritt had hit another nerve. Raines hated any allusion to his former good looks. Too many people had made the mistake of trying to get close to him because of them. A gay inmate had slashed his face after Bubba had kneed the man in the groin for trying to kiss him. Bubba had been able to take the makeshift knife from the inmate and nearly sever his hand before prison guards could break up the fight. Merritt knew of the incident. Ordinarily, he would have been reluctant to provoke Raines to violence, even if he did consider him to be only an errand boy, but his boy had just created a lot of problems for him with his associates, and worse, the possibility of a criminal investigation.

Raines reached into the truck bed pulled out the pipe and turned toward Merritt. "So, mush for brains. You go ahead and beat me to death. You do realize that there are some very big people who knew about our deal. The idea was to send a gentle reminder to play by the rules, not try to kill someone. City councils and local big businesses don't like it when the biggest entertainment venue in the area gets blackballed because someone nearly gets beat to death due to lack of security. You probably cost Dugganville millions last night. How many pieces do you think your body will be found in, or better yet, how is the thought of going back to prison for the rest of your life?"

Bubba continued to hold the pipe as he tried to grasp what Merritt was telling him. "Now, put that damn pipe back in your truck, so we can talk. You can fix this."

Bubba did as he was commanded, then waited with his arms crossed for Merritt to continue. Even when wavering between rage and intense fear, R.T. Merritt knew how to work people. Raines still hadn't said a word when he began talking again.

"I've met with the affected parties, and I am taking a lot of flak right now." Merritt didn't mention that the affected parties of whom he was speaking came to a total of two people, R.T. Merritt Senior and Robert Hightower.

"What happened at the arena will blow over as soon as a couple of big-name events come in and we can avoid any more fiascos." Bubba wasn't sure what fiasco meant, but he knew it had something to do with him. He continued to look silently at Merritt.

"Pretty soon, it will become old news to everyone, except for one very dangerous person. Tyrell Ramsey will not forget, and he won't let it go. Ramsey has some friends from his college days that are currently in the state senate. I know. I got tired of them telling me about his impressive success story. Make no mistake, Ramsey is going to contact those people and both of us are going to feel a lot of pressure. I don't like the thought of prison any more than you."

Raines finally spoke. "So, what are you going to do?"

"Not me. You. I don't care how it happens, as long as it looks like an accident. Ramsey needs to be the victim of bad luck. Don't forget, it was Ramsey who put that old man up to testifying against you, and the reason you have that scar."

Bubba scoffed. "So, you and your buddies wait for me to take out Ramsey, and then you point the finger at me. No way."

"Damn it, Bubba. No one ever knows where you are unless you want them to know. If anyone wants to know where I am at any given time, all they have to do is look at the schedule on my secretary's desk. I get it, though. You are the one taking the biggest risk."

Merritt paused a moment and said, "Twenty thousand dollars."

"Not enough."

"What? You've never made anywhere close to that for a job."

"I ain't never killed nobody for money."

"Ok. Thirty thousand. Ten up front and twenty more after I read in the paper that Tyrell Ramsey has met with a tragic accident."

"Deal. I want the ten thousand now."

"What? Bubba, this is the age of credit cards. I don't have that kind of cash with me."

"Yes, you do," Raines said. He had gained control of the negotiation.

"Ok." Merritt walked to the back of his Escalade and opened the lift gate. He looked up nervously when he heard the passenger door of Bubba's truck opening. He feared that Raines might be pulling out a gun, but when the door shut, he held only a pen and a single sheet of paper. Raines leaned on the hood of his truck and began writing. Merritt leaned over to open a lock box he kept hidden in the wheel well of his vehicle. He counted out the money, but kept one eye on the big man as he continued to write.

Bubba was still writing when Merritt approached the truck. "I've got your money. What's that you're writing?"

Raines stood and held the pen toward R.T. "Sign and date."

Merritt looked down at a surprisingly professional looking makeshift invoice, neatly printed in block letters.

> Job: R.T. Merit agrees to pay William Raines $30,000 for
> causin acidint to T. Ramsey. $10,000 now and $20,000 after
> it happins.
>
> Sign
> Date

Incredulous but grudgingly impressed, Merritt pointed at the note. "Bubba, I'm not going to sign that."

Bubba continued to hold out the pen. "Why not. If I get caught, I ain't goin down by myself. If I don't get caught, I ain't confessin just to get your worthless ass in trouble. And like you already said, nobody finds me unless I want them to."

Merritt shook his head and took the pen. He hesitated slightly before signing and dating the agreement. The absurd notion to complain about misspelling in a legal agreement flashed briefly in his mind, but he shrugged it off and handed the paper back to Raines.

"Gimme my money."

Merritt handed him the money, but Raines continued to hold out his hand.

"What?"

"Gimme my pen back."

Merritt handed him the pen and without further word, Bubba got back into his truck and drove off. Merritt felt a knot in his stomach as he watched the one good taillight from the old Ford disappear over the horizon.

Chapter 31

The Present – Rematch

Sunday

Sometime in the early morning hours, the rain stopped, leaving swollen rivers, downed powerlines, debris strewn streets, and death in its aftermath. The monster flood had decided to move eastward. The clouds had disappeared with its exit, revealing the last few stars of night before a happily released sun rose on the eastern horizon.

The arena-like parking lot of The Church of God's Redemption was unsurprisingly sparsely populated on the morning following the storm. On any other Sunday, parishioners having to park on the edges or in the remote lots could expect to be picked up by a parking shuttle and transported to the church. On this morning, only the first few rows were occupied by vehicles. Many members of the congregation were dealing with the immediate effects of the flood; wash-out roads, flooded houses, power outages, and a host of other challenges including human tragedy. Some, who normally attended, had decided to listen to the message from home. Still others, just saw an opportunity to sleep in.

Kirby Appleton looked out over the cathedral from his glass pulpit and breathed a sigh of relief. *"Maybe not many people at home are listening,"* he thought, hoping that the storm would dampen the impact of the message he was about to deliver. Over the years, his attire had gradually morphed from that of a repentant gang-member before shortly transitioning to a business suit, until it had finally reached the mature stage of the priestly robe his father had worn before him. It had become a long-established practice for the reverend to approach the dais and grasp either side, immediately sending a shower of sparkling light floating down on the congregation. Over time, he had added uplifting music that would begin at a barely audible level and increase in volume until Appleton would suddenly raise both hands and shout, "Praise God for his blessings." Upon which the music and lights stopped, the crowd shouted the phrase back to the pastor, and he began his sermon.

On this Sunday morning, there was no huge crowd. People were scattered throughout the huge enclosure, but could have easily sat in the first few rows. Almost all of the people in attendance that morning could trace their lineage in the area for generations. Most, in fact, belonged to families that had been part of his father's original congregation. Kirby had grown up with them and knew their names. The pews arced around the stage upon which stood the high-tech dais. Only a few rows from the stage and surrounded by empty pews, sat Robert Hightower, along with his wife and daughter. Although bigoted and the possessor of highly situational morals, the farmer had long been one of the biggest contributors to the church.

Sitting directly across from Hightower on the other side of the arc was Robert Thomas Merritt Jr. Appleton looked down and knew instinctively that Merritt wanted to make sure that Hightower knew he was there. Merritt sat displaying his best imitation of a humble man who was waiting to be inspired by God. Inside, he was laughing at what he perceived to be a human comedy. *"Damn, I love people. They park so close to each other to keep from walking a few extra steps and getting their feet wet, that they can't open their doors, but in here you would think they were staking out homesteads, they're spread so far apart. Yea, Bob, I know you see me."* He nodded slightly at the farmer.

Even Merritt was surprised when Appleton placed his hands on the dais and nothing happened. A feeling of discomfort could be felt among the skimpy crowd, as they waited to respond to their normal joyful call to worship. Instead, the reverend looked somberly down at his crowd. "My friends, God has sent us a reminder of his power over an arrogant people."

The storm hadn't yet hit when Merritt had written the sermon for Appleton to memorize. "*Nice intro Rev,*" he thought. "*You did do your homework.*"

"I look out into this holy temple of God that is usually filled with masses of people, and I see only the faces of the faithful that were here when my father started this church. Many of you helped raise me when he arrived, poor and broken in spirit."

"*A little off script, but I must admit that I like where the holy man is going.*"

It didn't take long for Appleton to get to the text Merritt had supplied him with. Most of the small audience peppered throughout the huge auditorium had been members long before Kirby Allen had taken the reigns from his father and could trace their ancestry directly to the confederacy. They nodded silently when the pastor spoke of an immoral element still living in the community that had historically disobeyed their rightful place in God's order and profited from filthy lucre while living in the shadows. The few members of the transient population that had made it through the flooded streets to attend church squirmed in their seats at the uncomfortable allusion to class and racism. Robert Hightower and a few others, nodded in agreement. A vision of Bubba Raines popped up in many of their heads.

Appleton then transitioned from the old evil in the community to a greater one that had grown its roots deeply before anyone had time to notice. The pastor paused and became pale before continuing.

"*I'm not sure if that boy is truly a master of dramatic effect, or if he might become ill right in front of us,*" Merritt thought. He was truly enjoying Appleton's discomfort, but he nodded right along with Hightower. He had also noticed the location of the cameras placed throughout the sanctuary, as they panned back and forth across the audience. Merritt had chosen his seat strategically. He knew that

Ben Johnson would be watching and couldn't miss seeing him or Hightower among the sparse congregation.

"We were once a Godly community, but Baal has moved into our gates. Foreign influences have moved into our homes promising wealth and easy living, but have brought with them sexual immorality and atheistic beliefs."

The timing of the cameras couldn't have been more perfect for Merritt's purposes. The camera caught the pastor in profile before zooming out to the audience where it caught Merritt appearing to nod solemnly. He looked directly at the camera for barely a second and almost imperceptibly tilted his head toward Hightower. After again crossing Appleton's profile, the lens came to rest on Bob Hightower and his family. Mrs. Hightower's expression was blank, but their daughter appeared to be on the verge of walking out. The camera quickly zoomed in and remained on Robert Hightower, showing him vigorously nodding in agreement.

Now, out of view of the camera, Merritt nodded equally as vigorously, while thinking, *"Get them fighting each other, and they will forget all about you."* It was a concept that had been passed down the Merritt line for generations.

By the time Kirby Appleton reached the end of his message, a few members of the already sparce audience, including Phyllis Hightower, had walked out. He was pale, drenched in sweat and seemed barely able to stand. Unlike his first church presentation, two decades prior, the perspiration was not a result of the lights, and the pain displayed on his face was not an act of thespian skill. Still, he continued, hoping that he might able to salvage something of the empire that he had built.

"Beloved, these are indeed perilous times, and we will continue to face challenges from the dark one. But, please, look up to God as you walk out these doors. He has brought us through one storm and given us a beautiful glorious day. He will take us through others. When Noah opened the Ark after it had been stranded on Mt. Ararat, the only living things left on Earth were those that had been brought into the safety of that sanctuary and protected from the wrath of an angry god. This church is our sanctuary, and we must remain safely wrapped in its love. God bless you, and go in peace."

"Well damn, Reverend Appleton! I am truly impressed and inspired. I may have to give you a bonus in your offering plate." Having sensed that he had averted disaster not only for his dealings, but for his life, Merritt was already mulling the possibility of a venture with Appleton. By the time he rose and walked into the parking area, it was empty. He couldn't resist raising his hands and shouting, "Praise God for his blessings!"

*   *   *   *   *

Also feeling extremely grateful on Sunday was Frank Bear. After breakfast, he had humbly asked Tia if he could borrow her brother for the day.

"Okay," she had agreed in resignation.

Frank, Jason, and Tunner took four wheelers out on the property to see what damage had been caused by the rain. Everything in their relationship suddenly felt different, but also as it should always have felt. They stopped at the spot where Jason had stood and screamed at the Elk only a few days before. It was now completely underwater.

"You ever seen this much water, big brother," Tunner asked.

"Not even close," Frank answered. "You know, these streams will be dumping water into the river for the next several days. It probably won't crest near Beaumont Island until Thursday or so. I wonder if the major has ever seen this much water."

Jason snorted. "Maybe we will get lucky and he will float down the river on his horse."

Tunner looked at his nephew. "Wow, that was harsh."

Jason looked slightly guilty. "Maybe. Grandma Sophie told me that it might take a while for me to let go of all the anger. Every time I saw R.T.'s parents, I had the Beaumont history rammed down my throat. Mom says the only historical evidence she has ever found of Raeford Beaumont, is that stupid book that his dad wrote.

Frank laughed out loud. He took his son's arm in a playful wrestling move, spun him around and wrapped his arms around him from behind. "Your mother is a better local historian than R.T.

Merritt senior or junior will ever be. I think I would trust her at her word."

Jason laughed, ducked under the embrace and performed a standing reverse.

Watching the exchange, Tunner was amazed at how naturally Frank and Jason had fallen into their new relationship. He found himself missing Sylvia Batten, badly.

* * * * *

Bubba's mood continued to sour. The limestone walls of the cellar had held solid and only minimal amounts of water had seeped in through the door. When Raines opened the door of his shack however, he discovered that the ceiling had completely collapsed onto the floor. Worse still, the poorly maintained septic system had backed up into the house, creating a stench that was overpowering even for him. He walked out without bothering to close the door.

"I'll knock it down and find me a trailer when everything dries out."

Monday

Bubba's mental state bubbled like acid by Monday morning, after having slept sitting up in the cramped cellar. *"Maybe, I've got some work,"* he thought, before climbing into his truck and driving off. After driving for only a few miles, he pulled up to a large iron gate and walked to a mailbox that stood near it. The box was the final anomaly to the hermit's filthy lifestyle. It was a USPS approved, locking oversized box that had been impressively set in native stone. It stood beside a driveway entrance that had been deeply covered in river rock. The heavy ornamental gate that had been erected across the entrance gave the impression of a fortress. A few such entrances along the mountain road had been erected since the influx of money into the area. One could rarely see where the driveways led because of dense forestation, but they usually terminated at the front door of an over-sized mansion built with the ostentatious goal of impressing anyone who may have been lucky enough to be invited in.

Bubba's entrance, however, quickly degraded from an attractive layer of rounded rock down to two-wheel ruts approximately forty yards past the gate, and then ended in a primitive campsite only a few hundred yards beyond that. The large tract of land had been acquired as part of another one of his shadow deals. He only came there to collect what little mail he might receive and hunt; illegally, since, as an ex-convict, he couldn't legally own a gun. He had built the impressive front entrance as another way to thumb his nose at the class of people he detested. The mailbox, in his mind, was another way that he gave the middle finger to the rich and powerful. Since he didn't have a phone, they had to come on his turf to make a deal and he controlled when to get back to them.

Although the specifics for making nefarious arrangements with the shadow class in the valley may have changed over the past century, the rules had remained the same. The shadow class, to which Bubba belonged, lived on the fringes of society. They only had value when they could secretly accomplish unrespectable tasks for respectable people. Those rules were, meet quietly, don't use names, pay, and move on. Bubba checked his mailbox regularly to see if any notes had been deposited. The contents of the notes were always the same; Short description of the job, payment being offered, meeting place, and time to discuss specifics. If Raines was interested, he showed up. If not, he didn't. Although he actually lived in a shack with no registered physical address, the box had also proven useful in meeting his probation requirements and for receiving his meager welfare checks. He unlocked the box and looked in, expecting to see the standard stack of junk mail, which he always carelessly tossed on the ground. Instead, he saw only three unmarked envelopes.

He opened the first. It was from Robert Hightower. "The deal's off! STAY AWAY FROM MY DAUGHTER!" RH

"No problem, Bobby." Raines sneered inwardly. He had taken pleasure in seeing the fear in Phyllis Hightower's eyes after she had made the mistake of trying to show him compassion.

The second read, "Your services are no longer needed." KL

The third, "Cancel the meet." TA

Both were from farmers with whom he had made arrangements several times and were friends of Robert Hightower. *"What is this chicken shit?"*

No one had ever had the nerve to back out of a deal with Bubba. Not even Merritt had ever tried. Frustrated, Raines felt the need to hurt someone.

Tuesday

Frank answered his phone while the extended Bear clan was having breakfast. "No, not today, buddy. I am going to hang with family another day. Be careful. There are going to be some rough spots, and if you hurt yourself, you know I'm the one who is going to catch it from Rose."

"Albert is going to inspect the trails and the gazebo, isn't he," Rose said, after her husband put his phone in his pocket.

Bear had wanted to share the news about Jason with Albert Floyd, but the family had made a commitment that no one else would be told until R.T. Merritt had been informed. "Yes, I am almost surprised he wasn't out there in the middle of the storm holding an umbrella over that gazebo. He is so proud of what he did with the kids at the center."

Frank looked around the table. "Where is Tunner? Since this is the last day that we are all going to be together, you would think he might come down to breakfast."

"I heard him get up and leave really early this morning," Janie said with a yawn, still not fully awake.

"Tunner, get up early? No way!" The entire family laughed at Tia's emphatic proclamation.

Frank simply shrugged. "Who knows with him. He'll be back."

It was still incredibly wet outside, so after breakfast the entire family, including the monster mutts settled down in the family room. They would talk more later about how to best deal with Merritt. Confronting his fraud in connection with the bit coin mine would be complicated by having to tell him that Jason wasn't his son. Tunner really needed to be present for that conversation, so, for now, it was a good time to simply enjoy each other.

Janie had reminded the twins for a second time to stop being so rambunctious with the dogs in the house when the door opened. Tunner timidly stuck his head in the room. "Hi guys."

Quizzical looks went around the room at his odd entrance. Timidity wasn't his style.

"I've got someone I would like you to meet."

He stepped through the door and held it open, allowing Sylvia Batten to walk in front of him. "Sylvia, you came!" Janie jumped up and ran to the new visitor to give her a hug. Tunner's younger sister and her sons were the only members of the family to have met Tunner's girlfriend. She was petit, redheaded, freckle-faced and exuded an air of perpetual energy.

"Well, I guess the rest of us need to introduce ourselves," Rose said, and walked toward Sylvia.

"That won't be necessary, Rose. I have a feeling that I know all of you better than any of you know me. I almost didn't go on a second date with Tunner, because all he did was talk about you on our first date."

Her second statement hadn't been truthful. Sylvia was an only child and estranged from her aristocratic parents. She had been sent to elite boarding schools from an early age and had long yearned for the feeling of family. When she had first met Tunner, it was she who had constantly pulled information from him about his large chaotic family, and it had been Tunner who had considered ending the relationship. Eventually he came to realize how much his family and Sylvia Batten meant to him.

Tunner dropped his head and grinned sheepishly. Both dogs stood in front of Sylvia, expectantly. She leaned over and stroked them under their jaws. "And that includes you, Monsieurs Takedown and Reverse."

At first, the shy family was slightly taken aback by her extroverted friendliness, as she went around the room giving each person a hug before naming them and sharing one piece of unique information, she had remembered hearing from Tunner. About midway through, she came to Jason. He had been standing back, assuming that Batten wouldn't know who he was. "And you are Frank's handsome son, Jason. I am so happy to meet you."

Frank's gut clinched, and he shot his brother a hard look. No one outside the family was supposed to know. A momentary feeling of betrayal was bubbling in his throat when Lisa screamed. "What is that on your finger!"

Lisa grabbed Batten's left hand and held it up. All of the females in the room immediately descended on the grinning redhead. A few moments later, the males caught on and looked at Tunner.

"I bought the ring months ago and was going to think of some really fancy way to ask her, but I couldn't stand it any longer. I had to get her out of bed this morning to ask her. And Fank, I didn't tell her about my new nephew until she said yes. I promise."

"He is telling you the truth, future brother-in-law. It was the first time he has ever had to wake me up, and I was too sleepy to say no. Honestly, I don't know what made me happier; his proposal or that story. It made me fall even more in love with your family."

She turned to Amber. "Amber, you are an amazing woman, and I am so honored to meet you."

The entire family started to group around the professor and admire the ring until one of Janie's sons called out. "Hey, you haven't finished telling the rest of us cool stuff about us."

"You are right!" All laughed and she continued going around the room, focusing on the children. Frank put his arm around Tunner and whispered in his ear, "I'm still pissed, but you did good. You're lucky that I like her. I'm happy for you!"

Sylvia saw them together and said loud enough for all to hear, "And Frank, I knew that he was a big wimp the first time I met him. He was just so darn cute!"

Bear put his little brother in a headlock. "He is also very lucky to have witnesses present."

The congratulations and hugs continued until most of the children, except for Tia, drifted back into their play. After happily declaring that she had gained a brother and an aunt in one week, she settled happily in Sylvia Batten's lap and listened in awe to the world traveler and natural story teller's tales of adventure. When all of the attention was focused on the new arrival, Frank slipped quietly into his library and pulled out his phone.

* * * * *

Although caution tape had been stretched and uniformed officers continuously reminded people to stay back, the crowd gathering on the opposite sides of the river bank from Major R.T. Beaumont, had grown considerably since Sunday. Rather than flowing to the worthless strip of land's north or south, the swelling river had surrounded it, and the statue once again stood on a true island; one that was shrinking quickly.

Merritt looked down at the scene below his office, but it wasn't the Major's fate of which he was thinking. He cared nothing if the inhabitants of Beaumont had to deal with a little noise, and he was ecstatic about the possibility of making Frank Bear miserable, but his father was right. He had roped several powerful people into this scheme. Those people had the means to make him disappear quietly if they thought he had cheated them. They wouldn't care if the flood had washed away the site on Twin Sisters Mountain. They would want their investment money back; money that he no longer had.

He had already sewn a seed of mistrust among them by having Ben Johnson witness the pastor's performance on Sunday. He was sure that Johnson had already spoken to some of the investors among the newcomers about his doubts concerning Robert Hightower's motives.

"How can I put Bubba right in the middle of this so that both sides are coming after him?"

Merritt was still mulling his strategy when his phone vibrated. He looked at it laying on his desk. *"Aw, shit! What could that little red toad possibly want?"*

"Yea redskin, what do you want. I really don't have time to deal with you right now."

"You are one stupid pale face if you don't," Bear said, returning the mindless insult. "I am trying to do the honorable thing by offering you the opportunity for a private meeting, but I will just let you find out the news when the police come to pick you up, if that suits you."

Frank's calm flat tone had always irritated Merritt. Now, it carried with it an ominous threat. Merritt wanted to end the call with another racial slur, but he knew Bear wasn't one to make idle threats. "Ok, so what is it," he said, trying without success to sound unconcerned.

"I'm not talking to you on the phone. When I tell you this thing, it will be to your face."

Merritt suddenly saw images of his plan being dismantled in front of his eyes. He had heard that Bear had been doing research about cryptomining. He had also been concerned as of late that Ramsey and Son had become increasingly popular among both Dugganville cultures and had recently landed an account with the tire factory, the largest employer in the area. *What does he know? What is he planning?* He had no idea of the true reason for Frank Bear's desire to meet with him privately.

"So, where do you want to have this meeting?"

"Otter's Point. It is half-way between you and me."

"The Point? That's in the middle of nothing. What you are you going to do? Have your tribesmen jump me?"

"Cowardly attacks are your practice, not mine," Bear said flatly.

The statement hit Merritt in the gut. He figured that Frank had been referring to the brutal assault on his ex-wife, but the narcissistic misogynist viewed his behavior from the long-ago incident as little more than an understandable overreaction, considering the strain she had put him under. Bear wouldn't be calling him about that. His fear was that Bear may have somehow learned the truth about the attack on him in the arena twenty years before, or worse, that he may know how Tyrell and Tabitha Ramsey had died.

"Ok, so when do you want this meeting?"

"In the morning. 10:00 am. There will be enough light for a white man to see the road. I wouldn't want you to accidentally miss a turn."

If Merritt had been in any doubt, Bear's last statement had washed it away. Still, if the Indian was going to expose him, why call a secret meeting? Why not just have him arrested? Merritt's mind quickly ran through different possibilities of Bear's purposes for the meeting, not knowing that the seeming connection between

Frank's insult and the Ramseys' death had been coincidental, and that he had not been alluding to the mysterious cause of the car wreck that had taken their lives.

"Alright. I will be there. Be careful, little boy. Don't get yourself in over your head." Frank ended the call without responding to R.T.'s weak threat.

Merritt walked to the window and looked down at the river below. It seemed that it had risen even more from just a few moments before. Hundreds of fingers suddenly pointed to the statue in the middle as the front edge dropped several inches and the major's horse looked momentarily as if he may take a swim. The statue settled however and the Gage continued to roil past. *"Damn! That's a lot of red. It's no wonder they call it the Blood River."*

* * * * *

Water was also moving past the corner posts of the gazebo at the trailhead. Albert had known that the entrance near a low water crossing would be an issue, but he hadn't planned on a hundred-year flood hitting the area so soon after the trail had been completed. After calling Frank that morning, he had headed out to inspect the site. Arriving before him, had been Bubba Raines. The angry man needed to do something that would make him happy.

"Dumb shit. Now, ain't it a shame that all that hard work is just going to fall down." Raines would have preferred to have flattened the site with his beloved grader, but the machine was currently surrounded by water, and people would have immediately known who was responsible if he had leveled the entire area. Instead, he grabbed a heavy sledge from his truck. *"A tap here, a tap there, and the water can do the rest."*

He would have to work quickly. Although the rain had stopped in the area, it was still raining heavily to the east, and the creeks feeding the Gage River were swelling rapidly. He was already preparing to swing the hammer when he heard, "Stop, you monkey ass sum bitch!"

It was Albert Floyd. Raines laughed in derision, turned his back on Floyd and brought the head of the hammer hard against the base of the post. He was preparing to strike the post again when he was struck hard by a full body blow from Floyd. The slightly built man weighed less than one hundred and twenty pounds, but the force of his charge would still have knocked the much larger Raines off his feet if he had been running from dry ground. Instead, he slipped just before reaching his target. Raines only stumbled, and Floyd floundered while trying get up. Raines picked him up and smashed his head against the post. Floyd fell limp. Raines looked at the hammer on the ground and considered the shotgun in his truck. *"Nah. Wouldn't want anyone thinking my poor cousin had met with foul play. It would be much better for him to suffer a tragic fall while keepin' the trails safe for the fine folks of Beaumont. I know just the spot."*

He could see that Albert was still breathing, but didn't figure that he was in any shape to be making any fast get aways. Raines slapped his head up against the post one more time for good measure before throwing his ragdoll-like body into the back of the bed. He got into the truck and started it, but then turned off the key. *"Damn, I almost forgot."*

After getting back out of the truck, he grabbed the sledge, sloshed through ankle deep water to the gazebo and struck the corner post one more powerful blow. It leaned, and the corner of the roof sagged. *"Poor construction, cousin. Poor construction. It'll come down before long."*

After driving slowly on a rock and mud road for nearly an hour, Raines pulled as far to the edge of a cliff as he dared, got out of his truck and looked down on his cousin, laying apparently lifeless in the bed. To his surprise, he heard Albert moan. "What's that cousin," he said, leaning over in order to taunt the broken man."

"Screw you," came the barely audible response.

"Cousin, I am disappointed in your attitude. What would your dear departed grandparents say about that kind of language?" With both hands, Bubba lifted Albert's limp body from the bed of the truck with no more effort than it would have taken him to lift a sack of flour. Raines had planned on carrying him to the edge and dropping him over to the rocks that lay a hundred feet below. The instability of the edge gave him pause, and he stopped a few feet from it. "Don't think I want to go over with you," he said to his now unconscious cousin.

"Bet I can throw him that far," he thought.

Raines grabbed the seat of Floyd's loose-fitting pants with one hand and the collar of his shirt with the other. After taking a couple of steps forward, he heaved the body as far as he could, but it landed a foot shy of the edge.

"Damn! That ledge ain't gonna hold my weight. I'll haf 'ta find a dead branch and push him over."

Only seconds after Raines picked up a limb that would be long enough, the weakened soil upon which Albert had landed, broke loose from the cliff. He woke up just in time to weakly try to grab at anything that might hold him, but there was nothing to grab, and he disappeared over the side. "Here cousin, grab this," Bubba snarled before tossing the limb over the edge.

* ** **

Rose saw Frank as he came into the family room and walked to him. "Better smile, Dad, or you are going to throw a blanket on the party."

He sighed, smiled and gave his wife a hug and a quick kiss before going to Sylvia, who was playing ping pong against the twins. The professor of anthropology had written scholarly books, but exuded the playfulness of a child. "I hope you know what you are getting yourself into with this bunch."

"This will be the best adventure I've ever been on," she said, meaning it.

Their last planned day together had the feeling of a family outing rather than a meeting to discuss the dangerous possibilities surrounding the mining operation on the mountain and the revelation of Jason's heritage. Frank found himself feeling comfortable with Sylvia being aware of it all. She was smart, and a fresh perspective couldn't hurt. They had decided to meet again in a few days. Unlike his little brother, the rest of the clan were early risers, and Frank knew they would be moving out after a sunrise breakfast, the next day. He planned to leave for his meeting with Merritt immediately afterward.

Dishes were being cleared from a huge lunch when Rose's phone rang. Frank and everyone else, saw the immediate change in her joyful mood when she answered.

"When?" a pause as she listened to the answer. "Mae, slow down. Do you know where he was going?" another pause. "Mae, you have to remain calm. You are carrying a child, and you have little ones there that need you. I am going to call some cousins. They are closer and will come straight to you. We will be there as soon as we can."

The entire family, children and adults, were looking at Rose when she hung up. "It's Albert. He hasn't returned home and she can't reach him by phone. They only have one car, and she has no way to check on him."

Frank was already on his way to get his car before she finished the sentence. Rose got immediately back on her phone and started calling her family members near Beaumont. By the time he came back into the house to collect Rose, the Bear family was organized. Amber and Sophia were staying with the children while the rest of the adults would help with the search. Frank looked at Sylvia Batten. "Sylvia, this is asking too much. Please, stay here."

"Frank, you really don't know me yet. I spent five years of my life living with indigenous trackers in South America. You can use my help."

Frank gave his brother a where-did-you-find-this-girl look. "OK, all we can do is say thank you, and welcome to the family!"

Rose called the sheriff's office on the way to the Floyd home only to be told that, due to the flooding, their resources had been stretched extremely thin. An officer would be sent their way when available. An hour later, Frank and Rose opened the front door of the Floyd home and were greeted by two worried little boys. A very pregnant Mae Albert sat on the couch in the small living room. It was obvious that she was struggling to remain calm for her sons' sake. They had asked everyone else to remain outside so that she wouldn't become overwhelmed. After trying to encourage Albert's wife for a few moments, Frank said to Rose, "Stay with her. I need to get this organized."

He couldn't have been more wrong. When Bear walked outside, he witnessed Sylvia Batten standing with Jason and Tunner on either side of her and in front of a growing search party. Albert Floyd was loved, and it hadn't taken long for the small community to gather when they heard that he was missing.

"Listen everyone, I want you to organize yourself in groups of three. The only time you are to separate yourself from that group is if you find Albert or if one of you gets hurt. Cell phone service in these hills is always spotty, and I've been told that a tower is down because of the storm. If you find Albert, two people will stay with him, while the third will go back to the trail head and report at the command center we will have set up. If one member of your team happens to get hurt, one person will stay with the injured person, and the other will go back to the command center for help. Tunner has told me that a big map of the area is posted at the trailhead. We can use it to assign search zones. Be extremely careful! It is still raining to our east and the streams are still swelling. A creek that you may have waded last week could pull you under today. It will be dark in a short time, and we may not find him today. Do not try to search at night. It is too dangerous. Mark your location and start back tomorrow."

Batten looked back and saw Frank looking at her. She read the question on his face, and answered it, aloud. "I was also on a search and rescue team in the army. You are the commanding officer. All I know is how to find people. You know all the things I don't know."

What she hadn't told him was that both Jason and Tunner had implored Batten to find a way to keep Frank off the trails. Accepting his limitations was an ability he didn't possess. A part of Frank knew that he was being played, but he was happy to know that the competent young woman would be with his son and younger brother. Her confidence reminded him of a teacher upon whom he had once had a crush.

He felt the need to contribute something and asked, "What about the trailhead. Shouldn't someone stay there, in case Albert makes it back?"

"Rose has some amazing cousins. Look over there." She said, pointing to seven women of various ages. "You are looking at the

Red Elk Command center and Rescue Station. They already have a tent in the back of their van, as well as food supplies and a generator to set up for the rescuers at the trailhead."

Frank was starting to feel like the little boy who everyone took care of, again. He was grateful though. Albert Floyd's rescue couldn't have been in better hands, and he had a rendezvous the next day that he had to keep. As soon as he walked into the Floyd home, Rose said, "Mae is trying to rest," before asking, "Are you going back home, tonight?"

"No, I was going to help with the search, but I think that I have been relieved of command. I guess, I will stay here with you."

Rose laughed and stroked her husband's face, "Sylvia's pretty awesome, isn't she? I think she is also hopelessly in love with Tunner. But listen, I can take care of Mae by myself. You need to rest before tomorrow. You can't do that here, so go back home."

Frank looked at his wife and realized that she knew about the meeting he had set up with Merritt. "Do all Indian Women have this telepathy thing, or is it just Bear and Red Elk Women?"

"Now, don't be racist. It's all women. Amber and I have already talked. I know you told her and Jason that the three of you would confront R.T. together. As much as she wants to show her ex-husband what a real father looks like, she is worried that Jason might not be able to handle it. She and Jason have been talking. Amber hadn't realized how much resentment he had held inside of himself after having been constantly snubbed by the man he believed to be his dad. She told me that, after getting over the initial shock of learning about everything that had happened, he has never been as happy as he is right now. I think she is afraid that he might actually get violent with R.T."

"Does Amber know where I am going in the morning?"

"I already told you," Rose paused. "Now what is it that Mary Briton calls her sister? Hmm, I remember, now. I already told you, Dippo! It's all women, or at least those who love their men. Of course, she knows. Now, you go, Commander. I can hold down the fort, here." She ended with a mock salute.

When Frank walked back outside, he noticed for the first time that Tunner and Sylvia hadn't come to his house in Tunner's classic Mustang, but in her Jeep Rubicon. They were now dressed in fatigues and hiking boots. Jason looked out of place standing between them in jeans and a tee shirt. Fortunately, he did have on a good pair of boots. Again, she interpreted his unspoken question.

"I was also in the scouts. Always prepared."

"Looks like we are both in good hands, little brother," he thought before smiling and going to his car.

As Sylvia had predicted, the quickly assembled search team had barely been able to start, before having to come back in for the night. Upon arriving at the trailhead, the ad hoc search committee discovered that the Gazebo had completely collapsed. They were able to salvage the large trail map posted at the site. While a few of Rose's cousins scoured the immediate area for signs of Albert, Slyvia laid out a plan for the following day. It was already dark by the time Frank walked into his kitchen, where Sophia and Amber sat alone, talking quietly with each other.

"Any news," asked Amber.

"No, but I doubt that there is a search team anywhere that could have a better organizer. I don't know where Tunner met his fiancée, but, present company and my wife excluded, Sylvia Batten is the most amazing woman I've ever met. Don't tell my sisters I said that."

"Be careful, Mr. Bear. You are a little old to be developing another crush," Amber responded with a grin.

The reaction to the quip from Amber started with a tiny giggle from Sophia, causing Frank to roll his eyes and groan, but the groan ended in a chuckle.

"I'm so sorry, Frank. I didn't mean that," but the snort and heaving sides, betrayed that Amber wasn't truly remorseful.

"I am so sorry for you, Amber. I am afraid you've been dumped," Sophia was barely able to finish before laughing.

"Mom!" Frank blurted the statement out in an attempt to sound angry, but his own laughter betrayed that he was enjoying the interchange.

"Oh, Professor Batten, everything thing else is but a fog whenever you are present." Amber swooned dramatically.

Sophia followed with, "Please, Dr. Batten, tell me one more story?"

"Stop, you are both, cruel!" Frank was still standing, but now had both hands on his knees from laughing. Takedown and Reverse had been upstairs asleep with the children, but came down to investigate. Frank put one finger to his lips.

"Shhhhh!" If we wake Tia, I'm blaming you two."

The sudden quake of laughter quickly subsided, becoming tremors of sighs and brief aftershocks of giggles. To laugh so hard in the middle of potential tragedy may have seemed odd, but it had been needed. A lifetime of change had occurred in only a few days. It was the first time in his life, Frank Bear had felt himself completely relaxed standing near the woman who had given birth to his first child. A new facet of his long relationship with Amber had emerged. Frank was now looking at a friend.

Sophia sensed the change, also. She rose from her seat and gave Amber a hug. She next went to her son, placed her hand behind his head and pulled it down so she could kiss him on the forehead. "I love you, son. We all do. That is my little blessing."

"That was a powerful Blessing," Amber said, "but, please be careful tomorrow. I know you aren't afraid of R.T. and neither am I anymore, but you know how capable he is of justifying any action that serves his purposes."

"I do, Amber. That is why I am meeting him in person, alone. He has no idea why I want to meet, but he is scared. I heard it in his voice. Gotta admit; I enjoyed it. I am pretty sure he is in over his head on this last scheme, and he may think I know something. I told him that he and I were the only two people who knew about the meeting, but he doesn't know what cards I hold. He may have set something up for afterward, but it won't happen there. Merritt will want to hear what I have to say first."

"I don't know, Frank. He is a very dangerous man."

"I have to do this, and the rest of the family, including our son, need to find Albert. Besides, like you said, Mom's blessings are powerful."

Amber smiled, stood up, and as she was walking away, said, "OK, get some rest. I love you, and I love being part of this family."

"We love you, too." Frank sat alone in the kitchen for the next hour, contemplating what lay ahead.

Wednesday

Members of the Bear and Red Elk families, along with a strong contingent of concerned friends from Beaumont, met before sunrise at the trailhead and waited for Sylvia Batten's instructions. She had barely started when Tunner and Jason up pulled up in the Jeep. In it, they carried the five spotting scopes from the community center. Lisa had reminded Tunner of them the day before, and he had driven to Beaumont to pick them up. Sylvia had already chosen locations for the scopes to be placed, and had also identified less physically fit volunteers to act as spotters.

The only exception had been Janie, whom she had also assigned to a spotting station. The sheriff's department had been able to free up Officer Tim Wentz for the search. Although the officer would have to remain close to his car, he would be able to take reports on the search unless he was called away on an emergency. Sylvia had thought it would be best to coordinate the search with the sheriff through a member of the Bear family. Janie had also recently started dating Officer Wentz.

After dispatching everyone to their assignments, Sylvia rechecked her gear and looked at her companions. Tunner had loaned Jason a pair of fatigues. Not surprisingly, they wore the same size. Sylvia looked at her search mates and shook her head. "I am really surprised that no one has ever noticed that before."

"What?" asked Jason.

"Just add a little black hair dye, brown contacts and a dark tan, and you look like your Uncle Tunner."

"You ain't this pretty," laughed Tunner.

"And, you're not this hunky." Jason shot back. It was Sylvia who laughed this time.

* * * * *

Merritt had risen well before sunrise, although he hadn't actually slept at all. He stood looking out the window and holding an empty coffee cup as the sun rose illuminating the river below.

"Aw shit!" He said aloud. "You're in trouble now, Major." For the first time in his life, the single tear rolling down his cheek was real. The river had crested overnight, and was now slapping forcefully against the sides of the horse. Various theories had been postulated over the years as to why the major and his horse had been erected heading west on the river. Some said that it had been a tribute to westward expansion while others joked that Beaumont was simply riding away from the conflict as quickly as possible. Neither theory would account for the major's current awkward position.

Red turbulent water had swirled and eddied around the front of the statue's base, carrying with it loads of clay and sand as it rushed past, eventually creating a shallow crater under the front half of the statue. Rising water from upstream had continued to slam into the rear of the horse, eventually pushing the front of the statue far enough forward to topple it into its new position.

The sight that greeted Merritt as he mournfully looked down on the river was that of the back half of a horse rising above the water. The horses head had disappeared under the river. The major was still visible, but barely. His face was only inches from the westward rushing flood. People were once again arriving to view the scene. Most just stood and pointed, but it appeared that a group of young people were having some sort of party at the major's expense. Before long another group pulled up, and a scuffle broke out.

"*Get the bastards,*" Merritt thought. "*I'm leaving you now, Major. Gotta take care of some problems of my own.*" He turned from the window and walked out the door of his office. Ordinarily, it would take him less than an hour to get to Otter's Point, but Merritt was going by Bubba's place first. Raines didn't like anyone coming to his shack and not many people had ever had the nerve to take the risk. This was an emergency. "*I wish that Neanderthal would get a phone.*"

He was beginning to think he had made a mistake in trying to get down the rain-soaked dirt road before he finally saw Bubba's shack. It looked even more pathetic and dilapidated than usual. Merritt assumed that Raines was there because his beat-up truck sat outside. After slowly turning his SUV around in case he had to make a hasty exit, Merrit got out and walked toward the shack. The stench from the backed up septic tank hit him before he reached the front door.

"Bubba!" He called out.

"Bubba. Come out. We need to talk." He called more loudly this time.

"Damn it, Bubba. If you're in there. Come out. We've got trouble," he yelled as loudly as he could, but still received no answer. Feeling seriously nauseous, he goaded himself to knock on the door. The door stood partially open and swung wide as soon as Merritt's knuckles made contact. A wave of sewage fumes hit him almost immediately. He stumbled off the porch and retched, nearly falling to his knees. Bubba had seen R.T. as soon as he had gotten out of his SUV and had watched the whole scene from just beyond his cellar. He laughed to himself, *"How ya like smellin' my ass, Merritt?"*

As Merritt walked wobbly legged toward his car, Bubba called out, "I don't like people comin' round my place, uninvited, R.T."

Merritt didn't need to be told. He was on Bubba's turf, and he was terrified. All he could do was stand up straight, and try not to let it show. "I know, Bubba. I would have left you a note in the box, but we have a situation that needs to be addressed this morning. I was afraid you wouldn't get it in time."

"We have a situation, or you have a situation?"

Merritt paused before answering. Raines was obviously in a worse mood than usual, if that was possible. "Alright, I will come straight out with it. Frank Bear called me last night and wants a meeting at Otter's Point; 10:00 a.m. He said he knows how Ramsey and his wife died, and that it would be wise for me to show up." Merritt's last statement was a lie, but he had to say something to get Bubba's attention.

"How do you want me to kill him?"

"I don't want you to do anything until I find out what he has to say. He's not stupid. Bear isn't going to tell me anything, unless he has some kind of insurance card. If you kill him before I find out what that insurance is, we could both end up in prison."

Raines knew better than to trust anything Merritt said, but he would rather die than go back to prison. "OK, so what ya got in mind?"

"The meeting isn't for another two hours. You leave now and find a spot where you can see the clearing. You need binoculars?"

"Got'em."

"OK. I don't know what the site will look like because of all the rain, but I know Bear. He will be there by the time I drive up. I will try to park as far as I can away from his truck. We will have to meet in the middle, so your vision won't be blocked by either vehicle. I will be wearing a red cap. If I leave it on when I walk back to my car, don't do anything. We have to wait. If I take it off, Bear needs to go. Don't shoot him, and don't do anything there!"

The panic in Merritt's voice had been more obvious than he had intended in his last statement. He calmed himself. "Look, it's no secret that neither of us like him. If they find him with a bullet in his brain, who do you think the police are going to come looking for? It's not the old days, Bubba. Bear has a lot of friends around here, including people with the sheriff's department."

"Yea, just make sure I keep the stink off of you," Bubba thought. His hatred for the man in front of him grew with each passing moment. He turned and walked away from Merritt.

"Where you goin'?"

"Gotta grab my nocs. I know the best look out spot for the bend. You best get over there."

Merritt got in his SUV and drove out. He didn't see Raines go behind the shack to the cellar and bring out his binoculars, along with the AR17 and short barreled shotgun.

* * * * *

As Merritt had assumed, Frank had arrived at Otter's Point, or Otter's Bend as some of the locals called it, well before ten that morning. Under normal circumstances, the point sat at the top of a bluff about twenty feet above the water. It had been formed over centuries by the erosive forces of the river below. The edge of the bluff was lined with ancient boulders, some taller than a man. Due to the historic rainfall, the water now ran only a few feet below the edge of the drop. The pie shaped bluff in the middle of the bend had often been the sight for daredevil diving contests from the boulders, under-age summer beer parties in the clearing, and lovers' rendezvous amongst the surrounding trees. The location was ideal for these activities because the heavy woods surrounding the area made the clearing hard to see from the main road.

When Merritt drove into the clearing, he saw that Bear had the same idea for parking arrangements as had he. The truck displaying the 'Ramsey and Sons' logo on its door had parked in the widest part of the pie wedge and as close to river's edge as safely possible. Merritt pulled his car to the opposite edge, leaving approximately sixty feet between the two vehicles. Both men wanted to give themselves time to assess the intentions of the other before meeting in the middle. A quarter mile away, on a tree covered hill, Bubba's truck sat hidden on the side of an old logging road. He looked down on the two men below as they walked to meet each other.

* * * * *

Officer Wentz had been able to supply six walkie talkies to the search effort. Sylvia Batten decided to post one with each spotting scope team, and she would keep the extra. The day had barely started before the radio squawked, and one of Rose's cousins came on. It was obvious that she was crying. "Oh God, Sylvia. I think I see his body."

"Where?" Sylvia's question was filled with urgency.

The cousin took a breath and brought her emotions under control. "I can see you, too. You aren't far away." Another sigh, and a pause as Rose's cousin tried to calm herself in order to give clear directions. "He is laying on a narrow ledge about fifteen feet below the lip of the cliff to your west. There is a lot of mud on the shelf. It looks like it may have stopped him from going completely down."

Suddenly, a burst of emotion came over the radio. "Oh, God! Oh, God! Oh, God! His hand moved."

Sylvia looked at Jason. "There are three coiled ropes and a machete in the Jeep. Get them. Now!"

Without responding, Jason sprinted to the jeep. It had taken him less than two minutes to get to the jeep, locate the items and return, but when he did, Tunner already had a set of four relatively straight six-foot-long branches laid out. Jason watched as Tunner and Sylvia wordlessly tied knots in the rope and trimmed the branches. Sylvia pointed to two trees near lip of the cliff and Tunner tied a rope to each. The pair looked as if they had been doing this for years.

Finally, Tunner looked at Jason. He had formed a makeshift holster for the trimmed branches and they now hung over his shoulder. He handed his nephew a pair of leather gloves, before saying, "Ok, Hunk. It's time to show us what you got. Sylvia and I are going to rappel down to Albert. Once there, we are going to use these branches to stabilize his body as much as possible. We're blind from up here and will have to figure it out while we hang. When Sylvia calls, 'UP', you are going to brace yourself against that rock and start pulling slow and steady. You need to know three words. Up, down, stop. We will be keeping him balanced, but all of the muscle work is on you. Got it?"

"Yes, sir." It felt strange to be saying, yes sir, to Tunner, but his new uncle had suddenly transformed himself into something more than a goofy tech nerd.

He walked to the edge where Sylvia was already waiting. She nodded, and the pair disappeared over the side. When they reached Albert, the precariousness of the situation was obvious. The mud that fell with Floyd was what had saved him. If the ledge had been in its normal state, his body would have bounced off and continued to fall, but the mud had acted as a type of mortar. When the semiconscious man's limp body hit the mud, it stuck.

His eyes were open, the fear in them, obvious, when Sylvia and Tunner roped down to either side of the ledge upon which he lay. He lay facing Sylvia, and she smiled calmly at him.

"Hi Albert, my name is Sylvia. My friend and I are going to get you off of this ledge." She had thought it best not to identify Tunner in fear that Floyd might react."

"Even if you can move, I don't want you to. If you understand me, please blink your eyes, twice." The gray eyes looking back at her, closed and reopened two times.

She pointed for Tunner to position himself immediately below the ledge. "My partner is going to be under you, if you start to fall.

You are perfectly, safe. The best thing for you to do is lie as still as possible. Do you understand?"

Two more blinks.

Jason could hear Sylvia talking to Albert Floyd from his position on the ridge. She purposefully spoke loudly enough for him to hear each instruction she gave to the fallen man as she and Tunner fashioned a make shift trauma stretcher from the branches and rope. Even though hearing each move they were making, it seemed to Jason that the process was taking hours. This was the first time he had ever doubted his physical ability.

The order finally came. "OK, Jason, UP"

Whether he had overestimated Floyd's weight or underestimated the amount of adrenaline flowing in his veins, the first tug caused the stretcher to move up with a jerk.

"SLOWLY!" The forceful command came in tandem from Sylvia and Tunner.

Jason's heart raced and his nerves tingled. "*It's just a match. Plan your moves. Pace yourself.*"

After a few seconds, the order came again. "UP"

The muscular teenager pulled slowly and smoothly this time. Sylvia continued to direct him, until Jason saw the heads of Tunner and Sylvia appear from behind the ledge. Soon afterward, the three of them lifted the stretcher carrying Albert Floyd and moved him to a safe place, away from the edge. He was obviously in bad condition and was unable to talk, but he seemed aware of his surroundings. His face registered surprise at seeing Jason and Tunner.

"You're going to be OK, Buddy," Tunner said. In response. Albert gave them a weak, but smiling, thumbs up.

Sylvia excitedly got on the radio. "We have him. He is responsive!" The cheer could be heard from all five of the observation points.

While she was continuing to check Floyd for injuries, Jason pulled his uncle to the side. "Tunner, can I ask you a personal question?"

"Sure, Jason. Go ahead."

"Exactly, what do you and Dr. Batten do on dates?"

Tunner laughed out loud. "I don't think you are old enough for that information, nephew."

* * * * *

Janie jumped up and hugged Tim Wentz as soon as she heard Sylvia's announcement on the radio. Wentz smiled. He had found himself developing strong feelings for Janie and her sons.

"I will call in the good news," he said, after giving Janie a quick kiss.

On the way to his patrol car, he stopped briefly to admire the spotting scope. He looked in the eyepiece and panned across the countryside.

"These things are awesome. I am going to have to talk the sheriff into buying some for the department."

Wentz stopped panning suddenly and adjusted the focus on the scope. "Hmm, I wonder what your brother, Frank is doing over at Otter's Point."

"What?"

"Yea, I see some old clunker among some trees on a hill, and that is definitely Frank's truck in the clearing. I see his logo. And wait, a really nice Escalade is pulling in."

Janie pushed Wentz away from the scope. "Let me see."

"Ok, I need to call this in anyway."

He walked to his patrol car, and as he was reaching for the door, Janie screamed hysterically. Less than a second later, the sound of the gunshots reached his ears. Without taking time to further assess the situation, he grabbed his radio.

"Shots fired! Shots fired! All available units, report to Otter's Point.

* * * * *

Frank and Merritt had gotten out of their vehicles and walked a few steps toward each other. Frank thought it odd that Merritt had on a cap. He had never seen him wear one.

"Now, this could be great scene for a wild west shootout, but that piece of paper you're holding doesn't look much like a six shooter or a bow and arrow." Meritt assumed that paper might be some type of legal action concerning the bit coin mine, or worse, something that indicated him in the death of the Ramseys.

"It's a paternity test, R.T."

"A what?" Merritt looked incredulous.

"A paternity test, showing that Jason is my son. Amber and I have known all along. It's time you knew."

Merrit laughed, scornfully. "You lying red skinned son of a whore. That's ridiculous. What are you and my ex-wife up too?"

Frank wanted to rip the man's tongue out for the vulgar allusion to his mother, but he kept his calm. He walked to Merritt, handed him the paper and stepped back.

"It's all going to come out soon. I am just letting you know, now. I am also giving you fair warning not to hurt Amber or my son. Leave them alone, and I will happily repay all of the pitiful amount of child support you provided to Amber over the years."

Merritt looked down at the paper, up at Frank, and back down at the paper. Merritt couldn't believe his good fortune. For two decades he had worried for no reason. He could destroy his ex-wife and Bear later, but for now he would focus on more important matters.

To Frank's surprise, Merritt actually seemed relieved. He laughed again, but almost joyfully this time. "Aww, Hell Frank, let's let bygones be bygones. You don't owe me a thing."

Without thinking, he pulled off the cap and scratched his head as he spoke. As soon as he did, a burst of gunfire came from the trees at the edge of the clearing. Frank instinctively tried to turn and run, but the sudden twisting motion sent a searing pain down his back and into his legs. He fell and scrambled toward the rocks on his hands and knees. He heard horrible screams of pain, and thought for a moment they might be his own. His senses came back quickly and realized that the screams were coming from R.T. He looked back toward the clearing. Merritt was laying on the ground, and his legs were covered in blood.

Another burst of gunfire came from the trees, hitting Merritt in the legs again. Frank turned toward the sound and saw Bubba walking from the trees carrying a long gun and a sawed-off shotgun. For the moment, he was focusing only on Merritt and ignored Frank. Before reaching Merritt, he tossed the AR17 to the ground.

Merritt's screams subsided to a pleading whimper as Bubba stood over him. "Why?"

Bubba, held the shotgun menacingly in Merritt's face. "So, you wanted me to kill Bear while you are sitting safely in your office. What were you planning on doing after that? Send the law to come and get me, later? I'm really tired of you thinking that I'm the stupid one!"

Merritt was confused. He had changed his mind about killing Bear. *"The hat,"* he suddenly remembered. He had told Bubba that he would take it off if he wanted Frank killed.

"No, wait. That was a mistake."

Frank had quietly tried to get to his knees and crawl to his truck while Merritt pleaded with Raines. He had only gone a few feet when Bubba saw him from the corner of his eyes. He turned the double-barreled weapon on Frank and fired with one hand. The gun was loaded with slugs designed to kill at close range, but it wasn't very accurate. The slug struck his side just above the hip, tearing out a hole as it passed through flesh and shattered a nearby rock. The poorly aimed shot hadn't hit bone or any vital organs, but had still been extremely painful. Bear fell to the ground while uttering something between a scream and a growl.

"You ain't goin nowhere, Indian," Raines hissed before turning back to R.T.

Merritt knew at that moment, that he was going to die, but still he pleaded. "Bubba, Bear doesn't know anything. You can go ahead and kill him, because he hasn't told anybody anything. Nobody will ever know."

"Oh, I'm gonna kill him. Next." Raines pointed the weapon at Merritt's chest and pulled the trigger on the remaining Barrell.

Merritt's body was considerably heavier than that of Albert Floyd's, but here, Raines had rock upon which to stand. Unconcerned about being covered with a dead man's blood, he slung the body over his shoulder and walked to the edge. He watched the water rushing by momentarily, before unceremoniously shrugging the deceased man into the river. He watched another few seconds as the river carried the body westward.

He turned toward his next intended victim. Frank had managed to rise to a half-stand in front of one of the point's larger boulders. He awkwardly stood in a crouched position with his right leg dragging behind his left. Blood from the shotgun wound darkened his side and leg. Both hands hung limply by his sides.

"Damn! The poor little Indian boy can barely stand up. I was hoping that finishing you off might be a little harder, or would you like to beg for mercy."

Even though the pain was tearing at his body, Frank's face showed no emotion. "You stupid coward. You're afraid to come at me when I can see you. You want me to turn my back first, idiot?"

Idiot had been the only word that he had emphasized. Frank knew that the taunt about his intelligence would enrage the man facing him. The former wrestler had won three state championships by appearing to be off balance in order to get his opponent to make a mistake. Raines charged and swung his right hand wildly at Bear's face, intending to smash his head and body into the rock at the same time. Frank ducked the hand and caught Bubba underneath the right armpit with his left hand. He propelled the charging beast forward by explosively extending his left leg and arm, while allowing his right leg to buckle under the force of Bubba's charge. Frank hit the ground as the combined forces of his shove and Bubba's forward momentum sent the attacker hurdling into an uncontrolled face plant on the boulder. He couldn't hear Bubba's skull crack against its surface through his own scream of pain. Bubba rolled over slowly and sat propped against the rock. He was already going into shock. The pain of so forcefully twisting his body, combined with that from the wound in his side caused Frank to momentarily pass out.

The events of the past hour struggled to emerge from the fog in his brain as he tried to will himself back to consciousness.

"Bubba! Where is he? Have to get back up."

He was still trying to sort his thoughts when the sound of a woman's screams came to his ears. "Frank, Oh God! Please God!"

He managed to open his eyes enough to see his sister, Janie, running toward him through the fog. *"No. Bubba. Stay away. Why is she still coming?"*

Janie fell to her knees by her brother. He was laying on his side in a slightly curled position. The force of his twisting throw had left him facing away from where Bubba's head had smashed into the rock. The big man now sat behind him, propped up by the boulder upon which he had collided. Blood poured down his face and shirt, mixing with that of Merritt's. His eyes were open and he was breathing, but was obviously struggling to make sense of his surroundings.

Finally, Bear was able to say, haltingly. "Janie, look out. Bubba's here."

He wasn't able to see the man standing beside his sister, but he thought he recognized the voice. "I don't think you have to worry about him, Frank," Tim Wentz said. "You can add another win to your record."

Bear's mind continued to clear, and he tried to sit up. "Please lie still," his sister said.

"No, gotta see. Help me up. I'm Ok."

As Janie was gingerly helping her brother to sit and turn, so he could see the man who had attacked him only moments before, Otter's Point became filled with the sound of sirens. Terrible road conditions had slowed the response time to the remote location. Janie and Officer Wentz had left their observation site immediately after the first burst of gunfire, but had not arrived in time to witness anything that had ensued afterward.

Two Sheriff's officers came up beside Wentz. One of them looked at Bubba and asked, "Mr. Raines, are you conscious?"

Raines looked at the officer through hate filled eyes. His response was slightly slurred. "Yea, pig. I'm conscious."

The officer immediately pulled his service weapon and pointed at Bubba, even though the big man had made no attempt to move from the boulder. The bleeding from his headwound had slowed but was continuing to ooze. "Bubba Raines, you are under arrest for the murder of Robert Thomas Merritt Junior and the attempted murders of Franklin Bear and Albert Floyd."

The deputy continued to Mirandize Raines, but neither he nor Frank heard anything after the phrase, attempted murders of Franklin Bear and Albert Floyd.

Bubba clinched his teeth. *"He can't be alive."*

Frank gripped Janie's hand and looked at her through hopeful eyes. "He's alive?"

"That's right, big brother. Sylvia radioed all of the lookouts, just a few minutes before –"

His sister stopped midsentence and trembled. Tim Wentz came to her side and put his arm around her. One of the other officers continued for Janie. "Frank, it's going to take all of us a while to process everything that has happened in the last hour. For now, just know that your brother, Jason Merritt, and a young woman named Sylvia Batten executed a pretty amazing rescue and pulled Albert off the side of a cliff. I just heard from dispatch that he is pretty banged up, but things are looking good for his recovery."

"Bear. His name is Jason Bear," Frank said to the officer.

A puzzled look came on the officer's face. "What?"

"Never mind. Just something else that is going to take a while for folks around here to process."

As they spoke, two ambulances pulled into the clearing. EMTs pulled gurneys from each vehicle, but the officer with his gun still drawn said, "Get up Bubba. You can ride in the back of my car."

Bubba snarled through clinched teeth. "Can't."

"Can't what?"

Raines stared straight ahead without looking at the officer. "Can't feel my legs."

The EMT had already begun preparing Frank to be lifted onto one gurney when the officer pointed at Bubba and said, "Clean him up too, and get him out of here. Make sure you strap him down real tight. Bubba, hold out your hands. You're still going to be cuffed."

Sylvia Batten's Jeep pulled into the clearing as the officer was giving his orders. Tunner drove and Jason sat next to him. Lisa and Emily sat in the back seat. Sylvia had ridden with Albert Floyd in the ambulance. Jason jumped out of the Jeep before it came to a complete stop and ran to Frank.

"Dad!"

"I'm OK, son. Just a little beat up."

This time it was Tim Wentz who looked puzzled. He took off his hat and looked at Janie.

"Tim, it's another long story that you are going to get to hear.

CHAPTER 32

The Present – A Visit from a Friend

Rose and Sophia sat alone in the hospital room with Frank, for the first time in the day. Two of his employees had just left. After the events of the previous week had made the news, he had been visited by a steady stream of well-wishers. He had appreciated their thoughtfulness, but he was ready to go home. His doctors had been amazed at how relatively little damage he had suffered from either the gunshot wound or the attack.

Sophia smiled down at her son. "Frank, I am so sorry, but there is one more family that would like to see you."

"Arrgh. Ok, but anymore and I may have to fake a relapse."

Rose said loudly, "Come on in!"

Bear wanted to jump out of bed when he saw Hefner Briton and his family walk through the door. He hadn't talked to him since sharing his news about Jason.

"What a great surprise. How did you know I was here?"

"Know? How could I not? You are about the hottest item on the news right now, even in Canada. How can one guy expose a crime ring, prevent an environmental disaster and be the cause behind a major historical find, all at one time?"

"You're stretching it on the first two, but I have to agree with you on the history thing. That was kind of crazy."

"Who do you think it was?"

"I have no idea. The university is being really hush-hush. I think that they are being very careful about not jumping to conclusions. We may not know anything for a while."

Hef shuddered slightly. "It will be interesting to find out, but that was a pretty gruesome way for Robert Thomas Merritt to prove that there really was someone buried on that island."

Lisa Briton shot her husband a disapproving glance for making the comment, and he guiltily looked out the window. In only a took a few seconds for Hef to see the opportunity to change the subject and escape his wife's ire. "Speaking of ancient history, I think I just saw some in the parking lot."

Even though Kirby Appleton was fatter, wore a designer suit and had an expensive haircut, Briton had recognized his old nemesis as soon as he had gotten out of his car carrying a huge get-well bouquet. The reverend had been under immense pressure since his last sermon and the subsequent news of the attempted murder of Frank Bear. Members of the congregation had called daily to express their disgust and to state that they were leaving the church. His secretary had quit and had threatened to expose his porn habit and affairs with multiple married women in the church unless she received a healthy payout, from the funds she knew he had hidden. Worst of all, he was being linked to Merritt's criminal activities. He had to try and distance himself from the late R.T. Merritt Jr. and hoped being seen visiting Bear in the hospital might help.

"Ancient history? What are you talking about?" Frank asked.

"Nothing probably," Hef answered, but in a few seconds a call came into Frank's room.

Rose was about to answer the phone, but Hef surprised her by picking up the receiver before she could reach it. "Oh yes! I would be delighted to see him. Please send him up."

Sarah Briton looked at her husband, slightly taken aback by his rudeness. Rachel shared her mother's look. Frank, Sophia, and Rose looked at each other, wondering what was going on with Frank's long-time friend. A grin was already starting to grow on the face of Mary, the youngest daughter, as she sensed something fun was about to happen.

Briton had worn a long sleeve sweater into the room, but he quickly pulled it over his head and now stood in his t-shirt. Glances were exchanged across the room, but Mary visibly bounced in excitement. Finally, Briton swapped places with his wife so that he couldn't be seen when the door opened.

The door swung ajar, slowly at first, and then fully as Kirby Appleton walked in holding the bouquet. "Frank, I came to let you know how happy I am to see." The pastor suddenly broke from his prepared speech. He had been so nervous that he hadn't thought to look around the room or to introduce himself. Appleton hadn't recognized the man with the balding head and rounded shoulders at first, but being beaten to a pulp leaves an indelible print on a person.

Hef stepped forward and held his tattooed arms out wide. "Reverend Appleton, it is so good to see a fellow sinner who has repented to become a man of God. Come embrace me, brother."

"I'm sorry. Must have the wrong room. Am, mm, mm, Bye!" Appleton dropped the flowers, before turning and running from the room.

Rose, Sophia, and Frank were already laughing before Rachel asked, "What was wrong with that man. Why did he leave so quickly?"

Mary scoffed, "Because he was afraid Dad was going to kick his ass, Dippo."

Aghast, Rachel turned to Sara Briton in a one-word plea for help. "Mom!"

Her mother sighed almost imperceptibly. "Thank you, Mary, for explaining to Rachel how someone reacts when they are afraid that their ass is about to get kicked. Now, please apologize to your sister for calling her a name."

Heff looked sternly at his youngest daughter, but also snuck in a furtive wink. She turned to Rachel with a giggle. "Sorry Rach."

Soon everyone in the room was laughing, except for Rachel, who never quite got the joke.

CHAPTER 33

The Present – The Trial

The case against Bubba was ready to go to trial before he had recovered from his injuries sufficiently to be able to sit in court. Not only had the boulder upon which he had collided, cracked his skull, the force of his body slamming into the rock had snapped a vertebra. Raines would be paralyzed from the waist down for the rest of his life.

The outcome of the trial would never be in doubt. The incontrovertible evidence against him was mountainous, even if Officer Wentz and Janie Bear hadn't witnessed him shooting Merritt. Both the shotgun and the AR17 used in the shooting were at the scene. Beyond that, Bubba's cellar was discovered during a search of his property by the Sheriff's department. The log book and the receipt signed by Merritt, clearly implicating Raines and Merritt in the deaths of Tyrell and Tabitha Ramsey, were also found. Curiously, the second logbook, created after Bubba returned from prison, listing records from Raines's dealings with many of Dugganville's established as well as nouveau elite, was missing from the cellar and never seen again.

Bubba was quiet, almost docile, the morning he was wheeled into the defendant's box by the bailiff. He was cleaner than he had been in years. The jail issued orange jumpsuit was clean and neatly pressed, but fit too tightly to contain the flab pushing from underneath its edges. Jowls billowed over his neck brace. Even the jagged scar running down the right side of his face made him look more pitiful than frightening. No one sitting in the courtroom that day would have believed that the ogrish hulk sitting in front of them had once inspired momentary hopes of romance from any woman he might encounter before being distorted to fear by the hate within him. The façade of beauty had melted away long ago, revealing the ugliness that had always been inside.

The trial was short. There were no witnesses for the defense. The only question in the trial came during the sentencing phase. Raines' court ordered attorney argued that, due to having lived a life of impoverishment combined with a limited mental capacity, the death penalty should be taken off the table. A small uproar arose in the courtroom when Bubba exploded into his only spoken statement of the trial.

"I want the death penalty, damn it!" Going back to prison was the worst thing he could imagine.

The matter was ultimately decided during the portion of the trial when the victims and their families were allowed to address the defendant. The judge was surprised when only two people had asked to speak.

The first was Albert Floyd. He would eventually go on to make a full recovery, but that day, he was also in a wheelchair. He rolled it to the microphone and spoke only briefly.

"Cousin, I hope that you do not get the death penalty. I want you to live a very long life in prison, knowing every day that you failed to hurt me and my family. Thank you, Judge."

Floyd turned his chair and rolled back to his wife, who was holding their new daughter. She was flanked by their two sons. Since they had been considered victims, the young boys had also been allowed in the court proceedings. Mae handed the baby girl to her husband and kissed him.

The only other person to speak was Sophia Bear. Raines had brutally murdered two people she loved dearly, and had nearly murdered her son, twice. The pain of her grief reached to every person in the courtroom as she walked to the dais and microphone set up for the victims. Sophia had already taken two steps past the dais before the bailiff realized it. He was normally a quick-thinking man and had stopped more than one violent behavior in court, but this mild-mannered woman's action had left him unsure of what to do. Likewise, the judge had suddenly found himself without a voice and couldn't tell Sophia to stop.

She did stop, but not until she was standing directly in front of the defendant's box. Tender eyes and a soft sad smile peered into the face of Bubba Raines. She spoke so softly that, if not for defendant's microphone, no one in the courtroom but him would have heard her words.

"I forgive you."

"*I forgive you.*" It was what Tabitha Ramsey had said to Raines before he had snapped her neck. Worse than not being feared, was not being hated. It was the only emotion he understood. You can't forgive someone and hate them at the same time. She wiped a small tear from the corner of her eye and turned to go to her seat. The only sound that could be heard in the room was Bubba's breathing over the microphone. Suddenly, he screamed and tried to lunge, but he could only move his upper body, and his arms were handcuffed to his wheel chair.

Tears flowed throughout the room as people watched the pitiful sight in front of them. Bubba felt their pity, and he hated even more. He continued to scream, but before the Bailiff could reach him, he suddenly collapsed into the chair. Paramedics rushed into the room. Raines's outburst had caused him to suffer a massive stroke. The judge sentenced Bubba Raines to life imprisonment, and he was placed in a prison care facility.

Raines was no longer able to speak or take care of his basic needs, but his mind was still intact. Each day, he was bathed, fed and toileted by trained prison staff. He quickly grew immune to the taunts and callous treatment shown him by the underpaid staff. His greatest punishment came in the form of a grandmotherly Catholic Nun and her weekly visits to his bedside.

"Hello William, I am so happy to see you today." He wanted to put his beefy hands around her scrawny neck.

She sat and read from the Bible or told him maddeningly happy stories from her youth. The sessions always ended the same. *"Don't say it, bitch! Don't say it!"* He screamed the words at her in his mind, each time she closed the book, because he knew what was coming next. The hatred in his heart manifested itself in the form of tears weeping from the corners of his eyes.

"There, there, William. There is no need to cry. God loves you and forgives you, and so do I."

Before saying goodbye, the Nun then did something that Raines had never allowed any other human being to do. After placing both of her hands on his chest, she leaned over and kissed him gently on the forehead.

"This is my little blessing. See you next week."

Chapter 34

The Present – Opening History

It had taken several more days for the river to recede to the point that horse and rider were fully exposed. A few scattered onlookers had continued to gather each morning to witness its retreat. Sometime in the night, the weakening sand underneath the base of the monument had collapsed, causing it to topple forward. The horse's head and withers had disappeared from view, and were now partially buried under the silt and debris that had been deposited back into the hole created by the rushing waters. Watching Major Beaumont desperately trying to keep his mount from plunging downward would have been a comical sight, if it hadn't been for the bloating twisted body laying partially embedded in the sand at the base of the statue. Instead, a rapidly growing crowd of spectators pointed and gasped in horror.

Word spread quickly after the first sighting. Both north and south banks filled again to watch the Sheriff's department patrol boat retrieve the body of R.T. Merritt. It was perilous work. The river was still running swiftly and carrying dangerous debris with it. While trying to extract the body from the mud, a deputy fell against the bottom of the base. It cracked and cracked again. A piece fell out, revealing that the base wasn't solid, but had acted as a vault containing something else. Calls immediately went out to the local archeological society.

By that afternoon, a casket was carefully extracted from the statue and transported to a university research center. The communities on both sides of the river were abuzz with theories and counter theories, and Dugganville's most mysterious citizen became the subject of news programs and talk shows. The coffin removed from base of the statue had been much too small for a man the size Major Beaumont was supposed to have been. It was simple, but beautifully built. The statue's base had acted as the coffin's crypt. Superbly engineered, the chamber had kept its occupant completely sheltered from the elements for nearly two centuries before finally being upended by the river. Even then, water had barely seeped into the cedar box that had obviously been crafted with loving care.

When researchers opened the coffin, they found the body of a young boy who had suffered from severe skeletal deformities. He looked to be around the age of twelve when he had died. He had suffered from a twisted spine, one leg that was several inches shorter than the other, and a malformed jaw that would have made it difficult for him to talk or eat solid food. The archeologists opening the casket hadn't expected for handkerchiefs to be important research tools, but they became immediate necessities when the scientists looked down at the body of a child who had obviously once been loved dearly.

They picked up the two items that had been placed on the body of the little boy with a sense of reverence. The first was a family Bible, printed in a language unfamiliar to any of the researchers, but three names had been scribed in the family record that were recognized as being Romanian.

Avram Albescu	Born – May 14, 1822	Died –
Loana Albescu	Born – March 7, 1830	Died – November 17, 1854
Bogdan Albescu	Born – December 24, 1852	Died – October 1, 1864

The second item was a neatly penned letter that had been tucked among the pages of the family record. Little information could be found in local genealogical records about the Albescu family, but enough to discern that Avram Albescu was a real person. His name could be found in a census taken shortly after the war, with an occupation listed as stonecutter. No record could be found of his wife or son.

Once translated into English, the letter would reveal the true identity of the proud rider on the horse.

My Dearest Bogdan,

I am enclosing this letter and Bible so that you will never forget who you are. Your name means gift, and that is what you were to your mother and me. We were so excited waiting for you to come. Mama was very sick before you were born and I didn't want her to have to work for the Beaumont family. They were cruel to her and looked down on us, because we were poor, and our English isn't very good.

I am so sorry, son. We had no money after coming to this country, and we both had to work for those awful people. Mama washed their clothes and cleaned their house until the day you were born, even when she could barely stand. Then, when they saw my beautiful baby boy, they called us monsters and made us leave. It was Mama that named you, son. 'My Gift,' she called you, each time she looked in your eyes.

We took all we had in our little cart and left the little shack that we shared with a slave family. She was so weak, but she took care of her gift. We were very hungry when the people in this little settlement found us and welcomed us. The women tried to nurse Mama back to health, but she was too weak. She was holding you in her arms when she died a little before your second birthday.

Everyone was so sad, but still they welcomed you. The mothers nurtured you, and their children played with you. We lost Mama, but still, we have a family. When you died, it was a man named Ramsey who showed me how to honor you. Together, with all the village, we sculpted a proud statue. It is my finest work. All these people worked together to build a raft big enough to float the statue to the island. Mama must have asked God to send more water to make it easier to send you to her, because a big flood came and widened the river. Never have I seen so much rain. The river pushed our vessel like it was a fine ark, and God's hand guided you to your resting place. When the water receded, you were in the middle of the island.

> *Ramsey is a woodcutter. It was he who built your fine coffin.*
> *It was also he who told me to engrave the name Beaumont on*
> *the pedestal and to give it a grand title. These people are idiots,*
> *he said, and think that names make people important. Each*
> *time they salute the statue, the people who hated you, will really*
> *be saluting Bogdan Albescu. Ramsey has a wonderful sense of*
> *humor. He told me to give your statue a very serious face, even*
> *though it is your smile that still fills my heart with joy. Now, we*
> *can all smile and laugh together, and they will never know it.*
> *Say hello to Mama for me.*
> *I love you,*
> *Tata*

The contents of the letter coincided with the known events of the time period, including a huge flood that would have occurred around the time the letter was written. There was also believed to have been a runaway slave named Ramsey that had acted as the unofficial leader of the settlement later known as Beaumont. Over time, evidence would continue to point to Avram Albescu as the sculpture of the statue and to his son Bogdan as the subject of his work.

At least two people in Dugganville were never convinced, however. As more details came out about the activities of Merrit Jr., the social influence of Merritt Sr. continued to wane until he and his wife found themselves largely isolated from the old elite of Dugganville. The decaying condition of their poorly maintained mansion reflected the state of their social standing in the community. Still, the old man published a series of unvetted and nonfactual papers, claiming that the discovery of the body in the monument had been a huge hoax perpetrated by Frank Bear, working in concert with the wealthy newcomers of the community.

EPILOGUE

The Future – New Mascots;
A New Monument

Life goes on for Frank and his extended family after that day at Otter's Point. He decides that building a successful company was but one chapter in his life. After consulting with Rose and Sophia, he sells his portion of "Ramsey and Sons" to his sisters and the family moves to Canada to Join Hefner and Sarah Briton in their work.

Whenever asked how he will be able to work with a Christian Missionary, Bear's answer is always the same. "Hef is my best friend, and people need plumbing and a family, regardless of their religion."

All of his daughters, except Tia, eventually move back south and join the ever-expanding family business. After a successful career in acting, Tia goes on to become a United States Senator.

Heff 's daughter, Rachel, becomes a best-selling children's author. Her most popular series entitled, "Dippo's Dilemma," about a brilliant teenage girl who must constantly keep her incorrigible little sister out of trouble, is eventually published in seven different languages.

After being faithfully tutored by Frank's daughter, Jasmine, Mary Briton earns a college scholarship for women's wrestling. While in college she earns back-to-back national titles before winning an Olympic gold medal in free-style wrestling. She is coached by her husband and former two-time Olympic champion, Jason Bear.

Tunner Bear and Sylvia Batten marry and become world class explorers; taking their three children with them wherever they go.

Amber retakes her maiden name and moves with her parents to Florida, where she accepts a professorship at the University of Miami. Professor Bronson becomes a widely respected lecturer in the field of education. She continues to keep close contact with the Bear family.

Kirby Appleton changes his name to Val Halla and moves to the west coast where he opens a used car dealership. Viking Val's commercials become widely known for their over-the-top theatrical effects.

Dugganville continues to grow and change, but pockets will always remain the same. It is still possible to find folks willing to take on shady side jobs for the right price. A few old men still tell their grandchildren about the big rasslin' match when the mafia put out a hit on Dugganville's most famous wrestler. A volume of "The Legend of Raeford Thaddeus Beaumont," can still be found in the public library.

The Gates River has mostly washed away any memory of that legend, however. Not only had the flood toppled the Major and his horse, it also had carried the island downstream. In a flood control measure, the army corps of engineers dredges and widens the river. Newcomers and visitors to Dugganville now see only a series of bridges connecting the north and south banks.

In spite of being in different states, the schoolboards merge and decide to tear down the old high schools because of age and overcrowding, and to build four new schools. Making an effort to avoid any carryover from the bitter rivalries of the past, none of the schools are known as North or South. Nor, do they retain their old mascots. Instead, the schools choose names associated with the geographical features of the area and Bears, Elks, Otters and Eagles as their mascots.

Over in Beaumont, Mayor Albert Floyd spends his days, speaking to its citizens and welcoming the many tourists who come through. Under his leadership, the little village transforms into a chic arts community. The home page for the city displays the two accomplishments for which Mayor Floyd will always be the proudest.

The first is the new library and the monument that stands in front. Major Raeford Thaddeus Beaumont and his horse are recovered after the flood. Using his organizational skills and Rose Bear's writing skills, Floyd launches a lobbying campaign that brings the statue, the Bible and the letter home to Beaumont. The major now points to Twin Sisters Mountain as he welcomes visitors to the library. In the library's foyer is a glass case proudly displaying the documents. An interactive diorama depicting how the early inhabitants of Beaumont may have floated the heavy statue down the river, occupies a large portion of the foyer floor and is visited annually by elementary schools from around the area. A growing collection of artifacts, donated by the ancestors of those inhabitants, surrounds the diorama.

The second, and the accomplishment of which he is most proud, is the new monument standing at the entrance of the Beaumont Community Center's state-of-the-art playground. The bigger-than-life statue depicts a smiling little boy, lying on his back and propped up on his elbows. His legs are sprawled in front of him. He is looking up at the faces of two people kneeling and smiling back at him. On the boy's left is a handsome physically fit black man, and on his right is a beautiful Cherokee woman. At the base of the monument is a simple plaque.

FAMILY
Hebrews 11:1